I0607391

Rafe's Every Wish Fulfilled

Sweet McKenna Book Eleven

Christine Young

ISBN: 978-1-62420-856-0

Credits
Cover Artist: Design by Ms G
Editor: Amanda Armstrong

Chapter One

Rafe Frasier sat in a chair provided for visitors, his fingers drumming on the cold wood of the armrest. The clock struck the hour of one. He'd been waiting three hours for an audience with the head of the magazine where Dallas was supposed to work. All he knew was that she'd been sent on an assignment somewhere north of here. Desperate, he had to discover her location.

His patience neared the snapping point. Restless, he wasn't used to waiting for important information. Dallas went missing from his life over a week ago. This was worse. Before that, he'd not seen her for months. On assignment, she told him he needed to remind himself of all the facts. This wasn't like the first time she went missing. How the hell did he know that? Gut instinct. In the present, he sensed her before she was gone. Vanished without a trace.

Those two words, 'on assignment,' didn't tell him anything he could sink his teeth into. To get this far into the building, Rafe had to lie. Told the secretary in the front of the building Dallas was his wife.

Not much of a falsehood.

Dallas would be his wife as soon as he could get her to a minister, say the necessary words then put a ring on her finger. She would need to agree. After the way she'd been acting, he was worried she would balk at the suggestion of marriage. Now, he didn't have any thoughts about what ran through her head. Before, he could always read her mind. Her eyes coupled with her facial expressions were an open book. He had to see her before he could read her special book. It was possible she learned how to block his thoughts. If that were the case… Damn, he didn't wish to think of that possibility.

When she disappeared a few months ago, he thought he would never see her again. At the falls he found her car. The trunk held her tripod along with her computer. Nothing else. Not her camera or the big bag where she kept all her necessities. Fool that he was, instead of leaving the car in the parking lot where she could get to it, he drove the car back to her house. She told him she had to hitchhike into Edinburgh for her interview. *Hitchhike! Good God, he put her life in danger!*

"Mr. Frasier…" He jerked to attention. Nerves snapped. Heart raced. A strangled gasp of air caught in the back of his throat.

He looked up to see the secretary standing in the doorway leading to the boss' office. "Yes! That's me!" She knew it was him. His heart turned over. Hoped he was about to get a few answers. He stood. The chair he'd been sitting in screeched against the floor and rocked before banging against the wall. He wiped his sweaty palms on his pants legs.

"Mr. Johnson will see you now. He doesn't have much time. You need to make this quick. State your case."

Just as McKenna suggested, Rafe drove to Edinburgh, to the office of the magazine Dallas mentioned she worked for. He waited for an audience. Cole McKenna, head of the Clan, suggested he do whatever was necessary to discover Dallas' destination. That's why he lied. Her boss would never give out information as to her whereabouts to just anyone. He needed to be someone. Someone who would be important to Dallas. A person who could be trusted with private information. In this situation, the lie was a necessity.

Blazes, he needed to see her. Hold her. Test their relationship. The spark they felt when he kissed her last time he saw her lit his insides on fire. With the sweet sensual contact, his body roared to life. Before the intriguing moment, there had never been anything substantial between them except an honest friendship. Yes, he loved her. Loved Dallas as a brother loved a sister. Now…now the feelings he harbored for her were far different. There was nothing platonic in the way he felt when he looked at her or thought about her.

After she told him she lived with the man who drove her to Edinburgh before her job interview, he went crazy. Was the name Scratch or Gordon? He couldn't recall. At the time, he thought he should shake a bit of sense into her. *Hitchhiking!* She wasn't acting with logic. Her rational mind tuned out.

She couldn't give up on them. Not now when there was something tangible they could both hold onto. He didn't intend to allow her to dismiss him from her life. Not after the kiss they shared. Not after realizing after all these years Dallas was his mate. In a hazy outline, Rafe began to understand what occurred. The universe was in the process of righting itself. He needed to hear more details from Dallas. If she could explain those months she was away, incognito, he would feel much better. As Cole told him, he needed to tell Dallas everything about him. She needed to understand shifters mated for life. He couldn't leave out one detail. Before they could move on, he would need to show her his cat.

"Have a seat." The man he came to talk with motioned to a chair.

Dear Lord, he'd been so caught up in thought he didn't listen. He needed to pay attention. This was far too important for him to mess up. If this man didn't give him Dallas' location, he didn't have anywhere else to turn. There were no clues as to her whereabouts. Nothing in her small apartment that would give anything away.

Rafe pulled up a chair then sat down in front of the big cherrywood desk that seemed to fill an entire wall. Windows behind the desk caught and held the light. The day was a fine one. Sunlight danced in the room.

"What can I do for you?" her boss asked as he appeared to be studying him. "Don't want any shenanigans. The last man who came in here tried to bribe me. Be apprised, I don't take bribes from young men. Dallas' whereabouts is privileged information. Can't be given out to just anyone. The young woman has put her trust in me. Privacy is important."

Rafe's hands were sweating. "I need…" He swallowed hard, a vague attempt to mask his discomfort. "I need to find my wife. No bribes. Just need to know where she is. She said she was going to call me when she reached her destination. That was how many days?" He looked out the window trying to figure out the day she left. "I've lost track." Wouldn't do to put his foot in his mouth over the day she left. "If she doesn't have cell service, she can't call. I'm at my wits end. Frantic with worry."

"Strange." The man tapped his pen on the desk. "You've misplaced your wife? How does a man misplace the woman he is supposed to love?

Where have you been for the last five days?"

A half-smile formed on his lips. That was a lame thing to say. "My texts…they don't go through. No cell towers. You see. I can only make guesses. I need real information." Rafe held out his hand's, palms pointing to the ceiling. "She told me she'd let me know when she arrived at the destination. Last night I gave up expecting a call. At least I'm assuming… It's possible she forgot her phone. Sometimes she's a bit scatterbrained." Rafe lifted his shoulders in what he hoped would appear to be a nonchalant gesture. He wasn't certain as to how much acting he needed to do. "Assuming she got where she was supposed to go. I'm apprehensive."

"Dallas…you are looking for Dallas Shaw."

"Frasier, Dallas Frasier now. We're married." He understood he needed to remain consistent.

"Frasier," he corrected himself looking skeptical. "Frasier, you say. That is what my secretary said. She is your wife. Why should I believe you? There were two other men in here looking for her. One of the men told me Dallas was his wife." His snow-white brows furrowed together while he appeared to study him.

Damn, he never thought of that scenario. Never believed for a moment those two bozos would be looking for her. Would come here. Why not? She did tell me she agreed to wed one of them. Was it Gordon or Scratch? Yes, believe she said Mathew Gordon. Must have known the mistake for what it was.

"They are lying. Both of them. I have proof of my claim as I'm certain they did not." Rafe pulled out a forged marriage certificate that Cole insisted he take with him. He was glad he listened to the McKenna. He thought the certificate would provide the proof he needed in order to gain the information. He handed the paper across the desk to Mr. Johnston's outstretched fingers. "This should provide the verification you are looking for."

Rafe sweated while Mr. Johnston looked over the certificate appearing to read every word. After what seemed an eternity, he gave him the paper. The man nodded.

"You should pay more attention to your wife. Those men who visited before you were…" he paused as if he didn't have the words. He went on, "So, the two of you are married. Miss Shaw marked single on her application. Why would she do that?" The frown lines on his forehead became deeper grooves as he looked for a plausible response. One he could believe. While the man waited for Rafe's answer, he sat back in his chair, his hands folded across his trim belly. "What do you have to say to that?"

The question was not as difficult as it might seem even though her application gave her correct marital status. Cole gave him the needed idea for the reply. He would have never thought of something so simple.

Rafe cleared his throat. Pointed to the marriage certificate. "What is the date on her application? That should tell the true story."

"Dallas applied in February."

"If you look at the marriage certificate, it's dated March ninth. Simple… When my wife applied for the job, we weren't wed. Now we are. I do need to locate her. Don't like her out of my sight. We've plans to go through the photos she's taken. Dallas likes my input. Did I say I am an artist? No? Well, I am. I've been worried crazy since she left. Sick to my stomach. Half out of my head. Haven't eaten. Don't know if she reached that part of the highlands or if she's in need of assistance. Her car isn't always reliable. It's broken down before. Plan on using the money she makes on this shoot for a down payment on a new car for her."

Mr. Johnston cleared his throat, tapped his pen on the top of the desk. "Your wife was sent to the Isle of Skye. I'm sure you are familiar with that area. Very touristy. Very photographic. I'm certain the photos will do the magazine proud. She is taking pictures of the Fairy Pools along with other highland scenery. The closest village is Carbost. That's where her base camp is located." He picked up a piece of paper then began writing.

Rafe hoped he was giving him the address of her hotel or place of residence. Dallas would pick a rental rather than a hotel to stay in for the duration. He needed to be with her. Must convince her they were meant to be together. His heart quickened when her boss handed him the directions. The breath he'd been holding while the man wrote left the back of his throat, moving in slow motion. Relief plummeted through him.

Taking a moment to read the information, he looked up. Smiled.

"Thank you. Thank you, sir. I'm certain Dallas will appreciate this. We work well together. Always have. I did make arrangements to join her. She's expecting me. Dallas would be disappointed if I failed to turn up. She would wonder why. In turn would be worried." He folded the paper before stuffing it into the pocket of his jeans, having the feeling he'd said too much.

"Is that all?"

"Yes." He rose to leave, making plans now to get to Dallas the next day, if possible, reached over the table to shake her boss' hand. Tomorrow evening he hoped to see her. Hold her in his arms. "Thank you again." Pleased with his accomplishment, he felt like whistling.

Rafe walked past the secretary, tipped his head in acknowledgement, then into the lobby. Outside, the air was warm. The day was brilliant with sunshine. A gentle breeze ruffled his hair sending an errant lock into his eyes. The delight he felt was tangible. He wanted to kick up his heels then howl his delight. He felt certain the trip would be speedy.

He reached his home in Carnoch in record time, berating himself for not packing his things before heading into the city. If he'd had the foresight to do so, he'd be well into the trip instead of working to get started. Two-stepping the stairs to his bedroom, once there he pulled out a travel bag then tossed clothing into it; underwear, socks, a couple of changes of both jeans along with shirts. Figured if he forgot something he could buy anything he needed in the village where she stayed. Grabbing his toothbrush and shaving paraphernalia, he raced down the steps, tossed his bag into the car.

He was headed north.

Behind the wheel, he tugged in a breath of air, gripping the steering wheel. Focused on the road. So much depended on this trip. He couldn't mess this up. After he explained his position, he would show her his cat. Tell her about shifters. With exact words, clarify his theory about why she was sent back to another century. Wondered if she believed in the old folklore. While he knew her better than any one of her acquaintances, he wasn't certain if she was superstitious. In the present, even north in the more secluded places of the highlands, shifters were rumors. Stories told in the night around campfires.

Where superstition was concerned, there were varying degrees. One could walk to the other side of the road to avoid a black cat...or not. If not, a person would test their luck. Take fate into their hands. He grinned. She always avoided walking beneath a ladder. For him, he didn't pay much attention to minor things. One made their luck. Established their fate. Believed all worked out well unless the universe stepped in to rearrange an accident.

On his way to the Isle of Sky, he mulled the thought over for a few seconds. While he'd never visited this place before, he heard the rugged terrain was beautiful, the Fairy Pools spectacular. She would take gorgeous pictures...absolutely amazing photos. Ones she could frame then sell. He brought his laptop to help her go through the photographs. Her next show would be in June. He tapped his fingers on the steering wheel. The exhibit would take place in Edinburgh. He never got a chance to see the pictures she took at the falls. Would be interesting if they shed any light on what happened to her. How was he going to get her to speak of that time? Maybe she would want to tell him all that happened. It might be that she wouldn't remember. That was a very real possibility.

The place where she disappeared from his life. Cole told him he believed she traveled backwards in time. The picture of a woman named Lainie with Cameron Roc Frasier in the McKenna keep haunted him. The woman sitting next to Roc looked enough like his Dallas to be her sister or a twin, they were so close in appearance.

One day, he brought a portrait he'd painted of Dallas to the keep. When he held it up to the one of Lainie for comparison...there were subtle differences. Dallas' hair was redder than Lainie's. Her eyes were a deeper blue. Lainie's breasts were larger. Her hips wider. Cheeks a *wee* bit plumper. He supposed Dallas kept her body's natural tendencies to become lush curves by exercise along with diet. If he had his way, she would stop torturing her body to be a shape it should never be. He loved all her lavish curves. When they made love, he wouldn't have to stumble around in the dark to find her feminine endowments.

When they made love...
That event was still in the future.

After the clock on his dash told him he should be in bed, he pulled over. Stopped at what appeared to be a café that might be open all night. Once outside in the crisp spring air, he stretched. Brought several stimulating breaths of oxygen into his lungs. A few minutes later after using the facilities then buying a large cup of coffee along with a sandwich, he was behind the wheel again. Planned on driving through the night.

The next afternoon, he stopped in front of the rustic log cabin Dallas had rented. His heart skipped a beat then another. He wiped his sweating hands on his jeans. Pulled at the t-shirt that stuck to his damp chest. Nerves seemed to splinter while he tried to breathe deep. Never in his life had he been this damn nervous. His steps toward the door faltered. Was certain his knees would give out before he could knock. With his hand in front of the wood he held back.

Courage. I need courage to face her.

At the front door, he knocked. Knocked again harder when there was no answer. Walked around the cabin so he could look in the windows. Pressed his nose against the pain of glass. As far as he could tell, Dallas wasn't there. He thumped his forehead with the heel of his hand. She would be working. He checked the front door. It wasn't locked. Rafe let himself inside, swearing at her stupidity. Dallas never remembered to lock doors. Either that or she didn't think securing the door was necessary.

He checked his watch. She would quit only after the sun disappeared for the night. He had two options. One was to cook dinner. He could have everything ready when she arrived home. At the last stop, he bought a couple of bottles of wine, chicken he could broil, along with a bag of salad. The second option was to take the trail to the Fairy Pools. Meet her. Help her with her gear. They could walk back after sunset. He opted for the first choice, thinking he needed to prolong the meeting he wasn't certain about. Had no idea how she would receive him. Would lecture him about the lie he told her boss. He needed to be upfront with her. Tell her all the truths. Answer any as well as all her questions.

A romantic dinner.

They would talk all night if necessary. Convincing her not to run from him again would come before speaking of marriage or showing her his cat. She might need to learn how to trust him. Rafe never believed between them trust would be an issue. As he proceeded now, he wasn't certain. He had a tendency to get things out of order. Knew there was always a proper order to everything. He just had to discover what that sequence was. He was by nature, far too impatient.

No mistakes tonight.

Whistling, he set about the preparations for the romantic dinner, positive this was the right choice for them. On the small table that sat in the corner of the kitchen next to a window, he spread a white tablecloth. Rafe didn't know why he brought the adornment. Now he knew. Even when he tossed clothing into his bag, he thought of romance. Stepping outside he picked a handful of wildflowers. With water and a vase, he now set the fragrant decoration on the table. Setting the mood was always important. When he thought about technicalities, he could be romantic.

Dinner was ready to be served. The candles were lit. Wine was poured. He paced outside to see the dying brilliance of the setting sun. He was impatient to see Dallas. His body hummed in anticipation. If he closed his eyes, he envisioned her marching down the trail while she struggled with all her equipment. She would be home soon. The tourist information he read said the roundtrip would take about an hour.

He saw her emerge from around a bend. Thought he should step lively so he could help her with the equipment. For the first time since he arrived some of his nerves vanished. This was his Dallas. He knew her better than anyone. Took her to the doctor when she had no one to help her. Understood her like no other just as she understood him. The two of them were meant to be together. She was his mate.

He knew when she saw him. Was overjoyed by the initial reaction. The smile on her face told him a wealth of information. The most important fact was that for at least one beat of her heart she was pleased to see him. Seconds later there was no frown. She stopped walking. Stood still for the longest time while she stared at him. Turned herself a bit to the side as if speculating various ideas. After what seemed to be a thorough perusal, she started to walk.

Rafe couldn't wait to reach her. To pull her into his arms then kiss her would be a dream fulfilled. His long strides ate up the distance between them. He was at her side, taking her camera equipment from her. The tripod he collected under his arm. Her large bag which held the cameras along with the lenses he slung over his shoulder. She didn't need his help. Even so, she looked as if she wouldn't refuse.

He grinned at her. Touched a wayward lock of hair that had come undone from her ponytail. Pushed the cool silken strand behind her ear. "Hello."

Again, the urge to tug her into his arms for the kiss he'd been waiting for, for what seemed to be his entire life, rifled through him. Wished he dared sweep her off her feet so he could carry her to the bedroom. Making love to her had been on his mind for the entire drive. In absolute truth, it had been on his mind when he kissed her that long ago day and discovered the inferno she lit within him. He had to be patient as well as realistic. She might not be ready to take that necessary step. Damn, but they had so much to talk about. There were months missing from their lives. If his, along with Cole's, guesses held merit, she'd been in a different century. She'd been righting something that went amiss hundreds of years ago.

Tilting her head a bit to the side, she spoke. Her voice soft, "I never expected to see you here, Rafe. Why did you come all this way?" She ran her tongue across her lips as if she too wished for that kiss he'd been thinking about. The erotic gesture left a trail of moisture behind. He needed to taste. Savor. *Damn.*

How could he tell her in a brief sentence? The whys of his appearance were long as well as varied. The reasons all involved her, coupled with what they meant to each other. The need to see her before she could make a mistake with Mathew Gordon part of those reasons.

"I'm glad to see you too." he ventured with the sarcastic comment instead of the explanation she wanted. She would bristle then retaliate. His Dallas wasn't a girl who would let anyone take advantage of her emotions.

Dallas brushed strands of hair from her face as she resecured her ponytail. Her brows were drawn together, sunset-colored brows he wished to trace with the tip of his finger. Her lips thinned as she fought to concentrate. "You know what I mean. Don't get flippant."

He'd started walking again, unwilling to give himself away. She caught his arm to stop his retreat. He turned to listen, hoping she would say something that would please him. With Dallas one never knew how she would respond.

"I'm happy to see you too." With a small giggle, she said "Needed someone to carry my equipment. Might as well be you." Dallas was skipping to keep up with his longer strides. "You don't have to walk so fast. Nothing is going away."

This wasn't what he would have liked to hear from her sweet, kissable lips. Though he did appreciate the small giggle. Before, when they did things together, she laughed all the time. Their relationship was carefree, never serious.

Her cheeks were pink, a slight sunburn marring her tender skin. He wished she would tell him how happy she was he came to help her work. "You forgot your sunscreen again." Someone needed to take care of her. He meant to apply for that job. "Your cheeks are burned."

When she replied she sounded in a huff. Dallas never liked it when he took it on himself to lecture her. She was always forgetting necessities as she was too caught up in her photography. "No, didn't forget anything. I applied sunscreen this morning. Been out all day. The stuff wears off. Got enough to carry without adding sunscreen to the mix." Her back straight she walked ahead of him.

Sunscreen didn't weigh very much. Ah well.

He loved to watch her hips sway. She was dressed in walking shorts, not her usual short, shorts that showed off her long legs to perfection. If she wore the smaller variety, he'd find himself treated to a glimpse of her fanny. Before she picked up her pace to walk in front of him, he was able to revel in the thrust of her breasts. They were large. Would fill his hands if he ever got another chance to hold them, test their weight, feel their delicate warmth. He shuddered recalling the last time he touched one breast. The lightning that leapt between them was tangible. His memory had him hard beneath his jeans, throbbing with need for this delightful woman who was his mate.

This meeting wasn't getting off to a great start. Not the one he imagined as well as hoped for. Backpedaling would be a good idea. He had put his foot in his mouth twice now. Doing so a third time was unacceptable to the path he embarked upon. He caught up to her. They walked side by side for a few seconds. He debated how to begin the next exchange without damning himself to her scorn. "I came because I was worried about you. That's one reason why I followed you here. Your friends, Gordon and Scratch, were asking about you at the magazine. Wanted to know where you were. Would you have cared if they turned up here to disrupt your assignment?"

"So, you thought you would lead them to me? Those two are the last two men I want to see. They make me shudder with revulsion. There is something evil about those two. Can't quite put my finger on why they give me those feelings. Though they are real."

They reached her door. He opened it for her, waiting for her to pass through. Catching the scent of lilies in the air as she entered, he was reminded of other times. As long as they were getting off on the wrong feet, he might as well add another damper to the evening. Dallas might not be too pleased at the romantic setting. She gasped when she saw the table.

The wine.

Candles.

The flowers.

Smelled the roast chicken.

"You cooked?" She reached up to brush a tender kiss across his lips. "Thank you, and you brought wine." Dallas walked to the table, her hands beneath her chin. After she looked at him, "The flowers are a nice touch too. Romantic. Didn't know you could be amorous."

He decided not to mention the unlocked door. That would have been the third *faux pas* of the day. Too many times to count, they argued about securing her apartment. She grabbed her equipment from him. Stowed the things away.

"I like to cook. You know that. Are you hungry? Not as creative as you." After splashing some into a glass he pulled from the cupboard, he handed her the wine. Stepping back to observe, he waited.

"Hmm… didn't expect to be treated as if I'm royalty tonight. Was going to have a peanut butter sandwich and a cup of tea. Intended to look at my photos then go to bed. Thank you. To answer your question, I'd like to take a shower first. Feel dusty as well as sweaty. I am hungry. Forgot to bring something with me for lunch. Do you mind waiting until I get a hot water treatment?"

"Take your time. Brought my computer. Do you care if I take a look at some of your pictures? We can start going through them tonight for your exhibition." Rafe found he was eager to see what she captured on film. Was eager to sit close to her while they combed through the pictures, debated which ones to use.

"You'd do that?" Her eyes brightened. Her hands were behind her back, unfastening her bra. From prior experience he understood she'd be eager to shed the garment. Didn't appreciate the underwire digging into her skin or the confinement. "Yes, please… Seems as if it has been so long since…" Dallas turned away as if she hid from him. Her shirt along with her bra slid from her. He saw the length of her back. Imagined the rest of her naked. Around him, she was always at ease with her nudity. He'd painted her nude form numerous times. She was his favorite model. They were like brother and sister. No longer. Soon they would be lovers, then husband and wife.

He huffed in a breath of air, stalling himself from action. The long line of her back beckoned to him. Damn, but he wanted to touch, follow the line of her spine with the tip of his finger then with his lips. "What's wrong?" He knew there had to be some reason for her to run off without an explanation. This was the second time he felt her abandonment, soul deep, unexpected. Now that he understood her position in his life, fleeing him was worse. "You are…different. Tell me what happened those last months. Maybe I can help."

She turned. For several beats of his heart, he saw her breasts. He sipped air.

"Rafe…please…not now." Her t-shirt held against her chest, she backed away from him. After she grabbed her glass from the table then drank, she fled to the bathroom. Left him staring at the empty space she'd occupied but a second before.

"Not now…" Rafe murmured, sifting air through his teeth. What did he do wrong this time? *Now, now!* His fist tightened. He needed patience. Told himself that time and again. It was just so bloody hard to watch her struggle with her emotions. To understand part of the conflict along with the turmoil she fought. In the past, Dallas would have confided in him.

When? When will she talk?

Over the last few months, they'd both been through more than any couple should be put through. Now she didn't want to tell him anything. Wouldn't speak of the months they'd been separated. He needed to understand what happened to her. Where she disappeared. Felt as if he stumbled around in a fog.

Damn…he found her car at the waterfall. He didn't see her again for over a month. After he saw her on the street, she vanished again.

Unexpected, she showed up at his door one night. When he kissed her that evening, held her in his arms, he felt the spark he'd been looking for all the years he'd known her. While she was gone from his life, she changed. Dallas told him she felt the same electricity between them. The leap of energy…the surge of adrenalin. Not more than a few minutes later, she told him she was living with some man. All she was doing in Carnoch was picking up her car. She fled as if she was afraid of him. How the bloody hell could this woman be afraid of him? He'd taken her to the doctor when she couldn't ask anyone else. Held her hand when she was in pain. She meant the world to him.

Patience.

More tolerance than should ever be necessary is what is needed now. If I want her, I must give her time to adjust to this new revelation. Give her time to come to me the way I hope. The two of us have always been friends…never lovers. Now I want something different from her. She might be afraid. Dallas is my mate. Soon my wife. Forever my life.

You can't expect anything from her on the spur of the moment. With no warning, you showed up at her front door. Surprised her. Cooked her dinner. Had romance in mind. She needs time to process this unexpected visit. You aren't her boyfriend. Never have been. What do you expect?

He sat down with his glass of wine. Nursed the drink. After his emotions slowed to small vibrations, he pulled out her camera then took out the card, put it into his computer to download the first images.

The tourist guide was right. This was a beautiful spot, magical. Her images captivated. Held him enthralled. He pulled a few aside for Dallas to look at after dinner. She had enough for the magazine article as well as her exhibit. He would help her choose those to frame.

She was out of the shower. He heard her soft singing. She always sang in the shower when she was at his home. For a lifetime then beyond, he could listen to her voice. Dallas walked from the bathroom in shorts, very short shorts, and a t-shirt. The kind he liked to see her wear. Hell, he painted her while she wore nothing. Now, she didn't wear a bra. Beneath the pink cotton T, he saw the outline of her breasts, the rose-colored nipples pressed against the fabric. Watched them sway as she walked. Around him, she still seemed comfortable with her almost nudity. Well, he wasn't as comfortable as he used to be. His penis jumped to life. Being around her was taking on a new angle, a hard edge he had to find a way to hide.

That was the nice thing about their relationship. They were at ease with each other in every way. Dallas posed in the buff for him. He did have a buyer for the last painting. The profit would have paid his mortgage for five years. He didn't sell. Couldn't part with the oil. The offer came to him while she was gone from his life. While he didn't know where she was, he couldn't bear to have the painting out of his hands. He hung her portrait in the attic where she posed, where he painted. At night he would walk the steps to the room. Gaze at Dallas. Wish for something he didn't think would ever be.

After she posed for him then dressed, she never wore panties, she would always stuff them in the big bag she carried with her. He wondered now if she wore anything beneath the shorts. If he guessed, he would deduce she wore nothing. The image sent more lightning ripping straight to his groin. He found he was damn uncomfortable. Needed an adjustment to his jeans. Nice that she was at ease. For him, the night was going to be a long one. What he hoped for on the long drive wasn't going to unfold. There would be no lovemaking tonight. Rushing her would never be advantageous.

Clearing his throat, he stood, "Ready to eat? I'll dish up. Give you a bit of everything." Rafe pulled out a seat for her then topped off her wine. "You've amazing pictures in the first batch. How many are you obligated to give the magazine? Do you have a choice?"

"Fifty. They have first pick of the photos. I've got so many it won't be hard to find ten or so for the gallery. More to wrap in plastic and mount on cardboard for possible sales. The wine is good."

After the initial conversation, they ate in silence. Rafe didn't know how to talk about the past months. How to broach the subject that seemed to send her off in a rush in the opposite direction. He supposed she needed to feel relaxed in his company again. As it appeared now, she was stiff, restrained. Didn't seem to know what she could or couldn't say.

She pushed the remnants of her food around on her plate. He gave her more than she would eat. Tried to convince her he loved all her curves. Wouldn't mind if there were more. Dallas was always careful about how much as well as what she ate. Made certain to exercise. Complained about the cellulite on her legs. If and when she ever gave him the chance, he would taste each tiny dimple.

With a long-drawn-out breath of air, she set down her fork then picked up the wine glass. "Look, I understand we've talk that needs talking about. I ghosted you. You should hate me. Want you to understand the ghosting wasn't intentional. I had no say whatsoever in what happened to me. Never meant to leave without telling you where it was I was going. In a blink, I was in another world sitting on my butt looking at a man I'd never met before."

That was a start. Maybe she needed to tell him where she was as much as he needed to learn the truth. "Where did you go?" His curiosity spun out of control. So far, she told him nothing about those months when he couldn't find her. This was the first hint of communication. "You could have picked up your cell. Called me." He braced himself with his forearms on the table. "I was worried. Terrified something horrible happened to you. Helpless. A man doesn't much appreciate that vulnerable feeling. You do realize how much I care for you."

She lifted her shoulders in a tiny shrug as if there was nothing she could do. The movement sent other parts of her in a visual dance treating his eyes along with his senses to a titillating display of female curves. "No cell tower where I was. Nothing. No electricity. Nothing. No cars. Only horses." Dallas shuddered. "I dislike riding horses. Found myself perched on one…a horse. The ground flew by. I held tight to his arm keeping me from falling."

"That's all possible. Were you on some kind of assignment you never mentioned to me? I thought, maybe, there was no service here which is why I couldn't call you. Why I didn't give you a heads-up that I would arrive this afternoon. Didn't mean to catch you unaware. You expected to be alone. I intruded. Do you want me to leave?"

She set the glass on the table, a strange look in her eyes. "How did you find me?" She topped off her wine. "Need something more to bolster me up. Somehow, I understand what you're going to tell me I won't like. So, let's get this over with."

"I lied to your boss." He didn't intend to make any apologies. Would do it again in a heartbeat. "Told the man you are my wife."

She hissed air in through her teeth. "He believed you?"

~ * ~

The bastard! At least her boss didn't believe Mathew. Even so, she was surprised to discover her boss told Rafe her exact location. Mathew was a sneak. Oily. Hateful. Not very much time passed before she understood her mistake with the man. On first meeting him, she trusted him to do what he said, helped her out of a tough situation. While he was a cad taking advantage of her weakness. He tried to coerce her into his bed. Only one kiss convinced her his bed was the last place she wished to be. The kiss disgusted. Left her to shudder with displeasure.

When he found her hitchhiking, she was so disoriented she didn't know if she was coming or going. She was confused. The world seemed to spin in too many different directions. After she hopped into his car, Tinley moved to the back seat. During the ride into the city, she had this uncanny notion she knew these two. The men were less than stellar. It was here, at the Fairy Pools, that she realized where she first saw the men.

At first, she was so muddled in her mind that Mathew was able to sweet-talk her into staying with him at his apartment. Within a span of a day and a half, she moved out. She could do so only because her boss at the magazine gave her an advance to meet her needs until she left for the photo shoot.

For too many days after she settled into the cabin, all she could do was walk the trail to the pools. She would sit for hours staring at the rippling, sun dappled water as the cold liquid spilled over the rocks. Tried to remember all that happened to her. Felt the breeze blowing off the craigs change as if something supernatural touched her. The sunlight dimmed. All around her the scene seemed surreal. Little things came to mind. A touch here. A caress there. The man who set her upon his horse was real, flesh and blood man. The first few days she believed this was the remnants of a dream. The dream wasn't a dream at all nor was the memory a nightmare. What she experienced was real. When she closed her eyes, even when she didn't, she saw the fantasy man's features.

The man in the mist rainbow behind the falls…his face was still etched into her memory. Why not? He could be a brother to Rafe. Tall, handsome as sin, the man captured her attention the moment she saw him, feet braced apart. His hands placed square on his lean hips. He came to rescue her from Scratch and Gordy. Gave commands. Laughed when she acted as if she wouldn't obey. Asked her if she would rather be with those two men. Until she started to retain her memory, she never made the connection between the two who accosted her in the glen and the two who picked her up on the side of the road. A cloud covered the sun. Shadows deepened. Tourists came and went. Laughed. Chatted. Spoke of the beauty. The enchantment of this mystical setting helped her remember some of her past. There were moments when she felt certain fairies fluttered around the pools. They would slip their toes in the water. Splashed each other. When she tested the water, the magical liquid was like ice to her fingers. Still, a few of the tourists braved the icy cold to swim.

Scratch and Gordy.

Tinley Scratch and Mathew Gordon.

Good God, to protect herself, she pepper sprayed one of them. Couldn't remember which man was the recipient.

Sunshine broke from the clouds. Chased away the shadows. Even so, given the eerie feelings surrounding her, she could not rid herself of the darkness in her heart that seemed to also possess her soul. The man who rescued her from those two, tossed her on top of his horse as if she weighed nothing. Nothing! A woman of her size? The ride through the forest trails terrified her. As she clung to his massive forearms, he whispered to her that he would keep her safe. Told her to relax when doing so was impossible. She recalled the cave where he took her. Where they spent the night and one or two after that. The exact time was hazy in her mind. Parts of those months she remembered. Some parts she did not.

She sat on a nettle. The man, Roc was his name, Roc Frasier. He rubbed cortisone cream on her butt. He touched her in ways no man ever touched her before. Mentally as well as physically, she felt the spark he ignited she and Rafe lacked. Reveled in feelings that were new to her. Found if he wished or asked, she would have let him take her virginity. In her large bag, she had all she needed to protect herself from disease as well as pregnancy.

While she showed as well as explained these things to Roc, she had the sudden feeling he was angry. Why would he be furious with a woman who wished to protect herself? That was something she didn't understand. He didn't like the birth control pills or the condoms. He was familiar with condoms not the pills.

Never would understand his position on the birth control. Rafe wasn't like that. Understood the necessity for both.

It rained the next day, forcing them to remain in the cave. While she wanted him to take her to Inverness, Roc refused. Told her in time he would take her to the city. She didn't remember how many days water fell from the skies. How many days they stayed in the cave and talked. When the weather cleared, she sat in front of him on his huge horse. They traveled to Carnoch. Discovered he lived in the same home as Rafe. By that time, it became apparent to her that Roc and Rafe were in some way related.

The Fairy Pool was silent. There were no tourists for the moment. The day was passing. The sky would grow dark soon. She needed to return to her cabin. With her bare foot, she kicked the water, sending sprays of glistening drops into the surrounding air. Watched as the tiny droplets fell back to the pond sending ripples across the surface.

It was in those first few days she began to forget things she should know. There would be lapses in her memory. She would begin to think something then stop, forgetting what she meant to say. It was during those first days that Roc swept her off her feet, literally as well as figuratively.

All these remembrances were things she should tell Rafe. He should understand why she never contacted him. She didn't know if he would believe her when she told him she traveled back in time to the year seventeen-fifty-six. There were days that she didn't believe the reality herself. Now, everything blurred together, the past along with the present. She felt as if she was evolving into a different person. The time in the past century transformed her personality.

He was right when he told her she changed. How could a person travel through time without becoming someone different? Sometimes she pinched herself in order to be positive she wasn't dreaming. Rafc couldn't understand. If she told him what happened to her, he would believe she was daft. She wasn't. What she went through wasn't a bad dream she would wake up from.

Rafe was here…in Carbost. He came to talk about their different relationship now that she returned from her adventure. Her adventure…one she fell into. Slid down a hill to land at the feet of a handsome Scotsman…a Frasier. She wasn't ready to talk. Didn't know if she ever would be prepared to spill her story. Didn't know if anything she told him would be true. All she seemed to have at her disposal were guesses. Her mind tripped from one image to another one.

After her shower, when she waltzed into the living room as if everything was the same as it used to be, she realized her mistake. Rafe's eyes seemed to glaze over while he stared at the outline of her breasts. He never before looked at her as if he wanted to devour her. She was reminded of the jump of adrenalin between them when they touched. The electricity that skidded from their fingertips. She even felt that spark when he touched her to take her camera equipment.

In their life before, he never paid much attention to her body parts. Never stared at her breasts. When she dressed this way in front of Rafe, she didn't think. All she wished for after a long day of walking and shooting pictures was to relax, to be comfortable. With bra along with panties beneath her clothing she would be anything but at ease. She opted for comfort. He was still staring. His gaze traveled along the length of her.

Good God, before she went to take her shower, she stripped off her bra along with her t-shirt right in front of him. Her breath caught at the realization she all but invited him to touch.

Now, with Rafe, this was all new to her. Never before had he been interested in her as a girlfriend, as a lover. Rafe never consumed her with his eyes. He was eating her up. Now his eyes kept focusing on her breasts. Her nipples hardened beneath his passionate examination. Through the thin fabric of her t-shirt, he would see her response. She felt as if she should cover herself. Instead, she tilted her chin up and decided that she would ignore the potent stare that flashed her way. Dallas intended to brazen this out. She understood what he wanted. She wanted the same. Terrified didn't do justice to what she felt having never been with a man in that way.

Earlier today when she saw him striding toward her, she felt as if a gigantic weight had been lifted from her shoulders. Pleased to see him didn't do justice to how she felt. She understood Rafe would listen to her. Attend to whatever she could tell him. Would never judge even though he might be a bit skeptical of what she was going to recount.

After she saw the candles, the wine, the vase of flowers... The romantic setting he created for their pleasure. Her heart filled with love. She understood they had some things to consider...to hash over before they could become lovers. Realized he would not believe she traveled through time... Assumed he would not believe Gordon and Scratch... He would imagine they meant her harm. That much they would be able to come to terms with. They would agree. Gordon along with Scratch were trouble for her. What Rafe wouldn't understand was why.

Her short time in the shower allowed her to regain a dash of composure. Hot water soothed her knotted nerves along with muscles that had been tense for months. She kept telling herself he would never commit her to some asylum for the insane after she apprised him of some mind jarring revelations. After all, he lived in the highlands his entire life. He would just have to understand her truths. Something unexplainable happened to her. She survived. Scotsmen were a superstitious lot. Maybe that rumor was just gossip. Rafe wasn't superstitious. So much for that thought.

"You've not said anything in the last twenty minutes." His voice came from out of nowhere, a soft melodic purr. "Where have you been? Your eyes have this glazed over look. You've been deep in your head. Can I help? Want to talk?"

Startled by his sudden intrusion to her musings, she jumped. "Oh! Oh, my…suppose I was caught up in my thoughts." They were looking through her photos. "I…my mind was on something else." She smiled at him hoping to ease the moment into something more doable.

Rafe sat back, his hands behind his head, a half-smile quirking his lips. Lips she now thought about kissing, as well as how they'd taste. "Care to share? Were you thinking about me…us?"

He was giving her the opportunity she needed to divulge her thoughts, memories, the time that changed her. She looked down, hiding her eyes from him. "No…I don't wish to tell you what's in my head right now. I…" She ran her tongue across dry lips. Drank long and deep of her glass of wine hoping the liquid would ease her parched throat. Nothing seemed to help.

Dallas wasn't surprised to hear him curse beneath his breath. He sat up straight. She'd heard all his words before.

"If you don't want to talk maybe you can explain these…" Rafe pulled up a page of photos. Pictures of Roc. "Who is this man to you?" his tone harsh. His words filled with anger. "Who the hell is he?" For some reason his anger didn't reach soul deep. She was glad of that.

My savior.

Unable to stop herself, she groaned. In the cave, she shot photo after photo of Roc. She wanted to have pictures to remember him by. Thought that with the exception of Rafe, he was the most handsome man she'd ever seen.

"That's not fair of you. I… It's not right that you question me about this man. He has nothing to do with me." Dallas couldn't tell him she fell in love with Roc Frasier. Now, she didn't recall enough about him to understand how that happened. If her feelings weren't deceiving her again, she was in love with Rafe Frasier. They looked so much alike. Acted very different. They were both demanding. There were more similarities.

"Not fair!" he shouted before quieting his voice. "Not fair… You take over one hundred photos of this man. Who is he!" Rafe moved away from the computer screen so she could see better. Pointed at the photos. "Who is this man? I deserve an answer."

"Someone...someone I met an eternity ago." She drank more wine. Let the liquid slide down her throat. Wished the alcohol would soothe her crashed nerves. "A man who is dear to me. A man who is in my past. I will never see him again except through these pictures. You've no business going through those photos. No business questioning me." She felt a sudden rise of moisture to her eyes. Pushed the sensation away.

Rafe placed her hands in his, his eyes focused on hers. His lips were pressed into a grim line. "Do you not recall giving me permission to take a look at the pictures on this card?" He set his finger on the plastic. "Rest assured, I would never go into your photo pool without authorization." He rubbed the backs of her hands with his thumb.

She felt the shimmer of heat glide across her skin. Knew the sensation as something new between the two of them. Lightning jumped across their fingers. Dallas tugged. Needed distance to think. For a few more beats of her slamming heart, he held her hands. With another curse, he let her go.

"Who is he? I would have you tell me," He demanded again. This time his words held no venom. He sounded resigned to the fact she took so many photographs because she needed to remember. "He looks a lot like me."

She doused herself with oxygen. Held the air inside until her lungs burned. Thought she couldn't hold it any longer. This...she supposed...was the time to begin the tale of her journey. "You will think I'm crazy. Everyone will believe I've lost my sanity. Suppose as my best friend you deserve to learn about my insanity first. I'm not certain even I believe all that I'm going to say to you."

"Who is this man who is plastered on this camera card? This man who you seem to be thinking about while we are working?" he asked again. Appeared he didn't intend to give up on that single question.

"His name is...was..." That was a great start. She could have said is... He was staring at her as if he was still furious about the photos.

"Is or was?" Rafe picked up on her misstatement which wasn't a misstatement at all. "Is he living?"

"Was. His name was Cameron Petroc Frasier. I called him Roc. He called me Lainie. The man rescued me from Gordy and Scratch at the falls when I was lost. Had nowhere to go. He saved me." The walls in the cabin spun. Darkness closed in on her. She closed her eyes for seconds inhaling deep breaths of air while she counted.

"Did you sleep with him?" his question sounded possessive…condemning.

A slap in the face could never have been so hurtful. Yet… did she sleep with him? She'd wanted to be in his arms, in his bed. There were several times he held her through the night because she was terrified as well as lonely. Understood she wasn't in her century. Didn't believe she would ever be able to return to a century she comprehended.

"How dare you?" She found a serenity in her answer she didn't expect. "What I did with Roc…"

Rafe held up his hands as if he knew he transgressed. Shook his head as if to give emphasis to his mistake. "Is none of my business. I understand. We've always been straightforward with each other. Imagine I trespassed into territory where I don't belong. Jealousy. The concept is new to me." He wrapped his fingers around the stem of his glass. "I'm sorry…" He drank.

The look in his eyes told her he didn't mean his words. The man wanted to know if she was intimate with this man. Not that she could remember. The long sigh she let out reflected her distress. She would tell him what she could. "Yes, I slept with Roc but not how you're thinking. At least I don't recall intimacy. I was terrified when I realized I'd… Never mind. Let's just say we never had sex that I can recall. That was the gist of your question. My mind was fuzzy after the first few days in Carnoch."

Dallas might have laughed at the look on his face if she wasn't so distressed from the question. If Roc had agreed, she would have gladly given him her innocence. She wanted him from the first sight of him. *Coup de foudre*…love at first sight. He reminded her so much of Rafe. Rafe, who could never love her. Rafe, who was always her best friend, nothing more…no flash. Nothing. Even though there was no spark, she would have given Rafe whatever he asked for.

When she caught sight of Rafe this afternoon, she felt that same sudden onslaught of lust. The feeling wasn't love. She already loved Rafe. Couldn't feel more for him than she already did. What she wished for was so much more. Love coupled with lust.

Lust.

Raw hunger for this man she'd known for most of her life was a new feeling. Desire. The need to be seduced by him. A real kiss from Rafe would never be refused.

"That you can recall?" The pause between sentences was significant. "I suppose that will have to do for now. I'm going to find a way to understand what is happening. It would help if you would speak to me."

He would know the truth if or when they had sex. It could be tonight. There was only one bed in the cabin. The couch would never be comfortable for either, less for Rafe since he was much taller. Dallas wasn't at all positive she wanted to share a bed with him. Her newfound feelings for him were just that…too new.

With a thready breath of air puffing from her, she felt resigned. "You've got the gist of it. Why don't you tell me what you've been doing all this time?" She was prepared to be out of the line of fire for a few minutes. This interrogation wasn't to her liking since everything she recalled or didn't was a muddled mess.

His broad shoulders lifted upward. "The same as always. My life didn't change when you left except that I didn't have my best friend to talk to. You are listed as a missing person. Suppose we should tell the authorities you've been found."

"That's been done. After I moved into my apartment, an officer came to interview me. Couldn't tell him much. I was here then I wasn't. Somehow, I returned but couldn't recall how." She found her hands were shaking. She didn't understand the emotions eating her up. "He…the officer blamed me for deceiving the good people of Scotland. He was going to charge me with…" She waved her hands in the air. "With lying. Deceiving the public. Using officers for my gain when someone else might have needed someone to help them."

"That day you disappeared; I expected a phone call from you when you reached Inverness. It never came."

"No cell towers…" she reminded him.

"You were going to have dinner at that restaurant you liked…" He stood. Began to pace the room. Rafe reminded her of a cat on the prowl.

"I slid down the hill behind the waterfall," Dallas blurted out, wishing she dared tell him more of her memories. "I didn't deceive anyone. Didn't hurt anyone or lie… Never lied to you. When all this happened, we were like brother and sister. Nothing more. Nothing less. No commitments or promises." Moisture threatened to fall for a second time. Her throat felt clogged. She headed for the door. Escape seemed preferable to answering questions. Distance from this was something she needed. She raced from the room, tears spilling from her eyes. Behind her she heard Rafe's muffled curse.

Outside, she didn't know where she was going. She headed down the trail to the pools before deciding that wasn't a good idea. She didn't want to encounter people. Had to get away. Needed distance to think. He confused her. One moment she thought she understood what was happening. The next she didn't know.

The night sky was darker than she expected. Stars twinkled high in the sky, shining, brilliant. A planet sat on the horizon. The moon gave meager light to the path. Oh, dear, she wasn't dressed to be running around where people could see her. She didn't care. She did though. Escape was what she needed. The night was too dark to see much of anything. She stumbled. Caught herself. Wiped moisture from her face.

Dallas heard his footsteps behind her. She stopped, knowing she could never outrun him. He would follow. Understood he was there to protect her from herself as well as the Gordy and Scratches of this world. Why didn't she have the courage to tell him all he wanted to learn? Rafe wouldn't care if what she told him was crazy. He was a patient man. He loved her as a brother loves a sister. While he might think she was a *wee* bit touched in the head, he would humor her.

After she stopped, he rested his hand on her shoulder. Squeezed as if to reassure. The touch was gentle. He stood behind her. She felt the warmth from him. Felt secure, safe. She recalled feeling much the same way with Roc. The two men, of two different centuries, were so similar.

"Come, Dallas, we should get back to the cabin. The breeze is cool. You don't want to take a chill." He nodded up the trail. Two men were walking toward them, talking, seeming oblivious to them. "Don't think you would like just anyone to see you wearing these clothes."

She sniffed. Brushed more tears off her cheeks with the backs of her hands. He was right about that little bit of reality. He turned her. His finger beneath her chin, lifted. Brushed a gentle kiss across her lips. She warmed. Heated all the way to her toes. Desire for this man she'd known most of her life flared. Was disappointed when he drew back. She craved more of a kiss. To her a million lifetimes passed by them. Now her life pivoted back to what should be normal.

"I want you. Don't ever doubt that, Dallas. Not tonight, not until we understand what happened to you. Since your disappearance, things have changed between the two of us. You asked what I did while you were away. I'll tell you. We'll have more wine along with some of the desert I brought. Instead of questions to you, I'll field questions from you. Would you like that? I will answer all the queries you put in front of me."

He turned her so her breasts pushed against his chest. His hands circled her butt. The men walked by. Nodded. Said good evening with smiles on their lips. The two gentlemen were gone. They were alone. His arm around her, Rafe walked her back to the cabin.

Once inside the warm interior, Rafe sat down with her. Needing his heat along with the comfort he offered, she snuggled into him, her head on his chest. Took consolation from the steady beat of his heart. The pulses of their hearts seemed to blend together. Almost as if they beat as one. She set her hand on his chest. He covered her fingers with his. With him she felt complete. Damn the questions. She didn't want to think.

"I hoped you would tell me more of your life over the last few months. Can tell now that you're too distraught to talk. I've the distinct feeling you no longer trust me with your secrets. That hurts. I will begin by telling you all of what I know. Some of what I guess. With Cole McKenna's help, we pieced together what we believe happened to you. A hypothesis of sorts. I needed a few answers."

"You did? You went to Cole? I do trust you. It's just that I'm afraid. As you said, things have changed. Afraid of what we might feel for each other. Uncertain too." She pushed away from him, looking into the silver blue of his eyes. "What…what happened to me? I remember some of that time. Understand a few facts that I wish I didn't." She almost sputtered that she traveled back to another century. Almost told him she fell in love with another man. If she said those words the sentiments would hurt him. Prudence helped her hold her tongue. The last thing she wanted in the world was to upset this man who'd given her so much.

"This could be a very long story. You realize that until you returned there were no sparks between us. We both felt as if there should be. To both our dismay, there wasn't anything. We loved each other. Even though you were willing to gamble on a marriage, I wasn't. For us, I acknowledged, there was too much at stake. Things have changed. Those flares I searched for are between us now. Not just sparks but flames, an inferno."

"Yes. Now I feel warmed through to the marrow of my bones when you hold me. Heat blazes. That small kiss ignited every part of me. I don't fathom the changes. None of this makes sense. If you can help me figure this all out, I would be grateful."

"Me too. I'll try to put some of this into its proper place. At the keep, there are portraits of all the McKennas, the Stewarts as well as the Frasiers. They line the stairway. The couples…let's just say there are some resemblances throughout the centuries."

"I've never been there. Is there some significance…in the portraits." She tilted her head while thinking. "Was I there? It seems that I…no…" If she heard the wobble in her voice, it was certain Rafe did too. "I just don't remember details. I see flashes of things. Then what I thought I saw or felt is gone. I don't believe I'm supposed to recall anything. There is something strange going on, seems eerie. Maybe the supernatural is at work. It's almost as if I was turning into a different person." Just like that. She snapped her fingers. "I'm me! I want to stay me…" she murmured.

Smiling down at her, he shook his head. "Nothing of what I intend to tell you will make a difference to us now. What I'm going to say to you is the fact your picture wasn't on the stairway when I visited the keep. I know in this lifetime; you have not been to the McKenna keep. Believe you were there…in the past."

"I…this lifetime…?" Perhaps Rafe comprehended more than she gave him credit for understanding. Did he guess she traveled through time…twice?

"Yes, when I was looking for you, I visited Cole. He showed me a portrait of Cameron 'Roc' Frasier painted with his wife Lainie. Elaine is your middle name. Is it not? Did you tell me he called you Lainie?"

"Yes, yes, he did. When I told him my name, he picked up on my middle name. Said that was what he intended to call me. Told me I didn't look like a Dallas. Whatever that is supposed to mean. So…?" With a start Dallas realized she was eager for Rafe to talk to her. The pressure to let out all her emotions vanished.

"Lainie resembled you so much you could have been sisters or passed for twins. Roc looked a lot like me. What do you think? Do I look like that man on your camera card?" he persisted in this line of questions. Maybe he knew more than he let on. "I should not have grown so angry. Suppose I was jealous."

"What I remember of those days it's true. The two of you are much the same. What does that have anything to do with it, except coincidence?" She remembered a story Roc told her when she mentioned she would return to this time. "Roc told me…he said…no…it's too unbelievable. He didn't wish to risk my life by sending me through that portal a second time. I didn't believe what he said. I was determined that he take me back to the glen where he first found me. I needed to find a way home. He didn't want me to leave. Didn't wish for me to go home. Even then, he spoke of marriage. I didn't know what happened to me. I refused to consider marriage." She gasped, realizing what she told him. Rafe had this way of drawing her out. She always felt as if she could tell him anything.

With his fingers supporting her chin, he lifted. Smiled with his eyes into hers. Bore deep as if he saw into her soul. Their relationship was all-encompassing. "What don't you believe?" His eyes focused on hers. He appeared so sincere. "You wished to find a way to return home? To this time? Roc was against doing so? Because he loved you. Sensed something else."

"You won't think I've gone insane?" Dallas was frantic with anxiety. This tale was so preposterous. Roc showed her his cat. Did he?

Was that a dream? He prowled around the bedroom just as Rafe prowled in his human form around this room a few minutes ago. In his cat form, Roc teased her. Could Rafe change into a cat too? Could anyone change shape? Was this all a product of her vivid imagination? Maybe she was crazy.

"I saw him naked." She thought her eyes would cross with the blurted revelation. She'd never seen Rafe naked. Never slept in a bed with him even just to be held. Until these last few minutes, never wanted to see him wearing nothing. Except…she always thought it would be fair if when he painted, he would do so without clothing. She never truly cared. Now she imagined how he would appear in the buff.

"Some of your memory returns?" Rafe chuckled as he bent to kiss her again. The brush of their mouths was soft, sweet. He was tender. "I believe I'm still jealous. Jealous of a dead man. That seems at odds with logic."

"How do you know that he's passed?" More questions. Her breaths turned ragged. The walls once again began to spin. She felt strange, the feelings bazar.

"I'm going to start with the beginning of this story. You've heard of the Clan Chattan?" he stroked her back. Touched one vertebra at a time as his finger traveled up then down the length of her spine.

Dallas began to melt at his touch. Was this how a man seduced? "Gossip…tales told to frighten children. Yes, I've heard of the clan of the cats. What does that have to do with anything? Superstition, that is all the tales are. Rumors passed down over generations." Dallas wished he'd get to the point. Bits and pieces of thoughts flashed through her head. Nothing she saw in her mind made sense.

"They, shifters, mate for life then into eternity. It's always that way. If something happens, future generations will not know their mates. Will never connect or feel the…spark of eternal love," his voice was so serious. He held her hands, rubbed the back of her wrists as if to soothe.

Curiosity soared through her. *Never feel the spark of eternal love? Rubbish.* "Shifters don't exist," she insisted. "How can a person change from a human into a sleek black panther? Doing so would be beyond the imagination…impossible." She felt as if grasping at straws would be easier. A niggling thought in the back of her mind began to take root. Again, flashes of remembrances warred with the present. Fought reality or dreams, she couldn't be certain.

"Or a tiger? There are other cats that change from human then back." His voice continued in a modulated rhythm. Continued to sooth, reassured even while she questioned. She closed her eyes for a few seconds more than a blink.

"I'm listening. It's obvious by the look on your face you're serious. Go on." If Rafe believed, she would have to find some way to also give credit to his facts.

Rafe ran his hand along the back of his neck. Heaved in a large breath of air. For the first time since she first saw him, he seemed nervous. Riddled with anxiety. Until now, he'd been confident. She sat next to him. He no longer held her. The crease of his brows told her he was apprehensive. His lips pulled into a thin line told her the same.

"We think… Cole and I believe that something happened to Lainie Shaw back in the seventeen hundreds. She was Cameron's mate." Rafe cleared his throat before continuing the story. "Shifters mate for life then on into eternity. Believe I just said that. If something happens and the male doesn't claim the female in his lifetime, they will no longer…"

"No longer what?" She thought he might be teasing her. Fought for answers. "Rafe, no longer what!" she cried out again as he seemed to be hesitating. This was something she needed to know.

"The male shifter will no longer be able to claim the female. They will continue living during other times, but they will never mate. They will continue to search for the one woman who is supposed to be theirs, never finding her. Maybe as in our case, finding but not realizing the truth."

She waved her hand in the air. Stared at him for a few seconds her insides fluttering. "That's utter nonsense. I've always known I loved you." Again, that feeling of his truth assailed her. She'd heard those same words somewhere before.

Imagination or reality?

"You fell through that time portal for a reason. Slid down the hill to land at Roc Frasier's feet. You had to bring Lainie Shaw home to Roc Frasier. Otherwise, Roc would never find his mate nor would all the following generations. I'm part of those ensuing generations as are you. Your presence in the eighteenth century righted our lives as well as many others. I'm guessing."

"No…"

"You are my mate."

~ * ~

On the stairway of the McKenna keep, Cole McKenna stood in front of the portrait of Lainie and Roc Frasier. Together, they seemed to smile down upon him. The two found happiness because fate stepped into their lives. Their story had been told through the generations of the clan. The tale was one of loss then discovery. Bitter despair then happiness. Roc worried over ever finding his soul mate just as Rafe did now. Dallas Elaine Shaw stumbled from another time to help bring Lainie and Roc together. The how didn't matter. The why was obvious.

Cole marveled at how destiny found a means to help the struggling couples. By now, Rafe would be learning about Dallas' adventure. Cole wondered what part of it she could recall. Bits and pieces…bits and pieces that would forever leave Dallas wondering about the past. He hoped the couple would find happiness. Now that Roc and Lainie came together, there was little doubt in his mind that in time, Rafe would marry Dallas, claim her so future generations would also find happiness.

A wedding soon in the keep would be wonderful. It had been a few years since a celebration such as this one had taken place. His older sister had been the last recipient of a clan marriage celebration. While his mother berated him to look harder for his mate, he waited with patience. Cole knew she would come to him in time. Indeed, he knew who she was. Too young at the moment for him to marry or claim as his as in the way of the clan. He needed to remain patient while he waited for her to grow up. In the distant past, he would not have needed to wait. Life was different now.

Striding down the stairs, he decided to take a look at the woman who would one day say vows with him. Who he would claim in the master chamber of his tower room. In the present, she was a little hellion, turned seventeen almost a year ago. At eighteen, he could claim her as if…he

32

would try to wait at least another year. Patience was never his strong suit.

As if she owned the place, she ran wild through the keep. Acted with a free spirit. On more than one occasion she'd been called a hellion. He did enjoy watching her. When she was younger, she would stick her tongue out at him when he reprimanded her for her unruly behavior before dancing away on a whim and a breeze. Once when she managed to upset a cart of apples and the owner slid on them, he threatened to take her over his knee to give her a child's punishment for her reckless gallop through the village. She laughed at his threat then dashed off in another direction. He could have caught her. Chose to watch her escape the scene of the crime. Didn't wish to give her the wrong impression. Despite his threat he could never lay a hand on her.

The girl was a flirt. Understood her female power over the males of her age. Knew how to lower her lashes as well as toss her hair over her shoulder. Coiled the young lads with care as well as wanton abandon around her little finger. She could draw them in if that was what she wished. Phoebe knew she was beautiful. She was used to getting her way in all she did. He needed to guard her well. When they wed, he needed to know that he was the only man who tasted those sweet charms she flaunted with carefree abandon. Her father was careless with her. Seemed he didn't know how to handle the wild child that she was. With a delicate touch, is what he had in mind. If she continued to test her wiles on all the young men of the village, he would need to revise his commitment to wait for her to mature. If she did show signs of maturity within the year, he would begin a tender seduction. Hell, he didn't know if he could wait another year. Eighteen was old enough to marry. Even in the modern world women wed younger.

Her golden hair she tied into a ponytail that hung down to the middle of her back. When the strands were not tied back, the silken waves tumbled around her shoulders all the way to her delectable, curvaceous rear. She wore shorts that showed off her sassy butt. Showed too much of her was his opinion. He held no sway over how she chose to cover her body. Even though he wished she would wear more, he would never dictate.

Her breasts were small beneath the tight-fitting top she donned this morning. Today, she went braless. The tight buds pushing on the fabric seemed to beg for attention. His attention. The tips were prominent for all to ogle. His hands fisted. Her legs long and well-shaped appeared to go on forever. He needed to talk to her father about moving her into the keep. Into the castle would be better. There were unused rooms in the north as well as the south tower. The two could live there in comfort. Would live beneath his, along with his mother's, observations. He would have a bit more control over her activities. If he mentioned the connection to his mother, she would take Phoebe under her wing. Guide her. Teach her what her father could not or refused to acknowledge. Cole wasn't certain.

As to date, she'd not directed any of her burgeoning charms his way. Had not flirted with him as she did the young lads who were closer to her age. She would think of him as an old man. He was ages away from being considered decrepit. The thought gave him cause to smile. He meant to teach Phoebe that he was hers. From time to time, he would remind her he was the head of the Clan McKenna. He wasn't certain what she knew about the Clan Chattan. Rumors still abounded. Most of the time, the clan hushed those rumors. Phoebe, he knew, was no shifter.

Phoebe's back was to him. Animated, she spoke to the school math teacher's son. He was a nice lad. Calm. Mature for his lack of age. Would never do for this woman who lived life with energy that would bedevil a lesser man. Her vitality overflowed her small form. Cole wasn't worried about the boy. What he lost sleep over was the football coach's son, Rex. Rex turned twenty-one a few weeks ago. Had his eye on Phoebe. He was a young man filled with his self-worth. He watched her with lust-filled eyes. If the young man seduced, the innocent that Phoebe was would lose her virginity to Rex. He couldn't allow that to happen. Cole wasn't at all certain how to go about keeping Rex away from his mate. Given some thought, he would come up with some diversion.

Bloody eyes, why did Phoebe have to be so young? So, beguiling as well as beautiful. He was twenty-six. Not that old but almost eight years her senior. By this time next year, he would be ready to settle down with this young woman. Doubted if she would be prepared for marriage. Seduce her. Take her off guard with his many charms. Make her want what he alone could give her. Perhaps he would begin the day after her high school graduation. He could take her swimming to the loch near the village. Perhaps show her how a man kissed a woman. Give her a small taste of something she might not wish to live without.

"Phoebe?" With long, determined strides, Cole approached her, sporting a smile. "You're looking very pretty today. Any new conquests to speak of?" He looked to the math teacher's son then back to her. The boy blushed a deep shade of red.

"Cole! What a pleasant surprise?" Her tone held a wealth of sarcasm. He supposed he deserved the mockery. In the past, he'd spoken few words to her. Had attempted to ignore her, along with her outthrust tongue. Though, it had been a few years since she resorted to that means to show him her dislike. This year, he saw major changes in her body as she turned from girl to woman. He did appreciate all her new curves, the shape of her hips, the bounty of her breasts. She should wear a bra.

"Not so much. You are always in this part of the keep after school. You are in your junior year?" He tried to put her age with the grade. He knew full well what grade she was in at school, as well as her age. Had been watching her for the last three years. Wished to see how she would respond to him.

"Senior year," she told him, while she tossed her hair then smiled at him for a beat, lowered her lashes. The smile was one of a siren. "You forget I'm almost eighteen. Will be so before graduation." Again, she lowered her lashes at him. Turned her shoulder a bit, giving him a full view of her shapely yet unconstrained breasts. When she opened her lashes again, her aquamarine eyes sparkled with mischief. Bloody eyes, the girl-woman could seduce a saint. He was no saint.

What was she planning now? He knew there was some type of plot hatching in her head. "I…" she moistened her lips. Let her tongue slow glide across the pink lips he'd like to savor. Smoothed the fabric of her tight-fitting top until it was stretched taut across her beautiful breasts. His body reacted. Her nipples accentuated by the calculated gesture. They were larger than he first thought.

Much to his dismay, he wasn't immune to her flirtations. His body began to tighten while he imagined tasting what she offered. "Want to go for a walk?" Cole held out his hand needing to feel the warmth of her flesh against his skin.

A walk with her might be a huge mistake. He wasn't ready to show his intentions. Before he could do so, she needed to graduate from high school. He needed to get to know her better. The time was coming when he would begin his quest for her hand with serious determination.

"Why, that would be nice. Would rather go for a ride…in your car," she amended with a flourish of her arms. "That convertible is…" She winked at him. "You know what I mean. Awesome."

The groan rumbling up through his chest had to be tamped down. He hoped he didn't know what she meant by the inuendo that she covered up with a quick addition to her statement. If she did understand, it might be too late. Maybe he didn't have time to wait until she graduated. The football teacher's son might have seduced her beneath the stadium. Shaking his head, he caught her elbow. Began to walk.

"You should not be making such scandalous inferences. Do you know what you're talking about?" he berated her. Of course she knew. Most young women understood the act of mating better than they should. He would like to be the man to teach her. Didn't want her to rely on social media for her information. "Come now, a nice walk through the rose garden will do us both good. I've need of some exercise. Saturday we can go into the hills. Maybe to the lock to swim." He needed to turn on his McKenna charm. Whether she was ready to wed or not, he must bind her to him.

"Why are you being so nice to me? You've never been pleasant before. Never asked me to go anywhere with you." She skipped along beside him, deciding not to take his hand. "You've always berated me for my behavior. Why the change?"

Before this she was a little girl. "Why shouldn't I be nice?" he questioned, rumbling different thoughts through his head for a decent answer. "You're a sweet girl."

She stopped, staring at him as if he'd gone daft. Her hands on her hips, those perfect breasts thrust forward, moving with each breath of indignant air she inhaled. Nipples hard, thrusting against thin fabric. Enticing. Her brows drawn together, leaving scowl lines marring her perfect forehead. To trace that soft line would be nice. "Liar. We both know

I'm not a sweet girl. So, I repeat, why are you being nice to me?"

"Just wished to talk." Guess he was not showing his charming side. Berating her did nothing to give him an advantage. She called out his lie.

"Talk about what? I'm telling you..." She was shaking one long delicate finger at him. "Even though you are head of the clan, I don't give away my favors to anyone. Not even you, Cole McKenna. Want the man I marry to be the only man to know me. Even if I say a few outrageous things, the words mean nothing. You hear me? Nothing!"

Cole couldn't stop the huge grin from framing his mouth. He would forever be pleased with her answer. "Don't wish to take anything from you that you don't wish to give. Indeed, that was one of the topics I wished to speak with you about…the way you flaunt yourself to the village lads." Well, he put his foot in his mouth again. Needed this beguiling child-woman to graduate soon. Oh, but she would give her favors to him. That moment was only a blink away. He could wait now that he understood her conscious.

Chapter Two

That night, Dallas slept in Rafe's arms. Security was something she longed for. Rafe had a way of chasing all her fears away while he gave her all she yearned for. While she understood the necessity of talk, of baring all her truths, she couldn't yet. Insecurity plagued her. She needed to first understand her feelings for Rafe. Unfortunately, though, her memory of that time in her life was fading. Each day she recalled less than she did the day before. Soon she would have nothing left to hold onto from that short time in her life. All she would have were those pictures on her photo card. Imagine that would need to be enough to last the rest of her lifetime.

The following day along with the next, they walked to the Fairy Pools. Shot pictures. Rafe swam. She didn't have the nerve to douse herself in the frigid water. All she could manage to let feel the chill were her toes. Her laughter at his antics in the pool surprised her. When he splashed water toward her, she needed to retaliate. Didn't. If she'd tried anything she would have ended up in the water along with him.

A week passed with little change in their relationship. They hiked. Visited places such as the Old Man of Stoor, a large pinnacle of rocks that was photogenic when the sun slipped into sleep. Shot more pictures for herself as well as the magazine. Took pictures of them together. Posted on Facebook as if they were a couple. Watched the sun dip beneath the horizon from various landscapes. They were able to witness the northern lights. All in all, the time spent was incredible.

Despite the amazing adventures, she grew more distant. He remained quiet as if that would help solve their difficulties. Silence didn't help. They were driving home tomorrow to Carnoch. From there they would take one vehicle to Edinburgh where she would show off her photos to her employer. They would sleep in her apartment. Rafe didn't want her to be alone with the two men still in the city. At the thought of Gordy along with Scratch being anywhere near her, she shivered with loathing. Rafe seemed certain she'd not seen the last of those two men.

After they pulled up in front of the structure where Rafe lived, she felt with a start as if she'd come home. The memory of the place in Roc's time was fuzzy. The house couldn't have been much different. Though the place would be *sans* conveniences. There were modern updates. Rafe did like to mingle the old with the new. Living without some of the things she took for granted seemed strange.

She stood in front of the two-story building, three if you counted the attic where Rafe built his studio. He was beside her, his hand on the small of her back. Heat penetrated through the fabric of her shirt. That week in the cabin he never kissed her. She wanted a kiss, maybe another one after that. Wasn't ready for anything more. Rafe told her if he kissed her, he would have the devil's own time stopping with a simple embrace. Since the first night when he told her a little bit about the Clan Chattan, they didn't speak of the past. He believed she traveled through time as did she. She understood there was a lot Rafe didn't tell her about himself. Before they could bridge the gap between friends turned lovers, he would need to be straight with her.

Dallas didn't have any confessions. She held the distinct feeling there was a wealth of information about himself he hid. Rafe brought up shifters. Told her they mated for life. Explained that was why she tumbled through time. She was the only one who could reset the path for Lainie and Roc. In doing so, also fixed their little problem.

No spark. Until now, kisses as well as touches meant nothing.

How the hell did she do that? Reset their destinies? He implied she was his mate. Never said so in so many words. She was baffled as to their relationship. Their connection wasn't what it used to be nor had the feelings between them progressed in a substantial manner to give her the confidence she needed to think of him in any other way than friend. If the tale about the shifters meant he could change form, he should apprise her of that fact. He should show her his cat. Tell her what would happen if they wed. She didn't know if she wanted her children to be little shifters.

"Shall we?" he asked giving her a gentle nudge. "Are you certain you don't want to see if you can get your apartment back? Don't believe any one has rented your space yet. You don't look as if you're comfortable here with me. We could call…"

Dallas interrupted Rafe. He needed to understand her feelings. "I'm not certain of anything except that I want to stay with you tonight. How I'll feel tomorrow morning, I can't say. Neither can I tell you how I will feel in a week or a month." She began the slow walk to his home. Marveled at how very familiar this place felt. The need to feel so much more assailed her.

Dallas saw herself walking up these same steps with Roc. They were different. The wooden steps were not consistent with what they were now. She imagined the steps had needed repairs over the years. The railings were now cast iron. She sipped in a breath of air while Rafe opened the door for her. A wealth of sensations assailed her. She felt as if a blast of images sped through her mind. The startled gasp surprised her. Swaying into Rafe, she closed her eyes. The grip she had on his arm tightened.

"Are you alright?" Rafe asked her, his voice filled with tender concern. "We don't need to stay here. What did you see? Feel?" His questions bombarded her just as the images did.

Shaking her head then nodding she stepped inside the entrance. The breath she tugged on was frail. "I don't know how I am," she managed to say through a wobbly voice. "I don't know anything. Deja vous, I suppose." Chills swept down her spine then back up. She hugged herself. Rafe seemed to understand as he pulled her close. Realized he offered warmth, much needed solace.

"Do you want to talk about what you're feeling? Won't judge. Just listen. Like the old days." His voice was compassionate. He held onto her while they walked farther through the house. "Do you want to explore on your own?" His tone changed, turning gruff as he thought on what she'd been through as well as seen. "You lived here with Roc. Didn't you?" Now, in not so many words, he accused.

He questioned her before about her relationship. "I don't know if we were lovers. Don't know if we married. Don't remember anything of that time. Think I might have lived here with Roc. Don't know. If that's what you're asking me, I can't tell you. Can't tell you anything with any certainty." She understood the underlying anger in his voice. If she was as he said, his mate, he would want to take her to his bed. Would expect her to be chaste. She couldn't answer him. Did she and Roc make love? Was it Lainie who was in his bed? Even more than he needed answers, she wanted to know. Dallas didn't believe she would ever recall all that happened while she lived in a different century.

What she did remember was that she wanted Roc to make love to her. That was when she was still Dallas. Those first nights in the cave if he'd asked or seduced, she would have given Roc one of her condoms to use. She'd wanted Roc Frasier to be her first lover. Was he? Before she never felt that aching need with Rafe. Now she did. Now she prayed that she never allowed Roc to take her innocence. She just didn't remember.

Rafe cleared his throat, changing the subject. He seemed uncertain. Uncertainty was never part of Rafe. "Before we take your photos to the magazine, we should go to the keep. Talk to Cole then to Father Richard."

"Why?" She felt shocked that he moved so fast...too fast for her battered mind. Even though she asked why, she understood he wanted to marry her as soon as possible. She wanted that too. Not as soon as possible. Time for her to sort out the mess of her memories was necessary. She didn't know if she could ever sort it all out. "I..." She turned to him. Set her hand on his chest. "Not yet. Maybe after we return from the city. I'll have to think about choices."

"Today or tomorrow morning, we will see Cole. Father Richard can wait. We need this because the talk will give us some insight into the path we should take for our future. From what I've explained to you about the clan, you do understand you're my mate. We will marry in the way of the clan as well as the way of the church. Father Richard will perform the ceremonies."

She shook her arm away from his grasp, turning on him, eyes as well as words spitting fire, "I understand nothing! Don't comprehend this mate thing. I'm overwhelmed, in case you haven't noticed. Considering our feelings, I'm not where you are. Marriage is impossible the way I feel. You would never have me agree to enter into a union I'm so uncertain of."

With a heavy sigh, he followed her. Unlocked the door. She

stepped inside, turning around in a full circle. Absorbed the room as it was now coupled with her vague memories of what it was before.

Rafe cleared his throat. "If you wish, you can sleep with me as we did before or choose any room you might like better," his voice was raspy, bitter as he set her bag on the floor. "I… geez Dallas, this shouldn't seem so impossible."

Dallas had no clue as to how to interpret his pique. She'd been as honest as she could be about her feelings. Seems he kept a great deal hidden from her. He expected her to marry him because he told her she was his mate. What the hell did that mean? "I'll sleep with you if you don't mind. It's what I want." Breath shuffled from her lungs then, "Whatever I did to create this anger I'm hearing in your voice, I'm sorry." She reached up to place a quick kiss on his cheek. That wasn't to be.

His arms circled her. Drew her close. A wealth of pent-up emotions battled through her. A soft brush of lips across hers. His hand on the back of her head to hold her unmovable. His tongue roamed between her lips. She parted for him, seeming to need this contact as much or more than he did. He thrust inside her mouth. Touched. Explored. Delved into the darkest recesses of her. Dallas sensed he wanted more from her. She gave him all she could.

This was heaven. The kiss was what she'd waited for all week. Her hands sneaked up to thread through his hair. She pressed her body against his. Felt his hard arousal next to her stomach. His hands cupped her bottom. Pulled her closer. She understood this was what she'd wanted. Part of what made her curt with him. They were both frustrated. Maybe this yearning was what orchestrated his anger.

There were still too many questions between them to commit to a lifetime together. Making love was a huge promise she couldn't make, not now. Not yet if she ever could. She wouldn't deceive him into believing she wanted all that he did. Not while she was still confused by the rapid-fire succession of events. Rafe must have felt her sudden hesitancy. His hold on her loosened. He set her down. Her feet touched the floor. Her mind spun. Stepping away, she stumbled. He caught her.

To explain herself was impossible. She didn't have the words. Her hands folded in front of her, she said the first thought coming into her head.

"I'll make dinner. Do you have anything in the cupboards? The pantry?" she asked, wondering what she could put together to fill their stomachs. She remembered. A flash of insight swept through her head. All the time she spent in the other century, she never forgot how to cook. Maybe Lainie also liked to experiment in the kitchen, to dabble with different ingredients.

Stepping back from her, he tapped her on the nose, a cautious smile on his face. "First, I don't regret the kiss. Second, I do want to have all of you as soon as you are ready. Need to understand your reticence better. As for the food, why don't you look. I've been gone a week. Don't have any idea what you might find. If you make a list of what you need, I'll make a quick run to the store."

Her feet seemed to attract her attention as she stared at him. After the surge of hunger the kiss created, she was once more left in a mindless fog. The potent caresses caused her insides to pulse. She felt alive as she'd never felt before. "I'm sorry. I'll say it again. Let's go see what there is. If you've frozen meat along with noodles or…" she left off speaking when his hoot of laughter filled the room.

"You've not changed in this cooking thing you love. That's a relief. I'll bet everyone back in the seventeen hundreds gained weight with your fabulous cooking. I know. I've cold beer in the fridge. Must have a few bottles of wine in the wine keeper. Know there will be ground beef along with frozen chicken. Won't take too much time in the microwave to thaw. Anything else you might need to create a delicious meal, I'll get for you."

Dallas found spaghetti noodles, along with tomato sauce. She made meat balls out of the thawed ground beef. While the meal wasn't fancy or romantic as that first dinner with Rafe at the Fairy Pools, the food was filling. She lit candles. There were no flowers. They drank beer instead of wine. It was more comfortable than tense with unanswered questions.

Relaxed in his kitchen, she recalled other times they sat at the table drinking a beer together. She in a pink robe with nothing on beneath. He in the clothes he wore when he painted…ripped jeans and tattered shirt. This was a cozy room. Nice. No romantic ambiance. She thought of the studio where she posed naked more than once. He was like a brother. No longer. In time, she was positive, he would be her lover. "Can I see the painting? The one you were working on before I slid down the hill behind the waterfall." What happened to her was far too similar to Alice sliding down the rabbit hole. "Before the world turned topsy-turvy for me."

As he lifted one eyebrow, she paused in thought. Tapped her fingers on the table while he seemed to hesitate.

"What painting?" he asked, with a seductive half-smile forming on his lips.

She understood from the past his little boy side kicked up. With her finger she tapped him on his chest. "Don't play dumb with me, Rafe Frasier."

"I've so many paintings of you, I've no idea which one you're talking about. You will need to be more specific. Is it the one where you are naked? One of the others where you are not?"

Unable to stop the snort, she spoke, "All the paintings you've done of me have been with me in the buff. This is the one you weren't going to sell because it looked just like me. Did you lie to me?" She tossed her spoon his way. He ducked, laughing. The spoon crashed against the opposite wall. "Did you sell it?"

Standing, he held out his hand to her. "I'll show you the one you are talking about. I've put it on the wall in my studio to remind me of you. Every night before I went to bed, I would look at it, needing you. Wanting you to show up at my door as if you'd never been gone. Somehow, I understood you would return one day. Kept looking even when I was discouraged. Also understood you would come back to me the way you were supposed to be from the beginning."

Without taking his hand, she headed toward the stairs, walking in front of him, eager to see his creation. When she stopped, he plowed into her. He grabbed her waist to turn her. She touched his chin. "He…Roc painted me too. Is that bad? I posed for him too. What do you think? Could that painting be somewhere in your studio. When he painted me, the studio was an attic. Told me no one would see the image save him. I believed what he told me. Can we look for it? Maybe in some hidden cubbyhole. He said he would never get rid of the painting. He intended to put the oil of me in a safe place." Dallas blinked a few times, realizing what she remembered.

"Who? Who the hell are you talking about?" Fury entered into Rafe's voice. The steel of his eyes was cold. Frigid. Looked as if he grew angrier with each breath of air he inhaled. "Who painted you. Not naked!" His hands gripped her tight.

Shaking her finger at him, "You're hurting me." His hands dropped away. "Don't you dare get angry with me, Rafe Frasier. I didn't think I would ever come back. Roc is a gifted artist also. Just like you. The two of you are too much the same. Naked? You know I'm a model. This was nothing to me as you well know. Other people besides you have painted me wearing nothing. Paid my tuition through school modeling, as you well know." Dallas felt the pain of the lost memory. While she didn't want to return, she didn't wish to forget either. The gentleness Roc treated her with, she hoped, would always be remembered as the visions faded. "No…" she moaned; her voice soft.

Rafe pulled her into his arms. His hand held her close. "I'm sorry. Can tell the memory was there and now it's gone. If he painted you in the buff, I wouldn't want to care. We are in ways the same person. I will have to accept that you shared parts of yourself with this man. Have to accept because we are one and the same. I, too, would have found a way to rid you of your clothing then paint all your beautiful curves. Just as I've done here in this century. I've…when I painted you in the past no part of me stirred. I know for a fact that now, if I looked at you to paint you, my body would swell with its need." He touched upon a tear slipping from her eyes. "I refuse to feel anger or jealousy. Feeling so doesn't seem right."

Hand in hand they walked the steps to his studio. The painting was framed and on the wall. Her heart fluttered upon seeing the splendid portrait. Rafe was indeed a gifted artist. Sipping in a breath of air, she turned to him. "How much did you lose by not selling this? Rafe, it's a masterpiece. Exquisite in every way."

"The selling price would have paid my mortgage for more than five years. Couldn't part with this last memory of you. Now, though…" he tapped her on the nose, his smile infectious, "that you're back, I might reconsider the sale. Would use it to…"

He looked surprised when she struck him in the chest. Pummeled him several times. "You can't sell this! The woman there," she pointed, "looks just like me. You promised to change the features. You didn't." Part of her was thrilled the painting was worth so much. The other part of her was appalled that someone would recognize her. "The painting belongs on this wall, only this wall. Nowhere else."

"I'm pleased you noticed. It is you. Wouldn't want the woman in this painting to appear as someone else." He was laughing too hard to listen to her sputter her protests. He would never sell. She didn't need to believe that.

"See if I ever pose for you again," she mumbled between her teeth. "I…"

Rafe swept her into his arms. Headed downstairs to the master bedroom. "I've got something else to show you. Tonight, you will learn more about me. Maybe more than you ever wished to learn."

"What?" She pounded on his chest again, laughing as he took the steps two at a time. "Put me down! I weigh too much for you to carry me. You're going to drop me. I'll fall down the steps. Break some part of me I'd rather was left intact."

"Not too much for me to carry. If you haven't noticed yet, I'm a strong man. I can transport you whenever it pleases me to do so. You do not weigh so very much. I wish to do so now. Protest all you like. You won't change my mind." He opened the door to his room with his shoulder before kicking the solid wood closed with his foot.

Once inside, she found herself sitting on his bed, her hair a disheveled mess floating around her shoulders. Never before had she been there, in his bedroom, on his bed. There had never been a reason. With Rafe, she spent time in his kitchen as well as in the studio. Mesmerized, she watched him as he began to disrobe. For a few beats, her eyes crossed. His fingers found the hem of his t-shirt. Surprise made her gasp.

"What are you doing? Rafe…you…you're taking off your shirt." There had been times when she modeled for Rafe, she thought he should also be naked…fair was fair. At the thought, she giggled. When she broached the subject, he told her she was being ridiculous. To Dallas it seemed the correct way to go about the painting. Wished him to paint naked so she could see him without clothing. Despite the fact there was never anything romantic between them, she'd been curious to see what he looked like beneath his clothes. He always fascinated her. Now he intrigued her more. Realizing now all her wild dreams might come true, she panicked. "Rafe!"

"Before I can show you my cat, I have to be naked. Well, I don't have to disrobe. Nonetheless, I don't want to shred these clothes when I change form. These are my favorite jeans. I do like the t-shirt also. What do you think? Would you enjoy seeing me without clothing considering the vast number of times I've seen you…naked?" He waggled his eyebrows.

She wished to toss something at him. "You're changing? Right now? In front of me? I don't believe you. Men cannot change into cats! That's not possible." She swallowed hard trying to dislodge the lump she found in her throat. A flash in her mind presented Roc in his cat form. He showed her his cat right here in this very room. "Rafe, you can't. Men cannot do this!" so freaked out by the situation, she repeated herself.

He lifted his broad shoulders. His broad naked shoulders. She'd seen his shoulders before. It was his lower half she was anxious about. Left her mind befuddled.

"What better time than the present? I've had the distinct, annoying fear you haven't believed what I've told you. Need to set everything right. By showing you what I can do, I will be a step closer to what I want…to what we both long for." His shirt fell on the floor. After that he hopped on one foot then the other to rid himself of his running shoes. When his hands fell on his belt buckle, she gave a little gasp. He was serious. This was going to happen. She would know what he looked like without clothing. If she closed her eyes, she wouldn't see. That wasn't going to happen. She fully intended to take advantage of this unexpected situation.

Dallas didn't know if the gasp was from fear or anticipation. She found her body pulsed with excitement at the chance to see Rafe wearing nothing at all. Heat flooded her. This moment was years in the making. Unless she saw Roc with nothing on, she had never seen a naked man. She wished she remembered. Losing one's memories sucked. A few minutes ago, she thought she had a flash of memory. The recollection was gone now. Had she seen Roc change to his cat? She didn't remember. Did she see him naked?

"Don't think you should do this…" Dallas was holding her hands out as if she could stop him. "Stop, Rafe. You cannot…" She was a pile of jumbled nerves. First, she did, then she didn't. "I've never…"

"Why not?" he questioned with a quirky slant to his lips. "I've seen you more than once wearing nothing at all. Seems only right for you to see me. Don't you think? We're going to do this today. Understand…" he paused for a few seconds. "Understand that not only will I be naked, but I'm fully aroused. You have this way of doing that to me. Seems I've been hard since I first saw you at the Fairy Pools. I'm not going to lie to you, Dallas. I want you. The catalyst between us is strong, all-consuming, the thoughts deep. As far as my feelings for you are concerned, the sooner we deal with this sex thing, the better. If we could arrange a marriage tomorrow, I'd be jumping for joy at the prospect." His jeans then boxers hit the floor. With slow strides he walked toward her.

Fascinated, her mouth gaped open. Could not keep her eyes from the most intriguing part of him.

"However, marriage or no marriage vows, I will make love to you. Not tonight. Understand you are not ready. Soon, Dallas. Soon, we'll be together in every way possible for a man and a woman."

What she expected she didn't know. Her tongue ran across her parched lips. She needed something to drink. Didn't think this was an opportune time for her to run down to the kitchen to bring up a bottle of wine or cold beers for the two of them. If she did, would the performance put off the inevitable. Dallas knew this was unavoidable. She knew that determined look on his face. He couldn't be swayed from his course.

"You wish to have something to drink. I can see it in your eyes. Feel as if at times I can read your mind. I've heard shifters can do that with their mates. Know what they think. I like the notion that I will know all your beautiful and sometimes wicked thoughts. You can't hide them from me, your mate." Buck naked he walked to a table in the corner of the room. His back was to her; almost as intriguing as his front. Dallas didn't know when he planned this scenario. It must have been when she was cooking. He poured them each a glass of wine. After handing hers to her, he drank. Set the glass down.

"Now, are you ready? Know that in my cat I'm quite large. Also, understand that I'm not dangerous to you in this different form. I would never hurt you. Gordon and Scratch are a different matter altogether. The pair will harm you if given the opportunity. I would rip out their throats if they tried anything."

Nodding, she watched with anticipation. Mulled over his words about the two men plaguing her existence. The transformation didn't take long. Before her eyes, he stood, staring at her. Grinning. Can a cat grin? She found she was trembling. Vibrated from the top of her head to the tips of her toes. Wondered what he planned now.

Rafe shifted!

My god, he changed!

She collected her thoughts into what she hoped was coherent speech. "Rafe? You didn't lie to me." Dallas reached out, her heart pounding in her throat. Her hand shook. She needed to touch. To feel. To understand all she didn't. Prove that indeed he was a large cat. A huge black panther. He prowled. His feet padded softly on the carpet. Memories flashed in her head. Recollections of another time, a moment when Roc was the cat prowling around her. The memory flashed then was gone. She blinked as if a strobe light went off in her head.

Rafe? Roc? Together as one soul. United by time.

This was about Rafe. This happened in the present not the past. He was real. Rafe was now. They were in the present. She shouldn't be trying to recall something in a distant surreal life. Something about another man. Dallas realized she needed to concentrate on her future. Their future. Needed to see Rafe for what he was to her.

"Oh!"

Rafe landed on the bed beside her. With his huge cat tongue, he licked the side of her face. Startled, she scooted back while he tipped his head as if questioning her reason for moving. Again, she didn't know what to think or what to do. She found she held herself tight. Her shoulders stiff.

"That's alright, big fella. Not ready to have you taste me. Don't lick me. Don't devour me. Your teeth are huge. You told me you didn't bite. You can't be so close to me. Not ready. I'm afraid." Dallas rambled. Her body shivered, shuddered with her fear along with anticipation to learn more. Before this strange event, she never imagined the rumors were true. The Clan Chattan was real. The people were real shifters.

He lay down beside her. As if he wanted her to pet him, he pushed at her hand. Licked her between her fingers sending his tongue along the sensitive insides. Startled, she jerked. "Oh…!" Unwanted, she felt a slow quivering deep in her belly. He turned, his raspy tongue on her wrist. Heat flared. Was that possible. He shouldn't be doing that. Should he?

"Rafe don't lick me!" She pulled her hand back. Bending. Cautious, she twisted close to him. "Can I pet you?"

Rafe nodded as if he understood her words. He must be able to hear, to comprehend. "Can you understand me?"

Once again, the movement of his big head told her he comprehended the words she spoke. Dallas reached out to run her hand along his back. Heard the purr of contentment throb with each stroke of her fingers.

Rafe rose beside her. His teeth closed around one strap of her top. Yanked until the strap slid down her arm. Turned his attention to the other strap.

"Rafe! No!"

He moved back, looked at her, at her breasts that were now bared for him. Self-conscious, she crossed her arms in front of her, knowing she hid little from him. All this added to the bewilderment in her brain. Still in his cat, he sat back again. Tilting his head one way then the other. Gazing over her. Studying her. She was stiff from embarrassment. Mortified to the tips of her toes. She understood he looked at her in a different way. Before there was never anything between them.

Put your arms down, Dallas. I want to see you. Don't hide from me. It's been so long since I've painted you. Looked at you. I need to be reminded of all your beauty. Think I've forgotten how beautiful you are. Join me. Get naked for me. Strip your clothing off. I might do the job for you. Promise if you are naked, I will turn back to human. I won't do anything you don't want. Understand you're frightened. Overwhelmed.

Dallas didn't comprehend what was going on here. She pushed back against the headboard. A cool breeze filtering through the open window kissed her flesh. She shivered. Goosebumps rose. The crowns of her breasts hardened. "No…" she murmured, as she tried to pull the straps of her top back to her shoulders. "No… you can't…we can't. I don't want to be naked with you like that." She was frightened. Terrified. Rafe didn't understand. All this was new to her. She wasn't prepared.

His teeth stopped her from doing what she wished. Kept her from rearranging her clothing. He licked her arm. She jumped. "Rafe no! Don't you dare!" The sensation of the caress he made shocked her. Heat spiraled.

I want to taste you. Savor all of you. Not like this. Need for you to feel at ease with me no matter how I look or how you see me. I'll wait. Imagine I should return to my human. Will you take all your clothes off if I do? Will you let me explore your beauty?

"No…" She felt her eyes glaze over. "Rafe, you are talking to me. I'm hearing you in my head. That's not possible. Did you know that you were talking to me. Talking to me in my mind? You want me to disrobe in front of you. I don't know what's real and what I'm imagining. The day is filled with new surprises. Too many surprises." Her reticence didn't make sense. Rafe had seen her naked any number of times. "I don't want to take off my clothes so you can ogle me with your cat eyes. Don't want you to lick me. Need to have you back the way you are supposed to be." She wasn't ready for any of this. "Rafe, please….please turn back. This is going to take me some time. I've known you all these years. You've never given me any indication you could…could change yourself."

If you take your clothes off, I'll change to my human. It will be just like it used to be for us. Before, you were never embarrassed. Never terrified. I assure you I'm the same person whether I look human or appear as a cat.

"Liar. Nothing is or ever will be just like it used to be for us. You are so huge. Your cat… What are you going to do if I take off…my… clothes?" She shivered. Wanted to be with him. Maybe this was too soon for them to be together. Perhaps the time was right. She hadn't changed her mind. Wasn't prepared for that next step with him. He wanted her. His eyes, even his cat eyes, told the true story. Told her, if she would let him, he would have sex. It seemed so much easier when she wanted to find someone who set her on fire. She found that someone. Now, she was afraid of being with him.

I'll have a glass of wine with you. Something to eat. Talk if you wish. After that we'll see what happens. We can sit on the bed. Sip the burgundy. I could pour a little on the parts of you I'd like to taste. You could...

"Rafe no...to the wine. Yes, if you'll return to normal, I'll take off my clothes. Sit here naked as well as drink wine with you." He'd seen her that way more times than she could count. What difference did it make if she wore no clothing? He'd seen her in the buff more than once. He'd seen her a myriad of times along with other people in her art classes at college. She used the modeling money to help her pay for her tuition. She wasn't a prude. She sunbathed in less than she wore now. Except her breasts were covered by tiny triangles. In the past, had thought nothing of disrobing for artists to draw or paint her. If anyone in the room bothered her, she would withdraw into herself. Enmesh herself in thoughts, mostly about Rafe. Thoughts that if things were different, they would have a relationship. Well, now things were changed. She had what she wanted. Instead of embracing the notion with both arms, she withdrew.

Before she could find the time to inhale a breath of air, Rafe strode to her in his human form. Sitting beside her, he cupped in his hand one large breast he had revealed earlier. Rubbed the tip with his thumb. With a heavy breath of air, he sat back. Their shoulders touched. He didn't say anything.

Dallas didn't know how she knew but she understood he waited for her to remove her clothing, what there was of it. She told him she would. While he waited, she did as she told him she would do.

After disrobing, she sat next to him, her glass of wine in hand, her legs curled beneath her. She never felt this vulnerable even though he didn't even look at her. He would though. "This doesn't change anything, Rafe. I'm not ready for sex with you."

"I understand. Tomorrow we will see Cole as well as Father Richard. The sooner..." he stopped when she spoke up.

"No!" Dallas didn't understand why she was so adamant about this. She was though. Time would heal her wounds. Wounds that confused her. "Talking to these people will just mess up my mind even more. I don't want reasons or facts that other people have decided upon. I'm, even now, while we sit close, unraveling one strand at a time." Her nerves were frayed. He pushed her too hard. Too fast.

Rafe turned to look at her. His eyes were steel-hard, gray. She was positive he was angry with her. He picked up her hand. Caressed the back with his cheek. She felt the stubble from the day's growth. "I want you to speak with Ruby, Cole's mother, you might be able to make some sense of this unique situation. Cole's mother is not a shifter. She married one of us. The woman will understand some of your fears. You don't have any ideas how you can move forward when I'm so different from you. I'm feeling that's part of the problem. Because of that fact, you don't know how to deal with the days in our future. How to be married to a man who is unique to all you know. Very few couples in our world are both shifters."

"I don't wish to talk to his mother. Don't want to go to the McKenna keep tomorrow." She tried to sound strong. Put emphasis on the, 'I don't wish to talk' part. She found she was weakening. Rafe would have his way. He would wear her down. He was right about some of her fears. She didn't think she had this trouble adapting to Roc.

"Please…give this…us a chance. I can be patient. You do recall, we waited more years than most should need to wait. Have I ever asked you for anything?" He was smooth talking. Niggling his way under her skin. Soon Rafe would have her wound around his little finger. Even while he pleaded, she weakened.

"No, Rafe, you haven't. I've always been the needy one in this relationship. No matter what was happening, you've always been there for me. Held my hand whenever I needed your strength. Can't say the same for me. I'm selfish." She tapped a finger on her chin. "Believe if you asked, I would go to the keep, I would have said, yes. Instead, you told me we would go. Not comprehending this arrogance of yours. This side of you is new to me."

"Does that mean you'll go with me tomorrow?" Now, he sounded eager, little boy enthusiastic. "We can leave first thing in the morning."

"I will. I will go after we have breakfast along with a shower." While she turned to him, her breasts brushed across his arm. She heard the quick inhalation of air. Felt the swift knife of heat. What she felt was fire. Her body quickened. His sex grew, hardened even more than when he first disrobed in order to change into his cat. She looked away.

"Thank you. You won't regret the visit. I know I won't. Want to show you the portrait of Roc and Lainie. When you see the painting, you will better understand much of what I've been saying. My words have all been true. We have the chance to unite in the way of the clan because you fell through a void into another world. By your unintentional actions the universe was set right."

A tick of the clock passed, then another, while she thought to risk everything by touching him. "I regret saying yes to your request. Doubt if anything that is said or done tomorrow will change my feelings. You will be putting me in a position where I'll need to defend myself." She leaned into him. "I'm terrified. Would rather we figure this is out together. Don't want or need outside help."

Rafe laughed before pulling her into his arms. The soft hair of his chest brushed across the tips of her breasts. She sucked air at the contact. Her body flamed hotter. Tempest roared inside. She almost changed her mind about the sex. She wished he would kiss her. Remembered the last kiss they shared. The touch had been so different. If he kissed her again, would she be able to say no to more intimacy?

As if he heard her wish, his lips formed across hers in a deep possessive kiss. One that spoke of longing. Desire. Hunger. A touch that spoke of the past as well as generations yet to be seen. She pushed on his shoulders. He threaded his fingers through her hair. The strands slipped around her, curled as he stroked her back. With his tongue he parted her lips. She felt as if she melted all over him. Refused to give in to her base desires. She wanted him. Didn't want him. He could persuade. No matter how he tried, he could not make her ready for this moment. She had to think. He pulled away to stare into her eyes. She could tell he sensed her withdrawal.

"Rafe. I don't want this...this kiss. Not yet. Not tonight. Need time to process, to come to terms as to what is happening between us as well as to me." Her protest was weak. He guessed her desire. Would he always know how she felt? He read her mind when he was in his cat. Could he do so as a human?

Liar. Your body as well as the thoughts I'm reading tell me a different story. Sex with you would not be force. Nonetheless, I intend to wait out the time you ask for. Give you the moments you seem to desire more than me. More ticks of the clock to come to terms with your passion. Want to have your present mind be one with me as well as the thoughts you seek to hide from me.

Dallas rested her head against his chest. Heard the soft cadence of each breath. Rubbed her cheek across him. Heard the hard pounding of his heart. Felt the warmth of his feelings. He was right about most everything. He had the advantage of knowing what she thought. The musky scent of him coupled with his aftershave filled her to near overflowing. He was correct. It was true. She did want him in the most primitive and elemental ways. Sometimes she believed he knew her better than she knew herself. He understood her mood swings. Comprehended what she required even when she didn't.

"I should sleep in a different room," she murmured as she began to rise. His hand settled on her shoulder keeping her still.

"You wish to sleep with me. I won't do anything you don't want. Promise."

"That's the problem."

Rafe cleared his throat before he spoke, his eyes a deep pewter. "We should sleep in this room together. You in my arms. Naked against my flesh. Want to proceed tonight as I would every night after this one for the rest of our lives. I won't take advantage of you. You told me no. This won't be different from the way we slept on your photo shoot. Every night I held you in my arms. Listened to each breath of air."

"I wasn't naked, and neither were you," Dallas retorted as if the words would un-muddle her mind. "This is nothing like those nights."

"I wanted us to be naked. Does that count?" he asked, that silly half-grin she adored flashing in front of her eyes. "Need more from you as you well understand. I can wait. Tomorrow we will take a few more steps in a positive direction."

"No. Don't know if I can sleep like this next to you," she murmured, as she found herself playing with the crisp dark hair on his chest. With curiosity, she touched one of his nipples. It was hard, taut. She heard the groan ruffle from his lips. Realized her touch affected him in ways that were new to her. This was something she'd never done before. Rafe would understand sex was new to her while sharing carnal pleasures was not new to him. He'd had women in his life. Even told her about the girls who he bedded. None of them meant anything to him. Would he grow tired of waiting for her? Would he grow bored with her just as he had the other women he told her about.

"I know one sure-fire way to fix that," Rafe muttered while he stroked the curve of her hip then down her leg. His caress lingered behind her knee before moving higher. "If you can play with me, I can play with you. It's only fair. You've always been the one to bring up fairness. What about now? I would have an answer."

Her body responded to his touch. Fire blossomed before spreading. An instinct old as time caused her to separate her legs for him. "You told me…agreed with me that we would not have sex tonight." She understood by caressing him, she was stirring up feelings best left alone until sex was what she wanted.

His hand fell away from her leg. "Stupidest thing I ever agreed to. I could even now seduce you. Sweet-talk you so thoroughly that you would respond to my seduction. Melt all over me like warm honey. You just opened up for me." He rose to refill their glasses of wine.

"Chivalrous," she told him, smiling at the look of painfilled distraught she read in his eyes. "I don't mean to be…"

"A siren?" he asked one brow lifting upward. "An enchantress or a vixen?"

"I'm not. You know I'm not any of those types of women. What I am is one who's mind is befuddled. One who needs a few answers before she can give herself to a man she cares for."

"Promise you tomorrow, you'll get some answers if you keep an open mind."

~ * ~

At the keep, Rafe was certain Dallas would garner a few insights into the Clan Chattan. Perhaps it was too soon in their new relationship for her to have seen his cat. In hindsight, considering the very real fear he felt emanating from her, he might have waited until after they made love for the first time. He thought of himself as a patient man. In this instance, with Dallas, he had no patience. He burst with eagerness. Shared a part of himself Dallas wasn't prepared to meet.

She had questions that he could answer. From all he surmised during the last week with her, he was the last person she wished to ask. He could have saved time. Could have given her a response to anything she wished to learn. So, instead of waiting for the question, he leapt right into her mind by showing her his cat.

Ruby's knowledge would help settle a few of her fears. Cole's mother would explain about the clan from her point of view. Seeing the portrait might conjure up a few memories that vanished. While she seemed to still recall her first few days with Roc, everything else seemed to be a blank in her head. Neither knew how long she, Dallas, had been with Roc. She didn't know when the real Lainie merged with her mind then took over.

Rafe didn't believe they would ever fully understand what happened over the days she went missing. The weeks. The months. Didn't know how she could change places with a woman who wasn't there but then she was. The abstract defied all logic. Ruby couldn't answer those questions for her either. No one could. All Cole's mother could explain would be her role in the marriage.

Light from the morning sun was just filtering in through the window. Dallas lay sprawled against him, one leg thrown over his. Her head nestled against his shoulder while her breasts fluttered across his chest with each breath she inhaled. He found himself aroused. Hard. Needing her more than ever. He could have her if he wanted. She would be seduced before she could tell him no. That would make him a cad of the worst sort. He would never put this to the test. After they made love, he didn't think she would cower before him again. Didn't believe she would stop him.

Holding Dallas in his arms, waking up with her head pillowed on his chest was heaven to him. Most of his life he'd never thought to have these wonderful moments with Dallas. Until she returned, he'd thought she would never be more than his best friend. A woman who was more like a sister than a lover. The problem he experienced now was that he needed more from her. She wasn't ready to give more of herself. Since he understood she was his, he wanted everything. All of her. The wedding. The feast. The claiming. He knew Ruby would have the white cape ready for them when they said a second set of vows in front of family. Stymied to figure out how to convince her, he groped at every notion that popped into his head. Now she played with his body. For the moment, her curiosity seemed to override her fears.

Unable to resist, he trailed a fingertip along her shoulder. Her satin flesh responded. Quivering with the pleasure he gave, she snuggled closer to him. Her thick gold-red hair tickled his nose. For the rest of his life, he needed to spend every night with her. Needed to hold her in his arms. Most of all, he wished to call her his wife, his mate as well as his lover. Prayed Father Richard would convince her this was the only path to take. Rafe didn't know how that could be accomplished.

Sleeping with her naked or not had both drawbacks as well as pleasures. All his waking moments during the night he found himself in full arousal, needing to make her his in every way. Needed to feel the velvet heat of her sleek wet channel. Even though sleep eluded him, he wouldn't give these moments up unless she insisted. While he explored, his fingers moved lower. Touched the tip of one breast then the other. Slid his hand along the curve of her hip to explore her delightful butt.

Dallas always thought she was too large. Compared to him, she was small, tiny in the extreme. Her curves were lush. Full. He loved the fact her breasts overflowed his large hands. Would love for her to allow him to bury his face between them. Her hips were wide, meant for his hands to hold. She despised the tiny dimples on her thighs she called cellulite. For him those depressions represented more places for his lips to find as well as explore. Soft flesh to tease with his mouth.

Rafe knew the moment she woke. Her soft sigh of pleasure ripped from her lips. He had no business exploring her curves. Couldn't help himself.

"Rafe…?" She pushed up, her hands on his chest. Mesmerized, he watched the gentle sway of her breasts. Grinned. Dallas looked confused for a few seconds. The look that came over her face gave him the first clue she was fully awake. "We should get up."

He didn't agree. They needed time in bed together. If they had become lovers last night, they would have early morning sex. Maybe tomorrow. It would be another day. After the meeting at the keep, Dallas might change her mind about taking the next step in their relationship. He hoped she would. Knew she'd always been open to a sexual relationship. Also understood she'd been waiting for the right man. The right man was here now. Ready for her.

"No. Wish to hold you for a few more minutes. Don't desire to rise just yet. We've got all morning. We aren't due in Edinburgh until tomorrow or the next day. That's what you told me. You have an appointment with your boss to show him your photographs. Today we can do whatever we please." He smoothed hair away from her face. Her deep blue eyes stared back at him. She lowered her lashes for a few heart beats.

"Alright," Dallas lay back down, her head on his chest, her fingers winding into the mat of dark hair on his chest. She trailed that lone fingertip down his body to his abdomen, farther, as if she meant to test his ability to remain still. She almost touched his sex before she brought her hand back to the middle of his chest.

Minx.

"You play with fire, little siren. Unless you wish to lose your virginity right now you should stop the exploration." Bloody eyes, he didn't want her to stop. This curiosity of hers could serve to get her into trouble, multitudes. Perhaps she was afraid to tell him what she needed. Thought she might be too bold.

"Don't you want me to touch you? I want to learn all of you. So? Tell me what you'd like me to do?" she queried as his body pulsed to life, still stroking him as if she meant to test his mettle. Her voice was flirtatious. Soft. Melodic.

"Only if you're willing…if you're willing, to take this to the next level then be my guest. Touch wherever."

Dallas withdrew her hand. Her eyes glazing over while she took the moment to think. "I should see about fixing breakfast."

She rose then pulled on the robe he left her last night on the chair near the fire. It was the one she wore when she modeled for him. She pushed herself way past her comfort zone then withdrew. He didn't understand how to bring her back. Dallas wanted to play with his body. There was no doubt in his mind.

He felt her withdrawal, the cold air flitting across him as the covers were moved aside. The next time perhaps. If not, then the one after that. He let a long breath of air leave his lungs. "Take the first shower. I need…" What he needed was to tamp down the raw hunger she created with a few tender touches. After that he needed to forget how fast her passion rose.

"Are you certain?"

He'd never been more certain. Time to breathe. Distance. Not waiting for his answer, she disappeared through the door to the bathroom. A few seconds later he heard the running water. He slipped his hands behind his head. Stared at the ceiling thinking that sharing a shower together would be nice. He was positive she needed to be out of his line of vision until he got his body under control. That wasn't going to happen if he saw her naked.

While she was still in the shower, he made coffee. Brought a steaming cup for her to the bedroom knowing how much she enjoyed that first cup of the brew each morning. He sat in a chair facing the fireplace, sipping his drink, waiting for her to appear. Wondered how she would dress this morning for the meeting at the keep. The water stopped. A few minutes later she walked through the door, her hair wrapped in a towel, another around her body. For his peace of mind, she should have dressed. A towel was too easy to remove.

"Coffee?" He held up the mug he brought for her. "Black?"

"You're wonderful." She grasped the cup with both hands, sipped, testing the heat of the brew. Sent him a devastating smile. "Thank you."

At times he also thought he was wonderful. He would do anything for her. Anything to make her happy. Anything except turn his back on her. He wasn't about to give up on them. On the relationship they could have. "My turn for a shower." He meant to give her space to dress. Last night he gave her no privacy. That was probably not well done of him. She didn't protest. If she'd said one negative word about disrobing in front of him, he would have backed off.

"Come to the kitchen when you're finished showering. Believe I saw some potatoes in the pantry along with bacon in the freezer. There were no eggs. We'll have to go to the store later today. By the time you're finished with your shower, breakfast should be on the table." She was bent over, towel drying her thick hair. He wished Dallas would leave it down. He knew she would tuck the long strands up in some kind of holder to keep the hair away from her face.

Left with his thoughts, he showered. Dressed in a pair of old jeans along with a t-shirt. When he came out of the bathroom, she was gone. He heard her singing. Seemed she always sang when she cooked. His stomach growled. Breakfast could wait. He needed to confirm a few appointments he had in mind for the day.

Picking up his cell he made two calls. The first one was to Cole. He apprised him of his destination this morning. Cole assured him he would be at the keep to greet him. Guaranteed him also that his mother would be more than willing to guide Dallas around the keep as well as answer questions that might arise. Ruby could ease Dallas into accepting the clan.

Father Richard was next in line. The man would have a great deal to say in the two ceremonies. He hoped when the tradition was explained the knowledge would not scare her off. Rafe told him as much as he could about what was happening between them. Explained in part her fears about him changing shape. The hesitation she had, as he saw, also stemmed from her time spent in a freefall to a different century.

The priest agreed that the sooner they initiated the ceremonies the easier he could rest. The fact Dallas wasn't a practicing catholic made no difference. Not even the reality she was closer to an atheist than being the least bit religious would ever stop the formality of the wedding. The good father elaborated that it wasn't a lack of faith but the way she'd been brought up.

Having finished the necessary conversations, Rafe stuck his cell in his pocket then whistling, made his way to the kitchen. He sucked in the wonderful aroma of bacon and potatoes. Didn't realize how ravenous he was. Last night his hunger had been for Dallas, not food. He ate, but not enough to satisfy his empty stomach. With all his plans falling into line, he could relax. Would be able to enjoy the meal. If, true to form, Dallas would have made enough breakfast to serve an army.

Just as he expected, Dallas had pulled her hair back into a ponytail. He could see the long heavy strands were still damp from the shower. He liked her hair better lose. Wished he dared undo the ponytail so he could run his hands through the long silken strands. Realized that with her hair hanging lose it wasn't the best way to cook.

"Smells delicious. Pleased you made a lot. Can you hear my stomach rumbling? I'm famished," he stated as he sat down. "Think I could eat half. Can you down the second half? Wouldn't want anything to go to waste."

Filling two plates, she brought them to the table. "I can't hear your stomach over the sound of the grumbles of mine," she laughed as she spoke. "Neither one of us ate much last night. I was too nervous. Most of the sauce from dinner I put in the freezer for another time. What would you like tonight? I can come up with something new and unique if you feel daring."

"You needn't be nervous around me. I'm sorry apprehension affected your appetite. You never used to be anxious with me." He scooped a forkful of potatoes. Chewed. "Exceptional as always. Did my appearance in my cat scare you?" He waited for a response. She would deny the fear. Stick her chin in the air.

"Don't want to be on tenterhooks. Your cat terrified me, if you wish to know the truth. I'm not going to lie to you. When you teased me, thought I would jump straight out of my skin. Didn't appreciate the mischievousness. I might get used to this other form of yours." She lifted her shoulders in a delicate feminine move. "I might not." With that being said, Dallas turned her attention to the plate of food in front of her.

While they ate, they spoke of the rest of the day. Most of the conversation was mundane until he brought up visiting the McKenna keep. When he did, she drew her brows together in a deep scowl. Told her he called the keep to be certain everyone they wished to see would be around.

She tapped her nails on the coffee cup. Brought her bottom lip beneath her top teeth. "Hoped you'd forgotten about that venture. I tried to put the thought to the back of my head. Does it matter that I don't wish to go? Don't you think I should have some say in this?"

"If I didn't bring the visit up, would you have?" Rafe wasn't positive why he asked when he knew the response she would give. When she told him as much just a few seconds before. "This is important to the rest of our lives," he added hoping that statement might make some difference in her feelings.

"No, of course not. Would avoid the conversation at all costs. The last bit is nonsense, closer to emotional blackmail than I care to think about. Don't you be doing that with me." She grinned at him. A smile that traveled in a beeline straight to his heart.

Rafe wasn't at all certain what to make of her words coupled with the smile. Maybe she wasn't as averse to this as she let on. "Before we can marry, we need to have the consent of Father Richard. Will need to speak with him before the wedding." With his words, he watched her stiffen. "We need to be told what will happen during the traditional procedure. No, it's important to the mating of the couple. I've never attended the ritual that will help you understand the Clan Chattan. Only family is there. We, you and I, don't really have family. If you like, we can ask the McKenna, along with his mother, to stand in our parent's places."

"I don't wish to go. Doing this only for you," she told him while she started clearing the dishes. "Not positive I want to marry you. All you've done so far is tell me how it's going to happen. A girl likes to be asked. You do know that little fact, don't you? You haven't asked." To Rafe, her voice sounded wistful as if she'd missed out on something important.

The moment Dallas pointed out his errors, he felt contrite. She was right. He was at fault here. Must be making this situation worse by his stupidity. He should have proposed. He needed to buy her a ring. In his haste to right all the problems that had kept them apart, he forgot some of the most important things to a woman. He found himself backing into everything instead of proceeding in the correct manner. He would have to rectify all that. Tonight. This evening, he would put a knee to the ground. Ask her for her hand in marriage instead of telling her they would marry. His grandmother left him the wedding ring his grandfather gave to her. He would rectify his mistakes.

Dallas would tell him yes. What else could she say? He knew she loved him. Had always loved him.

As for this morning, he needed to take care of business with the McKenna as well as Father Richard. Pleased she conceded to his wishes if reluctantly. "I called. Both Cole and the good father are anticipating our appearance at the keep sometime after breakfast. They've written us down in their schedule. We will spend time there. You may ask any questions that come to mind."

"You called? You called them? Why didn't you tell me what you meant to do?" She turned, plates in hand. For a beat of his heart, he thought she might drop them. Her hands shook, trembled with the weight she held. She sighed then, "Hoped they would be too busy to see us." After setting the plates and silverware in the dishwasher, she turned. "They are going to ask me questions I've no answer for. Do I love you? I don't know. This is all too new to me. Do you love me? Do you even have an answer? Shouldn't marriage be about love? All you've told me has nothing to do with love."

Her question stunned him. He'd never thought about love as part of this equation. Once he knew she was his mate, everything seemed obvious. Now, he questioned because she questioned. Well…of course he loved her. Didn't that go hand in hand with a woman being a man's mate through eternity? Before, he loved her as a sister. How did he feel now? This was too much to consider at this instant.

"Well?" she asked, tapping her toe on the hard wood floor. "Do you love me? Can you say the words that would help me make up my mind. By the look on your face, you don't have an answer either. How can two people marry if they don't know their true feelings? Keep in mind I've agreed to nothing."

Dallas was right. He felt stunned by the revelation. Shocked by the question. He needed to give her an answer. "I must love you. If you're my mate, then…" The words were not what she expected to hear.

She waved her hand in the air. A look of exasperation crossed her features. "See…see, you don't have an answer either. I'm not going to marry if I can't give myself an answer to that question. You just stop this mad rush of yours to the altar. We've just discovered something precious between us. Do these new feelings have to be hurried? Perhaps if we relaxed. Took a step back to enjoy what we can now have."

Two strides took him to her side. He reached for her hands. She turned away from him, presenting her back. He wasn't going to allow her to redirect this conversation. "I want you. Is that love? I don't know. I wish to spend the rest of my life with you then into eternity. Is that love? Again, I don't know." He set his hands on her shoulders turning her around. "You want me. You're my mate. In my mind that's all we need. We haven't rushed anything. We have been together in some way since we were children."

"Lust! This is all about sex!" She slammed the door to the dishwasher. Turned back to him, her hands on her hips, "I'll go with you today. I'm not going to make any promises as to weddings along with clan ceremonies that I know nothing about. You bet I'll ask questions." She tapped him on his chest. "Be advised, I'm not setting a date."

His Dallas wasn't pulling any punches. Honest to the point of saying more than he wished to hear. He'd hoped after speaking with both the McKenna along with Father Richard a date would be set. He had to take her words with the seriousness they deserved.

"I see. Well…as soon as we've cleaned up, we're on our way. Would you like to see the portrait first? Talk to Ruby? Perhaps Father Richard?" Confusion settled into his head. Of course, he loved her. She'd always been by his side. He'd always protected her. It might be he took his feelings concerning Dallas for granted. He shouldn't do that. He should be more animated more curious as to how she felt. They still had a great deal to learn about each other as far as love was concerned. Yet…he knew her better than any other living person. Knew her ups along with her downs. How she'd react when confronted. She knew him both inside as well as out. What more was there?

"Maybe later." He watched her lips thin then her hands shake. Dishes rattled. He took them from her before she could drop them. Set them on the counter.

"I'll finish these later."

"No, don't want to leave the dishes."

"What are you frightened of Dallas? The painting is a portrait of two people in love. Are you afraid you'll remember something? Worse, you'll wish to return to that time? Believe once we're officially wed, I'll paint a portrait of the two of us."

"Naked?" she blurted then giggled, her mood swinging from depression to amusement. She was a bundle of changes coupled with stretched nerves. He recognized the signs. One moment she was on the verge of tears, the next laughing. He wasn't at all certain how to handle the mood changes.

Indulgent to her whims, he would give her whatever she asked for. "If that is what you would like, though I would rather paint us wearing clothing. Could put it in the front room. Could do both. The naked one, I would hang it in the studio next to the one of you. I would stand behind you. Essentially the only naked body in the painting would be yours." Rafe grinned at her look of dismay. Seemed her joke was on her.

In a blink, she seemed to rally. "Rat! You would do that to me?" She was still laughing at him. "You wouldn't pose in the buff for me. I could paint that part of you…" she stopped what she was about to confess. His Dallas drew only stick figures. He could imagine what the painting would look like.

His hoot of laughter had her shooting daggers at him with her eyes. "Am I ruining all your fun? You would draw a stick figure of me with my penis protruding." At her look of acknowledgement, he held up his hands in surrender. "I'm not a professional model. Don't believe I would wish to be captured naked for anyone to see. While I love being naked with you, I'm not a man who would show all of himself in a picture." He realized the only one in the future to see him in the buff would be Dallas.

When the doorbell rang, they both jumped. Rafe couldn't think of anyone who would be calling on them without notice. It rang again then again. Insistent. Impatient. Loud. Obnoxious. Someone was leaning on the bell. The rude sound grated on his nerves telling him this was not a friendly call. "Stay here." His sixth sense kicking in a bit late, he understood the two men who tormented Dallas, in this life as well as the past, were at his door. They'd come to see if they could step into her life again. He wouldn't stand for that. Would fight with all he was to keep them from her.

Dallas clung to his arm, her nails biting into him. She stumbled when he started forward too fast. When he looked at her, her eyes were wide with apprehension. "You know who it is at the door? Don't you?"

He needed to find the words that would reassure. He didn't have them. As if she guessed the same as he, her face was a ghost mask leaving her with no color. Realizing he was her lifeline, her fingers held onto him tighter. She was shaking her head. "Rafe, I don't…don't want to see those two men. I've nothing to say to either person. Tell them to go away. Tell them not to come back."

"No, I don't know for certain, though I've a guess, as it appears you do also. Who else would lean on the doorbell? Not a friend. Only an enemy. Together we only have two enemies. I'll tell them anything you'd like." He started for the front of the house. She still held onto his arm, staggered into his back when he stopped. They were in front of the steps leading to the upper floors. He turned to her. "Dallas, let go. You need to stay where it's safe for you. You cannot go to the door with me."

"I'm not staying in this room by myself. One of them could come around to the back door. With you beside me, they can't do anything. Besides…" she paused for a few beats of his heart. She flashed him a hesitant smile and he saw she was biting on her lip. "You told me just last night you would rip out their throats if they tried anything. You could scare them. Run them off. Change to your cat."

His soft chuckle didn't mean he was amused by her statement. Perhaps she was coming around to believing in his shifter abilities. That part pleased him. Maybe she even wished it was possible for him to murder these men, even frighten them to death. Most likely the pair deserved torture if not death. They needed to understand he wouldn't tolerate them anywhere close to Dallas. In a different century, they threatened to rape her. If she'd not pepper sprayed one…if Roc had not appeared as if by magic… Dallas would not have been saved from their malicious intent. These two men wanted the same in this century. Nothing here was different. "To do so, I would need to change to my cat. That isn't prudent on the front porch in the middle of the town. I would need to be naked. Believe changing to one's cat is only for an emergency. We will make certain they understand they must leave you alone. Don't know how though, except to explain…"

"Maybe if I tell them I don't want to have anything to do with them, they won't bother with me anymore. One can always hope," she muttered as if she didn't believe what she said.

Rafe didn't like the surge of fear that settled in his gut when he thought about these two men finding Dallas alone and unprotected. He couldn't keep her confined to his home. She wasn't a prisoner. They were dangerous. Roc didn't have to abide by all the societal rules he did. With any luck what she said would be true. Experience along with instinct told him they would never be dissuaded by her statement.

"You can try," he said, his voice soft. Repeated for his benefit. "You can try. Believe we should seek out a restraining order. That might keep them away." The bell rang again. One long, loud nonstop wail. "Time to end this travesty."

"Don't think restraining orders work all that well. I'd rather you got violent with them. Can you just show them your cat teeth without changing? They are very big as well as threatening. Pull your lips back then growl. That should do the trick." She tripped along behind him, clinging to his arm. "We don't even know it's them at the door. Might be your neighbor asking to borrow a cup of sugar."

"It's them. We both know that for a fact. Stay behind me. Better yet, stay out of their sight. Don't want you anywhere near them." He turned to her, motioning her toward the stairs. "Please. Go on up to the studio. Stay there. I'll come for you as soon as I send them away. This isn't a good place for you to be seen."

Rafe was surprised when she did as he asked. He watched her race up the stairs. Breathed in a silent sigh of relief when the door closed behind her with a soft snick. He imagined her peering out the window to the steps below so she could see what was happening. Taking in a big breath of air before releasing the oxygen, he opened the door.

True to his thoughts, Mathew Gordon along with Tinley Scratch stood on his front porch. The pair were fidgeting, shifting from one foot to the other. The two men weren't certain. Weren't as brave as they tried to pretend. Rafe didn't understand how Dallas could ever get into a car with these two men. She must have felt too desperate to think. So distressed she was left with no choices. That had been his fault. He'd taken her car back to her apartment leaving her without wheels. He reminded himself by the time she returned, the car would have been towed. Still casting recriminations on himself, she had no means to get anywhere so she needed to hitchhike. Those two came along at the exact right time.

"Who are you?" He asked in attempt to put them on the defensive. Before this, he'd never seen them. Dallas showed him a picture she'd taken on her phone. These two didn't know that fact. Wouldn't understand he knew more about them than they would appreciate. "What do you want? If you're selling something, I'm not buying. See the sign? No solicitors." He started to close the door in their faces.

Mathew held his hand out to stop the forward momentum of the door. Rafe could have used more force. Didn't because he needed to hear more from these two men. Wanted to understand in plain terms what they looked for here.

"Not selling," Tinley said a sneer to his voice. "Not selling, though we'd be buying something if it's available. When you had enough of a taste of the girl, we would pay top dollar. Would share if you've a mind to do that. We could do it altogether if you *ken* what I mean?"

His stomach rolled at the man's words. "Don't know what you're talking about."

"Just want to talk to the woman. Lainie or Dallas, she changes names whenever the mood seizes her. Where is she?" Mathew asked as he tried to peer around Rafe's shoulder. "She owes me. I mean to collect."

"Dallas doesn't owe the likes of you two anything. Why would I let you talk to my wife? Be apprised of the fact, I don't share what's mine. Dallas is my woman," Rafe told them, cringing a bit at his one lie. Dallas would be his wife soon. If she stood beside him, she would have given him away by the shocked look on her face. She might have told these men she didn't intend to marry him. "As I asked before, who are you?"

"She's not married. Would've told us if she were. We're her friends. Picked her up off the road. Helped her when you weren't around. Some husband you are if it's true. Leave her stranded without a means to get anywhere."

"It's true," he said, as both anger, coupled with bitter annoyance began to build. "Would never allow the two of you to speak with Dallas even if I thought you were gentlemen. You're not. Don't explain myself to anyone let alone the likes of the two of you."

"Shouldn't you let her decide who she will talk with, as well as who she won't? Dallas did take a bit of a shine to the two of us. We do enjoy sharing our women folk. Threesomes are fun. Add another man, it might be even more enjoyable. We could have her spinning, moaning her pleasure as we rocked her until she could no longer move. Could be touching everywhere those sensitive spots on a woman." Gordon drooled as once more he thought to step around him. Rafe's arm shot out to stop him. "No! You're not entering my house."

"Can't stop us. Two against one."

"Best the two of you get on your way. There's nothing here for the likes of you. I can and I will stop you," Rafe snarled, doing as Dallas suggested, showing them his cat teeth. The act was an illusion they would think about. He needed to watch them sitting in their car, driving down the street. Rafe knew he'd not seen the last of these men. Wished he could send them back to where they came from. Let Roc Frasier deal with the pair of idiots. Seemed he had a better way to keep them at bay. He sent them with Dallas to belong to this century. Thoughts of the Kinnel Stones popped into his head. Maybe they wouldn't end up near either Lainie or Dallas.

"We'll find her," Tinley volunteered while he scratched his privates. "When you're not around to keep us from her. "We'll have our say. You just wait and see. The two of us will have her moaning beneath us."

~ * ~

"You say Rafe Frasier is coming to see us with his girlfriend?" Ruby asked Cole, who was staring at her as if she was daft. She always thought of herself as a patient mother. Had to be because her oldest boy said little. Kept most everything to himself. His thoughts remained private. She'd watched him the other afternoon with Phoebe MacAuliffe. Realized by the indulgent manner in which he acted, the young woman was his mate. Her boy would need to have the patience of a saint to deal with this little lady's shenanigans. She was a wild one, a hellion, that girl. Free spirit should have been her middle names. Ruby knew though from a few conversations she'd had with the girl, she was a sweetheart. At least she would be to the man she loved. Cole would see to it that she fell in love with him. A few more weeks and he could court her without feeling guilt. Phoebe needed to graduate from high school before Cole could see to their relationship.

"They are. Believe the girlfriend has found what she wanted all along but won't admit to the fact. Rafe's so enthusiastic that he found his mate after all this time searching, set this into motion without a care for her feelings. She is overwhelmed by all that's happened to her. He admits to the fact she needs a great deal of tender loving care. That's where you come in, Mother."

"Me?" Ruby felt both surprised as well as honored by her son's confidence in her. "What do you need? You know I'll do all I can. Tell me what's happened to her."

"You are a dear." Cole went on to explain to her what Dallas lived through. Her crazy ride into the seventeen hundreds after that, how she was hurtled back to the present century. Described her emotions when Rafe showed her his cat. "The girl doesn't know what to make of all this new information tossed her way. She's overwhelmed by all the truths put in front of her. Realities she thought were gossip."

"She fell through a rabbit hole, didn't she? Found herself in a different century. Do I have this right? She was supposed to bring Roc Frasier the woman, his mate. Only, Dallas wasn't that woman. It was Lainie Shaw. Can see why her mind is befuddled."

"Everything is a mess in her head, nasty business. You understand Dallas is no shifter. Rafe told me he showed her his cat last night. She is terrified of him. She might be able to tell you things she can no longer describe to Rafe. Rafe tells me, before this, she shared everything with him. He knows her better than he knows himself."

That was no surprise to Ruby. She'd been frightened of Cole's father when he first showed her his cat. She missed him every breathing moment of her life. Thinking about him never failed to bring tears to her eyes. If she could hasten her time to their next meeting, she would do all in her power. His death was such a tragedy. Something that might have been avoided. "I was there once, a normal woman…a man with supernatural abilities. Is that what you're asking me to do, to intervene on Rafe's behalf? Help explain the feelings that must be racing through her head?"

"You've read my mind. With all my heart, I'm hoping to see these two happy. Don't think their journey will be an easy one. They've much to deal with. He's impatient. She needs more time. In every way, except the sexual attraction, the two are at odds."

"Is there something you aren't telling me?" Ruby asked, while she strode with her son to the main hall. "I should be apprised of all the facts."

Cole turned to her. He smiled as if he understood part of the couple's predicament. "They are…*were* best friends before all this happened. Rafe tells me Dallas shared everything with him. The problem is, Rafe didn't reciprocate all the time. He was hesitant because he understood that at some time, he would find his mate. When that happened, they would need to put distance between them. Rafe felt his mate might not like his and Dallas' relationship."

"Hoisted by his own petard, was he?" Ruby gave a little snort of a chuckle as she thought about all the problems one encountered on their journey to love. She and Aaron had problems too. Seemed all couples found snares stopping them from reaching that goal with ease. "This should not be too difficult to overcome if they love each other."

Cole lifted a dark brow toward the ceiling. "Love, that's the other thing. Rafe has always felt love for Dallas. Now it's different though." Rafe paused, seeming to study the expression on his mother's face. "Love for a sister not a woman. The man doesn't know what he's feeling now except lust. He as much as told Dallas that very thing. Seems those words are something else that are keeping her from committing."

"Yeah, as you say, bet that went over well." Her sarcasm wasn't missed by her son who hooted with laughter.

The clock in the main room chimed ten times. "Those two will be here soon. We need to meet them. I'd like to make them feel welcome at the keep. I know Rafe is hoping for a wedding here along with the traditional feast."

Ruby pointed a slim finger at the couple entering through the huge front doors, thinking they were the ones in need of guidance this morning. "She is beautiful. I know I've seen her before. You say her name is Dallas?" Ruby tapped her chin as she thought back on all she knew about these two. Wasn't she supposed to be someone else in another time?

"Dallas is the spitting image of Lainie Frasier. You do recall the portrait hanging on our wall." Cole's hoot of laughter brought her attention back to her son.

"You did tell me she traveled back in time. Though what you are saying can happen, it's still rare. You said she found a vortex? She didn't go through the Kinnel Stones? While she is…she isn't the same woman as our Lainie in the portrait. There are subtle differences, easily recognized. I've looked at that painting hundreds of times as I have all the others."

"Rest assured, she is not Lainie. No one understands what happened, least of all Dallas, along with Rafe. They are living as well as dealing with the circumstances. Rafe is grateful for all that happened to bring them together again. What we do know is that Dallas is a separate person from Lainie just as Rafe is separate from Roc. All that happened here is that something supernatural stepped in to secure the future of the people who came to life after Lainie and Roc."

Starting forward, Ruby linked her arm through her son's. "Let's show them McKenna hospitality. I'm looking forward to helping plan the wedding. It's traditional for Frasiers to wed at the keep. This will not be different. When, seems to be the only question."

"Don't get your heart set on that. However, I believe Dallas might come around. Believe she does love Rafe. Show her all your charm, Mother."

"Of course, I'll be pleased to help in every way possible."

"Then…we will be having a wedding soon." Cole gave her hand a little squeeze.

"After they leave, we can speak of Phoebe MacAuliffe." She felt pleased by the sharp indrawn breath of air her son sucked inside. Felt his quick withdrawal. This was something she was looking forward to discussing. She needed to make certain Cole understood the parameters concerning the young woman. If he didn't, she would lay them out.

"Rafe." Cole extended his hand in greeting before introducing his

73

mother. "I assume you are Dallas. Pleased to meet you."

"Let's go see the portrait," Rafe murmured as he set his hand on the small of Dallas' back. "Seeing will help her understand her memory of that time before it fades."

Cole led the way to the stairs then forward to where the Frasier portraits lined the wall. Dallas' small gasp of shock didn't surprise Ruby. The two women were almost identical. The comparisons remarkable.

"While I expected this, you, Rafe, looked very much like Roc Frasier," Dallas murmured while she stared at the painting.

"I thought the same when I was here over a week ago. Before I met you at the Fairy Pools. The similarities are amazing. With all the other families, are their others that look so much the same they could be twins?"

"Not this much," Cole was shaking his head, smiling. "By looking at the portrait, you must realize how much the two of you belong together. The universe understands these things even if we, mere mortals, do not."

The sip of air into Dallas' throat was not missed. Nor was the stiffening of the young lady's shoulders. Ruby held the distinct feeling Dallas felt as if she was being pushed in a direction she didn't understand or wish to go. She seemed to dig her heels in even as they continued up the steps examining the portraits.

Ruby stepped up with a smile. "Dallas, would you come with me?"

Chapter Three

The nerves Dallas tried to hold in check started to snap. Her body shook, quivered both with irritation as well as with frustration. The portrait was the last straw. Showing her the painting was meant to influence her, change her mind. While Ruby seemed nice enough, she didn't want to be here. Didn't know what Ruby thought of her assignment. Was the woman supposed to convince her to marry Rafe? She didn't know what waited for her, what coercion this sweet lady would use to get her compliance in this matter of the heart. Dallas didn't care. What she decided was her business. No one else's. The first opportunity that presented itself, she would leave. She could call for a ride back to the town. She didn't need to rely on Rafe to take her home. There were options.

Ruby held the door to a large sitting room open for her while she walked inside. On one of the tables there was a tray with a pot of tea or coffee along with a plate of desserts. It was a beautiful room. Ruby was a beautiful woman. Her hair was dark. Around the edges there were hints of grey. Her eyes were a deep dark blue. They seemed to hold a wealth of wisdom within their depths, shimmered with the light of a woman who understood herself. After all these years she was still trim, her figure shapely. When Ruby looked at her, she felt welcome. It would be hard to remain aloof around Cole's mother, who received her with open arms.

"Would you like tea or coffee? My family seems to prefer the coffee while the rest of Scotland asks for tea. Have enjoyed coffee forever. Goes back to the seventeen hundreds when a McKenna, along with a Stuart, traveled to what was then the colonies. Among other things, they brought back coffee."

"Coffee, unless it's that horrible instant stuff." Dallas gave a small chuckle. "Rafe used to serve me instant coffee when I modeled for him. Did until I tossed the liquid in his face one day. The next modeling session,

I brought him a bag that I bought at one of those American coffee shops that seemed to have inundated all of Scotland."

"Coffee it is." Ruby reached for the creamer and poured them each a mug.

"Black. I like my coffee with nothing to ruin the wonderful roast of the beans," Dallas said, for the first time beginning to feel almost relaxed. Cole's mother had a way of calming her stretched temper as well as those same nerves Rafe provoked. She reminded herself the questions had not begun. The interrogation would put a damper on the atmosphere. Either that or Ruby would lecture her on the benefits of marriage.

After handing her the coffee, Ruby cleared her throat. "Cole told me you might have questions. Unless there is something on your mind that needs immediate attention, let me begin with a short story about myself. You might find the tale interesting. Would that be alright?" Ruby stopped to point at the tray of delicacies that were included. "If you like, help yourself to a pastry or two." Ruby cleared her throat then paused as if thinking. "I'm not going to try to influence you in any way. Feel safe with me, I would like what is best for you as well as Rafe. The two of you are the only ones who can make this decision."

Dallas nodded, feeling relieved this wasn't going to be what she expected. She sat back with a steaming cup of jo in her hands, ready to listen. Ruby didn't want to interrogate. Not yet. The moment between them felt right. "I'd like that. What's the story about?" Dallas assumed Cole's mother would be part of this tale she was about to recount.

"Who, would be the better question. What I'm going to tell you is about me when I first met Cole's father. Few have heard this before. Cole hasn't, though I did tell my daughter years ago, when she had a few questions of her own. He's gone now...my husband. Wish I'd fallen into his arms that first time I saw him. Wish I didn't waste time on trivialities, wanting him to convince me of what I'm certain now. We squandered almost a year of our lives together. A year we could never get back." Ruby looked down; her lashes lowered as if she didn't wish for her to see the moisture in her eyes.

Dallas wondered what it would be like to love a man as much as Ruby loved her husband. Wondered if what she felt for Rafe was love.

"What happened to your husband? A couple of months ago I heard that he'd died. Sometime before... I'm sorry for your loss." She was remorseful. If Rafe died, she would mourn him forever. Did that mean she loved him? Would always reflect on the lost time? Dallas saw a tear slide down Ruby's cheek. A shiver of acknowledgment slid down her spine. Was she reckless of the time she might share with Rafe? She didn't understand any of her feelings. She was terrified of his cat. Needed him in his human. Didn't like having her feelings so at odds.

"He was sick. Didn't realize it until it was too late to save him. Tried to get him to visit a doctor sooner...when he was complaining of a pain in his stomach. In his macho, arrogant way he refused to seek help. Thought the ailment revolved around the food he ate. The stubborn man thought he would live forever. Funny, I loved his arrogance. His self-assurance. Wish he would have listened to my advice." Ruby waved her hand in the air. "Enough of that. My story does have a great deal to do with my husband. Not his death, but his life is what I wish to speak of. How we first dealt with a few of the difficulties between a shifter who is fated to find a life with a normal person. It's rare, you know, for two shifters to come together. That happens upon occasion."

"I'm intrigued. I thought this talk would be different," Dallas told her with honesty. She was fascinated by something that seemed to affect her also. It appeared the men of the Clan Chattan had a great deal in common. "Rafe is arrogant. He likes to tell me he's confident; that the two descriptions are different. Suppose they are...still..." In many ways she enjoyed his arrogance. He would take charge of most situations. Today, she didn't appreciate the control he exerted over her.

"The men will all say the same. Cole is much like his father in looks as well as attitude. But that's neither here nor there. Men don't have any idea how to deal with women. They treat them as if they possess testosterone in the abundance of their male counterparts. Some, in time, learn to treat their mates with delicacy. Some can find a means to become romantic. Since you returned from your travels, I'm guessing Rafe has been far from romantic."

"When I saw him at the Isle of Sky while I was on a photo shoot, he orchestrated a romantic dinner. Brought wine, along with flowers.

That's where the romance began as well as ended. He thought I would fall into his plans. I was too confused. My mind jammed with worries along with memories of another time. Those memories are vanishing. I assume in the future they will all be gone from my head. Rafe doesn't wish to give me the time I need to come to terms with what happened to me."

"Since you returned?" Ruby questioned.

Dallas lifted her shoulders in a shrug that would answer Ruby's question. "How did you meet your husband? I met Rafe when we were in grade school. I fell. Scraped up my knee along with the palm of my hand on the playground. I was only six.' He picked me up then, sitting on a swing, he held me until my tears stopped. I've been half in love with him ever since. From that point forward, I thought of him as mine. In a sense he was. Later, we discovered we were not meant to be together forever. Now that has changed in Rafe's mind. He says we are meant to be together through all time. I understand the spark he looked for before wasn't there. Now it is. I don't think lust is a reason to marry."

"Half? Half in love? I believe you are all the way in love with the man." One of Ruby's dark eyebrows shot upward. She cleared her throat, seeming to think about what she was going to say next. "Only half in love? Never mind." She sipped her coffee. "That's none of my business. What you feel is between you and Rafe. I was about to tell you my story. How I met Cole's father."

"Please go on. I'll stop interrupting. Mother always told me I was too impatient." Dallas let out a long breath of air. She was impatient. Impulsive. Her mother was cruel about telling her. Always inserted some derogatory word with her comment.

"You, my dear girl, are welcome to stop me anytime you like. Your questions are good ones. They pertain to your feelings about Rafe. Much of what I relate to you has something to do with your circumstance." Ruby got this dreamy smile on her lips. She sighed softly as if remembering the day she was about to describe. "I met Aaron at the loch, at his invitation. I wasn't supposed to be there, was forbidden to go to the lake. Father insisted that the loch was not a place for good girls. He'd heard stories of girls losing their virginity at that place. Turns out Father was right. I didn't care though. I was so enamored of Aaron. I would have done anything to catch his attention." Ruby looked out the window. Sunlight brightened the room, glistening on the tears slipping down her cheeks.

So absorbed in her own problems, Dallas didn't notice how updated this castle room was until now, while she waited to hear the rest of the story. Clear windows let light into a space that might have been dreary years ago. Hardwood floors stretched from one wall to the other, covered with area rugs. All the lights were modern, as was the furniture. The McKennas were well off. They owned a shipping line years ago. They'd invested in businesses as they understood what would prosper along with what would not. Both the Stuarts, as well as the Frasiers, were also wealthy.

"I wanted to meet Aaron McKenna. Couldn't wait for him to pay attention to me. He was so handsome." Ruby paused, smiling, "Did I say that already? He was six years my senior. Tall. Handsome as all sin. Sensual in the way he moved. Yes, I'll keep saying the words. Handsome. When he stared at me with that look in his eyes, shivers would sweep down my spine. After that, heat seemed to take over. His shoulders were so broad, his hair so very dark. He kept it at shoulder length. Anyway, one day I followed him to the loch. Watched him leave the keep. It took me longer because I was on foot. Aaron drove his car. Seems he was going swimming. Saw him shift that day. Didn't know anyone could do that…change their form. Thought all the stories about shifters in these parts were tales passed down by women who had nothing better to do than gossip. I realized I was wrong."

"He didn't know you were there? Watching him? Don't they…don't they have this sixth sense that warns them about intruders. Rafe always knows when I'm close. When I'm thinking about him. It's unfair." From what she knew about Rafe, Dallas had a hard time believing the man, the shifter would not sense another person.

"At the time, I didn't think he did. Believed I surprised Aaron. He was even more gorgeous in the buff than he was wearing clothing. Felt the heat of embarrassment flame my face. I couldn't stop staring."

"You were wrong, weren't you? He knew you were there. Most assuredly knew you followed him. Maybe even wished for you to see him naked. To watch him shift." Dallas knew the answer before she asked. Of course Aaron knew Ruby was there. The man would hear her thoughts. "He stripped then shifted on purpose. What was he thinking to accomplish?"

"I was very wrong. Aaron did shift on purpose. Did it just to see what I would do. The man was curious about me, about my character. Aaron hoped I would be curious enough to stay…to watch him. He told me next time I spoke to him he thought I would hightail it home when he changed to his cat. He said he was shocked when I remained. Found out I was much braver than he expected."

Dallas found herself smiling then laughing. "You didn't leave. You surprised him. Did he want you to stay or was he hoping to get rid of you by shocking you?" From all Rafe told her about shifters, this was all Aaron's plan to catch his mate.

"Have more hutzpah than that. Aaron didn't know that fact though. Didn't understand me. He'd been waiting for me to get old enough to date. Thought I was a silly teenager who needed to discover who the boss was. The man knew I saw him without a stitch. He delved into my mind, so he knew I saw him. I'd been watching all the time he disrobed."

"Why would he risk showing you his cat? Isn't that dangerous?" Dallas was thinking about the few times Rafe talked about changing form. Those talks came after that first time in his bedroom. He wanted her to understand changing shape wasn't something most people would believe or understand. Very few understood there were shifters in this world. The ability was their secret to keep.

"Yes and no. He knew who I was. Had known I was his mate for a couple of years. He had to wait for me to grow up before he could act on his desire. That day at the loch he didn't plan on showing me so much of himself. It came about as an impulse, he told me later."

"What happened after that? You alluded to the fact that something…" Fascinated, Dallas waited to hear the rest of the story.

"When he witnessed the look of shock on my face, he decided to change back. He could talk in his human. Saw him. His front not just his back. The man had the gall to kiss me while he was buck naked. You see, after I didn't run away, he decided other tactics were needed. One thing led to another." Ruby held up her hands to stop the next question. "Before he turned back, he teased me. His cat taunted me. Rubbed himself on my legs. Licked my hand between my fingers. Tugged on me so I had to sit on the rocks. After I was vulnerable, he set his head on my lap. Nuzzled my stomach then higher so he rubbed his head across my breasts." Ruby put her hand on her chest. "I was so petrified my heart was beating so hard I thought it would jump right out of my chest. Strange though, in his cat, what he did also awakened me. I was too young to understand arousal. All I knew was that I was so heated I could scarcely breathe."

"That's about how I felt when Rafe showed me his cat. I wanted to run. Held my ground instead. When his tongue slid along my arm, thought I would jump out of my skin. What he was doing was too new. Too sensual. I just…" Dallas gulped in a lungful of air. "Are they all like that? Do they like to play so many games? Nothing he did that night in his cat seemed right. Yet…" she sipped air. "Yet…I liked what he did even though he scared me. Understood the cat was Rafe, I just couldn't…we haven't been together that intimate in his human form."

"Suppose the men are all like those two. Incorrigible. Uninhibited. Impulsive as well as impatient with their mate. They strut around naked as if that was normal. They have no shame when they are around their woman. After a few months with the man, I became more comfortable when we were naked."

"Highhanded."

"Full of themselves."

She was certain what Ruby told her would be true. "Too loveable to ignore. No matter how they tease, they always make sure their mate is taken care of."

"They walk around naked as if that was natural. They have no shame when they are around their woman. After a few months with the man, I became more comfortable when we were naked. I miss Aaron with every breath I take. In the middle of the night, I long to feel him holding me. Sometimes I can imagine and remember how we came together. Other nights, I'm cold. I long for him with such intensity, I hurt."

"So, what happened next? You said he kissed you? You also implied more than just a kiss happened that day." Dallas needed this story. The fact Ruby was also petrified by her mate's shifting reassured her. Rafe teased mercilessly. She'd never thought of anything like what he did. If Rafe was her mate, he would expect certain things of her. Dallas didn't know if she could give him all that he needed.

"In his cat, Aaron must have realized he was terrifying me, so he turned back. When he shifted, I saw his tight hard butt. After he changed back to his human, he faced me. I saw all of him." She breathed in deep. "All of him…never seen a naked man before that day except in paintings along with statues. Nothing prepared me for what I saw. He wasn't at all similar to what I'd seen. I wanted to touch him, to feel for myself…"

Dallas lowered her lashes. Her fingers wove together. "I understand. That sight must have frightened you too. You were a real innocent. I've never seen Rafe naked except the time he changed. He's painted me several times while I wore nothing. When he did, he never felt anything for me. Now, he has a hard time keeping his hands to himself."

"Aaron didn't give me a chance to wallow in fear. Pulled me into his waiting arms then his mouth captured mine. I forgot about everything except how I felt. Heated. Flamed. I remember whimpering. Cried out his name. Pleaded for him to show me more. His hand cupped my breast. I'd not worn a bra that day. Most days I didn't wear one. Didn't have much to support back then." Ruby laughed. "Not like... I'm sorry." Ruby looked away.

Dallas flushed. What Ruby implied was something she was used to hearing. She had more than a handful for any man. "Don't be sorry. We are all made in different ways. I don't like being this large, but Rafe makes me feel beautiful. He adores my curves. He's only touched my breasts a handful of times. That first day was the first time we felt the spark of desire. I stopped him from making love to me. He wanted me. I ran from him that night. He did make me feel as if I was the most beautiful woman on earth."

"That's how a man in love makes his woman feel. Treasured. Does Rafe do that to you?" Ruby asked, her dark blue eyes focused on her. "You must take everything into perspective. Must figure out what you want from this relationship. Compromise seems to be needed here. What do you think? Can you reach some type of understanding? Do you just need more time to come to terms with all that has happened in your life?"

Compromise was an interesting concept. More time would be wonderful. From the moment that lightning flashed through them, there had been no compromise in Rafe. He plunged ahead full throttle. She didn't comprehend the sensual intensity he projected to her. That fact might be the reason she put distance between them. "Yes, even before…before when we thought we were only to be friends. He treasured me. Helped me through all my difficult times as if deep inside of him he knew the truth of our relationship. If Rafe can compromise, I'm certain I can too. The man hasn't *asked* me to marry him. He's gone off on this tangent believing we want the same things and he's barreling through as if I'm right behind him. He assumes I'm with him in every aspect. I…" She ran her tongue across her lips thinking about what she wished for. "I need for him to *ask,* not assume. At present, the two of us are not on the same page. I want…need a real proposal. It doesn't have to be romantic; I just need the damn man to *ask* me."

Ruby's laughter surprised her. Swept into her as a breath of fresh air. "Give your poor, besotted man a chance. He loves you. I can see the sentiment in his eyes when he looks at you. When he speaks to you. Take a step back to see the situation in his shoes. Until now, Rafe is a shifter who has believed he will never find his woman, his mate. Now that he knows his partner is you, of course, he is going to speed forward." Ruby leaned toward her, smiling. "He's afraid too. He's terrified of losing you. Afraid some outside force will step in then whisk you away. It's not as if that hasn't happened before. You must see this in his eyes too."

Dallas looked away, a huge lump forming in her throat. She never thought of Rafe as fearing anything or anyone. What Ruby told her might be true. She could ask him. No, she would never be so bold. "I don't know…it's all so new. I need…"

"He's rushed you. That much is apparent. I think he understands. That's why he wanted you to talk with me. Tell him what you want, then how you feel about him. Those words will go a long way to reassure the poor man."

"Yes, I need time. Time to understand myself. Time to understand who he is. For so long, I thought he was someone else. Believed he was my best friend. Now he's pushing me toward marriage." Dallas did want marriage, did need to be in love. She'd always thought she was in love with Rafe.

"Damn it! I do want him to ask me. He needs to buy me a ring. I don't care what he spends. Could be a crackerjack ring for all I care. I need for his knee to hit the ground. Need a bit more of the romance he showed me that first night. He should get down on one knee to ask me. We could have a candlelight dinner. I'd even cook the meal. A bottle of wine, a few shared kisses…would be appreciated too. We've hardly kissed." She touched her lips needing some type of reassurance.

"Tell Rafe what you just told me," Ruby urged with a smile on her beautiful face. "He will give you everything you ask for."

"If I tell him everything, I won't know if he's performing to get what he wants or if he's taken my suggestions to heart."

There was a light tap on the door. Both women turned to look at the door, waiting, anticipating. Dallas was certain the knock signaled the arrival of Cole along with Rafe. They would be there to retrieve her, to take her to the priest.

"It's the men," Ruby told her as she rose to open the door then greet Cole and Rafe. "I imagine they believe we've had enough time to gossip."

Dallas wasn't certain she wanted the conversation with Ruby to end. She wasn't ready. She knew the choice was taken from her when she saw the two men standing in front of the open door. They both seemed to be insecure. Rafe held his hands behind his back while he rocked on his feet. His face a mask to her, so much so she couldn't read his thoughts.

"Can we come in, Mother? If you tell us no, Rafe would jump down your throat. He's said to me he's waited long enough," Cole said, a wry smile on his handsome face. "What have the two of you talked about? Assume the conversation has been enlightening. Has it been about us? Father? Just Rafe? Should my ears be burning?"

Ruby stood aside as they entered. "That is something we women will keep to ourselves. What have the two of you been up to? It's been almost an hour."

"Been talking about women. What else?" Cole laughed. "How they can turn a man upside down when they least expect."

"Cole has been telling me how to proceed with my mate. It's not as if he has vast experience with a woman. He's yet to claim his mate. I could give him much needed advice."

Cole gave Rafe a good-natured slap to his back.

"But…Cole does know who his woman is just as you understand the role Dallas will play in your life. You both need patience," Ruby suggested, a wicked smile gracing her lovely features. "Let this take its natural course. Opt for some romantic moments. Woo your brides to be." Shaking a finger at her son, "You must let her grow up before you proceed in haste."

To Dallas, at the mention of romance, both men blanched. "Romance is nice, as are traditions. Romance can make a woman feel special." She hesitated to say more. Decided this was time to begin the telling of her truths. "If you expect me to fall into your plans that include traditions I've never heard of, well then, it is time for you to practice more standard traditions. You need to think about how I feel."

"As in…?" Rafe questioned, perplexed by her statement. "You could try elaborating. A man shouldn't have to guess what it is his soon-to-be-wife expects. As to thinking about how you feel, that's all I've thought about over the last hour."

She wasn't about to elaborate on what she wanted. Rafe was a smart man. He should be able to guess. If she told him what she needed, she would never think what he did came from the heart. As to the exactness of what she wished for, she meant to remain mute on the subject. Feeling stubborn, she lifted her chin to a tilt.

"You'll need to figure all that out on your own time. Coffee?" she asked, as she rose to pour them each a cup. "There are delicacies left over on the tray if you're feeling hungry." She almost mentioned the priest. While she'd rather Rafe forgot about that visit, she understood he would not.

"No. No food or coffee for me." Rafe spoke up, a glint in his dark blue eyes. "We have an appointment with Father Richard. He is waiting for us at the rectory." He extended his hand expecting her to take it. "Shall we go? I would not like to be late." His words spoken softly sent more conflicting feelings into her head.

This was the appointment she'd been dreading all morning. She didn't want to meet with the good father. This was too soon for her to make an assurance of an event she was traumatized over. After they spoke, all would seem so finalized. Permanent. Enduring. How could she make her opinion clear to the priest when she couldn't explain herself to Rafe? She didn't want to set a date for the wedding. That was what Rafe wished for. Before any date could be put forth, she hoped for a real proposal. Needed him to go down on one knee. It seemed he overlooked the obvious. Until that happened, she wasn't about to pretend they were going to marry. He never asked, he told.

Dallas looked to Ruby as if she could lend support. Ruby nodded her head then smiled. An encouraging gesture, nothing more. This was not her affair. Advice had been given. Now it was up to her to decide her future. She set her cup on the silver tray.

Ruby did speak. "You must do what is best for you, as well as Rafe. Talk to each other. Confide your feelings. That's my only advice. The two of you will figure out what is the best course." Her smile was beautiful, lighting up her face along with her eyes.

Stepping up to Ruby, she extended her hand. Her heart beat hard, her hands were sweaty. She stole a moment of air from the room. Ruby stood. She wished her mother was more like Ruby. Wished she could talk to Ruby more often. Cole's mother knew how to listen…how to give advice without judgement. "It was nice to meet you. What we talked about gave me new insight as Cole and Rafe thought it would. They were right in bringing me here. I'll have to think about all I wish to do. Thank you."

Instead of shaking hands, Ruby hugged her. Spoke close for only her to hear. "You are always welcome in my home. If you ever have the need to talk, give me a call. I will never fail to find time to meet with you. Talk to your young man. Think about all the wasted years in your young lives. No one knows how many beats of the clock they have in this world. If you do end up planning a wedding, come see me. The Clan McKenna are expert wedding planners."

"Thank you." She felt as if she rambled. "I just might take you up on that invitation. If there is a wedding, I'll come to you first for help." Dallas slanted Rafe a hard glare. She hoped he understood the meaning of the scowl she shot his way. The man had known her long enough, there should be no surprises between them.

They left Cole and Ruby to walk down the tower steps to the keep below. Rafe held her hand, wrapping his fingers between hers. The touch, erotic in ways she couldn't imagine. He'd never done that before, held hands with her. As friends not lovers, they never thought to do something so simple. What she needed was for the man to date her. In her life, she'd never had a boyfriend. Never met a man who appealed to her except for Rafe. The only man she'd ever had dinner with was Rafe. Those meals were not dates. She missed so much. Now, he still meant to take those moments away from her.

Dallas enjoyed the feel of her hand engulfed in his larger one. The notion that the small, loving gesture generated surprised her, as well as awakened her senses to the man. Marrying sooner than later would have benefits. She told herself countless times if she ever found a man she wanted, she would never wait for sex. In this day and age, one didn't need to wait. All the sensations sweeping through her now screamed to her. In the most elemental way, she wanted Rafe Frasier. Wanted sex with the man. Would he insist on waiting until the wedding night? She hoped not. Perhaps she could seduce him to think the same way she did.

He leaned in close to her. Whispered his question as if the shrubbery was listening. "What did the two of you talk about? You seemed absorbed in each other when we entered the room. You two would still be visiting if Cole and I had not interrupted." He asked several questions, his voice nonchalant. "You can tell me. Confide in me. Just as you used to do."

Dallas drew in a long deep breath of air, searching for the courage to talk to Rafe. "A lot of things. We spoke of many different topics. Ruby told me how she met Aaron. Told me how much she missed her husband. There were other matters. Don't know if things were said in confidence or not. I won't repeat any of the sentiments Ruby told me. Except the one obvious fact, she loved her husband...still does. How did you and Cole spend this hour?" Dallas meant to turn the tables. Wasn't ready to share all her feelings with Rafe. Perhaps tonight, after dinner, she could confide more specific details. She would try to follow Ruby's advice. Would tell him how she needed time. That she wished to have a bit of romance in her life before they were married. She could tell him how much she wanted him. One didn't just jump from being simple friends into marriage. Rafe was far too eager to fit into her comfort zone.

"Much the same as you. Just as I have realized my mate, Cole has met his mate also. She is too young for him. All that will be common knowledge after she turns eighteen, then graduates from high school." Rafe told her. "That's one of the reasons Ruby told us both to be patient. Cole must wait for her to mature. Ripen, he told me. Thought that was a strange sentiment."

"I'm not eighteen. Don't need ripening," she said, sarcasm tinging her words. "I just need to have you more receptive to my needs. Ruby suggested we compromise. Can we do that? What would you give me in return for something you want? We can confer on this. Negotiations."

He stopped, the expression on his face one of startled confusion. "If I could I would give you the moon along with the stars. What do I want? I think you know what that is. However, I will give you time to adjust. This is new to both of us. You've been hurtled through time twice. Now, what I would like in return for giving you anything you wish for is to set a date. Can we come to terms with a day in the future for our marriage?"

Dallas didn't expect that. She still needed a proposal. A real proposal. If not, then date or no date, there would be no wedding for them. If this would be the one and only time she wed, she meant to get everything she ever dreamed about.

"Next Christmas?" she asked, ready to see the look on his handsome face. Needed to see the shimmer of anger in his steel-gray eyes. What if something happened and she was wasting time? What if they never got to make love because she was foolish. What difference did a real proposal make? Damn it, she wanted him to understand. Take the initiative then ask her for her hand in marriage. He sipped air. He wasn't responding. "You do know it takes a year to iron out all the details for a wedding?"

"If that's the amount of time you need then so be it." Scowl lines were forming on his face. His brows had drawn together. Almost a straight line now. His eyes flashed with annoyance. Obvious to anyone who knew him he was angry. She knew him better than anyone. "A year…at the

McKenna keep the plans for a wedding wouldn't take more than a week. They would work together unencumbered by the threat of time."

"I would like to shop for a gown." Dallas understood this might be asking too much. A wedding gown should be in her future as a bride. She deserved to have everything she'd always wished for.

"You could wear…"

She understood he would have an argument to everything she proposed. "So be it," she murmured, wishing she had more backbone. With little said between them, she caved. It was the look in his eyes that made her wilt to his plans. "I will set a date but not this morning. Need to hear what the good father has to say about our suitability for marriage."

"He won't judge us."

"You don't know that. You don't have any idea what he will think about our circumstances. He might think I'm not good enough for you. I'm not Catholic. For that matter, I'm not anything. He could wish for you to have someone more appropriate."

"Since you are my mate, your religious background will make no difference," he growled his anger.

~ * ~

Rafe didn't know what to make of her reticence. Rushing her to the altar had never been part of his plans. Now that he understood they were meant to be together, he didn't want to waste time. He needed to figure out how to help her understand the cold facts. Every beat of his heart away from her was time he could never retrieve. All the years previous…wasted years. Dallas wasn't in a hurry to hear wedding bells. He needed to figure out how to change that fact.

While Dallas was sipping tea with Cole's mother, he and Cole walked through the keep, then found a small tavern on the outskirts of the village. They ordered beers along with appetizers. Found they both loved deep fat fried pickles as well as mushrooms. The young lady who took their order flirted with Cole. Batted her long sooty eyelashes at him, stood with her chest pushed out. Rafe watched with interest. This must be Phoebe. On the way to the tavern, Cole told him about finding Phoebe.

How he knew the first moment he looked at her she was his for all eternity.

He tapped his nails on the top of the table where they sat. "Seems I've rushed Dallas. At times I think I don't understand why she is holding back, then there are moments when I understand some of her fears. Since realizing Dallas is my mate, I've done everything wrong. She is holding herself away from me. The time spent on her photo shoot was different. We were busy with the pictures she took. We found common ground. Forgot about her encounters with time travel. Doubt if she would model for me now if I asked."

"How so?" Cole questioned him as his beer was set in front of him. Phoebe bent over to set Cole's drink on the table. He would receive a nice view of the valley between her breasts, more might be possible. When it came to Cole, Phoebe didn't hold anything back. He thanked her. She moved on.

The McKenna sat back, watching him with hooded eyes, appearing to think over what was said. He would also be thinking about Phoebe. Almost as if Cole understood all the reasons he would give. Cole spoke, "Dallas isn't thinking along the same lines as you. I understand the sentiment. Her agenda is different. You need to figure out what she wants or needs before you continue to struggle in the quicksand of your making."

Rafe leaned back, pushing the chair to settle on its back legs, his hands splayed on the table. "I should have proposed to her. That was my biggest mistake. Instead of proposing, I told her we would marry. We've only kissed a couple of times. Never the way I wished to kiss her. She held back each time. Stopped me from pursuing more heated caresses. Even then she was afraid of her emotions. Dallas always told me if she ever met a man she wanted, she would give herself to him. I know I'm the man she wants. Yet…she holds herself back, which is the opposite to her statement. What the hell does that mean?"

"She hasn't done that with you? The two of you have never…?" One of Cole's eyebrows shot up. "I'm surprised. You need to…" Not finishing the sentence, Cole paused in thought. He took a long drink of his beer. "…perhaps not. Making love to her now might prolong making the commitment. On the other hand, she would learn what she was missing."

"I told her she shouldn't keep condoms in that big bag of hers.

Doing so was inviting trouble she might not be able to dig herself out of. She told me she needed them for protection in case the right man came along. Believe now, she spouted a great deal of nonsense. She's a virgin and afraid of the act. Saying she would give herself to the right man and doing so are two different ideas.

"Dallas thought I was being too overprotective. After that was announced, she asked me if I carried condoms in my wallet. Of course, I do. Only would need them if I knew it was my mate I was talking to. Knew when I found my mate, we would marry. For me the situation is right out there. Not only does she have condoms, she uses birth control. Has for a long time now. She would never get pregnant unless she stopped taking the pills." He remembered taking her to the doctor when her periods were so intense she had to stay in bed. "We could have sex without worrying about conception. She doesn't want me." Rafe didn't like admitting to that fact.

"Gather you know Dallas better than anyone. Why do you think she's holding back? You need to turn that around," Cole told him, while he watched his mate sashay around the room, her delicious looking butt swinging back and forth. Phoebe served drinks to other customers. Teased. Flirted. Cole's fists tightened then relaxed. He stole a long drink of air.

"I believe I do know her better. Know all her mood swings. All her little habits. Can tell when she's nervous. When she's hungry or tired. Thought about that question for the last week. Longer if you count that evening when we first kissed with sparks flying. Thought we would make love that night. She told me no. Said she had to think. She rushed from my home as if...as if she caught on fire. That's her answer to everything. She has to think."

He did know his Dallas better than any other person, including her parents. Her parents never cared much about her. Once she left for the university, they ignored her. Seemed to him, they were more than pleased when she found a place to rent and moved out.

Phoebe walked by, a tray in her hand. She paused a moment to stare at Cole, who smiled then tipped his head in her direction. The little wanton flounced across the room to the bar, swinging her hips. Rafe watched perspiration bead on Cole's forehead. Heard the small groan.

There was more going on here than met the eye. Cole would need to claim this woman before she found herself in trouble. Rafe didn't envy the journey ahead of them.

"You told me you never proposed to her. Do you plan on doing that? Proposing?" Cole asked as his gaze remained focused on Phoebe.

A half smile curved Rafe's mouth. "Yes, I have a ring for her. It was my grandmother's. Hope she will like the piece. If not, I'll have her pick one out tomorrow or the next day. Tonight…" He let out a slow breath of air. "Tonight, I'll get down on one knee. Ask her to marry me. Hope that's what has been troubling her. If so, most of my problems with her will be solved. She said she would cook dinner this evening. Maybe we can take this one step closer to that ceremony." He thought about a little seducing while she was cooking. A kiss here. A gentle touch there. A bit more in other places.

"If you wish for the wedding to happen sooner than later, don't make love to her. Charm her, sweet-talk, do everything except…leave her needing more. Tell her you're saving yourself for the wedding night. Whatever seems to bring her closer to you, do it."

"What?" Rafe was startled by Cole's statement. Until this moment, he'd not had one intention of waiting. "Begging? Doubt if I can do something so coldhearted. Is that what you're doing with Phoebe?" He understood he should not ask that question. It was too personal. Too intimate between partners.

Cole turned away for a beat then raked his hands through his hair. "No, Phoebe doesn't know what she means to me, not yet. As our relationship stands now, she's flirting with me. I'm pleased that she's interested. Means a lot to me to see her bat her eyelashes at me, swing her hips, pose with up thrust breasts. I'm biding my time." He cleared his throat, forcing his gaze away from Phoebe. "Back to Dallas, make her want you until she's begging. Tell her you wish to wait to have a real wedding night. Don't create the ecstasy she deserves. Does she have any notion of what will happen on the wedding night? How you will claim her?"

Rafe found himself shaking his head. While wishing he wouldn't need to explain everything, he grimaced. "No, doubt if she understands.

Except for me, she knows no shifters. Would not have an occasion to discuss something so personal with anyone except me. She was shocked out of her skin when I changed to my cat. Again, I rushed things. Should have waited. She told me she needs a year to plan the wedding. How can I wait a year?"

"A year, you say? Damn. Don't talk to her about the claiming. Knowledge will only serve to terrify. Discovering what you intend on the wedding night might make her back off even further. She could prolong this marriage for years if she has a mind to do so." Those were Cole's words of wisdom. "Mother, along with the other clan wives, will be with her before you can take her to bed. They will help her understand what is going to happen."

"First, Dallas needs to agree with me. Tonight," Rafe reiterated. "Tonight, will be my time for romance. Put into action all your suggestions."

"As I said earlier, seduce, charm, kiss her until she can't breathe but don't make love to her. Don't let her feel that final ecstasy. Make her want you enough to set a wedding date within the month. If you continue to insist on a real wedding night, she will come to you sooner than later."

Rafe tossed all of Cole's advice around in his head. Smiled. He needed to fix this. Didn't want to wait longer than necessary. He stole air from the room. "Good God! She told me she needs a year. Tells me weddings take at least a year to plan. She doesn't need that long. What the hell is there to do that would take that long? I would think a week would be enough time. A wedding dress might take longer than a week."

"That's nerves about sex talking. As I said, do away with the nerves. Be romantic along with patient. Seduce as well as charm. Dallas will come around. If you heed my advice, the little lady will see Father Richard before the month is over. She will be in a hurry to set a date. If luck is on your side, maybe sooner."

"Can I get you gentlemen anything else?" Phoebe was at the table smiling at Cole. She swept her tongue along her bottom lip. Posed with her hip jutting out. Cole swept his gaze along her body, lingering at her breasts. Hunger lit his eyes. If Rafe was right, Cole wanted to drink of all her assets, to devour every sensual part of her.

As far as Rafe could tell, she begged for Cole's attention. When he decided Phoebe matured enough, she wouldn't know what happened. She would find herself charmed as well as seduced. She would lose her virginity before the wedding night. "Nothing for me," Rafe spoke up, pushing his chair away from the table then dropping a few bills to cover his share of the bill. He had a mission to accomplish. He checked his watch. The priest would be waiting for their interview. "If you wish to stay…" Rafe left the sentence hanging while he watched the interplay between the couple. "I can walk back to the keep by myself."

"No… Nothing better to do." Cole grinned at Phoebe, then he too pushed back his chair leaving money on the table to cover his bill along with the tip. "The extra is for you, Phoebe." Cole turned back to Rafe, "I will walk with you. Wish to speak to mother about an important matter." He slanted Phoebe one last look. In obvious retaliation to his abandonment, she tossed her long golden hair over her shoulder.

Once outside, Rafe let out a bark of laughter. "You and Phoebe, I see why patience will need to be a virtue. At least Dallas and I are not so far apart in age as the two of you. How many years? Not that you need answer. It's not my business. You're certain that little girl is your mate?" He found he couldn't stop laughing.

Cole slanted him a scowl. "Eight years, give or take a few months. She hasn't even graduated from high school. Believe me, I understand she's going to be a handful. The way she flirts has possible suitors climbing the walls. I have to chase them off. So far, I've been able to do that with a scathing look. She understands what I'm doing. What Phoebe doesn't understand is why. She might not think I'm interested. So far, I haven't shown her too much interest. I'm waiting until graduation to start the courtship."

"You've less than a month until she puts schooling behind her. Does she have any thoughts to her future? College? Trade school? You'll need to allow her to chase her dreams. Give her a few years to mature." Rafe was pleased he and Dallas pursued the same type of work. He was also grateful she agreed to model for him. As he recalled the times she sat in front of him naked, while he sketched then painted, his gut clenched while his body heated. If she consented to model for him now, he wasn't positive he could keep his mind on his painting or his hands to himself.

Even when there was no spark between them, he believed she was the most beautiful woman he'd ever set eyes on. Her hair radiated the colors of the sunset. Her cornflower blue eyes never ceased to sparkle. The innate sensual beauty of her voluptuous curves never set him on fire as they did now. These days when he looked at her, the sight caused him to burn with desire. All the time, every moment of every day, he hungered for her. Before, if he touched, brushed his hand across the tips of her breasts when he arranged her hair, no part of him stirred. Now, when she looked at him, the shimmer of her beautiful eyes stimulated all his male parts. The way her breasts bounced when she walked ripped heat through him. Seducing without taking everything she might want to give would be harder for him than for her. Doing so would leave him gasping.

"She doesn't have thoughts along the line of a possible career. Phoebe is moving into the keep in a few days. I've a room being prepared in the south tower for her. It's far enough away from mine to keep gossip at bay. She can't be living with her father. I've heard he's abusive when he drinks. That won't do at all. Won't let anyone hurt my mate. She also needs protection from herself along with all her ardent suitors. In a few weeks, Phoebe will be under my protection. All will understand that fact."

"You have realized she's a flirt? Right?" Rafe asked as he thought about the future problems awaiting Cole. "No wonder your mother has advised patience. When I look at you coupled with Phoebe, seems you need to possess that virtue more than I. Believe that with a few tucks and nips on my behavior, I'll have Dallas in the palms of my hands. Your advice seems sound and logical."

Cole didn't laugh as Rafe though he might. Instead, deep scowl lines formed on his forehead. "I must give her time to grow up. Need to protect her from herself, her father too. Figure if I spend as much time as possible at her shifts at the tavern, that will help keep the young pups at bay. You're right though. Phoebe enjoys the game of flirting too much. The boys she set her sights on leave drooling. She trifles with them. Enjoys watching them squirm. She won't be able to do that with me."

"You don't have to wait that long. Many women are wed at eighteen," Rafe suggested, watching the play of emotions on Cole's features.

"Phoebe is not ready. She's never had a true beau. I plan on being that man, acting the part until I deem her ready for marriage. If we tied the knot now, nothing would be right. I have to give her a bit of room to grow up. If I don't, she'll come to resent me. I want our budding relationship to be perfect."

"Perfect doesn't exist. I take Phoebe isn't a shifter?"

"No…she's not. That fact creates a problem to deal with…the showing of my cat. Appearing as my cat can't happen until I'm certain she is mine and am positive she loves me. Mother will help when the right time appears on the horizon."

That was one of the things Rafe did wrong. He showed her his cat before she was ready. Was impatient. Having acknowledged that fact, it was time to move on.

They were walking up the stairway to Ruby's suite of rooms in the tower. Rafe stopped at the portrait of Roc and Lainie Frasier. Gazed at the painting while Cole continued. Despite all the difficulties, the two ended up happy. They were smitten with each other from the first minutes upon meeting. He was enamored with her counterpart, Dallas. Fell in love with her on the playground that day he comforted her. Rafe felt certain that if Dallas saw their past lives together, she would realize what they meant to each other. If that happened, she would never be so hesitant as she was now. It wouldn't happen until the clan's traditional ceremony.

True, he terrified her by showing her his cat then playing with her. The showing was too much too soon. Teasing her made the reveal worse. At first, he didn't understand her fright or why. His cat was such an integral part of him. He expected that she would understand the cat was him. She didn't. When he teased her, by caressing her arm with his tongue, he heard her startled gasp. Felt her draw away from him. Heard the revulsion in her thoughts, afterward the terror. Combating those two feelings was too important to overlook. He wouldn't shift again until after they were married, until after he made love to her.

Rafe saw her now sitting in the living room with Ruby. Heard her thoughts. She wouldn't know he could hear her. If she learned, she would take umbrage with the fact. Shifters were always able to hear their mate's thoughts when they reached out to them. Understood she hoped to compromise with him, discuss terms between them. She wasn't going to agree with the marriage until he put his knee on the ground. When it came to romance, he needed guidance counseling. Didn't know of anyone except perhaps Ruby who could help him in this endeavor. Damn, but he needed a swift kick in the butt.

He always thought romance would be easier to navigate. Perhaps he confused romance with lust along with the hunger that drove him to possess her. Before Dallas returned from the past, he never felt intense lust for a woman. The dinner he brought when she was on the photo shoot was romantic. Flowers. Candles. Wine. He needed to do more of the same. She appreciated the gesture. Didn't want to overplay the romance. She might think he was sappy. How much was too much? That was a question he didn't have an answer for.

They needed to visit Father Richard. It was their next appointment. Set a date for a wedding she hadn't agreed to yet. Pushing for a date…needing to set the time…he wasn't going to mention that insignificant little fact. Didn't intend to act over eager for a date. He would agree with all she said. First, they would speak with the priest. What he would tell them, he had no idea. Would there be counseling? Would Father Richard see through her hesitancy?

Together they walked from the main building into the courtyard. He held her hand in his. Slipped his fingers between hers. Felt a tiny tremor of pleasure shoot through her into him. Heard the soft sigh ruffle through her mind. She enjoyed holding hands. This was the first step in the wooing of Dallas. As he hoped to please, he would do more simple gestures. As Cole suggested, he would seduce as well as charm. Certain he could sweet-talk her. How would he compromise? Negotiate? He couldn't…wouldn't give her all that she asked. There had to be a common thread between them.

Compromise.

Negotiate change.

Tonight would be the first night of this new relationship he planned to embark upon. In his dresser he had the ring he intended to give her. If she accepted the proposal, it would be hers. He would slip the ring on her finger The jewelry was still in its original box. His grandmother saved everything she believed to be important, including boxes. He didn't know if the box was that important to save for this many years. The fact made the giving easier for him. What he didn't know was if she wanted something new, more modern or if she thrived on tradition. They could shop together for a ring if that was what she wished for. Money wasn't an issue.

Before they left for the keep, he ordered the dinner ingredients she told him she needed, along with two bottles of red wine. She'd said to him that she would cook the meal. He planned on helping until she shooed him from the kitchen. She would. When it came to cooking, he enjoyed the task but was not so talented as Dallas. He grinned. Didn't think he would leave tonight even if she tried to shoo him out of the kitchen. He thought of all the seducing he could do when her hands were otherwise engaged. He would make certain her wine glass was full. He could touch, caress, whisper in her ear. Dallas was always fun when she was a bit silly with wine.

They walked through the rose garden. As of now, nothing was in bloom. He brought her hand up to his lips. Kissed the back. Her thoughts pleased him. She liked the soft kiss. Wished he would do more of the same. Rafe decided listening to her contemplations could help his cause. She didn't know she gave her emotions along with her thoughts away. A man could use the upper hand when it came to romance. He needed every advantage he could find. Until now, he hadn't listened often enough.

She would learn about his ability to read her mind. Would be angry as well as irritated at the invasion. There was nothing she could do to change that little fact.

Before that time, as well as after, he would reap the benefits.

"We are here. Are you nervous? I am." He didn't give her a chance to answer the question before he stepped forward. She held back. He heard the ripple of unease shift within her head. He tugged. She resisted, then gave in to his efforts. "It's going to be fine. I don't intend to force anything at this interview. You need not set a date. We will be honest about your hesitancy."

"Thank you," she mouthed to him when he looked at her.

"You're welcome." He tucked a flyaway strand of hair behind her ear. "From this point forward, what will happen with us is for you to decide. I will stand by all of your decisions even if I disagree. We can discuss any differences later, when the moment is more convenient as well as more private."

The door to Father Richard's office stood open. Rafe peeked inside. Father Richard stood. A smile was on his face. The father was clean shaven and bald. His belly was round and his legs short. Rafe knew him to be a shifter. All the priests who performed the clan ceremony had the ability to shift. His cat could not be large. The man was jolly. Ready to smile as well as laugh, he seemed to find humor in most situations. He could be solemn also. Took his faith with the seriousness demanded by his profession.

"Welcome," Father Richard extended his hand in greeting. "I'm pleased you are on time. Tells a great deal about young couples if they can't be at appointments as expected. Rafe Frasier, I haven't seen you in church for a while, I trust you have a valid excuse. Should I expect to see you and your friend next Sunday?" He shook his hand then turned to Dallas, a beaming smile on his face. "You are Dallas Shaw?"

She nodded then, "Yes…"

Rafe felt the trembling of her body. Saw the quick intake of air when she thought about attending church.

Farther Richard hmphed. Paused for a few ticks of the clock while he seemed to study them. "A long time ago I knew your mother. She's a lovely woman. Nice, very nice." He gestured into the room. "Come, sit down. We can talk about whatever is on your mind. Heard there might be a wedding. If that is true, we can speak of particulars. The two of you have known each other how long?"

Rafe flinched when the priest spoke of Dallas' mother…her uncaring mother. Heard her thoughts on the topic. Mrs. Shaw was a woman filled with hate and malice. Long ago, this wonderful woman discarded her child, telling her she was worthless. Part of the issues Dallas had was the fact her mother disliked the way Dallas looked. Hated her beautiful feminine curves. Venom spewed from her lips while she berated Dallas to eat less. Thought she should purge after every meal. Those hateful words affected Dallas. Hurt her to the depth that she tried starvation to lose weight. He'd stepped in, telling her that her health was more important. He picked up the shattered pieces with soothing words, comforting words. Rafe loved the way she looked as well as acted. He didn't believe she should change anything about herself.

Dallas didn't like to admit that her mother was part of her problem with her weight…most of her problem. Dallas didn't weigh too much. She didn't overeat. Genetics played a huge part in the way she was built. Even starving herself, the curves never vanished. Rafe loved her curves… always had…always would. He enjoyed the tiny dimples on her thighs she bemoaned. Most women had cellulite. She wasn't alone with that characteristic. Watching certain parts of her body move when she walked delighted him. She was perfect just the way she appeared. With his thoughts, a certain appendage of his responded. He was hungry for her. Could think of little else than this evening while she cooked for him.

Dallas' face turned the shade of ashes with Father Richard's comment on her mother. A soft snort of disdain followed. She cleared her throat to speak. "My mother is not a lovely woman. If there is a wedding, she won't be in attendance, nor will my father give me away. They are both hateful to me. Haven't seen the two of them since I left for college. Don't wish to see either parent."

Father Richard looked at him as if for confirmation of her statement. Rafe didn't like that. He should accept whatever Dallas said as her truth. She was capable of speaking for herself without being questioned. "They are…hateful," he said, agreeing with her assessment of her parents. Rafe rubbed the back of his neck. Tension built in the tiny office. As if he felt it necessary, he continued to speak with honest sincerity. He began, "Toward Dallas, the two have never been loving parents. If she doesn't wish them to attend the wedding, they won't receive an invitation. As it stands now, Dallas and I haven't decided there will be a wedding. I am hopeful she will come around to my way of thinking." If she didn't, he would claim her. He could never allow them to go through this life without the claiming ritual. While he didn't like the notion, it was something he had to do.

"If there is to be no marriage, why are the two of you here?" He tapped his pen on his desk. His eyes narrowed as he looked from one to the other.

"That's a good question," Dallas spoke up before he could say a word. "We jumped the gun a bit. I've…well…" She caught her lip beneath her teeth worrying the soft flesh for a few seconds. "We just don't agree on certain aspects that need to become clearer before we can commit. We haven't been a couple much more than a week, though we've known each other since what seems to be forever. I need…" Dallas looked to him as if seeking an answer. "I need more time to get to know this man as we are now. Don't want to lose my best friend. Don't want to rush into something that is forever if it's not meant to be. In my mind as in Rafe's, marriage is forever."

He was pleased with her sentiments. He needed to remind her that just because they loved each other didn't mean they would no longer be best friends. He sensed she was coming around to his way of thinking without too much convincing on his part. Reaching for her hand, he scooped it into his then squeezed. Wound his fingers between hers. Felt the soft sigh of pleasure the gesture elicited. Wished to tell her there would be more of that, much more. He liked all those sensual mercuric sounds rippling from her lips.

"Dallas is right in everything she is telling you. When I called you this morning, I was in a hurry, a rush to set what happened between us right. Dallas has a great deal to learn about me, as well as the clan. I believe we will decide sometime in the future to become husband and wife. When we do, we'll be back. More confident. More certain of our lifelong promise." He saw the bewildered expression on her lovely face. Dallas didn't know what to think about his comment.

"Then…well then…you do not want to make a commitment today? Do I have this right? The two of you don't wish to set the date for your wedding." Father Richard sounded flushed. Confused. Baffled in the extreme.

Looking to Dallas, Rafe waited for her to answer. He nodded then gave her another encouraging squeeze to her hand. She gazed at him as if befuddled by his obvious turn. By these few moments, he understood he needed to listen more. Should assume nothing without asking Dallas for her opinions. He should seek her true thoughts by listening to her muddle about over-thought ideas in her head. When they began their trip to the keep this morning, she would not have expected this turn of events.

"I would wait to set a date." Dallas nodded her agreement. "As Rafe told you, this is too soon for me. Just getting to know Rafe in a different way than before everything went topsy-turvy is too important to skip. Maybe in another month we could visit again. Set a date. I'm sorry for wasting your time. My sincerest apologies." She paused. Focused her gaze on him for a few seconds as if seeking confirmation then turned back to Father Richard. Silence in the room seemed to muffle all the thoughts that were flying through her brain to his. "Can you tell me about the clan ceremony…anything? Something?"

"She should…" Rafe began but was cut off before he could voice his thoughts. He tried to understand her fears. As of yet, she didn't know the claiming would cause her pain. Had no idea she would be naked during that one part of the ceremony. She'd been naked numerous times in front of him. Last night was the first time he held her in his arms when she was in that state. He would during this ceremony. All her precious curves would be pushed against him. Flesh against flesh, the thought rifled within.

Father Richard waved his hand though the air. His smile turned grim. "No…that's impossible until there is a commitment between the two people. As I see it now, there is none to speak of. Am I right? Outsiders can never know about the ritual that brings two of the clan together. It is sacred to our people."

"Yes…" Dallas admitted, with a whole lot of reluctance in her voice along with her thoughts. She'd wished to be told what to expect. Hell, he didn't know what to expect through the ceremony. The fact they would stand together naked surrounded by a cloak was all he understood. "I've not agreed yet. Though I'm certain if given time to adjust, I will see things Rafe's way. You are right to keep the secrets from outsiders. That's what I am…an outsider looking into something I've no right to see." She sucked in a deep breath of air. It was clear she was annoyed with the circumstance.

"When you do wish to commit to life with this man, come see me.

I'll explain whatever you would like to know. You will understand all before the ritual. You will not be surprised by anything except the true revelations that pertain to your life with young Frasier." Father Richard was standing, dismissing them. It seemed there would be no more questions. "Call me whenever you are prepared to set a date for the wedding. These things the clan does quite well. The celebration can be planned in record time. A week at the most. Why, I've seen them come together for a wedding celebration in three days. Once you decide there is no need to wait, Ruby will help you with all the details."

~ * ~

Cole poured his mother a cup of tea before sitting down beside her with his brandy glass in hand. He needed her advice, yet the thought of discussing Phoebe with his mother discomfited. After seeing Phoebe in the tavern, he needed something stronger than tea. His body jumped to attention while he watched her glide across the floor. He had a myriad of questions to ask both his mother as well as Phoebe. One of which was to discover what his mother told Dallas. Even though he understood the conversation between the two was none of his business, he meant to ask. She would tell him whatever she could. He also realized he was opening the door for her questions pertaining to Phoebe. That was all well and good. He had plans that would soon be out in the open. His mother should be first to understand his intentions. Phoebe would be the next one to learn about his ideas when they developed to the point where he was satisfied.

With no reluctance on his part, he understood he needed advice as to how to handle the flirtatious young woman who was his mate. His mother's guidance could go a long way in how he handled the precocious young woman. He barely knew her. Phoebe already found a place in his heart. Cole understood if he was too highhanded with her, she would bristle. She would hold herself in reserve. Despite her father's failings, she appeared to be both independent as well as stubborn. She would not take him with the seriousness he would demand unless he treated her as if she could think for herself. That would be no trouble. Cole relished learning more about her thoughts…her aspirations…her dreams. Just because she wasn't off to the university didn't mean she had a lack of goals. He meant to discover her likes along with those things she disliked.

He began, his voice soft. He wasn't certain how to phrase his question. "So, you spoke quite a while with Dallas. She appeared more relaxed than when they arrived here. I gather the discussion was worth the time."

His mother shook a finger at him, a wicked smile flitting across her features. "I know my son very well. You're trying to get me to speak of things Dallas and I talked about. The words we shared are none of your business, as you've guessed. What I can say is that Dallas is a lovely young woman who is head over heels in love with that bounder, Rafe Frasier. He doesn't have one clue as to how to court his mate. He thinks she will fall into his plans just like that." Ruby snapped her fingers, still grinning, enjoying the scenario that was created long before Dallas visited. "If she hasn't done so yet, she won't. He needs to treat her with gentle concern instead of running rough shod over her."

Cole hooted with laughter. "Mother, you're right. As usual, hit the nail on the head, so to speak. Rafe needs to have someone shake a *wee* bit of sense into him. Where Dallas is concerned, the poor man is flummoxed. Confused as to what he's doing wrong. As it concerns his mate, he doesn't know whether he is coming or going. The fact he can focus in on her thoughts will help him navigate that road to the altar he is pining for. I did give him a few suggestions. He seems to believe the advice valid."

"Flummoxed…good word for your friend. At least he isn't almost eight years his mate's senior. Did you see Phoebe at the tavern? She's such a pretty little thing. You will need to treat her with gentle concern. Don't do what Rafe is doing to Dallas…"

"What is that?"

"As I said, run rough shod over her, just because you are older and, you believe, wiser," Ruby told him. "She has feelings…unique to her."

"Can't hide anything from you, Mother. Yes, of course I saw her. The pretty little flirt showed me the swing of her hips as if shouting out my name. Batted her eyelashes as if I'd fall at her feet and pay homage to her beauty. She was calling to me along with every other male in the tavern. Rafe couldn't be bothered. That fact hurt her feelings for a few seconds." Rafe had thoughts of Dallas. No one else. That was good.

"Phoebe wants to see you jealous. She flirts when you are in the vicinity so you will think she is more adult than she is. The girl knows there is something between the two of you. Is a bit terrified of your age as well as unsure of herself." Ruby snorted then chuckled. "She is much like I was at her age. I was after your father even though I never understood why. I flirted. As you say, batted my eyelashes at him. Tried to seduce him by swinging my hips when I walked away. He watched me from the corner of his eyes just as you focus on Phoebe."

"You were a little flirt?" Cole asked with startled disbelief. "You? I can hardly believe that." he questioned again then hooted with laughter. Another chuckle before he spoke again, "I would have liked to have been there. Father reeled you in, didn't he? Knew what he was about."

"I wasn't a fish," she huffed.

"Reeled you in," Cole repeated with another bout of laughter.

"It wasn't long before you were with us. I was afraid to inform your father. He knew the moment it happened. Shifters *ken* that sort of thing. Of course, it took me a couple of months before I understood I conceived that day. You were more than a thought in our heads before we were wed. What I didn't know was that Aaron was waiting for me to grow up. Just as you wait for Phoebe. When he thought I was old enough, he seduced me, charmed me. I became pregnant with you the first time we made love. We took no precautions. I didn't think of taking any. He didn't wish to. Then…" she paused, tapping her beautifully manicured nail on her chin. "Because of you, I was privy to his thoughts. The fact befuddled his male brain for a time until he spoke with a few others and learned that through the *bairn* I carried, I could hear his thoughts. He didn't appreciate that fact one bit. Enjoyed hearing my thoughts but when it came to him, I found he was quite annoyed."

"You are wicked, Mother. Are you trying to tell me I should seduce Phoebe and have done with waiting? We both know she's too young for marriage. She would rebel at the notion. I do intend to keep a close eye on her comings and goings. Won't let her get into trouble with those young drooling idiots who surround her."

"You should do that. Also, you need to become a part of her life after she graduates. Take her out to eat. Maybe to the loch, but don't seduce her there as your father did me." With her lashes lowered she sipped her tea.

"You think I should step in that soon?" He massaged his neck, not too certain about his mother's plans. Where Phoebe was concerned the tension was ever present. "Take her out to eat? We could go to Inverness for an evening. I did think earlier today while she was sashaying across the tavern floor, I should start the courtship the day after graduation."

Ruby shook her head. "Yes, to the day after she leaves high school behind. No, to taking her to Inverness. That's too far away too soon. There are several nice breweries in Carnoch. Take her to one. Buy her a beer along with dinner. Walk with her in the moonlight. Hold hands with her. A kiss or two would not be inappropriate if she agrees. Nothing more until she is older. Wiser to your ways, a man's ways not a boy's. You could take her to the bonfire. Let her cuddle up against you. Your father and I did that. Roasted marshmallows too. Those are simple things a woman that young would take a great deal of enjoyment in doing."

"I believe I would take pleasure in any time with her. If she wants to be with me…" He didn't know if he could keep his hands to himself after sharing kisses with her. He would need to figure out how to do that.

"From what you've told me, she does want to see more of you. She's flaunting herself to get your attention. What you need to do is make certain she knows she has what she wants. All of your attention. Let her understand she doesn't want another man, especially not a boy; one with no experience to guide him. Patience. Take the wooing slow. Phoebe is very young. Don't frighten her. As with all young women in this era, she is aware of far more than she should be."

"Don't I know it. Young. How could my mate end up being so much younger than me?" Cole rubbed his temples in an attempt to assuage the growing headache that always exploded in his mind when he tried to figure out what to do with Phoebe until she was mature enough for his plans.

"You do understand that in the past…the far past…most young women were much younger than their husbands. It might take many more centuries to catch up to the fact that women tend to marry men who are closer to their age. Dallas is younger than Rafe. Not eight years but…I believe at least four years his junior. It's possible she is five years younger."

"I will have patience as you suggest. For now, I'll find something to do until the end of her shift. I was able to get that information from the owner. I'll walk her home. Perhaps, I'll start the wooing a bit sooner than after her graduation. Maybe I'll hold her hand. Slide my fingers between hers."

He left the room whistling, feeling much better now than when he came to see his mother.

Chapter Four

The ingredients for tonight's dinner were on the doorstep when they reached his house. Rafe carried the box inside. Dallas marveled over the conversation with the priest. Rafe seemed to give her what she wanted. He never argued when she insisted on waiting. She'd slanted him a look of bewilderment when he fell into her plans. After he told Father Richard they wouldn't be setting the date for the wedding today, she almost blurted her surprise. A tender smile graced his lips when he met her gaze.

Before she began to cook, she meant to change into something more comfortable. This day in May was unseasonably warm. While huge trees shaded his three-story home, there was no air conditioning. The upstairs studio would be blindingly hot. Good thing there wasn't going to be any nude sketching this evening. If there was, she'd be sweating. Rafe called that condition of hers glowing.

Skipping up the steps to Rafe's bedroom, she unbuttoned her shirt, slipped the blouse from her arms and unfastened her bra. She tugged it off, letting the garment fall to the floor. She reached into her dresser to pull out a halter top. Quickly, she tied the back. Next, she got rid of the skirt along with her panties. She pulled on short shorts that were light as well as comfortable. Perfect for the hot kitchen.

Dallas knew he would never interrupt her dressing. They had an unwritten rule between them. If one was changing clothes the other would wait outside until they finished. She smiled. Not that it mattered to her. He'd seen her naked many times. For her pleasure, she wished they didn't have that rule. She wanted to see Rafe wearing nothing at all. Many times, thought the whole thing was quite unfair.

She'd seen him once.

"It's your turn," Dallas called out, as she strode into the kitchen prepared to cook the meal they'd been waiting for. To her surprise, a glass of wine sat on the counter next to the stove. The vegetables had been washed then set on the cutting board. "For me?" She asked pleased with the fact he thought of her needs. She sipped. Swallowed and sighed with pleasure at the taste of the wine he gave her.

"For you," he spoke, his voice low as well as soft. "Enjoy. We've two bottles. I like your outfit," he murmured, as she whirled, giving him a full view of her. "It's skimpy. Do you have something in mind?"

"You do? You like what I'm wearing?" she asked, surprised by his comment. *Do I have something in mind? No…?* "Are you going to change into shorts and a T?" His usual clothing.

"I believe I will. I'll be back in a few minutes to help out with whatever you need."

She watched his back as he strode through the kitchen door then murmured. "Please, don't plan on helping too much. You can cut vegetables for the salad and the stir-fry." *I doubt if you could get into too much trouble chopping.*

"I heard that."

The glass of wine stopped midway to her mouth. "I didn't say anything," Dallas shot back, confused at his statement. She didn't say anything out loud. Did she? A little wave of guilt blasted through her. She didn't mean to say anything negative. Even though he enjoyed cooking, Rafe did possess two left hands when it came to helping out in the kitchen. When they were together, instead of cooking he always cleaned up. That part was nice.

Tonight, she wasn't doing anything fancy. A simple stir-fry would be quick. He seemed to have romance on his mind, which suited her just fine. She wanted him to pay attention to her. Needed him to care about her feelings. As soon as he got down here, she would have him chopping the ingredients for the meal. The cut pieces of steak would go into the wok after the oil heated.

She hummed while she poured a generous portion of olive oil into the pan. Sipped her wine. Cut the steak. She felt his fingers on the back of her neck before she heard him. She must have been caught up in her thoughts. He pushed strands of hair to the side. His lips brushed across her nape. He toyed with the tie holding her top in place. She held her breath.

He left it alone…the two bows were still in place.

Kisses raffled across her neck then along her shoulder. She shuddered with the pleasure the butterfly caress gave her. "You could cook naked for me," his whispered words floated across her. The sensation was light, airy. She felt his tongue play with the lobe of her ear. Heat shimmied. Lashed into secret places. She swallowed air.

"Rafe!" She loved what he did but if he kept it up there would be no dinner. "Stop!" Good God, she didn't want him to stop. Who needed dinner? His hands settled on the tie at her waist, but he left that alone, and then one fingertip touched each vertebra on his way upward.

"I need dinner," he told her, as the heat from his body left her. She felt both disappointment as well as relief. "Are these the vegetables that need cutting?" Rafe held the big chopping knife in one hand while he waited for her instructions.

"Did I ask if you needed dinner?" Dallas inquired, beginning to wonder if she imagined thinking the comment and not asking. That was the second time it seemed he read her mind. Could he do that?

"You did," Rafe told her while, per her instructions, he began to cut broccoli. "You said 'who needed dinner.' I heard your voice ask the question. There is no one else in this room." He stopped to look around as if he searched for another person. "Hope not."

He would need to do the same with the snow peas and the carrots. There was one zucchini to chop. She had him order watercress along with water chestnuts which were her favorites.

"I'm not cooking naked for you!" Until now she forgot his earlier comment. "I draw the line at modeling for you. Besides, one of your friends could show up at the door. Your mother or father might decide to visit. I'm not going to be caught standing naked in your kitchen." She huffed out the last statement.

"No one will visit. You know Mom and Dad never stop by unannounced. They would call first," he told her, slanting her a wicked grin as he winked.

"There is always a first time for everything," she muttered, while she thought about the way his lips felt on the back of her neck. She wanted him behind her again. Needed to feel his kisses. Since that first time she told him no, he'd not touched her. Had not kissed her. She wouldn't tell him no again. Not when she needed him so damn much.

"I would enjoy dinner so much more if I could look at all of you. I still believe the best way for you to cook would be without the benefit of clothing." Rafe set piles of vegetables for her to use when the time was right.

She was still cooking the meat. He finished with the vegetables and stood behind her again. His hands ran along her ribcage. Up then down. His fingers touched upon her torso just below her breasts. Spirals of heat flamed where his hands roamed. One more time, he brushed his lips on her nape. She shivered. Her hands shook.

"If you want dinner, you need to stop doing what you're doing." He'd never been so forward. She felt his fingers at the bottom of her shorts. He touched tender territory. The curve of her butt. Over then over again, he swept his finger where he had no business touching. He slipped his hands to the front of her. Unfastened her shorts. With his large hand, he covered her lower belly. Her muscles clenched. His fingers glided lower until he was so close to her darkest secrets.

"Do you have anything else for me to chop?" he asked, as he nipped then laved as if soothing the small hurt. "I want you naked."

"No…" she moaned as his hands moved to her thighs then back to her ribs.

"Yes…"

"No…

"Just a little bit, for a few minutes." The tie at her waist fell away. "Maybe not all the way naked." His hands found tender places. When he placed them on her stomach beneath the fabric of her shorts, again her muscles contracted. "So soft. Precious. I want you…Dallas… You know that though."

"Everything is going to burn. Rafe! Not now! Oh! The rice is boiling over!" She reached for the pot to pull it off the high heat; she forgot to turn down the knob. His hands slipped beneath her halter top. Held her breasts in his hands. Her top fluttered loose. "Tie it. Please," she whimpered as she flamed beneath his touch. He ran the palms of his hands across her. Explored lower and then back to hold her.

"I want to undo the top too. I want you naked to your waist. Nothing between me and my sightseeing fingers. I want to charm you, feel your sensual response." His thumbs stroked her nipples, tugged on each one until she moaned low in the back of her throat. She closed her eyes realizing the intense urgency of the moment. "Would like to suckle you, drink of you. Devour you."

Her knees weakened. Dallas didn't think she could remain standing. Couldn't cook. "Please…oh…this needs to wait." Dallas didn't know if she was relieved or disappointed when his hands left her and he tied the halter top.

Rafe backed away. Ran his finger down the line of her back. "You're right. We do need dinner first. Don't want you to lose any of your generous curves from malnutrition." He topped off her glass. "Drink your wine. Finish cooking. I am starving. After we eat, we can play more. Do whatever you might like. I'll let you take charge of our entertainment."

He'd not given her a chance to drink anything. She was a perplexed mess of rolling emotions. Her brain, along with her body, was in turmoil. He did that to her. She'd never felt anything like what he orchestrated in her life. *Of course, you haven't. You've never had a beau. No man has ever touched your breasts to seduce except Rafe.* Until tonight, he only touched once. Now, he seemed to have an agenda.

I ran terrified. I'm still running terrified. I want him, then I don't want him. I need to give the man a chance. His cat frightens me. I don't understand what to make of him.

As if he wasn't affected by anything that transpired for those few unguarded moments, Rafe sat down at the kitchen table to watch. He set his feet on the chair opposite. He was relaxed. Grinning. His long fingers wound around the stem of his glass while he studied her. "You're beautiful when you're confused. Did you want me to stop? I'm not certain."

In one gulp, Dallas drank half her glass of wine. She spilled more into the crystal goblet. When she looked at the dining room table, she realized he brought out the best dinnerware, along with the crystal glasses. The silverware was indeed the silver set that his grandmother owned and had given to him before she passed on. Was this his way of trying to be romantic? Part of it was romantic, the other part seemed to be… Dallas wasn't certain. It seemed he started to seduce then quit.

"Yes," he said with tenderness as if he heard her thoughts. "Yes, I want tonight to be romantic. Want it to be all about you. You're also right about the seduction. I don't wish to rush you. Whenever you are ready. I'm certain you will tell me."

This time she knew she didn't say anything. She turned on him. Her hands fisted on her hips. "How did you know what I was thinking? You're listening into my mind? Is that another characteristic of shifters?"

He shrugged, lifting his shoulders as if it meant nothing. "I've known you a long time. Just as you might know my thoughts from time to time, I know yours. I'd like to be everything you want me to be. I wish to give you whatever you want. If you don't tell me, well then…well…I need to ascertain things about you that you aren't telling me." Again, he lifted his broad shoulder in a half shrug. The corner of his mouth twitched as if he was trying not to smile. "I don't know how to be romantic without directions. You explain to me how to chop vegetables, which in my mind is not all that important to romance. However, you won't or can't give me your expert advice on romancing you. It's obvious to anyone who knows me, I'm lacking in the romance department. I'm factual. I live with notions I can measure and weigh. I don't know how to be abstract except when it comes to painting. Even my paintings are not abstract. They are concise. I would give you anything along with everything you want. Telling me what is significant is also important to me." He stopped as if he needed air. "I'm repeating myself. Guess I need to do that so I can make certain you understand."

She stared at him, mouth agape. He reached out to close her mouth. Her teeth clamped together. She didn't recall a time he'd ever said so much in such a short amount of time. He wanted to learn about romance. Romance comes from the heart. "It seems to me," Dallas spoke with a slow smooth voice as she tipped snow peas into the wok, "that if I have to tell you what you should do, the romance will vanish. The spontaneity would be gone. I…" She turned to him, her lips thinned, as she tried to figure out the words she needed. "I don't know what you want of me." She spread out her hands. "This…this…all of what you have done…is romantic. Even while seducing the cook, you were romantic. I did enjoy the attention. Will enjoy more as the evening moves on. I would like to know what you've planned."

The relief she saw on his face almost made her giggle. He must have been tense, worried about his actions. "I've succeeded? I don't have a lot planned for the evening. A little more of the same. Maybe."

"Yes. You have achieved your goal if you had one. You knew that." She stepped up to him, her hands around his neck, tilting her head so she could see into his eyes. She moistened her lips hoping she was being a little charming herself. "Would you kiss me? Kiss me as if you want this one to last forever. I know I do. After you kiss me, we can eat. Drink more wine. I'll wait for more of this romance thing you are doing tonight. Surprise me."

"I'd like to surprise you, plan on doing just that. Need to see your eyes shimmer with emotion. The smile on your face when something I do pleases you. I wish to give you pleasure in more ways than one."

The smile springing to his face surprised her. At the impact, she sipped a gasp of air. His hands once more settled on her waist. She hoped he would untie the top again. Instead, he chuckled as if he heard her thoughts. "Perhaps not tonight. Maybe tomorrow we'll pursue this further." His mouth captured hers in a butterfly light caress. He swept his tongue across her bottom lip as she parted her mouth for him. Tangled and danced. Played as well as toyed. She rubbed against him, pushed herself as close as she could. There was nothing between them except too much fabric.

His hands on her rear, he pulled her against his body. "Feel what you do to me. I'm expanded with need for you. Needing so much more that only you can give."

She pulled back, looking at him as she felt a hard ridge against her belly. Dallas wasn't certain. Had never known what to expect. She was too old to be so innocent. The feeling wasn't something she wanted. "I…is that you? I…I…" she stuttered, her eyes widening as she saw the slow rise of his grin. In the back of her mind, she recalled the same sensation with Roc when he held her close.

"What else would it be?" He laughed softly, as once more he caught her mouth with his. He explored her, touched her lips with his tongue which glided in then out with a slow smooth motion, penetrating then retreating.

She wished for this to go on then on some more. His hands roamed up her back then down to hold her. She didn't want the slow motion of his body against hers to stop. The sensual pull touched every nerve. "I…"

"We should eat." Rafe set her aside. "After dinner I have something to ask you. Something important."

"Oh?" To Dallas, the tone of his voice told her he was worried. "Why not now? If you don't, I'll be thinking about what that question might be. I won't be able to eat or enjoy the meal. You should ask me now."

"Damn… I've screwed up again!" He stalked through the kitchen into the dining room then back. His hands fisted. "Fuck…" he muttered to no one. "Needed this to be perfect."

Baffled, she watched him pace. Understood she needed to do something that would put his mind at ease. Didn't know what that could be. By her unthinking feelings, she hurt him. He'd put so much effort into making this night impeccable for her. With a few unthinking words… She reached out to him.

"I'm sorry…" Dallas blurted, knowing that wasn't enough. "I'm sorry. I'll…I'll eat. I'm just curious. You know nothing can stop me from eating when I'm hungry. You didn't screw up. Waiting is fine. It will make the reveal all that much better. More exciting."

"You might be more curious than hungry. Hell…this isn't what I intended. If I do this now, after I've been swearing, the deed won't be romantic. Will that matter to you? I'm worse with romance than I am with cooking. I have to tell you. This poor man is trying. Even got a bit of advice from Ruby as well as Cole. Now…" His broad shoulders tilted upward as did his eyebrow. "Can we wait?"

Rafe looked so stricken she needed to reevaluate her position. "Of a certainty, we can wait. I'm being selfish. Let's do this your way. The way you planned." The stricken expression on his face turned to relief. A small smile flitted across his handsome face. "I am hungry. If left, the food will grow cold. I'm sure your plan is the way it should be. The perfect order you understand."

For this one moment, Dallas thought she might have said the right thing to him. Rafe was giving so much of himself to her, for her. She had no right to infringe on the way he intended to proceed.

"Thank you. The table is set. I lit candles. There is a vase of flowers on the table courtesy of the florist in town." He watched her and his silver eyes darkened. "More wine?"

Dallas noticed her glass was empty. She didn't recall finishing the glass. She felt a *wee* bit lightheaded, but she wanted to make whatever he planned right for him. By making the ensuing moments unflawed for Rafe, she was making his plans seamless for her. "More wine. Yes, that would be nice."

He escorted her to the dining room table, his hand placed lightly on the small of her back. After that he brought the plates he dished up in the kitchen to set at their places. He went back for the bottle of wine.

"You're up to something, Rafe Frasier." She bit into the food. Savored the hot spicey flavor of the dish. Drank more of the wine. Tried to absorb the ambience of the meal. This evening was turning into a special night between them. Many times, they enjoyed a beer in the kitchen or a delivered pizza. She made dinner here many times. They never ate in the dining room, always in the kitchen.

"I'm attempting romance. That is what you wish for? Am I correct? A romantic man? I do try to please," he told her, his voice bland, casual in the extreme.

"Yes, as you must have guessed by now, with all my heart. I resigned myself to something less than amorous from you. Now you are surprising me at every turn." She bent her head then looked at him. "Thank you. I do appreciate everything you've done tonight."

"Good," he held out his hand for her. "Surprised is nice. Keeping you on your toes will be fun. I might be able to accomplish that. Shall we go outside to the patio and start a fire in the firepit? Bring the wine along?"

"Is this what you were planning?" Curiosity, coupled with anticipation, was getting the best of her.

"Sit down." Rafe filled the glasses with more wine and smiled. For a heartbeat his brows pushed together.

She wished she understood what he was thinking. "Alright…"

After she sat and he was in front of her, his knee hit the ground. The smile left his face. She watched his Adam's apple move up then down as he swallowed hard. Clearly, he was nervous. Rafe was always confident, never anxious. "What is it?" She was both concerned as well as questioning. He appeared so serious.

Only one thought crossed her mind. Dallas was having a difficult time believing what she was seeing. This had to be her imagination working overtime. She didn't dare say one word. Waited. Kept her breath inside her lungs for as long as possible. He held her hand in his. His thumb circled a few times on top. His eyes were the color of dark blue smoke. She tucked her lip beneath her top teeth. "Rafe?" The single word wobbled in the thinning air.

Again, Rafe rubbed his thumb across the back of her hand while he reached into his pocket. Time seemed to stand still. He held out the box to her, flicked the lid open with his fingers and cleared his throat. "Dallas?"

She tried to say yes. Her hand leapt to her throat. She looked at Rafe then back to the diamond ring sitting in the box. The words wouldn't form. He hadn't asked. This could be her imagination working overtime. The ring was beautiful, an old setting, but beautiful. One large square cut diamond was surrounded by small ones. The diamonds were set in silver, not the traditional gold of the era.

He cleared his throat. "Dallas…" A tiny pause, then, as if he gained courage by the second, his gaze never leaving contact with her eyes. "Will you marry me?" His slow look of apprehension surprised her. His hand trembled. This usually self-confident man was anxious. Rafe should know what her answer would be.

Her heart forgot to beat, and then with startling speed the organ thundered beneath her chest. She slid her tongue along the fulness of her bottom lips. So stunned by his actions she was having trouble forming a response. She wanted to yell yes. Scream. She drank in air. Tried to slow the violent beat of her heart. "I…"

"Dallas? If you don't like the ring, we can shop tomorrow. You can pick out anything you think would suit better." He pulled the exquisite piece of jewelry from the tiny box, from its blue velvet confinement.

"No…I…I meant, yes, to the marriage, then yes again. I love the ring. It's exquisite." She watched a flicker of relief sweep over the firm set to his jaw. Saw his eyes close then open again as if he felt right with the world. "Yes, to marriage. It's what I hoped for. A proposal." Perhaps, he did listen to her. Maybe he wouldn't continue to dictate everything in her life.

Slipping the ring from the box, he placed the small token of their commitment on her finger. "There…this ring is right where it belongs. It was my grandmother's. She gave the ring to me, saying she hoped I would find the woman of my dreams." He turned her hand over. Kissed her palm. Lingered for a moment then touched with his tongue. Startled, she jumped at the potent contact.

"Did you?" Dallas asked, hoping he would say more. "Find the woman of your dreams? Am I that woman?" She prayed the words were true. He was, after all, the man of her dreams. He fulfilled every one of her wishes. She couldn't tell him as much. Didn't want to admit to her love for him. She'd loved him now for a very long time. Believed she fell in love with him when she was just a small girl.

"Yes, you are my mate, the woman I've searched for my entire life. Funny thing…" He stopped as if thinking of the right words. "You were always with me. Always a part of my life. Always, ever since I picked you up off the playground where you took a spill. Comforted you. Held you in my arms while you sobbed. Always knew you would be special to me. Our relationship stumbled for a few years. Now, it's put right."

"It fits?"

Dallas held up her hand to stare at the ring, amazed.

"I borrowed one of your other rings to get the size. The jeweler told me the ring should be fine. If it's too tight or too large, we can go in then get it sized properly."

"When?" Dallas didn't know when he could have found the time to get the ring sized. "When did you do all this?"

"Yesterday. I would have proposed last night but I didn't have the ring back. It was delivered today while you were changing into this provocative little outfit you have on. Did you hope to tease me? Charm me with your lack of clothing? Do you wish for me to caress certain sensual places?"

Heat rose to her face. He'd seen her in less. When she was around him, as far as picking her clothing, she thought of comfort first. Before she answered, she held her hand out to study the new ring one more time. She liked seeing the symbol of his intentions on her finger. Wished she had people to show the ring to. She didn't have parents who she would like to call with the exciting news. "You've planned this for more than a day?" Dallas was feeling as if her world was slowly righting itself moment by moment. She loved that he seemed so worried before the proposal. Worry on Rafe was a new emotion for him. He was always so self-assured and confident. He must have guessed she would accept.

Pulling her to her feet, his hands set on the sides of her head. Strong fingers wove into her hair. Standing on the tips of her toes, she wrapped her arms around him. His lips found hers. A soft tender touch greeted her. She felt the tip of his tongue sweep across her mouth. She parted her lips. Savored the warmth of Rafe as he brought her closer. He slid his hands down her back to cup her rear. He tasted of mint, along with the wine they drank. Her breasts pushed against the hardness of his chest. Her nipples tightened.

He pulled away from her to look down on her upturned face. The kiss ended far too soon. She didn't want him to stop, hoped he might take this farther than just kisses. "Dallas, you make me happy. I give you my promise."

"What is that?" His words puzzled her as her voice whispered out in a thin glide of air. "I don't understand."

"A promise that I won't rush you. Now that you've accepted my ring, we are one step closer to a life committed to each other. Ruby told me to be patient as did Cole. I plan on being more tolerant than ever before. Well…I was never patient. When I want something, I need it now. Don't like to wait. Don't forget, I want you, Dallas. Have for more than a week." He swallowed air. "That's more patience than I've ever had."

"Their advice is sound. We need to get to know each other as a couple before we bind ourselves to each other for life. I want you to always be my best friend and I'm afraid if we become husband and wife that won't continue." Dallas thought about her words to him. They were all true. She prayed they would always talk. Always laugh together.

"There is no reason to ever think we would not remain the best of friends." His whisper was close to her ear. She hoped that was true.

With a start the ground left her feet. She found herself held in his arms. He sat down with her on one of the patio chairs. The small firepit sent out its heat to warm them. She set her head against his chest listening to the steady beat of his heart. Hearing the sound of each breath. Soaking up the scent of spice coupled with man. His hands ran the length of her arms. She hoped he would touch her like he did in the kitchen. She would not complain if he untied the halter top.

She heard Rafe's chuckle. His hand settled on her belly. "I'm glad you enjoy my touch. Not too much more stimulation tonight though. We need to take this courtship slow. As you implied earlier, I don't wish to rush you. If I had my way…" Rafe broke off before he finished the sentence.

She pushed against his chest, flustered, embarrassed, feeling heat rise to her face. "You do not know what I'm thinking, Rafe Frasier. You do not! You can't. I don't like this. You make assumptions." She punched his chest. He grunted. Dallas knew she didn't hurt the man.

Running his fingertips across her eyebrows a pensive look on his face. "I do… Dallas, don't get angry. I do know what you're thinking. I'm tuned into the thoughts of my mate. Shifters do that. They understand emotions as well as the thoughts of their partner. You have no secrets from me."

Outrage flashed. Anger brewed. She felt the tempest inside her surge at his outrageous words. "You cannot! It's impossible." She felt as if all the anger she felt at the first moment when he told her he listened to her without her permission, spilled out of her.

"I can. Not by choice, mind you."

"Doing so is impossible." Her fury now simmered at a low boil. "One person cannot look into another person's mind and know things…personal things."

"Hush, love. No, it's not impossible. You were hoping I would touch you as I did while you were cooking our wonderful dinner. Am I wrong?"

Trying to push off his lap, she needed to hide. Felt the shame of embarrassment heat her cheeks. He held her tight. Wouldn't allow her the freedom to run from this important conversation. Mortified, she didn't think she could sit while listening to him spout this nonsense. What he told her was just a lucky guess. She hid her face against his chest, understanding what he told her was not nonsense. "It's all wrong. All of it. You've no right to intrude on my thoughts."

To her further frustration, he lifted her chin so she had to look at him. With a small grin, he elevated his shoulder in a pure male gesture. "Comes with the territory. Shifter territory." He ran the tip of his finger across her forehead, moving strands of hair aside. "I have to be able to protect you at all times. Nothing can happen to you on my watch. Not even a scraped knee."

"I'm not in danger of a scraped knee or anything else," she muttered with a gruff voice. She saw the silver shimmer of his eyes, the tenderness this conversation evoked. "I should be able to have my thoughts to myself."

"In theory, yes. Your thoughts should be your own. You might at some time find yourself in need of me. Gordon and Tinley are still a small threat to you. They weren't pleased when you left them to be with me. Were furious when I didn't allow them into my home to see you. They remain a danger in your life."

Unable to stop her mind from spinning in the direction Rafe sent it, she mulled his words over for a few minutes. She looked at him with a scowl and he yowled with his laughter. She cleared her throat to keep from hearing his laugh. "I don't think they will return here. You made it clear we didn't want anything to do with them. They are not stupid." They weren't all that bright either.

Strands of her hair ran through his fingers. She felt the erotic pull. "If it were me," he paused as if in thought, brought the strand of hair in his fingers to his cheek, to his nose, "I would always return for you. I need you. You understand. You are a part of me I could never leave behind. My sixth sense tells me they are not through trying for you. Take care where those two ruffians are concerned. Until we understand their plans for you, you are not to go anywhere without me."

Who thought the man couldn't be romantic? Now he was being

autocratic. She covered her mouth as if she spoke the words. You heard? She questioned him silently. Crossing her arms across her chest, she spoke with a cadence meant to tell him about her feelings on the topic, "I don't like this. If I could keep my thoughts to myself, I would. I don't want you in my head."

"I understand. I would feel the same. The fact might be unfortunate for you. However, I believe there is a purpose in my understanding what you are thinking. Perhaps you will even get used to the notion. I would never mind having you know my thoughts." He was shaking his head. "Even if I could stop myself from hearing the ideas banging around inside here," he tapped her head, "I would not. In this we can't compromise."

"You cannot? Is that the truth? You cannot keep from hearing me?" She drank in the air. After that, she decided she needed more wine. She reached for her glass. Rafe handed the crystal goblet to her. She gulped then set the glass down.

"It's the truth. I'm not going to lie to you, Dallas. As I just said, even if I could block the words you are thinking from my head, I wouldn't."

His big hands smoothed circles on her back, soothing her temper. Warm languid heat suffused her. "I wish I could read your thoughts," she blurted, her voice strong. She did feel that way. "Though…" she paused touching his chin. "It's an invasion of my privacy, don't you think?"

~ * ~

He found himself nodding his head, agreeing with her. Listening to her thoughts…she was right on all counts. That little fact made no difference in his mind. He would never stop listening to her feelings. "Yes, an invasion of privacy. Yes, a necessary ability. I'd rather learn if you're in trouble when we are apart than not know the truth. What if you've lost your cellphone? What if you fall through time again?" Good God, that couldn't happen another time. Could it? Would the universe be so horrible as to send Dallas back into that other universe? It wouldn't, because if he had a say about the event, she would never return to those falls.

"Is there any way I can learn to hear your thoughts? If you are going to delve into all the dark recesses in my mind, I should have the same ability. Don't you think? What if you needed protection? If I didn't know, I wouldn't be able to help." Dallas asked, while she explored his jaw with the tip of her finger. The nail scraped across day old stubble. His body reacted. Jumped to life in response to the small tender strokes she stimulated with expertise. Wondered if she meant to awaken his need. She did request more from him, more caresses, more kisses. Maybe he should take her up on the offer. He did, however, recall Cole's advice.

Dallas turned the tables. Could she learn to read his thoughts? Was that something a person could discover? He liked her quick wit. The instant comeback from her. "If you're trying to seduce me with the tiny tip of your finger, you should know it's working." He caught the tip between his teeth. Bit. Laved. Felt the tremor slide through her. That was what he was supposed to be doing. Seducing. Charming her until she squirmed. If she kept this up, he would be the one twisting with pressing desire. In need of the ecstasy her luscious body could deliver. She was a sensual delight.

"Is that what I'm doing to you? Seducing? Charming?" She ran a second finger across his mouth. "You must have heard me think that I wanted you to kiss me again. Did you? What else was I thinking? You should tell me. If you don't, I might fail to believe you capable of what you claim. Perhaps those earlier suggestions were lucky guesses. I should never have confirmed your conjectures."

"More caresses are what you wish for, your breasts, your belly. You wish for me to stroke, as well as investigate, tender flesh, sensitive, places. Would you like me to explore more secret intimate parts of your beautiful body? Your darkest most valued mysteries. If you ask, I might do so tomorrow night. I told you we've done enough this evening." Good God, he needed to get out of here. Had to have some space. Distance between them was the last thing he wanted. "We might pursue this conversation further in a different setting. I find I'm more willing now that you've aroused me than I was a few minutes before. You could smooth your hands over me. Explore any parts of me you wish. I would allow you that privilege." Rafe understood he started an unquenchable fire. If they touched each other more, he didn't know if he could keep his promise to himself. Didn't know if he cared.

Standing, he set her feet on the floor and held out his hand. She tilted her head in a charming way. She didn't understand what it was he wanted. "Go for a walk with me. The weather is warm. The evening will be beautiful. Might be able to see the northern lights, though the bonfire is not that far from the city. We could walk to the firepit. It's an easy stroll. After we get there, I'll hold you in my arms. Believe from what I'm hearing rumbling around in your head, you would like to find yourself closer to my body, to me. If you're really, really nice, I might consider some of the other notions you have tripping through your mind. Might caresses you in those soft places that call to me."

"You would?" She blinked a few times. He found the expression of uncertainty amusing. Fascinating in the extreme. "Can we take the second bottle of wine with us along with two mugs. I don't want marshmallows, but more wine would be nice," she murmured, darting her gaze from his eyes to his groin. Dallas reached out as if she wished to touch him. Another thought held her back.

Rafe cleared his throat. Resisted the urge to adjust his pants. If the little vixen had any idea how fast she awakened him he would be in more trouble. At this point in time, she was the one charming his socks off, not the other way around. He didn't know if he liked not being in charge of this affair. If Dallas kept this up, he might not be capable of taking Cole's advice. Abstinence, until she begged him to set a date. "We can…I told you earlier, I would do most anything you wanted. If you wish to touch me, you can." If she did… Rafe found himself shaking his head. This bargain of waiting until the wedding night was never going to work. The sight of her beautiful body coupled with her succulent curves sabotaged all his good intentions.

"Except kiss me again. You told me no to the kiss when I asked," she muttered, while she started for the door, her hips swaying with each step. He saw the rounded bottom of her delicious butt. Had the urge to follow the soft contours with a fingertip. All her feminine charms would be moving with her hasty walk. Her breasts would dance in front of her with a delightful, tempting bounce. She was off. A determined woman. Onto the lawn. Not waiting for him.

The long line of her back intrigued. Fascinated him to the tips of his toes. This would be a worthwhile excursion for them. He did want to hold her, touch her more than he had already done. Explore those assets she was thinking about right now. See how fast her passion blossomed. Needed to create raw hunger within her. He held back the chuckle that threatened to turn into a bark of laughter if he didn't keep his raging lust in check.

Rafe swept up the bottle of wine before rummaging through the cupboard for two sturdy mugs. He grabbed two blankets, one for sitting, the second for covering, caught up with her a few minutes later.

Slipping his fingers on her arm, he said with an affectionate voice, "You don't need to run from me. I'd like to hold your hand." In this, he didn't give her a chance to turn him down. He slid his fingers down her arm then through the fingers of her small hand. Heard the swift intake of air as she shivered from the sensory connection between them. Their connection was potent. Fast. All encompassing. When they finally came together as one, he would feel the raw passion that was his Dallas. They would set each other on fire. The flames would soar. If given the chance, burn down the night. Her hunger for life impossible to resist. The desire for adventure an aphrodisiac to his soul. She always jumped in with both feet first. He loved her that way. Adored her impulsiveness.

"I wasn't running," she snapped at him. Stopping, she turned to him. Set her free hand on his chest. "Sorry. I'm out of sorts thinking about you listening to my thoughts. I'm going to figure out how to block you from doing so."

He set his hand on top of hers. "You can try." He grinned at her. Delighted with the spunk she exhibited. Unless she was a shifter, she would never be able to block his thoughts. To the best of his knowledge, as well as Dallas', she couldn't change her shape.

"What's that supposed to mean?" her voice softened.

He brought her hand to his lips, kissed the back then the heart of her palm. He lingered there for a moment before he searched her eyes. "If it's any consolation, I'm not listening with a purpose in mind. I don't want to know everything that's in your head. I only wish to know your thoughts when you need me. Only another shifter would be able to keep me away from their thoughts. That shifter would need to be very powerful to do so.

My instincts are strong."

"You don't? You're not going to listen all the time?" she asked, as her brows came together in a straight line.

He smoothed creases in her forehead. Ran his knuckles along her cheek, reveling in the silken texture of her skin. "I didn't say that. You did. I will always listen. What you think is just as important to me as the words you say." With possessiveness, he placed his hand on her neck, his thumb touching on the rapid beating of her pulse.

"I don't appreciate the intrusion. It's disconcerting to know you can decipher everything from my mind. If it was your birthday or Christmas, I wouldn't even be able to keep a present a secret from you. You would ferret out what I got you."

His shout of laughter made her eyes widen then narrow with displeasure. "This is not funny. Nothing to laugh about. Suppose you enjoy ruining surprises."

He touched her mouth with the tip of his finger before she could voice another round of discontentment. "Dallas, I do agree with you in part. Privacy is important, even between mates. I'll try not to invade your thoughts if you try not to have so many of the carnal nature. When you reached out to touch me…" He looked down. Her gaze followed. She stiffened. Heat rushed to her face, to the tops of her breasts. "That was…" Rafe didn't know how to explain what her naivety did to him.

Her lips thinned. He chuckled. "How do I do that? I want to learn more about you. After all, you've seen all of me numerous times. You know my body by heart. I've not had that advantage…only once."

Her question was an honest one. Rafe wasn't certain he could respond with any truth. "Maybe you should not think about touching me…my penis, even though my most masculine part seems to intrigue you." Rafe saw her face flame hotter at the word he used. He couldn't think of any other way to say what was on his mind. "That would help. I'm as hard as a rock hearing all your lustful thoughts about my male parts. Makes me hope to see to your pleasure before you're ready. I don't intend to do that." He held up both her hands. With the movement, saw the delicious sway of her breasts. "Those are…no, I am pleased you want me that way. Nonetheless, you could try to keep your ideas a bit more subdued. Less graphic in nature. Though I do appreciate the fact you'd like to taste me…my…"

He appreciated the color rising to a vivid shade of discomfiture. He didn't think she could become any redder. Her face was near crimson. Embarrassing her wasn't something he intended. Though all her thoughts were a delight to his senses. When they were just friends, he could say anything to her. She never blushed. Perhaps she never listened to the words he spouted. Never associated carnal pleasures between them as something in their future.

"I was thinking about everything you said. I do wish to see you without the benefit of clothing. You've seen me numerous times. Painted me in different poses. You know that because you are hearing my thoughts. I did tell you once that you should paint wearing nothing while you looked at me naked. Thought it was only fair. Seems at that time, you disagreed."

"I enjoyed every second you posed for me. You do know I love all your curves. I've also told you the same, numerous times. Even while we were just best friends, I enjoyed watching you do things. You're graceful. Your body moves the way a woman's is supposed to move. While you were cooking when I held your breasts in my hands, I almost didn't stop. Was ready to pull your shorts down then set you on the kitchen table. Our first time shouldn't be that way. If I did something so carnal, the romance would be gone."

"Our second?" she questioned with a huge smile, seeming eager to have that first along with the second time. "The spontaneity would be nice. I don't like to think of everything having to be planned."

They started walking again. She kept thinking about wine. What to cook for dinner tomorrow. The sounds of the night surrounded them. She heard the croak of a frog. The bark of a dog. Somewhere close the hiss of a cat floated on the wind. In a way, Dallas was blocking her most basic thoughts from him. The ploy would not always work. She was concentrating so hard on the chirp of the crickets, he found it difficult to hold back another yowl of laughter.

He thought he might try a different tactic; one that would send her mind reeling in a different direction than the night sounds. He needed to show her that keeping her most important thoughts from him would never be easy. He rubbed his thumb along her wrist. The contact startled her. Blurred her deliberations about the night. He felt her heart race. Knew the instant she thought of his kisses they shared. The way he held her breasts. Ran his palms over the hardened nipples. Refusing to give himself away, he managed to keep his laughter to himself. His Dallas was precious. She would always challenge him as well as surprise him.

This was what both Cole as well as Ruby talked about. Patience in the face of his lust for a greater purpose…marriage. If he could keep his hands from…keep his body from giving into the primitive need to make love to her, she would set a wedding date. He had to direct his thoughts, take charge of his swollen male parts. Needed to hold firm to the vow he made. Hard to stand true when she seemed to lust after him. Cole even warned him against bringing her to her own release. He could do that. Give her the ecstasy her body would learn to crave.

Sex was powerful.

He intended to hold firm.

They reached the bonfire. Thankfully, so far, no one else decided the night would be perfect for burning marshmallows. They would be alone with their passion. By themselves, to explore more carnal pleasures that could exist between them. He hoped the bonfire would stay private. Monitoring her thoughts would give him something to think about other than sex with her.

In order to spread out the blanket, he let go of her hand. Popping the cork on the new bottle of wine, he sloshed wine into the cups, filling each halfway. There was a boulder to lean against, along with small stone tables on either side to set their mugs.

The setting was impeccable, the night air pleasant. The logs, as well as the kindling, was prepared. One of the McKenna employees kept the bonfire ready for any of the clan who wished to enjoy the evening at the pit. After he set the fire, he sat down. Spread his legs so she could sit between them. He wanted to feel her rump pressed against his sex.

With a strange expression on her face, one he couldn't read, Dallas looked sheepish. Hesitant. Seemed she was all bold thoughts but unable to put action to the ideas in her head. Appeared she lost the ability to tease him. Now that he suggested something more. She held back. This was new as well as an interesting side of her.

"Come here. Don't be shy," he whispered, his voice deep, a bit raspy from his potent need. A need that would not be assuaged this evening. Rafe patted the spot in front of him. "You can sit here, between my legs. I would enjoy holding you. Watching the fire burn while we drink our wine." He didn't know how much to tell her. Decided he would take this from one moment to the next.

"Alright." She sat where he suggested. Crossed her legs. Leaned against him.

"Have some of your wine. All of a sudden you seem tense. Enjoy the evening. Relax. Think then do whatever you like." He meant to be cautious in the extreme. He felt the tension. "Do you truly like the ring? It's a bit old-fashioned, I know." He held her hand in his, while he stared at her long slender fingers. He never did understand how she ever thought she was overweight. It was her parents who did that to her. They wanted a daughter who was runway model thin. Dallas was perfect the way she was. Didn't need to change for any reason. A perfect fit for this man.

She turned to him. Touched his chin with the finger the ring encircled. Pulled back to look at it. "Yes, it's beautiful. Don't be so insecure. I would never wish for another one. Never." Dallas shook her head as if to emphasize the point she made. "This is what I would have picked out for myself. The fact that it was your grandmother's makes the ring more special than I could ever tell you with words. I'm blessed to wear this in memory of your grandmother. Was she also a shifter?"

"I'm glad. You make me happy. Don't know why I didn't ask you sooner. No, my grandmother was not able to change form, only my father and father before him. Farther back, I've no idea who was, along with who wasn't. Suppose with the Frasiers, this tends to run in the male line," Rafe found he expressed thoughts that he might have kept to himself. His hands slipped beneath the top he untied while she was talking. He splayed them across her stomach. Felt the contraction of her muscles. Unfastened the button on her shorts then lowered the zipper. Her heart sped. The breath she inhaled caught in the back of her throat. She arched as if she wanted more. He would give more but not everything. Not until the date was set and the plans for the celebration were begun.

Her head rested against his chest. Because of the arch of her body, her breasts pushed forward. He heard the soft sigh of pleasure along with more titillating thoughts. The lush globes he so adored rested against the back of his hands after he skimmed them higher across her warm flesh.

Dallas' voice was soft when she spoke next. He felt tension sweep throughout her. There was a new revelation she just realized. For a few seconds, she stopped breathing. "You heard me thinking about wanting a proposal. Didn't you? When we talked to Father Richard, that's where my thoughts were centered. You didn't come up with the idea on your own."

Rafe new then he needed to tell her the absolute truth. "Yes, I heard you. How does that make you feel? I never denied the fact that when it came to *amour*, I'd been absent from the receiving line. Must have been playing hooky when that trait was doled out. Cole also suggested I treat you right by asking. Told me you would need something other than a demand for you to accept an engagement with me. Ruby gave much the same counsel."

"It pleases me that you're not denying the truth. Once I began to understand what you were telling me about the fact you could read my thoughts, I put it all together." She rested a finger on her chin. "How does that make me feel? I don't know yet. I'm thrilled you proposed. Would never have set a time for a marriage if you kept demanding. I don't like that characteristic of yours."

"I'm sorry… I apologize for not being able to think of it on my own." He *was* sorry. Wished he had more insight into what a woman thought was romantic.

"Don't be," Dallas was quick to say, her hand resting on his forearm. "You gave me what I wanted. Doesn't make a difference how that came to be." She turned around to face the fire. "You were right when you talked about instructions. If someone doesn't know what to do, it's up to another person to give explanations, to teach. Perhaps a man such as yourself can be taught how to be romantic."

"You're not angry I didn't think of it by myself? I needed coaxing from several different people." He stroked her stomach. Brought his hands up to cup her breasts. "These are beautiful. I'd like to taste them. Suck on each one. What do you think? Would they taste like succulent peaches or the ripest strawberries. I could push down the blanket then your top. They would be right there for me."

"Not angry at all. Suppose there is one good thing about this ability of yours. You will always know what I want you to do. A girl can't complain about that too much." She lifted her shoulders in a mini shrug. *I think you should do all you just said,* she pointed out to see if he would react.

The palms of his hands floated across the pebble hardness of the tips of her breasts. She sipped air. Her hand on his thigh tightened as she pushed back against him. Leaned into him. Thrust her breast into his palms. He tugged. Then twisted. Skimmed his thumb. Her whimper of pleasure delighted him. A small sound rippled from the back of her throat.

He brought his hands back to her stomach. "That's enough for now."

No...

"Yes... There will be more later. I promise." He wanted her melting all over him just like warm honey.

Alright. He felt her relax against him. She reached for her wine. Drank of it. He did the same. This was heaven as well as hell. He heard the conversation before it registered in his head that they were about to have company. This evening's privacy would end. He recognized the voice of Cole. Seemed he was jumping the gun with Phoebe. What did a few weeks matter? She would be out of school soon, a matter of days. He should begin the courtship now. She was eighteen. Old enough for a small amount of flirtation.

"Who is that?" Dallas turned in his arms. He brought the blanket higher to cover her. Didn't tie the halter back into place.

"Do you wish for me to tie your top?" he whispered against her ear, hoping she would decline. His tongue swept across her lobe, then darted inside. She shivered against him. Her body quivered. She was so damn responsive. Damn, but he didn't want company tonight. "No one can see anything. They won't be able to tell that I'm holding your breasts in my hands. That the tips are hard buds waiting for me to taste. Do you mind?" He needed to make certain she was comfortable with this new situation. There would be no more privacy.

In response, she ran her fingernails along his legs. He would tease her. Chat with Cole along with Phoebe. Rafe wondered what Cole's intentions for tonight were.

"We saw the bonfire, Phoebe wanted to walk up here. Hope the two of you don't mind the invasion. You probably want to be alone," Cole said, while he brought Phoebe around to stand in front of him. "I've brought marshmallows, and chocolate, along with graham crackers. I have plenty. Would you like some?"

"No thank you," Dallas murmured when she held up her mug of wine. "We ate a big dinner just before we walked here."

Rafe shook his head. "We don't mind company," he said with a grin, as he set his hand on her belly just above her womb. He moved his fingers. In her head she yelled at him. Dallas pushed her little rump hard between his legs. His body caught fire with the sudden inflaming gesture. Though his Dallas might be innocent, she was a quick learner. She did know what she was about.

"Oh!" her cry of surprise was a soft sound in the silence of the night.

Nonetheless, the sound caught the attention of their uninvited guests. Cole grinned then nodded as if he approved. Phoebe tilted her head as if questioning what made Dallas cry out. The two found a place to sit. Cole wrapped a blanket around them. As Dallas sat between his legs, so Phoebe sat in front of Cole. Together they made a handsome couple.

Rafe picked up her hand. Held it aloft, showing off her ring finger. "See, I'm not such a dunderhead as you thought. I proposed after dinner. Dallas accepted. The ring was my grandmother's. And we love the company."

Cole nodded, his smile spread across his face, "Congratulations are in order. You two celebrating the evening? The wine, the soft sounds of nature. There's nothing better."

"The ring is beautiful," Phoebe sighed. Her wistfulness didn't go unnoticed.

Dallas was embarrassed from the unwanted attention. Earlier through thoughts in her head, she told him she was disappointed she didn't have anyone to show off the ring to. He was just helping her out.

Cole brought out the metal sticks he brought for the marshmallows while Phoebe ruffled through their sack of goodies to find the other necessary ingredients for their evening treat. While she was searching, her jean clad bottom was in the air. It caught Cole's full attention, and he grinned while he watched the movement.

"You guys certain? I've got a second stick." He held one up after placing a couple of marshmallows on the two-pronged metal he meant to stick in the fire. Cole found a nice spot where there were embers and no flames to roast the treat. Phoebe sat on the ground staring at the flames.

Nothing more was said as the treats were cooked then eaten. Dallas lay against Rafe, absorbing his caresses. When he touched her, Dallas' body responded. He enjoyed her thoughts. He wished the company would depart even though he understood this was for the best. He couldn't get carried away when he had an audience.

"Since..." Cole licked his sticky fingers. "Since you've proposed...gave Dallas a ring, are you going to set a date? This seems to be happening too fast after the earlier conversation." Cole grinned as if he understood he was putting them on the spot.

Rafe set his fingers on her lips. He'd heard her bristle inside. Knew the question infuriated her. He meant to turn this around. "Hush, love..." Then to Cole. "We are going to take a year or more to plan the wedding if that's what Dallas would like. I'm no longer in a hurry to set a date. The two of us can relax. Talk about what we want along with what we don't want. Don't know if Dallas would like the venue to be at the McKenna keep. She might wish for a different venue. We could always search out other idyllic places. The Isle of Skye is beautiful. What do you think of a wedding by the Fairy Pools?"

Rafe was pleased with the rapid-fire change of thoughts in her head. After he mentioned a year or more to plan the wedding, she balked. She didn't want to wait that long. With his thumbs he brushed the hard pebbled tips of her breasts. To protest, she shot her elbow into his stomach. He grunted. This sound also caught the attention of their guests with the same reaction from the first little 'oh'...

"I don't think we'll wait a year," Dallas murmured with a soft retort.

In response to the pleasing statement, Rafe caressed the tips of her breasts again, rubbed his thumbs along the bottom curves.

"Not wait a year?" Rafe queried with as much innocence laced in his question as he could muster. "I think we need that much time. Don't you? Since you would never ask your mother, Ruby might enjoy taking you to Edinburgh to pick out a gown. I would go but doing so might be bad luck for us. Not supposed to see the bridal gown before the wedding. I'm superstitious you know."

"The seamstress in Carnoch is very good. It would only take her a few days, maybe a week, to fashion a gown for me. I don't want anything elaborate. Simple is best."

"There is a small bridal store in Inverness. My sister used it before she was wed. It has beautiful gowns. Not too expensive. You must have a budget before you visit. I could go with you; I love shopping for wedding gowns. Maybe Cole could drive us," Phoebe offered with a sweet smile. She looked to Cole as if she sought approval.

"I would enjoy that," Dallas said.

"Of course, I would drive." Cole looked to Rafe for a reaction.

He shrugged.

Rafe felt the slow easing of tension in her body. When the conversation turned to the wedding, the wine was no longer serving as a relaxant. Yet, he heard the reluctance in her thoughts to wait for an entire year which was her first prerogative. Also, he listened to the excitement when Phoebe spoke of shopping for a wedding dress.

"I would need to come along too," Rafe said, unwilling to let Dallas too far from him at any time. "Cole and I can find something to do while you are trying on gowns. We could make a day of it. Have a nice dinner. Perhaps stay the night."

"Oh…" Phoebe seemed startled by that. "Don't think I should do that…stay the night."

"She's right. A nice lunch then we can make it home before it's dark. Phoebe won't be staying the night in Inverness with me. It would damage her reputation. We, Phoebe and I, don't want that to happen." Cole hugged her. She looked at him with love-struck eyes.

She is smitten.

Rafe heard Dallas' comment. He wanted to return the sentiment to her, but she couldn't read his thoughts. *He is smitten too.* Or could she? That last comment from Dallas hit him as odd. Only other shifters could read their mate's mind.

Dallas never looked at him quite that way…the smitten way. He felt left out. Perhaps it was because they'd known each other for so long, had thought they were to always be best friends then nothing more. She was right. They were just beginning to learn new things about each other. While their relationship wasn't as young as Cole's and Phoebe's, they were at the beginning of what was still to come.

"Do you think Ruby would come too?" Dallas asked, as she focused on Cole. "The other day your mother seemed eager to help me with advice. Told me a little about your father along with their courtship."

"If Phoebe is part of the entourage, mother would love to be included. She expressed to me that she'd like to get to know her better. What more perfect way than to spend an entire day in her company?" Cole hugged her again. Ran his hand along her arm. "Are you cold? There are goose bumps here."

Phoebe was shaking her head, smiling. "No, it's just that… I can't say…" She looked to them before lowering her lashes.

Evidently, Cole was doing a bit of seducing beneath the blanket himself.

"When would you like to go, love?" Rafe bent close to her ear. Touched the lobe with his tongue. "Next month maybe, or the one after that? We do have a year or more so you can take your time. There is no rush."

She turned so fast the cover slipped down her arm. With as much haste as possible he brought the fabric up to her shoulder. He didn't like the idea that anyone else would see any part of Dallas or what he was doing beneath the blankets. He felt the heat of her blush. Heard the small catch in the back of her throat.

Cole looked away. Phoebe's eyes were wide pools of surprise. She saw. He saw. Well, it would be no surprise to Cole. He was, after all, taking the man's advice. Cole might need to explain to Phoebe what was going on with their friends. That thought presented Rafe with an inward chuckle.

It's not funny that he saw what you were doing, Rafe Frasier.

From a male standpoint it is. From yours not so much. Just like you, I don't like him seeing any part of you that is normally covered. The parts of you that are for my eyes only.

Rafe was shocked. Through his mind he was talking to Dallas. She must be a shifter who had no idea what she could do. This was something else that might present a setback for them. He needed to look into this new development. It might also be knowledge that could push them forward at a quicker pace than they were going now. Rafe half expected a comment with those thoughts.

He got nothing.

Heard no answering reply.

When he played with her beautiful feminine charms she didn't seem to be as receptive to what was rambling around in his head. He would need to think about that. Maybe this was a simple coincidence that could be explained away. If not, at times he would also need to block his thoughts from her. He would be able to do that even though she couldn't. Rafe imagined there was a solid reason for his abilities.

"As soon as possible would be nice. I don't wish to waste time. The gown I choose might need to be fitted. Alterations. I am…"

"Quite lovely. Don't you ever forget that." Rafe was exhausted with the fact she continued to belittle herself, her figure. She was perfect for him.

"I'm tired…" Dallas said with a soft sigh. "We should let Cole and Phoebe have a few minutes of privacy before they too need to start back. Mine as well as Rafe's schedule are flexible. Ask Ruby then the three of you decide on the day to go."

~ * ~

"I don't know what you're thinking coming back to this horrible place. Just standing here at the bottom of the embankment gives me the shivers and shakes. I remember Roc's cat rushing toward us. Thought we were going to be ripped to shreds. I, for one, don't want to be swept into the big dark hole that took us away that day. Who knows where we might turn up," Scratch said while he rubbed his stomach, then lower as if to make certain all his parts were there. "I don't want to return to our time. Don't want to lose all the comforts we have here. Like having hot running water, toilets that flush, ovens you don't have to put wood into. There is more."

"If you haven't noticed, we no longer have comforts…any comforts at all. No roof over our head. Have you forgotten? We were kicked out. We're homeless. We need jobs to maintain our apartments. Don't have any type of oven. Can't pay the rent. If you don't wish to return to the time we both understand, then you need to find a job. Working at a fast-food establishment won't pay the rent or put food on our table." Gordon didn't want to work, had never worked a day in his life. He didn't want to start now. He didn't know how to find a job. His life back then was just fine. He liked living the way he did. Nobody expected anything from him. He could go to bed whenever he wished, get up when he felt like starting his day.

Scratch threw up his hands in frustration and shot him a scathing look of disdain. "I don't know how to work, never worked a day in my life. Neither have you. Do you have any other brilliant ideas? This place won't ever take us back. We need to figure out how to live like we used to. I want to do what I feel like."

"No. No ideas. Just understand that we need to return to a simpler time. Need that black hole to sweep us up then take us home. All the cars whizzing by me while I'm driving makes my head spin. Everyone honks at me. I'm not going to drive any faster no matter how much noise they make." Gordon felt like crying. Felt the rasp of moisture in the back of his throat. He would cry soon if he couldn't find a way to return to a place he could understand. Hated this world. Despised his life within it. This was a living hell.

He didn't mind not having a roof over his head while the weather was decent. Back in their time they had a home of sorts. Some would call the ramshackle dwelling a hovel. They didn't have to pay rent on the one room structure that sat back in the woods. No one bothered them. Kept the rain off their heads. Back then he didn't have to pretend to be someone he wasn't. He couldn't read. In this place reading was necessary to find a job.

He didn't like to bathe. No one would talk to either of them because they stunk, one man told him.

Back in the era where he was meant to live, they hunted for their food. The water was free. All they had to pay for was their whores along with their whiskey. They made enough begging on the streets of Inverness to do that as well as dipping their fingers into the pockets of unwary gentlemen. A monogramed lace handkerchief could buy a bottle of whiskey. Two could give them a poke with one of the whores on the waterfront. There were also women who would give it away free for a drink of their whiskey.

He sighed, thinking that life would be easier if he could go backward. The life was a simple one. Nothing like this world where everyone was in hurry to go nowhere. Everything cost so much, even whores.

"If we can find a way back, I'd not be goin' anywhere near that Roc Frasier or the rest of his family. Mean to keep my distance." Scratch was tending to an itch on his belly, then lower, rubbing his privates. Someone walking by blasted him a look of disgust. "We shot Roc's woman. She jumped right in front of the man. She must have thought she was invincible. We taught them a lesson. Neither one might be alive."

"You thinkin' about that gal, Dallas. She's a lot like Lainie, who as you just said might no longer be around. Dallas could go back with us. We could take her along to live in our home with us. Maybe even cook us dinner. That would be fun. She wouldn't have no one to protect her like she does now. Lainie was better though. She was a bit plumper. Her curves more abundant." Gordon was thinking about all her lush breasts and hips. Her butt was pretty fine too. He discovered he was drooling. Those plump breasts of hers would overflow his hands. Just dreamin' about her he was certain he could taste her. Wanted to have her. She was just what he needed right now. Maybe to get that black hole to open they needed the woman. Just as all three of 'em came though the strange space back then, all three had to be there this time around.

"That Rafe Frasier is possessive of the gal. He's not goin' to just hand her over. Might be more trouble than it's worth to try to get her to come with us. Doubt if she'll be a willing lass. Won't let us poke her.

Didn't seem to like either one of us too well when she was around us," Scratch was shaking his head while he mused aloud.

Gordon understood the disillusionment. He wasn't happy either. His stomach rumbled. They hadn't eaten yet today. Yesterday, before they drove out here, they rummaged scraps from one of the restaurants in a nearby village. Climbed into the huge garbage can just to get their hands on food other people threw out. Wrestled with a dog over a half-eaten burger. If they decided to return to Inverness, they would have to hitch a ride.

"We can grab Dallas some time when Rafe isn't watching her. He can't stay with her all the nights as well as all the days." Gordon thought they should have stayed in Carnoch, closer to the girl. Inverness held more possibilities.

"Let's see if we can get a ride back to the city," Scratch suggested. "The car is worthless with no gas. Don't have any groats to buy gas."

New thoughts sprouted in Gordon's head. "The car's not worthless. Don't know how we got it, but we can sell the damn thing. We'd have some money." Once that was gone, what then? They'd be back where they were now. With nothing.

"How we goin' to get gas? You think of that?" He held out his empty pockets.

"Yeah, doubt if it will be as hard as getting Dallas to come with us."

"How we goin' to get gas first?" Scratch asked again.

"Beg…that's how we get lots of thing…by begging. People around here feel sorry for those who are down on their luck. We are down on our luck. Don't know of anyone more down than us." Gordon continued to hatch plans in his head. If they couldn't find that black hole, they would need to figure something else out. They could go to one of those homeless camps. Maybe find a willing woman there, as well as food. They might need a tent. Selling the car could buy them a few things. They'd make certain they found a place on the waterfront. Lots of activity on the waterfront. Lots of women, homeless women. Women they could charm with their delightful selves.

Pleased with their endeavors. Gordon was right on all counts. They begged for gas money then found the car lot closest to the waterfront. Sold it without blinking an eye. They collected the money then set off to make their new living arrangements.

Chapter Five

A week later, as planned, they all set off for Inverness to find a wedding dress for Dallas. Rafe drove. Ruby sat in the back of the car, Phoebe beside her. He had his arm wrapped around her. His hand hovered over her breast. That night after the bonfire, Rafe refused to sleep with Dallas. Since her return from the past, he held her at night. Now, he told her he wouldn't sleep with her, telling her he meant to wait for the wedding night. Waiting would make everything better, sweeter.

Dallas found she wanted him to change his mind about the sleeping arrangements more each day. She couldn't keep her thoughts to herself. He always understood what she wanted. Sometimes she thought he knew before she did. That couldn't be. If she didn't think something, he couldn't possibly know her mind. Rafe wasn't giving in to her wishes. He seemed more determined than ever to keep her away from his bed.

In the evenings, he would sit with her. Talk to her about various things that he liked and didn't like. He would kiss her. Touch her. Whenever she cooked, he would stand behind her, teasing her body to a point she had trouble breathing. When he taunted her, she also had trouble thinking. Trouble cooking. Once she burned his meal. He laughed. They ordered pizza.

Rafe never asked her when she wished to set the date of their wedding. If she brought anything up of that nature, he would either change the subject or talk about a day next May. A year from now as she first stated. Before, she'd been scared. Now, she just wished he would listen to her pleas. When she told him she was ready, he explained to her she wasn't. There were times she wanted to shake the annoying man until his teeth would rattle. Tell him a month would be just fine. Speak to Ruby so that she would start planning the celebration. One time she mentioned going to see Father Richard, Rafe told her seeing him was too soon. They should go after the New Year.

One night recently, she sat on his lap in the big plush chair in his studio. As often happened, his hands slipped beneath her shirt, cupping her breasts and warming her skin. Her response was immediate. Urgent in the extreme. That day she wore a tank top over a short skirt. He brushed his lips along the back of her neck. Sipped tender skin.

"Raise your arms," he whispered, touching his tongue on a sensitive place behind her ear. The sensation evocative; her pulse leapt with the gentle caress. He was tender. He left her shivering; her muscles constricted.

When she did as he requested, he pulled her top over her head. Ran his hands along the slope of her neck. Warmth swept through her. Dallas understood he would tease until she ached. She wanted that. She didn't want it. His fingers slid down her spine then back to her bra. After he unfastened her bra, his finger once more trailed down her spine to the waistband of her skirt. A tiny sound in the back of her throat ripped into the sultry evening air.

This was so different from her modeling days when all she did was slip from her bathrobe. He undressed her with slow, tender concern. Her breasts swayed. Her body heated, flamed with desire. His caress on her back sent a tempest of fire surging through her. Running his palms across her shoulders then down her arms, Rafe pushed the straps of her bra from her. He tossed the garment on the floor.

"I love your breasts," he told her. His hands closed over the twin globes. Held them with gentle reverence. Touched with a tender caress along the undersides. "Told you before, I needed to taste them. Sip the tips to hardened pebbles. Suck them deep inside my mouth." Just the words sent more pleasure rushing through her. Sweeping her into dreams of enchantment. Creating an ache that hinted at pleasure.

Rafe turned her so she straddled him. Her legs rested on the sides of his legs. She felt the rough fabric of his jeans against softness of her flesh. Felt the hair on his legs against her calves. His hand went behind her head and his mouth framed hers. He ran his tongue across her lips leaving a trail of dewy moisture. She parted her mouth, inviting him inside, into the darkness of her heat. His exploration within her mouth sent myriads of tremors to her core. She pulsed. Vibrated with longing. Melted into him. Needing more than he would give. She wished he would take this to its proper conclusion. Unless he changed his mind, he intended to wait until the night of their wedding. This was what all her dreams were about. Rafe. His hands. The mercuric tenacity of his caresses.

Their tongues touched, rubbed, danced.

Whimpers.

Sighs.

"Please…" she moaned as he caught the soft sound within his lips.

"Please what?"

Begging would do nothing to change Rafe's intentions. She arched, sending her breasts against his chest. Felt the softness of the cloth rub the tips. He wore his t-shirt. She slipped her hands beneath the cotton fabric, needing to feel the heat of his body. Smoothed her hands along his ribcage then across his hard abs.

"Take it off."

His arms rose in the air. She slid his shirt up then over his head. The tips of her breasts brushed against the crisp dark hair of his chest. She moved her body, making sure he felt her nipples dance, once then twice. Delighted in his groan of pleasure. Pushing back, she ran her hands across his chest, across his shoulders, reveling in the heat of his flesh. Moved her palms across his nipples until they were hard. His muscles contracted and rippled when her fingers caressed. She looked down. Thought it might be possible to touch him. She wanted to hold him in her hands. Touch her mouth on him, sip until he could hold nothing back. Her fingers fumbled with the fasteners on his jeans.

Dallas wished to seduce Rafe until he could no longer keep from making love to her. Understood how impossible that would be. Even now Rafe would be reading her thoughts. Thinking of ways to deflect her intentions. He would be prepared for any sensual assault she might initiate upon his person. He didn't talk to her. Not yet. He might soon tell her he wouldn't allow her to touch him.

Not until the wedding night.

Rafe cupped one breast in his hand. Held the globe with what seemed to be devotion. Smoothed his thumb across the sensitive flesh. The movement sensual. "I love your breasts. Have I told you that? Of course, I have." He lowered his mouth. Swirled his tongue around the tip. Sucked. Nipped. Laved.

"Y...yes... please Rafe."

"You taste better than I expected. Spicey as well as sweet. Wicked and naughty. A virgin temptress. You want me in the most elemental way. Admit it. You respond with wicked abandon when I touch you. Kiss you. Suck you into my mouth. Here. There. Different delicate places. Sip your sweetness. You can be tart. You can be sweet." He kissed his way to the valley between her breasts, exchanging one for the other. Treating them the same, he continued his attention, giving her exquisite pleasure she would never deny.

"You know I want you inside me. Need for you to make love to me. To do more than give me sweet words. Why do you want to wait? I'm not in danger of conceiving. You understand as well as I." Dallas thought she might know the answer. She didn't though. Was confused by his change of heart. Thought it might be a clan thing. She knew that wasn't true. Heard enough rumors to disprove that notion. Most all the shifters enjoyed their mates before the marriage. Many gave birth before they'd been married nine months. She didn't care. Dallas wanted to have his child.

Her nails slid into his hair as she arched, giving him better access. Her breasts traveled across his chest. While she clung to him, his hands slid beneath her skirt then roamed up her legs. He splayed his fingers across her belly. She moaned, sighed her ecstasy. He created magic. The whimper came from the back of her throat to enter into his mouth. He touched his tongue on hers. He assaulted her everywhere. The sultry air in the studio captured the sounds of pleasure he evoked from the depths of her heated core.

A gasp. He nipped across her lip. Her breath caught in the back of her throat. He slid the tiny piece of fabric away that protected nothing from his advance. His finger parted the sensitive folds between her legs. Touched her where she'd never been touched before. She parted her legs farther, giving him more access to that part of her she wanted him to explore. He gave tender attention to the hardened bud that brought her arching against his touch. Tremors vibrated throughout.

"Rafe…" she moaned his name. "Oh…" Her core constricted, then did so again while he continued to increase the ecstasy that had been hinted at before but never taken this far. She thought she was at the peak of her pleasure. Believed she was about to splinter into oblivion. Her body hummed. Pulsed with vibrance. Blood pounded then roared through her ears. Just before she thought she would fragment into hundreds of tiny shards, he withdrew from her.

"No…" her voice trailed off in a desperate plea, she understood he would not give into her. She heaved, desperate for air. Tears pricked the back of her throat. Threatened to fall from her eyes.

His head rested against her forehead. He slid his finger down the column of her neck. "That's it, Dallas. No more. Not until…" He tucked her head against his chest. Held her. His hands splayed across her back. Continued to warm her. He moved then, whispering soft words in a husky timbre, trying to sooth her shattered nerves.

She whimpered. Thought she would die right then. "Please…"

"No, love, we can't. Not until we are married." This time Rafe finished the sentence.

Not until they were married.

Dallas tried to reach into his thoughts. She could not. Thoughts of pummeling his chest crept into her head. She told him she was ready for his lovemaking. Refusing to believe her, he told her she wasn't prepared. Dallas found she didn't understand anything. Couldn't fathom how he thought. Not too long ago, Rafe was rushing her to the altar; angry with her because she hesitated. Furious with her because she was uncertain. Now, it seemed, he didn't want to marry her. All he wanted was to bring her to such startling pleasure then deny her. He taunted as well as teased. His actions were not well done.

"Why?" the single word was a slow moan. Still, she felt the sting of tears in the back of her throat. Her body was on fire, needed a release she knew he could give her. He refused. "We've…" she ran her tongue along her lip then caught it with her teeth, worrying the soft flesh. She sucked in a huge load of Rafe scented air in an attempt to calm herself. Nothing worked. Her hands shook. She didn't think she could walk.

"Yes, you deserve a few answers." He moved damp strands of hair from her face. "We've talked about sex when we were nothing but friends. For the two of us, sex was different then. It wasn't about us. Never believed it would ever concern the two of us together. I want our wedding night to be special in every way. The way a wedding night is supposed to be." He flashed her a huge, male domineering grin. One that made her wish to wipe it off his face.

The way he smiled angered her. Infuriated all her senses. "You just want to be in charge. The male dictating all that would happen. You don't care how I feel. What I think should count too." She pouted. Didn't want to stop. Tried to get inside his head. She couldn't. He wouldn't allow her access. She wished she could do that to him. Block her thoughts.

Hoping to change his mind, she kissed his chest along his collarbone. Lower to sip on each of his tight nipples. Lower still, following the line of his chest hair to the band of his jeans. Felt the hard muscles of his belly constrict. Saw the evidence of his hunger beneath the fabric covering him. His fingers sifted through the length of her hair.

He groaned when her hand rested on top of that evidence. "Dallas, I won't change my mind, no matter what you do. We need to get dressed. Phoebe and Cole will be here for dinner very soon. You knew that. The dinner…"

Snatching her bra from his hands she put it on then her top. She was not calm. Unable to move, she shot out her words directed at him. She was shaking. "Dinner will be awesome! Don't worry about the meal." She was furious with Rafe. He had no business teasing her until she all but exploded in his arms. Women's magazines wrote about climaxes. An orgasm was an amazing experience. She wasn't certain but she believed she'd been so close. Almost there. Another few seconds of his caresses would have sent her over that sought after threshold. So close she couldn't believe Rafe left her needing him. He was awful. Horrible. Despicable. She despised how he ended things. Understood he was doing so with a reason. What that motive was alluded her.

She struggled off his thighs. Puffed out a frustrated breath of air. *I'm going to burn your part of the dinner! Only yours. Everyone else will enjoy a wonderful meal.*

He hooted his laughter. "Don't see how you can burn just a fraction of the meal. I'll wait and see." He slipped on his shirt then held out his hand. He let it fall to his side after he realized she wasn't willing to touch him again so soon. She couldn't touch. Not now, not when she was still struggling with the fire he orchestrated.

Not on your life, Rafe Frasier. Not taking your hand. Your peace offering is unacceptable. There will be no peace between us right now.

As she marched out of the room, he let her into his thoughts. She read them. Pleased with what he heard, and now what he saw, he watched the sway of her hips, the movement of her breasts beneath the top she wore. He would have rather seen her storming out of the room naked.

Fat chance I'm going to ever let you get me naked again, mister macho. Not going to allow you to touch me. Not until the wedding night, Rafe Frasier. You can't keep doing this to me. It's not right or fair.

Rafe reached the kitchen two steps behind her. Ignoring her comments to him, his hand on her shoulder, he turned her. Captured her lips with his. Sucked on her bottom lip. Nipped then laved the tender spot. Left a trail of moisture. By her ear he whispered. "I love your tiny string bikini panties. I don't even have to remove them to touch you. Just push that slip of material to the side. I've free access to your most secret place. Dark. Hot. Wet."

The punch to his belly elicited an oomph. Nothing else. She started banging pans around as if that would make him feel different one way or the other. Dallas wanted him to understand how furious she was with the man. He could starve for all she cared. If they weren't having guests, she wouldn't cook for him.

"What are we having and what can I do?" he asked with soft spoken words as if he needed to make amends. "Cut the vegetables, I assume?"

"That would be nice, they are all in the strainer. I washed them before you took me upstairs." Dallas brought her thoughts from last night back to the present. They were driving to Inverness. She was going to pick out a wedding dress. Still, she couldn't seem to get thoughts of the evening before out of her head.

Are you still angry with me about the other night? I don't like it when you shut me out.

What? No. Yes! You must know. You can read my mind. Can't hide anything from you. Have to shut you out. If I don't, I'll be a trembling...mess...

Dallas crossed her arms in front of her. The GPS was telling them which exit to take. Rafe was grinning. Ruby was talking with her son and Phoebe as if they might have been making out in the backseat of the car. How could they with his mother sitting so close to them. Given the opportunity, she was certain Cole was just like Rafe. He would do what pleased him. Touched when he thought it would be advantageous to his needs.

This was chaos! It was messy.

She needed to focus on this day, not what happened the other night. What she did know was that she no longer wished to wait a year for the marriage. In contrast to what Rafe said, she was prepared in every way possible. Didn't understand why she ever decided such a long engagement would be what she wanted.

She told him. He never listened. His mind made up. They would wait a year. He thought waiting was what she wanted.

When she witnessed Rafe in his cat, the sight frightened her. He was huge. She never expected something so unique. Seeing him she should have been in awe. Should have understood he would never hurt her. Didn't quite have the words to broach the subject. She'd like to see him change again. He could tease. Dallas didn't think now that he...she wouldn't be afraid. Right now, she knew he was listening into her thoughts. Now, with company this was not the time to speak of something so personal. Next time they were alone, she might ask if he would show her his cat again.

Rafe listened to the directions. Exited the highway before following the instruction right to the front door of the wedding boutique. While he smiled at her, Rafe picked up her hand. Squeezed. The small token did encourage. She would rather be doing this with him. Didn't believe much in superstitions such as this one. Wished for his opinion.

He kissed the back of her hand. "Call me when you're finished. We'll be at the tavern we passed a few minutes ago. We can pick you up then we can decide where to have our late lunch. Anywhere you would like."

"Fine…" She started from the car; Rafe pulled her back. Kissed her hard and fast then let her go.

I love your little pouts.

Go to hell, Rafe Frasier!

"What was that all about?" Ruby asked as they walked into the shop. When she sent her a withering look, Ruby spoke up. "Oh my, too personal. You two having a lover's spat?" Ruby laughed.

"Lover's spats aren't funny," Phoebe pointed out, as if she'd had her share this last week with Cole. Dallas didn't enjoy the arguments. Rafe won every time. He would do everything his way. Maybe…just maybe, she should visit Father Richard without him. She would set a date. Today she could talk to Ruby. See how much time she did need to arrange the celebration. Her guest list wasn't huge, but Rafe had a lot of family in the area.

"Fifty years later when you look back on those conflicts they will be amusing. You can lay in bed and talk about the trying times." Ruby suggested with a sly smile. "The cad, he's been listening to your thoughts. Hasn't he? That's why you're so furious. I understand, my Aaron used to do that too. Thought it was his prerogative."

"Says he doesn't have a choice," Dallas said as she sniffed in a large dose of oxygen. "His listening in on my thoughts is only part of the issue. He eavesdrops but he fails to hear the meaning of my thoughts."

"He knows what you're thinking?" Phoebe asked, curiosity in her voice. "That's not possible. Is it?"

Ruby set her hand on Phoebe's shoulder. "It is, child. Soon my son will explain certain things to you. Perhaps you will be able to understand better because of this conversation." With a lift to her shoulders. "Then again, perhaps not. Men can be so elusive. Obtuse sometimes. I remember with Aaron I was hard pressed to believe any of the things he first whispered to me. He was very gentle, tender as well as patient. Seemed to understand that in time, I would comprehend all that was possible."

"Men!" Dallas said striding through the doors. She stopped. Stared. The gowns were amazing. Beautiful. All so very unique. All the ones on the mannequins were ones she might like. She didn't even need to look through the racks. Her heart started to beat harder. Her breath caught.

"Can I help you? Which one of you is the bride?" The woman was all smiles. She was looking over the entourage. "Is this the mother of the bride?"

Dallas found herself lifting her hand as if she was still in school then saying. "Me…I'm the bride. No, my mother isn't here. She won't be coming. Ruby is like a mother."

"Hope everything is fine, you do look a bit flushed." The woman laughed softly. She was nodding her head. "I've felt the same many times about my husband. I've had brides looking for dresses muttering those same sentiments. Don't worry about your men. I'm certain you will figure out many different ways to get around him. By the way, I'm Sarah. If not your mother, who do you have with you?"

Holding out her hand, "I'm Dallas," she turned to Ruby. "Ruby is the mother to my fiancé's friend, and this is Phoebe who is his friend's girlfriend. Sounds a bit complicated. My best friend is also my fiancé. Don't wish to test my luck by having him with me today. Though I would value his opinion."

Sarah nodded. "Understand completely. Tell me a little about your wedding. What's the venue?"

"It…" Dallas turned to Ruby. She nodded with a smile. "The wedding will be at the McKenna keep in Carnoch. The clans McKenna, Stuart, along with the Frasier, will all be in attendance."

"A huge affair, I presume. I'll pull a few gowns that might be wonderful for this occasion. Meanwhile, look around. Take your time. When you find a gown you'd like to try, let me know, unless you already have something in mind. I might be able to save some time. We should start with several dresses. Different styles. You might discover the one you thought wouldn't do at all is perfect. That happens all the time, which is why I encourage my brides to not be too set in their minds about what they would like. Sometimes they are surprised at what looks best on them."

Clearing her throat, Dallas tried to put her thoughts into perspective. "Something simple is what I'm looking for. Not a lot of lace or pearls. No bling. No ball gown. Mermaid…maybe. Something that fits close to the body. Think Rafe would like that. Don't want to call too much attention to me…" She didn't like speaking of the parts of her she always thought were too huge. "My breasts."

"Self-conscious?"

"Yes… my fiancé…" Dallas left off, not wishing to delve into the more personal side of her relationship.

"Of course," Sarah pulled out a few gowns. Phoebe found some. Ruby looked through the selection then pulled two more. Dallas found a few dresses she would like to try. When she entered the dressing room, the array of gowns hung in different places around the room. Deciding which one to try first would be difficult, next to impossible.

Dallas loved all the gowns selected. She supposed what she chose depended on what looked best on her. She seldom wore dresses. Never dressed up. How would she know? That's why Ruby and Phoebe were here. They were supposed to be Rafe's eyes. Would know how he would see her when she walked down the aisle.

"Some of these need to be laced up the back. You will need help. Let me know when you want assistance. As soon as you are ready you can show your friends."

In the end, the choice came down to two gowns. One Phoebe selected; the other was one of the ones picked out by Ruby. Dallas loved them both. They both flattered her curves. She discovered her waist was narrow even though her breasts along with her hips were larger than the norm. She turned sideways then looked over her shoulder at the back of the dress. The back was exquisite.

Ruby stood aside watching, her hands clasped beneath her chin studying first one gown then the second one. "You are so lovely. Either dress will steal Rafe's breath right from his lungs when he sets his eyes on you. Which one do you like best?"

Dallas just modeled Phoebe's selection. Now she stood on the small platform wearing the one Ruby picked out. She found herself shaking her head then shrugging her shoulders. She did love them both. "We need someone to break the tie, I can't decide." She turned to Sarah. "I adore both of these gowns. I can choose only one. Which one of these wonderful gowns do you think looks the best on me?" The woman had experience with gowns such as these. She had no reason to say anything but the truth.

"You wish for me to break the tie? I'm flattered. For me, Ruby's is the best for your figure. The shape flatters your curves the most without over shouting the size of your breasts. The other gown is also exquisite. You can't go wrong with either choice."

"Now that you point it out, I agree," Phoebe said, her voice soft. She turned her face one way then the other. "Wish this was going to be my wedding we're planning. I know which gowns I would try on."

Ruby set her hand on Phoebe's back. "You are too young to marry." Then she held up her hands. "I understand girls your age wed. Many divorce a short time after saying their vows. Believe they are in love with being in love. A few years of independence from your father will do you well. Use those years wisely. Once they pass by, you won't be able to retrieve them. A girl should never have regrets."

Phoebe was nodding, seeming to take in all Ruby said.

"I think this is your lucky day. My seamstress just walked in the back door. She wasn't expected for another twenty minutes. We can fit you in this dress today if you wish…or…we could order a new gown. That might take another month. Somehow, I sensed you were eager for the wedding to take place. Am I wrong?"

Dallas felt her smile grow. "I'd like that. Today would be fine. I am eager. Rafe and I have been friends for years. We've only just discovered there is more between us than just friendship. This gown would be less expensive, yes? Not that it matters to me. I've plenty of money. We stayed within budget. Still…"

"Showroom gowns are always less expensive. Are you certain?"

"The gown is gorgeous on her. It's as if the gown was made especially for her." The seamstress spoke up while she set her bags on a nearby table. "Is this the one you've chosen? I can fit it to you right now if you've the time." She circled her, making little noises as she studied her. She seemed to be making notes in her head. "All this gown needs is to be nipped in at the waist. Your waist is so tiny. Won't take long. Every other part fits to perfection. I'll get my pins. I'll have it finished for you this time next week. Will call you if I get the gown done sooner. I'm thrilled you picked this one, it's one of my favs. I designed it to fit a figure such as yours."

Dallas stole a breath of air. "You're the designer? I... I feel privileged."

Dallas hoped she reached Rafe with her thoughts. She was eager for him to know about her success. *You're not going to believe this. I found the perfect gown. It's beautiful. Thank you for taking me today. I'm not going to tell you anything about the dress. Bad luck and such, you understand. It will be ready in a week. Cole's mother picked this one out. Would like you to make an appointment with Father Richard? I would love to meet with him. Set a date.*

Glad you found the perfect gown. No, it's too soon for an appointment. Don't wish to rush this marriage you've been so hesitant about. Think we should wait at least six more months. Need to be certain this wasn't some type of cosmic mistake. Don't wish for you to be disappointed or change your mind.

Dallas discovered she was furious with his new attitude. She fumbled around in her head for the right words. *Rafe! If you don't, I will. You can stay home when I meet with him. For all I care you can stay home during the wedding, the celebration as well as the night!*

That was a ridiculous comment.

You can come to the wedding night. That's why I want the marriage to take place AS SOON AS POSSIBLE.

All three were standing outside the bridal boutique when Rafe pulled up with Cole. Rafe grinned. Going over Dallas' words to him during the drive, made his heart light. His ploy seemed to be getting under her skin. She would be ready for marriage by the time her dress was finished. She said a week. They could set the date between that day and the end of the week. It would need to be a Saturday. She told him the gown was beautiful. He couldn't ever recall her wearing a dress. This would be a treat for his eyes.

How he would give in to her with graceful aplomb to her demand to move up the wedding date to just two weeks from today was yet to be figured out. He had time to think on what he would say. Everything looked to be working out the way he planned, the way Cole advised. Her reaction to his admission that they should wait six months was perfect. Better than he could ever have suspected. He supposed he could mention three months next time. In all reality another two weeks was all he could wait. Since the gown wouldn't be finished for another week, that left a second week for planning. They would need to see Father Richard soon. He didn't know if his body could take much more stimulation without giving into his needs.

He also should discover the truth about her ability to shift. Just because she could listen to his thoughts didn't make this newfound ability of hers iron clad. He did enjoy talking to her in his head. Didn't even need to be in the same vicinity to do so. There were other possible reasons why she possessed this trait. If it turned out Dallas was a shifter, he could teach her how to change forms. Wondered which of her parents tossed the gene down to her. It was possible one of her grandparents possessed the characteristic, neither parent being able to change into their cat. He heard of that happening before. In those cases, the little shifter would never be taught the basics. Would be discouraged if they were ever discovered. The fact Dallas was so baffled when he shifted gave reason for him to believe she had no recollection of changing form. Most little ones discovered their ability at an early age. Enjoyed changing. What was Dallas' story?

When she slipped into the front seat, he smiled. Reached out for her hand to squeeze. "So…you found the perfect dress? It isn't red, is it?" He almost told her what he thought if she chose some weird color. He was able to hold the words back just in case she did. Dallas didn't need any more disappointment.

Dallas' little gasp of surprise pleased him. Her eyes widened as if he was a crazy man. He wasn't crazy, just cautious. Didn't wish to make assumptions that might put him in the doghouse. "No! Whatever would cause you to ask that? A red wedding gown?" Her full lips thinned in disapproval. "I'm too traditional. I didn't see a black gown. The owner told me she could change the color of most of the gowns if I didn't wish to have white or ivory."

Rafe lifted his shoulders in what he hoped was a deceptive shrug. "I've watched some of those wedding shows. Sometimes the bride wants a red dress. Saw one where she bought a black gown. A very pale blue would look wonderful on you. I'd rather you stayed with traditional. Did you? You did say you wouldn't tell me anything about the dress."

"It's pure white, virginal, just like your bride to be," Ruby interjected, taking matters into her hands, seeming to have guessed part of the argument between the two of them. "Your heart will stop for a second or two when you see your bride walking down the aisle to you. She is exquisite."

"She's beautiful wearing the gown," Phoebe said with a soft sigh. "Wish this were my wedding. Oops." She covered her mouth with her hand.

Through the rearview mirror, Rafe watched Cole bring Phoebe's hand to his lips for a quick kiss. For both of them life was moving on as planned. He saw Cole silently say the words. "Soon, in another year or two." Rafe didn't know if Phoebe heard.

Rafe wasn't certain how much to ask. He understood Dallas wasn't going to speak of the dress. That was fine by him. He'd been told by Ruby more than he expected. And he knew the dress wasn't some crazy color. Not for a moment did he think Dallas wanted to draw that kind of attention to herself, nor did she wish to make some type of statement that no one but her would understand. Time to move on to other things. "Where do you ladies want to eat?" Rafe asked, looking from Dallas to the people behind him. "We can go anywhere that pleases all of you. I could be happy eating just about anything." That was the truth. He couldn't think of one type of food he didn't enjoy.

"Your choice," Dallas said, her voice soft. When he looked at her, she was leaning back, her eyes closed. She was breathing deeply. "Deciding on which gown I wanted exhausted my decision-making skills. Suppose we see what other people wish to eat. I'm for fish and chips along with a cold beer. Anyone else?"

"Sounds good to me," Cole spoke up from behind them with a wink directed at his rear-view mirror.

Both Ruby, along with Phoebe, agreed that fish and chips would be good. Most Scottish taverns had other selections. Rafe didn't want to go to the tavern they just came from. Wanted one with a bit more ambiance than the one downtown.

"I know a place down by the waterfront that has great food. We can sit out on the deck. Watch the water along with the coming and going of the boats while we eat. The fish and chips are great. They also have an assortment of salads, shepherd's pie as well as corn beef and cabbage if fish and chips aren't your first choice."

They spent the next few hours eating and chatting, getting to know each other better. Rafe found that Phoebe was delightful, if not a bit young. Cole was right in putting off the wedding. The girl needed to grow up more. Everything she said and did yelled out high school. Not that there was anything wrong with that. The biggest problem was that Cole was almost eight years her senior. The man could be patient. Would need to show considerable restraint.

Ruby seemed to enjoy the time as much or more than the two couples. She regaled them with stories of her wedding as well as those of some of the other clansmen, her daughter's wedding too.

Rafe was somewhat disappointed when he brought them home. The conversation had been lively during the travel back to Carnoch. He would take Dallas into the city in a week to pick up the gown. She told him he would have to stay in the car while she tried the dress on just to make certain everything was perfect.

The week sped by faster than he thought possible. Dallas received a new assignment from the magazine she worked for. This one had her working closer to home. She was supposed to cover the highland games in Glasgow. They planned on making the day an outing with Cole and Phoebe. Ruby packed a basket of food for them to take with them in the car. She understood they would sample many varieties of food from the Scottish vendors and probably wouldn't eat a bite of what they packed.

On that day, the sun was bright and the sky a beautiful blue. A slight breeze flowed from the river that slipped through the city. The chatter and laughter during the drive was contagious. The two couples got an early start. Arrived at the games as the doors opened. Bagpipes played. Men in kilts marched along the university track. There was a mile race for the men wearing kilts. Booths were set up around the perimeter. All kinds of dancers competed for top prizes.

Cole and Phoebe drifted in one direction while Rafe took Dallas' hand walking in the opposite way. They stopped for food. She shot photos. Watched the caber toss then the highland dancers. Dallas took more pictures. They bought beers. Talked about everything including their possible visit to Father Richard's. So far nothing had been planned. Nothing committed to. No date set.

After she had enough photos for the article, Rafe found a shady spot to sit. He wasn't certain how to approach the subject on his mind. "We need to talk," Rafe began by picking up her hand. He wove his fingers in and out of hers. The sensations erotic. Tantalizing. He brought her fingers to his lips to give a gentle caress, felt the slight tremor of her response. This last week he'd been careful with her. The kisses shorter. His seduction of Dallas worked out. She did what he hoped for, moved her thoughts of a year of waiting to two weeks. Rafe thought he might even make it to the wedding without exploding when she touched him. So far, they'd not met with either Ruby or Father Richard. If they were to be wed in two weeks, the necessary arrangement had to be seen to.

"Do you think any of these pictures will work for my exhibit in June?" Dallas held the camera for him to view the photos as she flipped through them. He leaned in close, looking over her shoulder as she dashed through her selections. There were several candid shots of the men tossing their cabers, along with the women as well as with the young ladies who participated in the dancing. He pointed out a few he thought she could use for the upcoming gallery show. Some that would have to be given to the magazine for their article.

Resting his chin on the top of her head, he spoke with a soft cadence, his voice husky, whiskey smooth. He desired her. His hunger needed to be tamped down. "We can look on the computer tonight or tomorrow. You do have to give the best to the magazine." His hands ran along her arms.

She sighed; her breathing easy, restful as they relaxed beneath the canopy of the old oak tree. "They'll only want about fifty or so to choose from." Dallas leaned back against Rafe while his hands came around her. His fingers spread out just below the rise of her breasts. When he looked down, he saw cleavage. Enough to send a bolt of adrenalin to his groin.

He knew her taste along with her wonderful scent. The urgency he always felt with her was almost impossible to contain. Wished he dared hold her large globes in his hands. She wouldn't appreciate him doing so in public. He tamped down the rising need the best he could.

Changing positions, he caressed the curve of her hip. Ran his hand along her rib cage then down her leg. His palm passed over the inside of her thigh and he felt the quiver of her exhilaration. Was pleased with the gentle whimper cascading from the back of her throat. His restraint was vanishing.

"Your exhibit wasn't what I needed to talk about. We both understand your shots are the best." Before he carried this sweet-talking so far neither of them could think, he needed to keep his hands from moving on her body. Once they were married, he planned on keeping her in bed for at least a week until they were both sated.

"What then?"

"You know. Maybe you don't. There are two things we need to discuss. The wedding and the fact you can hear my thoughts when I allow you into my head." He wished he could see her expression. Needed to witness her reaction to his words as well as listen to them in her head.

She sat up, turning to him. The swell of her breasts brushed across his chest. He felt the pebbled hardness of the tips. Tilting her head back and forth she blinked then smiled, touching his chin with a gentle caress. Her eyes were vibrant, alive. Questioning. She was curious when she asked, "How so?"

Rafe touched the pulse thundering at the base of her neck. Enjoyed knowing he affected her that way. He'd not expected her to react with so much intensity. Perhaps this wasn't the right time for discussing something that might bother her. He needed to make the effort now. At home, they always managed to find themselves too distracted with each other for any lengthy discussion. Here, there was the public to run interference in their amorous pursuit of each other. He cleared his throat wondering where he was going with this.

"Let's begin with the wedding. What do you think? Is that a good place to start. Something we both might be able to agree on. Would you rather tell me how it came about that you can read my thoughts? Hmm…"

"Fine. The wedding would work well. I would know why you changed your mind then changed it again. Don't know what to think about the date. So far, nothing has been done." The sound of her voice tightened. Her shoulder stiffened. That light in her eyes that never failed to tell him she was furious grew hot.

"It's not bad." Unable to stop himself, he passed his thumb across the tip of her breast then the other one. "I'm not going to put the wedding off again. Don't wish to do so. Seems we've been through that issue numerous times. We will wed as soon as we can make the arrangements." Rafe smoothed some of her long hair behind her ear. She bristled as if she didn't believe his words.

He saw her shaking her head. Disbelief clear in the shadowing of her eyes. He'd put her off kilter by his declaration. She now didn't know what to think. "Are you leading me on? Once again, have you changed your mind from two weeks to three weeks. I'm fed up." Dallas started to get up. "Maybe we should never get married."

He knew she wanted to walk away from him. Understood her distress. He'd done that to her. Making amends to her without telling her his motive imperative. Before she could get on her feet, he grabbed her hand. Tugged. "Sit!" The single word came out too harsh for his liking. She needed gentling combined with reaffirmation of his intent. He needed to soothe her with his voice, together with a soft cadence of words.

Dallas whirled on him, her eyes flashing fire. Her brows drawn together. "You've no right to restrain me!" She looked to his hand wrapped around her wrist. They'd spent the last two weeks frustrated with sexual tension. Now that same frustration overflowed into fury. Rafe understood. He doubted if Dallas knew why she was so defiant. He felt the tension just as much. It was all he could do to stop himself when he gave her pleasure then kept her from shattering in his arms. Hated himself for his callous behavior while knowing that same conduct was what brought them to the altar. He needed to see her eyes when she reached her release. This had gone on too long. It was going to end soon.

"Tomorrow, if you're free, we can make an appointment with Father Richard as well as Ruby." He liked the way her eyes softened. Dallas never told him no when he kissed her, charmed her until she panted with her frustration. Never told him no when she understood he would stop short of her climax. He could never stop his hands from roaming places that would evoke carnal pleasure. This needed to end before he couldn't stop himself from taking what he wanted before the wedding night. Once the date was set, they would have to curtail their explorations. It might be best for Dallas to move into the keep. That way she would stay chaste until the wedding night.

"Tomorrow?" she whispered, her voice hoarse.

He tugged her onto his thighs. She still didn't believe his words. "Tomorrow," he breathed the word next to her ear. Tapped with his tongue. Nipped with his teeth. "Tomorrow. What are you doing in the morning? Are you busy? I can make the appointments for the afternoon if that suits you better. You tell me what it is you would like."

His Dallas was hesitant. *This isn't some sick joke? Didn't think you would ever agree to a wedding sooner than later. Believed you were still stuck on six months. Though, that was better than waiting a year.* "Going over these photos. E-mailing them to the magazine. What are you doing?"

"With you by my side, setting up a day for our marriage to take place. Will that work for you?" He didn't expect a negative answer. He ran his knuckles along the column of her throat. She shivered. He brushed tender kisses from one side of her mouth to the other. Wished she would open for him. Rub hers against his.

Wide eyed, she continued to stare at him. "You are serious? I wasn't certain. Didn't think that was something you would tease me about." Dallas still appeared not to believe him. Still seemed to hold back what Rafe hoped was a celebratory whoop.

"Very serious. I need to have you in my bed every night. All night. Wish to wake up with you in my arms every morning. So…" He tapped her on her nose. "We need to make wedding plans. You will have your dress soon. Ruby has said she wishes to help with the celebration, which leaves the actual wedding. We will have one in the church with all who wish to attend, then the one traditional one which will bring you into the arms of the Clan Chattan. This ceremony will be conducted with only family around."

"Now that I think on it, I might believe you. We are going to visit the good father along with Ruby tomorrow?"

She seemed to ignore the rest of what he said. What she should know about the clan ceremony, he wasn't certain. "Yes. If they don't have time tomorrow, then the next day. What do you think? Is that a yes from you?"

She nodded. A soft smile graced her mouth. He wanted to kiss her senseless.

"Just what I hoped to hear."

"What was the other topic to discuss. Something about me being able to hear your thoughts? Does it bother you? It bothers me that I can't keep you out at certain times. Other times, I like to just talk to you without anyone else hearing."

"Yes, to the topic and no, your ability doesn't bother me, you're quite good at leaping into my head to hear my opinions on various topics. I can block you when I don't want you knowing what I'm thinking about. If you were able to get through my veritable blockade you would have known I want this marriage sooner than later. Needed to make certain you weren't afraid of my cat or of a commitment to me. For a while, you had me puzzled about what you wanted." As soon as he stopped, he understood he didn't say enough. She questioned with her eyes.

"I'm not afraid of you or your cat."

"Fear isn't what this is about. Except you were visibly terrified when you first witnessed my cat. Both physically as well as mentally, you distanced yourself from me." That much was very true.

"If it's not about my fear, what then? Don't understand what you're getting at."

"Do you know of any man or woman in your family background that was a shifter? Did anyone speak of something like that. Were you always bombarded by the notion shifting was a rumor to be ignored? Is there anything in your subconscious that screams out at you? Maybe when you were little…a toddler learning to walk as well as absorbing other knowledge?" He watched her eyes cross for a few seconds while she thought about his question.

"Why?" She moved, squirmed. Her distraught was clear. "Now you are frightening me. What are you getting at?"

Rafe needed to understand if this was fear. "Any shifters in the family, black panther or otherwise?" He couldn't allow her to change his train of thought. With a swipe of her tongue across her lips she could do that to him. He'd focus on the dewy trail of moisture the gesture left. At that juncture he'd be lost. He didn't wish to deviate from his intentions. Tonight, after they were home, he would show her how to shift. She must have missed out on that when she was a child. Children shift. Instinct drives them. Someone must have stopped her. Could have forbidden her to change shape. Told her any number of things about doing so that would have deterred her. Her mother came to mind. Her father might also have been against this ability. Not if he was a shifter himself.

Dallas was rubbing the sides of her face with her fingers. When she looked at him, her hands stilled for a second. Time seemed to pass as if there was no concern for the immediate. He tapped her beneath her chin, urged her to meet his gaze. "Not that I know of. Why?" she queried again. "No shifters. Mother always told me thinking about something like that wasn't good to dwell on. Talk about shifters was nonsense…nonsense talk. Rumors that weren't true."

That was his first inclination. Instead of being nurtured as a child to understand her abilities, she was forbidden. "Why? You ask. That is a fantastic question. First off, we both comprehend talk of shifters is not nonsense talk. Your question is one that is easy to answer. I believe you might have the ability to change your shape. Probably do. Might is too weak of a word. This evening, after we finish searching your photos, would you like to try?"

"No."

Why wasn't he surprised? Her immediate reaction to the negative disappointed him. He'd hoped she'd be eager to see if she possessed the skill. He let out a breath of frustrated air. Her response was to be expected. Dallas was frightened of his cat. "Yes," he countered. "I do expect you to try. Attempting is something that must be done. If you fail, we'll try again sometime." Calm was the only way to proceed in this endeavor. Beside him, he felt her tremors. She might be better off not ever knowing the truth. In the end, once discovered, he was pretty certain she would be proud of her ability. Would thank him for insisting. This was another gamble.

She bristled. The movements giving the sway of her breasts a new meaning. The tips hard against the fabric of her shirt. "Rafe, you're crazy. I can't shift. Never knew anything about shifters until the other day when you frightened me so much I thought I would jump out of my skin. You can't possibly imagine…"

He picked up her hands. They trembled within his. He held tight. More than anything he needed to reassure her. "I don't believe I'm crazy at all. I trust what I'm telling you has the ring of truth to it. Don't know any other reason that you're able to read my thoughts. Christ, Dallas, we can talk to each other without speaking. Carry on long, drawn-out conversations. That's not normal for most humans. Doesn't that fact make you curious as to why? We couldn't do so before. Now that you traveled back from the past, we can. That alone should make you inquisitive."

She tried to tug her hands from his. He held on tight. Rafe wasn't about to let her go until she would agree to at least attempt the feat. He needed her reassurance. Now, she was running from the notion. Shaking away the fear. That was imperative to her well-being. "I'm certain there are other possible reasons. I can't do it. Change. Don't want to do it. Don't know how. Not going to try."

"I'm sorry. I should have waited longer to spring this on you. I'm always too impatient with you. Tonight, I'll show you how to change your shape. You will love doing so. It's fun. I promise changing won't hurt. There is nothing to be afraid of."

If anything, her quivering became more apparent. He pulled her into his arms, holding her, absorbing her terror into his big body. She pulled away to better look at him. He saw the moisture filling her eyes. This conversation was not meant to make her cry. Beneath his breath he cursed.

"I would have to strip in front of you. Take my clothes off. Not going to do that." She sounded determined. Adamant about what she would and would not do. Didn't think to put her comment into the perspective the words deserved. She was fumbling with her excuses. He could point out that he'd seen her many times and for hours on end without clothing.

His short bark of laughter brought the creases on her forehead together. Her lips thinned. He didn't dare run his thumb across her mouth. She might not appreciate the gesture. Might bite. She was drawing away from him. One more time she tried to distance herself from him. He wouldn't allow separation. "You've stripped for me many times…too many to count. You never felt even the littlest bit shy. Never bothered you before. I've touched every beautiful part of you. Kissed most of you. Would like to tell you I've tasted all those places, but I haven't. On our wedding night I will. Undressing in front of me should be easy for you."

"I won't."

"You will."

"I won't try to change my shape. You can't make me." She continued the dialogue. Sounded like a child. "I won't strip. Won't change my shape. Like me just the way I am, thank you. Don't want to be different. It's okay for you. I can't…"

She was a stubborn little thing. He admired that quality…most of the time. He did love her shape the way he saw her. That wasn't enough for him. "Then…" he paused, wondering if he dared make her angrier.

"Then what?"

He supposed she took the decision from his hands. "Simple…you try your hardest. Must convince me you are working your darndest to shift… I'll understand if you can't. You might be right in your assumption that you can't possibly be a shifter." He fumbled for words…for the right words. Wished he dared force her. Maybe this was just one more thing she needed extra time to deliberate about. Maybe he needed to approach this from a different angle.

"If I don't?" Her chin pointed into the air.

"We won't make those appointments we spoke of earlier." The words came out before he could hold them back. For a beat, they caught in the back of his throat. He didn't want to forego the meeting he meant to arrange first thing tomorrow morning.

"That's blackmail!" she sputtered, outraged. Furious, her eyes blazed with intensity. "Right now, I don't like you, Rafe Frasier. You can just go jump in a bloody loch somewhere and drown. I'll push you in if you give me the chance. You could freeze to death. The water is freezing this time of year."

"What did you do this time, old boy?" Cole and Phoebe came up to them. They were both smiling, standing in front of them. Cole held Phoebe's hand in his. He brought their hands to his chest. She closed her eyes with a soft sigh.

Rafe was finished with this conversation. Couldn't continue in front of an audience. There would be more time later to renew the dialogue between them. He would find some means, without the threat of holding the wedding over her head to accomplish what he wanted. He wasn't going to blackmail her with sex again. Those times were done. They would either proceed in the fashion they both wished, or he would forego sex with her.

"None of your business," he grouched out. "Imagine it's time to leave. We've got our pictures. Unless there is something more the two of you would like to see or participate in. I believe it's time to make our departure. So far, I've experienced my fill of these games." Rafe stood. His long strides took him to the entrance. He didn't stay to help Dallas to her feet. Realizing she would never accept the help.

From the beginning, he understood speaking to her about shifting wouldn't be easy. He should have waited until he was seducing her. Until he had her panting with raw hunger. He would have had a better chance of convincing her he was right. She would be almost naked or perhaps she would be naked by the time he broached the subject. A few shakes, a turn of her head, more concentration…she would become a beautiful black panther. He'd like to swim with her, wrestle, run… The list of things he'd enjoy doing with her in her cat form lengthened. She denied something that would give her pleasure.

Dallas trailed behind him. Her walk lethargic. Cole and Phoebe walked behind her. The air was rife with tension. He understood her anger…tried to appreciate how she must feel. She was both furious as well as defiant. She wanted her way. Well…the hell with it, she wasn't going to have her way in this. Not if he had anything to say about her learning to alter herself. He had less than he wished. He couldn't keep the enflamed thoughts in his head. Reaching out to her, he gave himself more reason to contemplate the very real fact the woman, his mate, was indeed a shifter.

You are acting childish. Just like a little girl that didn't get her way.
He lashed out. Regretted the words as they left his head.

And...you keep tossing out accusations. Do you think demeaning me by calling me childish will improve this scenario? You're acting like my mother. Thought you were different. I have the right to my opinions as well as feelings. Who are you to blackmail me into doing something I don't wish to do? Maybe this wedding should not go forward.

I am different...very different from your mother. In this instance I'm speaking the truth. You aren't thinking straight. Your mother must have something to do with your denial of the facts that are right in front of you. Listen to yourself speak to me. Hear me talking to you. No one else hears our words to each other.

In your point of view, that might be true. In mine, I'm neither childish nor thinking wrong. I don't agree with you. In my wildest imaginations I've never wished to change the shape I'm in. Didn't when we were just friends. Don't now that we understand we mean more to each other. I won't try. Damn the wedding. Let's forget about marrying. It's obvious we can't agree on anything or get along more than a few seconds.

From my thoughts...no, you're right. I shouldn't push you. Never thought you would be afraid to try something different. Didn't take you for a coward. Maybe learning about who you are just takes time. I've been thinking about the possibility since the first time you forged straight into my head. Imagine it's too soon...too big a gamble for you to undertake. I'll give you time to consider the possibility, but I won't let up. You are a shifter, Dallas. Deep in my heart I know that scenario for a fact. You aren't going to rebuff that ability.

So...you won't cancel the appointments? Despite the fact you told me you would make them tomorrow. I know you made them before we left this morning.

You were in my head? Rafe didn't realize she'd been within him. He grinned to himself. She was good. He didn't intend to give her more encouragement along those lines. She was right. He was an ass. He would need to work to rectify the way he acted toward her. Dallas didn't come right out and say the word. She implied with great strength.

I forgive you. At first your description of yourself is fitting. I'm going to think about what you've suggested. Not making promises. Give me time.

That's my love.

"The two of you involved in communicating silently? Isn't that a bit rude?" Cole asked as they reached the car. His chuckle wasn't missed by either of them. "I've asked you several times if you're still seeing mother tomorrow. Suppose you made an appointment with the priest." His question unnerved Rafe. He shouldn't be so perceptive. Cole knew they carried on a conversation between themselves.

In unison they replied. "The appointments been made!"

Cole hooted his laughter. "Good. Love weddings. Can hardly wait for this one. Bet the celebration will be full of surprises." He brought Phoebe's hand up to kiss her knuckles. "Don't you? You will come with me. Be my date? My plus one?"

Phoebe turned a sweet rose color. Blinked twice while she stared at Cole. Rafe wondered what they'd been doing all afternoon. If a man was ingenious, there were lots of private places to steal a kiss or two. There was also the public realm.

"I…" She smiled at him. Her eyes love-struck. "Yes, I'll be your date."

"Hope the ride home isn't as silent as the walk to the car," Cole said as if he understood that between Rafe and Dallas, there had been nothing quiet. The conversation had been nonstop.

. ﹍ * ﹍ .

"Did you see them?" Gordon asked as he continued to search the area. He was cautious. On edge. Didn't trust anything in this godforsaken place. The people in this part of Inverness weren't always the best. He hooted. The sound echoed in the narrow alley. Neither he nor Scratch were model citizens. "Those two, Rafe and Dallas, were sitting out on the deck, holdin' hands, sipping on their beers and eatin'. Just as if those two don't have a care in the world. They're all lovey-dovey. Would have been kissin' if the other couple wasn't there. Makes me sick to watch them, even though my stomach was grumbling mighty fierce. Could have used a bite of those meals that were only partially eaten. The waiters picked them up then tossed them away. Certain the rest is in the dumpster."

"We're never going to get our hands on Dallas. She's too protected. That was a McKenna…The McKenna that was with those two. Those men are ruthless. Protective of their clan. Frasiers are related to the McKennas. They must be drivin' back to Carnoch now. We sold our car. Can't walk that far. Need to forget about that girl. See what we can find here. Make the best of what we have. Saw some homeless women. Those women won't be too hard to charm out of their britches. Need to find some means to gain more money than just enough for whores and whiskey."

"Could stick out our thumbs to get a ride to Carnoch. Don't have to walk," Gordon said while he thought about different ways to make the trip. He stretched his back then turned his attention to the ships in the harbor. "Not giving up on the girl. She's got too much that I can't get out of my head. Need to get a taste of those big titties of hers before I give up on her. Stick my rod into her wet pussy. Listen to her moan with the pleasure I'm givin' her. Would like to see you rock her between her white thighs. Now that's what I intend on us both doing. If I can get us to Carnoch, I get her first. You can have what's left over. If there is anything left to dally with."

"The way you tell the story, makes havin' Dallas all seem possible. My mouth's a watering. Maybe I'm with you. Maybe I'm not." He stopped talkin' to stare at his hand. "What you got there?" Scratch kept staring at what his best friend in the entire world was holding in his hands. "Looks like candy."

Gordon leaned against a post sticking up from the dock. He held out some pills. "Bought these from the gent down the street there. Cost too many groats. He told me they would make us feel real fine." Gordon handed Scratch one of the pills. "Try it. Won't buy any more if they don't work. Need to feel real fine. Need to forget all my problems."

For a few shakes of his head, he waited before saying, "Don't much like pills. How can that candy colored thing make my hunger go away? Give me a good night's rest? Pleasure me when I can't find a whore. Don't need pills. Need a woman then food, before all that a good bottle of whiskey." He waved his hand dismissing the prospect. "Don't want no pills."

"Try it," Gordon said grinning. "Might be surprised. The man told me they would make me feel better than I've ever felt before. Now that might be a *wee* bit of a lie. What's there to be a losin'? We're just goin' to try."

"Fine. I'll be takin' my chance with this candy. If you insist, who am I to tell you no." Scratch grabbed the candy-colored pill, tossed it down his throat then waited.

"What be up you thinkin'?" Gordon wasn't going to take his chances with the pills if Scratch had a bad experience. He'd heard about the pills back when they be livin' in that apartment in Edinburgh.

"Dinna do anything for me. Doesn't even taste good or fill my belly."

"Wait." He held out a hand. "Maybe it just takes some time. Maybe we be needin' more than just one."

Gordon did the same. He swallowed the pill. It took a few minutes for the effect of the pills to kick in. Euphoria. He felt detached from himself. Whirling in a vague pool of nothingness. The hunger in his stomach vanished. He didn't care about anything. Didn't care about finding a whore for a little dalliance. Decided if one pill was good, two would be better. Tossed the second one down his throat.

Conscious decisions were difficult. He felt dizzy. Disoriented. Floating on air. Felt different, as if his body wasn't connected to his head. Didn't think anything he took would be different than when he drank too much. This sensation wasn't the same. Figured he needed to get some place safe while he could still walk. "Scratch," he spoke while he tried to balance himself. "We should find our tent. You remember where it is?"

"Yeah… Think I do. It's over that way." He pointed in what Gordon thought was the general direction.

The two stumbled their way along the sidewalk careful to stay away from the street. The two did find the tent. Staggered inside.

Gordon was happy. No pain. No thoughts of going home. No hunger. He could get used to this feeling that nothing mattered. A couple pills remained in his pocket. He thought he'd take them too, as soon as he could move.

~ * ~

"You took Phoebe to her room? Trust you didn't linger there very long." Ruby spoke, focused on her son. He grinned at her. Knowing his mother's curiosity was meant to protect Phoebe from him. Phoebe didn't need protecting. Cole didn't intend to do anything Phoebe didn't wish for.

He lifted his shoulders for a short breath while he tried to figure out what he could tell his mother, along with what was too much for her to know. "Long enough," Cole said, sidestepping his mother's question. Before Cole left Phoebe, he kissed her long and sweet. Touched her tongue with his. Heard her breathy whisper of desire ripple into his mouth. This was the most intimate they'd been. She melted into him, smooth and warm, reminding him of honey heated by the sun. He touched her cheek. Her flesh was silken, soft. He imagined she was ready for more. She was compliant, eager to have him hold her hand, wrap his arm around her. She liked him to kiss her. Touching her intimately with his tongue was more than he planned today.

At her door, they talked for a while. He leaned against the frame while he studied her posture. Phoebe was beginning to open up to him. Told him things about herself. Private things. Spoke of her father. She didn't care for the man. Told him she wasn't positive he was her biological dad. He liked the fact she told him things no one else knew. She missed her mother, who passed away when she was seven. Her aquamarine eyes reminded him of the color of the Mediterranean on a hot summer day. He enjoyed the knowledge she wanted to marry someday. Have kids. The trip to the wedding boutique brought on that topic of conversation. He set his sights for the marriage in two years. She'd be twenty. If she asked for more time, he would give her whatever she needed. He hoped she wouldn't ask for the concession.

"Kissed her, did you?" Ruby asked, a sly smile on her beautiful face. "Was it as good as the smile on your face is telling me?"

His mother delved into notions she had no business asking. She understood that fact. Did it anyway. He imagined she would be able to read a lot by the expression in his eyes. He'd never been able to keep secrets from his mother. She was far too intuitive. "Not that it's any of your business, mother. Kissed her, yes. Need to bind her to me in ways she won't want to break. Make certain her attention doesn't stray to some other man."

"It won't. She senses herself with you. Is she a shifter? Do you know that yet?"

He poured himself a drink. Offered one to his mother. She declined. He sipped. Savored the brandy. In time, Cole meant to relish all of Phoebe. Too bad she was so young. "Don't know for certain about Phoebe. Time will tell. What I do know is that Dallas is one. A shifter. She's fighting the fact. Rafe wants to teach her more. She's telling him a resounding no to learning. Could tell those two argued silently about her shifting most of the way home. Glad they came together about the wedding. The sooner those two find some relief from the tension that bristles between them the better off everyone in their vicinity will be. Rafe has taken my advice. He hasn't made love to her. He's torturing both of them. I'm not going to do that with Phoebe. When we are ready to come together physically, we will."

Ruby tapped her nails on the arm of her chair. He was the focus of her gaze. "So, Dallas is a shifter. Doesn't come as a surprise. Suppose the ability to shift jumped a generation. Unusual, but I've been told it happens. Both her grandmother and her grandfather could change to a cat. Seems our little girl has talents she doesn't know about. Wonder who's going to win this argument."

"Rafe." It was obvious to Cole that Rafe wasn't about to give into Dallas' fears. "He wants her to reach her full potential. Doesn't want her to be afraid of anything about herself."

"Tell me more about Phoebe," Ruby encouraged.

Cole was hesitant. "My mate does have aspirations beyond marriage. She told me she'd like to become a nurse. Also told me she didn't get accepted into the university. Says she's not a good student. Doesn't much like books. She enjoyed sports. Loves to swim. Finds volleyball a nice challenge."

"You think she's serious about nursing? You could help."

"Don't see how. Can't change her grades. I'm not certain that was the complete truth. Imagine she was trying to impress me with the subject. Would rather she remain in Carnoch where I can see her every day as well as court her."

"Maybe that's for the best."

Cole understood Phoebe wasn't a chatterbox. Drawing her out of this self-imposed shell wasn't easy. Kissing her was a delight. Tasting her proved to be contagious. He didn't know how long he could keep his hands from exploring more of her secrets. Wasn't certain he wished to wait. In a few minutes, she said she'd meet him downstairs. They were going for a ride. This night there would be a full moon. Romantic. Charming the young lady would not be difficult. He knew the perfect trysting place. He meant to see how much she intended to give away of herself. Tonight, if she allowed him, he was going to take his explorations one step farther.

After checking his watch, he bent to give his mother a kiss on the cheek. "Have to go. I've a date this evening with Phoebe. We're going to take a moonlight ride. Walk along the stream. Hold hands. Kiss, if she's willing." Holding up his hands, he continued to grin. Seems since moving his mate into one of the tower rooms he couldn't stop smiling. "Don't ask what I plan. Something else that you shouldn't know about."

The all-knowing smirk on his mother's face told him she guessed more about his intentions than he wanted. She'd always been a person who was willing to seize the day. Didn't like putting anything off. "Enjoy your evening with your mate. Don't overdo, be patient. Don't frighten her. You've got time. Proceed with caution. Damn the torpedoes and full speed ahead is not always the wisest tactic when courting a young lady."

"From what I've heard that wasn't the gist of your advice to Dallas. Told her not to waste what time you have with your mate. Never know what tomorrow will bring. Which is it?" He sauntered to the door. his hand on the knob. "Rest assured, I'm not going to force her to do anything she doesn't want to do. I'll take all my cues from Phoebe."

He was gone. Heard the sound of his mother's quiet chuckle as he closed the door. Cole whistled while he strode to the other side of the keep. At the entrance to Phoebe's room, he stopped. Ran a hand through his hair. She must have sensed him standing in front of the door as it was opened, he saw her sweet smile. The sight sweet, intoxicating, he was pleased that she was his.

"You're early."

"I'm eager for that ride. Keen to be with you. Are you ready? I'm only five minutes at your door too soon." He looked her over. Ran his gaze along the length of her. The jeans she wore hugged her body to perfection as did the top. All her curves were obvious. The long length of her blond hair curled around her shoulders to dip lower. In this beat of his heart, he needed to taste the full lips that he kissed a few hours ago when he left her at her door. Phoebe's legs were long and slender. Ankles small as were her wrists. She was finely built, small boned. Fragile. He wanted to cup her sweet butt in his hands while he pressed her against his aching groin. Wished for her to understand how the sight of her affected him. Her sweetly rounded breasts inflamed him. Before now, he'd tried not to look at her body too close.

Graduation ceremony was last week. Phoebe was no longer in high school. He meant to see her more often as well as in private settings. Didn't understand his change of plans. He imagined taking his mother's advice about waiting would prove beneficial. Waging her reactions, he planned to move forward one second at a time. After they stopped to stroll in the moonlight, he would give her the one rule he would work with. The word no or stop should be in her vocabulary. If she ever said either word to him, he would cease whatever it was he was doing.

Cole understood he could never wait until this child-woman turned twenty to taste all of her. She was too ripe. Too succulent. She was his mate through all eternity. He'd known her before. The exquisite release he knew would be his when they joined, loomed in his mind. Realism hit him in his gut. He could never remain celibate for two years while he anticipated her twentieth birthday. Phoebe was his mate. She was meant to be savored by him. Two hundred years ago the age difference would never have mattered. They could have been wed today. He would have wed her the instant he identified her as his. The next second he would have made love to her. Would never have waited to bed her. Most McKennas didn't wait for the ceremony.

This wasn't two hundred years in the past. This was the present. Life along with rules were different. Cole held out his hand to her. She slipped her fingers between his. Allowed them to glide through. The sensation erotic. Evocative. Titillating every nerve he possessed. He ran his thumb along the underside of her wrist. Felt the slightest quiver. She answered with a small whispering sip of air. He tormented himself further.

She hesitated for a moment before asking. "Where are we going? You said we would take a ride." Out of breath, panting, she skipped along beside him. She seemed eager to keep up. He was impatient.

In such a hurry to get to the stable, he picked her up. Cradled her in his arms. Hers circled his neck pushing her breasts flush against him. He didn't wish to admit he was shocked. He was. "You're not wearing a bra. That's naughty." Even for his flirtatious Phoebe. "Do you have any idea what that does to me?"

She laughed, her smile sending heated sensation to every male part he possessed. "No…but…you could tell me. I like to be comfortable."

The sound of her laughter was low, deep. Throaty. Not a giggle or a female trill. He liked the way the noise vibrated the air. The laughter caught his attention then held. "Had no idea you were so innocent. Perhaps later this evening I'll explain a few things to you." Lord, the way she trifled with him. Sent out messages Cole didn't think she realized. She had to understand something about the male body. Didn't they still have classes that would tell her… Cole shrugged. She told him she wasn't very good with class work. Either she couldn't be bothered to listen while attending her sex education classes or she didn't understand what was being said. Wondered too, what she thought about when the teacher lectured. He never expected for his mate to be so innocent she didn't have any ideas about sex. Not in this day and age, not with movies along with books that portrayed so much that should be left private.

"I'm not innocent," Phoebe bristled with his comment, her eyes flashing sparks. To his ears, she sounded indignant. "Don't you believe it. I'm not naive. I'm not one of those girls who play as if they don't know anything. I do."

He kept the hoot of laughter from bellowing out against his better judgement. "Trust me, you are. My words were not meant as an insult. I rather like you just the way you are. Don't want to change or pretend something that isn't true. Your first reactions tell me a great deal more than your words. Do you ride?" he asked, wondering if she'd ever been on a horse. If she couldn't, he might need to drive. He didn't intend to dwell on the other connotation that could be construed from his simple question.

"I don't know."

He groaned. His horse needed exercise more than he did, "You've never been on a horse." With an inward sigh, he wondered again if it might not be better to drive to the spot he was thinking about. Driving was not what he had in mind this evening. A midnight ride seemed to be much more romantic. They could ride double, or…

"Never…I want to learn." She brushed her mouth with his. Smiled up at him. "I've always been good with activities…sports. Will you teach me?" she asked into his mouth as he brought the kiss to a different level. His tongue swept across the full bottom lip she presented him with.

He pulled back. How could he refuse a request when asked with the sweet touch of her lips against his? Phoebe initiated the kiss. That pleased him. "I'll teach you everything you need to know."

Phoebe was a quick study. Once mounted, she followed all his instructions. She didn't seem to have any fear of the horse or him. After they reached the glen, his hands around her slim waist, he helped her down. He'd been so caught up in looking at her breasts, he didn't notice her tiny waist along with the gentle flare of her hips until his hands were there holding her, wrapped around her waist. For a few beats of his heart, he held her against his length before he let her feet settle on the ground.

Cole needed to clear his throat to speak. "Let's walk." He needed to distance himself from the raging hunger her body next to his created when he lifted her from the horse. His arm around her shoulder, he guided her down a narrow path that skirted along a small creek. There was just enough room for them to walk side-by-side. He relished the feeling of her hip bumping his.

"For your first time, you rode well. I was pleased as well as surprised. You're a natural." His fingers dangled close to her breast. He wanted to reach out to touch her there. Run a finger across a nipple. He could see both. They were hard tight buds pushing against the fabric of her top. Before they returned, he meant to uncover those lush secrets of hers. Unless she told him no. That was as far as he meant to go this outing. He didn't wish to frighten her. He didn't think anything he could do would scare her, even changing to his cat. She was tenacious, up to everything he might put in front of her.

"While my book learning was never anything exceptional, I did do well in all the activities at school." She lifted her slender shoulders in a delightful feminine movement. He watched the tips of her breasts slide against the top she wore. Intrigued, he hungered for more. He was a man grown. Had been celibate since he realized Phoebe was his mate. There was no relief for him expect within her slender form.

"Activities are good," he murmured, his breath whispering across her ear. He touched the lobe with his tongue then tugged with his teeth. Felt her shivering response which wasn't derived from the chill in the air but the warmth of his tender seduction. He let the tip of his finger glide across the covered crest that protruded against the fabric. Caught her quick sip of air. "Activities are very good," he murmured his voice soft.

It seemed she tried to cover her reaction to his caress by asking a question. "Where are we going?" the words were uttered in a husky wobble.

"Nowhere in particular," he pointed towards the path. "Just walking. If you don't want to walk, we can stop." Cole wanted to be farther along the trail before he stopped to kiss her. They were too close to a place where anyone could find them. What he planned was meant to be private. He needed to hold her breasts in his hands. Savor each delicate globe for a few beats of his heart. Needed to learn her reaction.

"I want to be with you. I don't mind walking; I like to walk." Phoebe leaned into him. Her head rested on his shoulder, her hand on his chest. She moved her fingers as if doing some exploring of her own. He appreciated her curiosity.

A few minutes later he stopped. The creek widened here into a small pool of water. A fish jumped as if they startled it. Cole pointed to the crystal-clear water. The dying light of the sun turned the ripples silver. "When I was a kid, me and my sister used to swim here. We skinny dipped. You ever do that? Swim without clothing?" He didn't have long to wait for her reaction.

"Good God, no!" She turned to face him. Eyes wide. With her hands on his chest, she steadied herself. "You swam naked? That's a *wee* bit decadent. Don't you think? What if someone came along? I would not want anyone to see me…" Even with the waning light, he saw the rosy tint color her cheeks.

So, she didn't want anyone to see her naked. He wondered if that anyone included him. He hoped not. The soft color of her cheeks delighted him. "I did swim naked. No one intruded. We," he pointed to her then him, "could do it sometime. Not tonight, the water is too cold. In July and August…the temperature is refreshing." With his thumb beneath, he lifted her chin. His mouth framed hers. With her gasp of surprise, he traced her lips, sent his tongue deep inside her mouth. He'd kissed her before, but the contact was a soft brush of his mouth on hers. A flutter of breath, a moment of tenderness. Now, he meant to taste her secret darkness, savor the sweet mint taste of her. Teach her a kiss was so much more than a gentle caress.

He sensed her hesitancy. To his surprise she opened wider, accepting him fully inside her warmth. His fingers wound into her unbound hair, sifted through the length. Let the strands glide between the sensitive insides of his fingers. Silk to his touch. Fire to his soul. She pressed closer. Her breasts touched upon him. The firm round globes, tempted. Provoked every male part of him.

Phoebe tapped her tongue against his, mimicking his foray into her. He sucked hers into his mouth. Rubbed. Danced. His hands on her delicious butt, he pulled her close. Wanted her to feel his hard arousal next to her belly. Cole didn't know if she would understand the significance of what she felt. In time she would learn.

The kiss went on, deeper, longer. He couldn't taste her enough. Needed to feel more of her. He was drowning in his need. On fire with the tender lust she orchestrated without knowing. Hell…he wanted to strip her then come deep inside the heat of her. This evening, he might be in over his head. He wanted her so damn much. The thought flashed across his starved brain then sizzled through his famished body straight to his groin. His appetite voracious. He was hungry for Phoebe. His hands slid beneath her top. Met soft skin. From the back of her throat came soft feminine purrs of pleasure. He needed to taste then close the door on his needs before he took her here in the glade with the rippling water as a backdrop.

His hands traveled the length of her back then down to the top of her low-cut jeans. Her flesh was silken to his touch. Warm. Resilient. Soft.

The sound of her sigh of pleasure filled his heart. Touched an ache deep inside. Phoebe could be his right now. He sensed she would never tell him to stop. He needed her to say the word. She'd been put in charge of her destiny.

"Tell me no," he whispered near her ear. Nipped the lobe. Between them that was familiar territory. He brushed hair from her neck. Swept light, airy kisses down the slender column of her throat then to the hollow between her collarbones.

"Yes…" she murmured. "Like…"

He enjoyed the sound of her breathy yes. He wasn't going to stop just yet, unless that was what she wished. "Lift your arms, love. I need to see you." To his surprise, she didn't hesitate and did as he asked. Her arms were in the air. With quick fluid movements, he swept her top over her head. Let the fabric float to the moss at their feet. Looking at her, he couldn't breathe for a beat. The twin globes swayed, oscillated as she moved her hands to his shoulder to steady herself. Chilled by the spring breeze, the peaks were pebbled, hard. The shape of her breasts were flawless. Round. Firm. They were larger than he expected. Cole looked at those delicious twin globes then into her eyes. "May I?"

"Yes…" Her eyes were focused on his. Her lips slightly swollen from his loving caresses.

Surprised once more, she didn't realize what he wanted. She gave him *carte blanche*. "Touch you. Taste then savor the tips. Hold you in my hands." He looked down. Ran the palm of one hand across the crests. With slow precision, giving her time to stop him, he lowered his head. He wrapped his tongue around one turgid peak then the other. The taste of her charmed. Fascinated. All his senses hurled him into the tempest he would be hard pressed to prevent if she continued to allow him everything he asked for. Her scent was more provocative than anything he experienced. He knew he needed to halt. If he didn't do so soon, he would take this farther than he planned or was prudent. Before they left, he wanted her to feel him. Needed for her to understand how much he hungered for her. Prayed if she touched him even through his jeans, the contact wouldn't terrify her.

Cole held her hand in his, brought the palm to touch him. Phoebe looked up to him, questions in her beautiful aquamarine eyes. She trembled and moistened her lips. "This is…?" There was question in her voice.

"This tells you how much I want you. This is…" Cole had no clue as to the words he should use. He ran over several in his head, dismissed all. She should know. He didn't wish to be crude.

"This is what you…?" She touched her top lip with the tip of her tongue as if she was thinking.

He nodded. "We should walk some more. It'll be dark in another twenty minutes. Should be on our way home before then. If you weren't new to riding, the journey in the moonlight would be wonderful. Maybe another time. We can practice more. I can take you along with the horses into the hills."

Chapter Six

Dallas was both furious as well as irritated when Rafe insisted she try to change form. With no idea, other than the fact she could talk to him without speaking, he set himself full speed ahead into thinking he could force her into doing whatever he wanted. That wasn't at all like Rafe. He'd never even pretended to force her to do anything she said no to. With emphasis, she said a resounding no to changing form. Still the man bulldozed ahead.

Her temper flared when he tried to blackmail her into acting out his wishes. Said he wouldn't see Ruby or Father Richard unless she attempted to do what he asked. She was independent. Had been for years. She possessed a ready mind of her own. Realized what she wanted as well as what she didn't. Could think for herself.

Rafe never told her what to do. Never coerced or attempted to take charge of her life. Never tried to beguile her to his way of thinking. He'd been right to laugh when she told him she'd have to strip. The statement on her part had been ridiculous. She could admit to that fact now. Even if the notion of stripping was preposterous, things were different between them than before. The idea of taking all her clothes off while he watched, didn't sit well with her. She had no idea why she was hesitant. She just was.

After their meeting with Ruby, Cole's mother suggested she come to the keep until the wedding. Dallas didn't want to be away from Rafe. With him she felt secure. Protected even when she didn't need his protection. Rafe agreed with Ruby, taking the decision out of her hands. That wasn't something she appreciated. Another black mark on the list as far as she was concerned.

Against her wishes, all her belongings were transported to a room in the keep. When he moved them, with the help of Cole, she was out of the house speaking with Ruby. Cole's mother had this way about her. She managed to convince her moving was for the best. After the meeting with Father Richard, the date was set for Saturday. At that time, the ceremony was five days away.

She went with Rafe, along with Ruby, to pick up her gown. There was one last fitting. Ruby was shown how to pull the corset laces so the dress would fit her to perfection. The word was spread to all the Frasiers, Stuarts, and the McKennas as to when the wedding would take place. The celebration would go on in the clan tradition.

Despite her wish against informing her mother and father, Ruby sent an invitation to her parents. She never heard if they sent an RSVP. Dallas supposed that was good of her. Perhaps even the right thing to do. She doubted if either parent would put in an appearance at the ceremony. They weren't invited to participate. Rafe's parents would attend. Their appearance would have to be enough.

At the meeting with Father Richard, he spoke with few words about the ceremony where only family would attend. Rafe couldn't tell her anything more. He'd never attended the ritual. Both Cole and Ruby told her it wasn't their place. The good father must have told her all he felt she would be comfortable with. The words did nothing to assuage her fears. To no avail, Rafe tried to give comfort.

Now, she was in a tub in the room where they would be shown to after the final celebratory feast. They feasted this morning for breakfast. Yesterday evening, there was a huge dinner after the rehearsal. For the last two days, she thought all she'd been doing was eating. In this room, wine along with snacks were brought. Far be it for anyone to go hungry. Her dress was hung on the wall waiting for her. If she kept eating, the gown might not fit. The bouquet sat on a corner table.

Cole's sister, Rosalyn, along with Ruby were puttering around the room outside the bathroom. She could hear them talking. Dallas was shocked when her mother's voice filtered through the door. She heard Helen tell Ruby she brought a gift.

Furious, Dallas rose from the bath. There were too many people in the outside room. A towel was quickly wrapped around her. At her mother's sudden appearance, she was tongue tied. After drying, Dallas slipped on the same silk wrapper she used to wear before she disrobed for Rafe to paint her. She tied the sash, stalling for time, having no idea what to say to a mother who most of the time chose to ignore her. When she wasn't snubbing her, she was verbally abusive.

Stepping into the room, "Hello, Mother. Why are you here? You don't have an interest in my marriage. Never have you liked Rafe. Always told me I could do better than a poor, starving artist. Was never certain what you meant by those words. Rafe makes a great deal of money from the work he does."

Both Ruby and Phoebe gasped. Dallas imagined their start of surprise came from both the tone of her voice, coupled with the stinging words. She was angry. Angrier than she'd ever been.

Helen stepped back; her brows creased together as she seemed to assimilate what was being said. She opened one of the boxes she held then pulled out a necklace. "I wore this on my wedding day. The pearl necklace is for you. I hope you will wear this; it is special to me." Helen soaked in a breath of air, holding the oxygen for a moment. "I spoke to Rafe. He wanted you to have these." Her mother handed over another box, this time a small one. Inside were pearl earrings surrounded by tiny diamonds.

"You collaborated with Rafe?" This was one more shock to her system. A shock she didn't need. Her nerves were stretched thin as it was. Ready to snap at the least provocation. Why now? Rafe never cared for her mother. She supposed that because they would now be family, he reached out to stem some of the differences as well as hostility between them. The gesture would have come from the heart.

Her mother looked down before she met her gaze to address the question. "He came to me. Asked me if I intended to be at the wedding. We spoke of several things. I told him that when I heard of your marriage to him, I thought of the necklace. Showed the piece to him. The rest he did on his own. Since he couldn't be here now with you, he asked me if I would give the earrings to you. Something new for the bride. Believed the gesture to be thoughtful."

"I didn't think you would come." When Dallas walked out of the bathing room to see her mother, she felt blindsided even though she'd heard the voice.

"Ruby sent me a message. She thought we should be at your wedding. Asked me if I could put whatever issues there were between us aside for this special event in your life. I agreed. Ruby has this way of convincing a person to do whatever it is she wants."

"I get the idea. You were, in a sense, forced. If you're feeling uncomfortable, you don't need to stay on my account. I never expected to see you here." Dallas no longer understood her feelings which were shattered into two parts. On one hand she felt pleased her mother showed up for her wedding. On the other, there was still a huge rift between them. They never got along. She recalled all the days her mother called her fat. Urged her to try to lose weight. She attempted. Failed. Struggled again then again. She purged. She starved. All to no avail.

"I would like to be here for my daughter if she will accept my presence. Ruby is right. This is a special day. You might not believe me. I am thrilled you found the man for you." The words sounded as if they came from her heart.

"I see…" Dallas didn't understand the cascading emotions. The seeming change in her mother. "Cole agreed to give me away. I wouldn't change that. We practiced yesterday. I want someone beside me who can give me the confidence I need. I don't want Father to walk with me. I never saw that man as a father figure."

"I didn't expect you to change your plans," her mother replied, the tone of her voice cynical. "You've never been close to either of us. Now that you're marrying a Frasier, I suppose the distance will increase rather than decrease. The Frasiers have never had any use for the Shaws." At that point Helen stuck her nose in the air.

In her opinion, her mother's last statement was backwards. "Yes…" Dallas thought about the fact Rafe was a shifter. Wondered if her parents would understand that fact or assume he was because of some misbegotten rumors that weren't so ill-conceived. She imagined that in this small village, the gossip would state the fact that Frasiers were shifters just as the McKennas and Stuarts were. Bringing that up was out of the question. "Even though you are family, I don't want either of you at the second ceremony that is meant only for family. It's been so long that I've felt part of your family. I don't feel in any way connected to the two of you."

Her mother blanched at her comment. She nodded. "So, it's true."

"What? What is true?" This was where all hell was going to break lose if something wasn't done.

"Helen," Ruby stood beside them. She held her mother's arm as if she intended to escort her from the room. "You should go now that you've delivered the gift. There is no reason for you to dally. Dallas needs time to dress. The lady doing her makeup is here along with her hairdresser. The wedding should begin on time."

"You've arranged all this," Helen's voice was tight, menacing. Her mother was winding up to say something regrettable. "In lieu of the mother of the bride. I suppose you accompanied her when she picked out her dress too. I should have been asked. Given a choice."

Dallas cringed; her heart accelerated at the tension that never failed to be a companion with her when her mother was near. She was afraid her mother would cause a scene.

"Mother, please go. You're making this difficult for me. I don't need anyone here who is…who is," she wasn't sure what to say. Couldn't think of the words.

Ruby took Helen's arm, then with gentle finesse guided her to the door. "I will see you in the church. You will sit in the front as is expected for the mother of the bride."

After that was said, she closed the door, turning to Dallas. She frowned. "I'm not making any apologies for asking your mother to attend. Helen needed to be informed of the event and I realized you would never tell her." While Ruby talked, she poured Dallas a glass of wine. Handing the crystal to her, she said with a soft reassuring tenor, "You will need this. I will tell you true. I understand what Rafe spoke of when he asked me to inform her of the wedding. They will be at the church. Just as we have practiced, Cole will give you away. Phoebe will be your maid of honor while as you know, Rafe has a friend of his who will serve as best man."

"Phillip. Phillip is his name. We've known him for years. One of Rafe's best friends, yes." Phillip had always been a buddy. He understood their relationship. Always wondered at the distance between them. When he was told they were going to marry, he'd been ecstatic. Pleased that, after all these years, they figured out the true direction of their relationship.

"Yes, now that you remind me, I recall. Not getting any younger," Ruby murmured as she looked into a mirror, touching her graying hair.

"You're not that old," Dallas snorted, grinning at her. In the few weeks she'd known Ruby she was more of a mother to her than her own. Ruby was a friend who seemed to respect her needs. "I understand why you invited her. I just wish you hadn't."

"Now dear, don't let her snide words ruin your day. A mother must be at the wedding of her daughter. What you must keep in mind is that this is your day. Yours and Rafe's. Nothing else matters."

"Mother has never liked Rafe. Is it because he's a shifter?" Dallas held the distinct opinion that might be a true fact. As her new life with Rafe progressed, it seemed so many issues revolved around his ability to shift.

"Yes, you see, I'm not at all certain how to say the words. Rafe believes you are a shifter too. Neither of your parents are. Seems the trait skipped a generation. I realize you are hesitant to accept that startling fact as truth. What I can tell you true is that both your grandparents on your mother's side had the ability. I know that for an absolute fact. You will have to decide what to believe. Perhaps given enough time with Rafe, you will come to realize your abilities. If one takes a few minutes to stop to think on the fact, the ability to alter your form is quite remarkable. Don't you think?"

Dallas didn't understand how Ruby could be so positive about something that was always kept so private. While she sat for her hair along with her makeup, she thought on all that had been told to her between Ruby as well as Rafe. Spent time reminiscing about her childhood then her early teenage years with her parents.

It's true. All Ruby has told you is absolute fact. The fact you're talking to me, tells me you are my mate, and also that you are like me, a shifter. Given enough time, you will accept your fate. When you do, our lives together can take on another twist. Acknowledging the truth is always for the best.

Don't you have something better to do than listen in on my thoughts? I would appreciate some alone time. My nerves feel as if they will snap at any moment. Getting into my mind is not helping. Between my mother coming here and you harassing my thoughts, I feel as if I need to scream.

Don't you have anything better to do? It's not my fault you were talking right now. You reached out to me. All I did just now was answer back. You were looking for me. Seeking comfort. I would never deny you.

Nothing. Nothing to do. I'm letting other people do for me. They are fixing me up, so I look ravishing for your inspection. Didn't fathom why I was seeking you. Guess my doing so was in my subconscious.

I should let you go. The wedding starts in thirty minutes. Do hope to see you ravishing. However, you are always gorgeous to me. Don't be late. Father Richard has never enjoyed waiting on the bride.

What are you doing? I'd rather be with you than here. We should have eloped. We would be married now.

Hush, sweetheart. Don't say something so blasphemous. The clan would never forgive an elopement. For now, I'm also getting fixed up for your inspection. Need to look my best while I'm standing at the altar watching for you. Heard your conversation with your mother. Not surprised. You handled her well. Felt your anger when you first saw her, then your confusion at her presence. Not going to make any apologies for listening in on your conversation. Had to be done. Besides, I needed for you to receive the earrings. Telling Helen was the best way I could think of.

I know. While I can't block you from my thoughts, the people are done here. If you want me to be on time for the wedding, you need to let me go. I still have my gown to put on. Ruby needs to lace me into the dress. Cinch me up tight, she says.

Good that I'm not with you. I would take it off rather than dress you. That's for later on this evening. Looking forward to everything.

Don't understand why I'm shy. Never was before, when we were just friends.

It was then Rafe blocked her from his head, but Dallas realized he could still hear her thoughts.

When she next saw Rafe, he stood at the end of the aisle, hands behind his back, feet braced apart. He was resplendent in his kilt and all the traditional Scottish attire. His dark hair was tied in a cue. She was glad he didn't cut the locks to mark the occasion. Phillip stood beside him, grinning. Rafe appeared nervous. He wasn't alone with that sensation. She felt as if she might jump from her skin.

Now Cole stood at her side. Nodded when he lent her his arm. She placed her hand in the crook of his elbow. Phoebe shifted on her feet. Dallas thought Cole's girlfriend was more nervous than she was. It seemed strange that Phoebe was her maid of honor. She'd never had that many friends during her school years. Rafe had always been the person she would turn to. Rafe was the one she spent her spare time with. Other than Rafe as a friend, a few girlfriends flitted through her life. There was no flower girl or ring bearer. Phillip held the rings in his vest pocket.

The music changed.

Cole leaned down to whisper for her ears only, "This is it. Certain you want to marry that fellow down there? He might not be good enough for you." He chuckled, seeming amused at what he said. After his words, he squeezed her hand. The reassurance was comforting. Her stomach churned. Not so much because she was afraid of the marriage. She was terrified of the clan ritual that would come later. From hearing bits and pieces of conversation she recognized, for her, tonight there would be pain. She didn't like pain.

Watching from this distance, Dallas felt her love swell for Rafe. She would go through anything to be with him for the rest of her life, then into eternity, as he told her. Maybe she should do as he asked…try to change her form. Tonight, or the next if he pursued the notion. If she made the attempt, that would please him. Just as he wished to please her, she felt the same about him.

"I've never been more certain of anything." She nodded, thinking she'd waited a lifetime to do just this. Marry Rafe Frasier. She smiled, looking down the aisle to the man she would spend the rest of her life with. "I do want him. Yes, I do."

"You'll have to say those words to Rafe in a few minutes. Try not to stutter over them. You'll hurt his feelings."

"You've a wicked sense of humor, Cole McKenna."

"That is the truth."

Phoebe walked down the aisle, her steps slow just as they practiced last night at the rehearsal. "Phoebe is beautiful, you know. How long are you going to wait for her?" Even though Dallas asked. She didn't expect an answer.

"Not as long as I planned at first. She's in my heart as well as my soul. The seed has been planted. I need to nourish the feelings then watch them grow."

"That's what I assumed. You will seduce her. Won't you?" Dallas paused for a moment to look into his eyes. Not that it was any of her business. "You have already?"

"No. No, I haven't. Not yet."

Ahead of them, Phoebe stopped at the altar. She turned to the entrance of the church, her eyes were for Cole, no one else. She gulped air.

"It's our turn," Cole told Dallas as he guided her down the aisle. Once there, she handed her bouquet of daisies to Phoebe to hold. She stepped up to stand facing Rafe.

He held her hands. His were warm, giving comfort. She sent him a hesitant smile. *I've got you now and forever. Lean on me if you like. I'll keep you steady for all the days of our lives. Hold me accountable for your happiness. I will always put you first. We will grow old together. I should have realized what you meant to me sooner. Though…I also comprehend the way of our clan needed to be set right. The world needed to be put in order before we could have our day.*

I've needed you since I was a little girl. You recognized the fact ever since I met you, I've always leaned on you. When I needed help, I found you. When I needed reassurance, I came to you. You are my rock. I hope I can do the same for you.

You are so beautiful to me, inside as well as out. I've yearned so much for there to be a spark. Until you returned from the past, there was nothing between us except the friendship we shared from day one. Now, it's impossible for me to keep my hands to myself. I want you every time I look at you. When I watched you walking down the aisle to meet me, I imagined you naked.

Well…I did the same. Problem is, I've not seen you enough times with nothing on. My imagination has nowhere to go. I would hope that after we are married, you'll stop being so shy. She heard his silent hoot of laughter. The amusement at her words.

Tonight, you will. Will you shift for me?

Maybe, if I can. I promise to try. Ruby helped me see this from your prospective. I respect your wishes. Don't know if I'll be able to do what you ask of me.

At her admission, she heard the catch in his breath. Calm fell over him.

The priest's words wove their way into then out of her head while they spoke to each other through their minds. Silent, as well as sincere, they gave their vows to each other. Rafe squeezed her hands when it was time to say the words they practiced. They'd said them to each other in their minds. She repeated most of what she told him. He did the same. The earlier exchange gave them confidence.

In the end, the 'I dos' were said. They were pronounced husband and wife. There was no receiving line. The greetings, along with the congratulations, would happen during the celebratory feast after the clan ceremony. Even as maid of honor, Phoebe wasn't allowed to attend this ritual. Once the witnesses to their marriage exited the church, they walked into a large back room. It was special for this ceremonial. Chairs lined the sides of the room. The only people in attendance to witness this were the McKennas. Rafe's father attended too. His mother was absent. She declined the opportunity since she was not a shifter.

Dallas's hands were moist with sweat. Her body trembled, quivered with both her fear as well as anticipation of the sacred event. Her breath was shallow. Ruby walked forward with two white capes, holding them out as she approached. First, she wrapped one around her shoulders, the second around Rafe's. She backed away from them, smiling.

This is the way we were meant to be. During the ritual we will wear nothing. There will be nothing between us. You didn't know this. I'm going to help you remove your gown. After that, I will take my wedding finery off...or...you can do the task for me. I would be pleased if you undressed me.

I'm going to do what?

Undress me if you like. No one will see us. We won't even see each other. You will feel me. I will support you when you are weak. Just as I've done in the past. If you need me, I'll be there for you. You go first. Pretend you are getting ready to model for me. Understand I'm not going to look at you except to draw. There are no other designs on you. No one in this room will see you.

She tried to do as he said. Her hands shook. Fingers trembled on all the fasteners. When she touched upon his waist band, she withdrew, unable to undo anything more. With quick movements, he finished undressing then turned his attentions to her. A few minutes later, beneath the white cloaks, they were naked. This was intimate. More familiar than they'd ever been before. She swept in a huge breath of Rafe scented air. He stroked her back, soothing the shattering nerves.

Her nipples brushed across his chest. She felt the rasp of his dark hair against the hard tips. His hands surrounded her waist. Father Richard stood beside them. In a soft voice he began to chant. Dallas didn't understand the words. The cadence was soft yet firm. His voice rose then fell at varying intervals. The people watching whispered. Their words stirred the surrounding air. The hem of her cloak floated, swirling around her ankles.

She listened as if she might catch the meaning of the mantra. Unlike the first words said by the priest, these were all in Scottish Gaelic. She understood nothing of what was being said. The sounds fascinated her. She felt as if she was drawn into another place and time. Surrounded by something that only a few would understand.

A new dimension. She'd been part of a different dimension.

The drone of his words seemed to go on and on. In Rafe's arms she swayed. Her head fell against Rafe's chest. She smoothed her face on the warm flesh. Heard a low hum rumble up from his lungs. She enjoyed the feel of his short crisp hair touching her face, along with the closeness of their bodies. This was so nice. She didn't want to move. Didn't wish to listen to the rhythmic words of the priest. Closed her mind to everything except the feel of Rafe.

She liked the press of his body next to hers. Together they shared so much. Never anything like this. Rafe seemed distant; his mind preoccupied. She couldn't get into his head; didn't believe he was keeping himself from her at this time. Some other power or being took over his mind as well as all his thoughts. Dallas didn't like not being able to rely on him. She tried to shake the threatening presence from her head.

Seeming to sense something was wrong, Rafe pulled her closer. She felt his arousal press against her belly. Wondered how he would look if she could take a step back so she could peek at him. She gasped at the brazen thought ruffling into her head as if it belonged. She heard his light chuckle as he must have listened in on her thought. Her lashes fluttered across his chest while her knees didn't intend to hold her up.

Rafe... She cried out to him. Fear penetrated the deepest part of her. She needed to hear him talk to her. Needed the reassurance he always gave. Know the sound of his voice. The distance between them grew with each passing second. *No...no...!*

Hush, you're fine. I'm here for you. Don't hide from me again. Lean on me. I'll hold you up. You're resisting the chant. You need to close your mind to everything except me, as well as the words. I will do the same. Relax. Let it come.

I'm resisting?

Yes, I can feel you fighting, not me but the process. You are afraid. That's believable. Let me into your mind. Did someone warn you about this ceremony? Poison your mind? Counsel you against the ritual? Did your mother say something?

Not this afternoon, if that's what you're asking. You heard the conversation. I don't know about before...when I was a child. Can't remember that far back. Tears slid down her cheeks. He touched one with a fingertip. She tried to wipe them away but didn't have the strength.

You must open your mind. Must allow the words Father Richard is saying into your soul along with your heart. I'm worried what will happen to us if you fail to see the past. The woman always sees. The man cannot. There will be no reassurance we existed together before this moment in time unless you see for yourself. This task is yours. I don't know what will happen if you fail.

I'll try. I don't...don't wish to disappoint." She slid her arms around him. Breathed in deep of his essence. Rafe was always there for her. She needed to do the same for him. Needed to somehow find a way to become his rock. Roc Frasier… he'd also been there for her. He rescued her from the likes of Gordy and Scratch. All of this was interconnected. Rafe told her she was resisting the chanting. Closing her eyes, she allowed the words to flow over her and then within her. Concentrated on the mantra.

Hush, love. I feel you coming around. No longer feel the opposition that was there before. Your barriers are falling. Words are unbroken. I sense the chant is beginning to work. Let the refrain find its way inside you. It must touch your soul; the very essence of what makes you the person you are.

I'm sorry. This is all my fault. For once in our lives together I want to be here for you. To make you happy. To please you. I'm failing. Maybe this was never supposed to happen. I might not be your mate.

Hush. You're wrong on that score. Don't try so hard. I want you to realize that you always please me, Dallas. That's why we are here now. You need to understand that your mother poisoned you against this tradition of the clan. Taught you to despise, as well as fear, everything about the Chattan. I'm thinking now that the trait didn't skip a generation as Ruby insisted. I believe one of you parents is a shifter. Do you ken who that could be?

My father? That seems the logical choice. My mother would have made certain to belittle him at every turn, just as she belittled me. She despises the families who are well-known in some circles to be shifters.

That's a possibility.

A possibility? You think the shifter is my mother? Why would she poison me? Try to influence me against the clan if she is one of you? At that thought, her heart lodged in her throat to stick there. Nothing she knew about her life made sense.

Helen has been sabotaging you from the day of your birth. Of the two parents, Helen would have been the closest to you. I'm certain you played the little games all shifter toddlers do. You delighted in changing form whenever you were naked. She shot you down. Told you how horrible shifting was. Perhaps she used other words to dissuade you from your innocent games. I don't understand her thought process, if she grew up with shifters, was taught to revere the ability. Her parents weren't strange in that scope. We should talk about this later. You are going to see our past lives together. Are you feeling better?

No…I don't know. Yes. I imagine so.

Dallas closed her eyes, doing as Rafe asked. Let Father Richard's voice seep into her soul. She understood that was what was needed. The sacred words needed to take hold of her mind. They must lead her in the direction she was intended to travel. She wasn't alone any longer. Rafe was with her. He would never abandon her.

Once she relaxed, her mind gave into the gentle sway of Rafe's body with hers, and the room began to tumble. No longer was she afraid. With a start she realized all was coming to right itself.

This was the way it was supposed to happen. The ceremony would go on as planned. She no longer fought what the world planned for her.

~ * ~

Rafe felt the moment Dallas understood she no longer battled herself. She knew her mother was the driving force behind all her fears along with her failures. For too many minutes, he was terrified the words would not bring forth the desired results. If that occurred, all would be for naught. Dallas was meant to see into their past. She resisted with an iron will. He'd never sensed her so desperate to keep the force of the clan at bay. The reasons had to be deep seated.

Throughout the chanting he sensed her different reactions. Felt cold sweep through her. After that, her body stiffened. She held back with all the power she possessed. Instinct told him they were in trouble if he couldn't change her attitude toward the ceremony. When he couldn't get a reaction from her, his terror intensified. When he reached out, she didn't speak to him. Ignored all his gentle coaxing. He'd heard she would experience the earth changing, coupled with the fire that would fan flames. In the end, water would douse the flames. The ritual was pagan in nature. Yet…yet all the women before him had been through the same experience. They all survived. There were never issues keeping them from seeing the past.

All he had to go on was hearsay. He waited for the privacy of the wedding suite to be able to speak with Dallas about her experience. Experienced a dire need to learn everything. That part he looked forward to. The rest was something he'd rather not deal with. Tonight, he would hurt her twice. Sinking his claws into her tender flesh was not pleasing to him nor was breaching the fragile barrier proclaiming her innocence. Now, she pushed herself into him. Pressed herself against him. He experienced her entire body against his, all her sumptuous curves. Whimpered as time seemed to melt around them. They must be coming to an end. It seemed hours passed. There was no way for him to tell how long Father Richard spoke.

The chanting ceased. Rafe didn't know how long he'd been holding Dallas. Didn't have any idea as to how she would feel. He did know Dallas was weak. She couldn't support herself. Inside the room, there were no sounds. When Father Richard stopped, it seemed to him that all held their breath. He was holding Dallas. They had sunk to their knees. The floor was cold. Dallas' skin felt as if icicles coated her flesh. Her body drooped. It seemed to him as if she'd become boneless. Did not have the ability to hold herself upright. He heard the others leaving. Father Richard blessed them, and, after that, he too walked away. They were alone in the stillness of the chamber. He listened to her breathe. The warm air flowing from her lungs ruffled across his chest.

"Dallas," he whispered. "Dallas…talk to me. I need to hear your voice. If you don't have the strength to talk, reach out to me with your mind."

When he looked up, Father Richard stood beside him. Everyone had not left. He waited for some word of encouragement; something he could grasp to help him understand what was happening to Dallas. What occurred here had been unexpected. He thought all would go on as normal. Discovering what transpired between Dallas and her mother was important. What happened to Helen to make her despise the clan? Someone would know the truth. His first thought was that Cole's mother might shed some light as to the depth of Helen's hatred. Father Richard had been the parish priest for years. He also might know. If so, why didn't he give them some warning?

"I sensed much of what your woman has gone through. This was not easy for her. She is very weak. I told the others not to expect you at the feast for some time. No one will come looking for the two of you. It will take her more than a few minutes to recover. Don't rush her. If you want answers, come see me in a week or two. I believe I can shed some light on why this was so difficult. It has been years. At the time, no one wished to speak about what happened. Now, I feel the truth needs to be heard."

What truth? Oh, dear God, he needed to help Dallas first.

By now, Rafe was sitting, holding Dallas against him. Her body flush with his. If not for the slow steady beat of her heart, he would be worried. The soft swelling of her breasts as she sipped in each needed breath of air told him she would recover her strength. He would be there for her. Her strength. Her rock.

For Dallas this had been more of an ordeal than he'd ever thought possible. Both physically as well as emotionally drained, she was in need of reassurance. Rafe tried to reach into her mind. Found her thoughts all in a jumbled mess. Her imaginings flitted from the conversation they had about her mother, then to Ruby and how she wished Cole's mother was hers. He heard her speaking of Lainie then Roc. Dallas must have seen him in his cat form. Heard mention of the bonfire. Then the cold stream where she fished with Roc. His Dallas didn't like to fish.

They would talk later. For now, he needed to make certain she would recover as swiftly as possible. Even though the good father said he would inform the people celebrating their wedding they would be late, there was still the possibility Ruby or Cole would look for them to see if either needed help.

You did wonderful, Dallas. We did get off to a rocky beginning. We will discover the truth. The reasons behind your resistance. I promise you. Rafe stroked her back. Touched on each vertebra as he smoothed his hand along her silken skin. He imagined the wedding night, making love to her for the first time. *There is no hurry for you to wake up. Rest. Recover. That's your job now. Father Richard said getting stronger would take some time. He would make our excuses to the clan. I won't rush you.*

In his arms she stirred. Moaned softly. Created a gentle noise with the breath of her air. She rubbed her cheek against his chest. A soft purr rippled across him. Even like this, she aroused him. He smiled down, seeing only the white cape, and ran his fingers through her hair. Strands reminding him of a sunset sifted through his fingers. While he waited for her to gain strength, Rafe let his thoughts wander to those years when she was a child. He wondered if there was anything he could do to bring back her memories. Speculated the problems they might have if she recalled. Perhaps it was best to leave all her memories in her past. Maybe not.

He didn't understand why it seemed so important to figure out who the shifter in her family was. By the nature of their relationship, he was positive it was her mother. If so, why had she been so cruel to Dallas when she discovered her child with the aptitude? He didn't know if that was important to their lives. Dallas no longer wished for an association with her mother. She'd been adamant on that fact when they discussed sending her an invitation to their wedding. Ruby overruled their decision, seeming to sense something no one else did.

With all her soul, Dallas resisted the clan ritual until he spoke to her during the ceremony, encouraged her to lower her inhibitions. Her back had been against the wall. The mind can play tricks on a person. Maybe the mind didn't play games as much as put-up obstacles. Dallas had no idea how to break that impediment.

"Rafe...?" With her hand she pressed herself away from him. When she looked at him her eyes were dazed, sleepy. A half-smile formed on lips he wished he could kiss. That's, he thought, what Dallas would look like in the morning after waking up. Tomorrow he would know. This was the culmination of all his dreams.

"Yes. I'm here for you." He kissed her forehead then the tip of her nose. "You're waking up. That's good. As soon as you feel stronger, I'll get you dressed. What do you say? Are you hungry? Would you like to greet all those who came to our wedding. They'll be ready to congratulate us. Celebrate with us."

"No...I'm dizzy. Not yet. Your face is spinning, moving, coming in then out of focus. The floor won't hold still. When my eyes are open, I feel sick to my stomach." She placed her head back on his chest. He felt her lashes move as she closed her eyes. Her breath rippled across him. The tips of her breasts enticed. He sucked in a deep breath of Dallas scented air, hoping to quell the stimulation her tiny sounds, coupled with her body so close to his, created.

"Dizzy, you say. Rest. Hold on to me until you feel strong enough to dress." He continued massaging her shoulders, smoothing his hand down her back. He thought of more, of the wedding night, then reminded himself Father Richard told him this would take some time.

"I would like to get dressed," she told him. "Don't think I can do that yet. My legs aren't going to hold me up."

"Soon, we'll do this together." He intended to encourage as well as give aide. "I'll help you when you're no longer dizzy."

Rafe heard each breath, coupled with the sounds of the night. Father Richard left one light on when he exited. The room was growing chillier than before. His arms were growing numb. He thought a nice big lounge chair would work much better for them than the cold stone floor they sat on. There was no comfortable furniture in this barren room.

Not too many more minutes passed before she repeated the process of opening her eyes. Dallas looked much better. Color was returning to her face. The pasty white gone to a soft ivory. There was a hint of color on her cheeks. She no longer had that sleep dazed look. He pushed wayward strands of hair from her face. "Are you still dizzy? Do you think you can stand?"

"No, you aren't spinning. Neither are the walls. I don't know if I can stand."

He was ready to put the cold floor behind him. "Should we see if I can get you dressed? If we stay here, you might catch a cold." Her gown wasn't simple. Before the ceremony, he didn't have trouble unlacing the back. Pulling the strings taut so the dress would fit would be much more difficult. He thought of her lush curves falling from her gown if he failed to lace the back in the correct manner. He would need to ask Ruby for assistance once they were in the great hall.

"Hmm… I'm doing much better," she told him, failing to meet his gaze with hers. "I'm frozen. You're right." She pushed back as if to focus on him. "You must be exhausted, cold too. How long have we been sitting on the floor?"

"I've no idea. A while I imagine. At first, I was too worried about you to care. As you started to revive yourself, well, I started feeling my aches and pains. If nothing else, we should get up off the floor." He grinned when her cape fluttered open. Her breasts moved as she attempted to sit on her own. The tips were hard nubs, waiting for his mouth that was watering at the thought of tasting each one. This wasn't the time to get amorous. Their first time on a cold floor in a barren room, wouldn't do.

With her hand she groped to find her gown then her underthings. They were where they'd fallen when he slipped them from her body. When she tried to dress, numb from the cold, her fingers fumbled. He heard her embarrassment. Realized he would need to help her more than anticipated. Rafe reminded himself he was her husband.

"You're beautiful. If we had a bed right here, we could forego the feast waiting for us. I could make love to you just as I've dreamed about."

She scowled at him. He ran his thumb across her mouth feeling the moisture there left by the sweep of her tongue. "Can you help? I'm certain I can't do this on my own. I do think with your help, I can stand."

"Very well." He was resigned to the fact she would not be able to put her clothing on. Even if she could, he would still need to draw the strings in the back of her gown.

Rafe got her dressed. Decided he did an admirable job on the cords pulling her dress snug on her body. Still naked, he stepped back to give his appreciation to her in a slow gaze down the length then back to rest on the beautiful thrust of her breasts.

"You should, umm…" *This is a first. I'm dressed and you are standing in front of me naked. You are…you are more than I imagined or remembered.*

He hooted his laughter as she perused his body just as he did hers. He heard her thoughts. Appreciated the fact she liked what she saw. With as much speed as possible he dressed in his formal wear. Wished he had a pair of jeans along with a t-shirt to slip on before they left for the celebration. The kilt was a *wee* bit airy for his taste. Though that fact fostered ideas.

Before Dallas could protest, not wanting her to expend energy, he took the ground from beneath her feet. Held her in his arms. Twirled her in a quick circle to celebrate. She wasn't going to expend energy walking across the keep. He needed her recovered for the ensuing festivities.

Refreshed for the wedding night ahead of them.

"Rafe!" She cried out a protest but the small noise she made was weak. "What are you doing? Put me down." She pounded on his chest before clinging to him. Her head in the crook of his shoulder, she spoke, "I can walk."

"What does it look like? Doubt if you can take more than a few steps without crumbling to the ground. Don't want to risk that. So, I'm carrying you to the hall where food will be stacked from one end to the other. I'm starving. Thirsty. Need to eat. Dance. Cut cake. Give you pleasure. Not in that order, mind you." He was thinking of the clan tradition of giving pleasure to the bride during the feast. This was a tradition that had gone on for centuries. No one knew when the custom began. He intended to participate.

"I can walk!" Dallas persisted, even as she wrapped her arms around him before nestling her face against his chest again, bringing in a deep breath of air. *I like the scent of you. Love the way the hair on your chest tickles my nose.*

"You were having difficulty standing a few minutes ago. As I just said, I want my bride to be able to dance with me once we finish eating our fill. Need to ravish you in front of family as well as friends while we are sharing a plate of food. I'll feed you. That is also a clan tradition. The new wife will find her pleasure during the celebration."

"No!" *I won't allow that, Rafe Frasier. You cannot do something so decadent in front of a hoard of people. I would be too embarrassed to ever look at anyone again. Everyone in the hall will know. They will...*

"Yes...all true, nothing you can do about my plans. They cannot be changed. If you try to stop me, you'll make a scene. Everyone's attention will be on you...us. Which means..." He touched his forehead to hers. "They will all see and know more than you would ever wish. If you don't call attention to yourself, no one there will comprehend when..."

"I don't want attention turned in my direction. Is this tradition sacred? Is it something... well, if you didn't, people would still believe you did. Wouldn't they? We can pretend we did."

"I don't wish to pretend."

"You'll behave yourself?"

"You, my shy sweetheart, will do as your devoted husband wishes." He couldn't stop laughing. Tried to stall when her beautiful brows drew together, and her lips thinned. Soon Dallas would recover. She was on her way as they spoke. The two of them would dance. As acting mother, Ruby would take her away to prepare her for the wedding night. He would pace until he would believe he walked ten thousand steps. Drink too much ale as he waited. Listen to the vulgar wedding jokes tossed his way. Would enjoy everything.

Once she was ready, the men would hoist him onto their shoulders then carry him to the bridal chamber. He couldn't stop his blossoming grin. That moment couldn't come soon enough in his mind. The night he envisioned was still a long way away. He tugged in a deep breath of air before exhaling oxygen in a slow stream.

"I always behave myself. It's you I'm worried about. Can you keep from crying out when I give you your pleasure?" The question was baited. She might do something unexpected. Might say what she was thinking. Could blurt anything from that sweet mouth of hers. He would prepare himself for anything.

This was just what he wanted. He would seduce. Charm. Sweet-talk. She would have her first climax in front of the clan. Her face would turn crimson. He felt inspired. The rosy blush of embarrassment on her face always made him smile. Made him grin even more when his sensual words made the impact clear. She turned her head into his chest. Hiding from him. Protecting her emotions.

Stepping into the great hall filled with friends along with family, he carried her to the dais where a banner was draped announcing their marriage. The table was set. Candles and a multitude of flowers adorned their place. He set her down. Ran his fingers through her hair, letting the long strands sift between the sensitive flesh. He needed to feel the length tangled around him. The silken strands would caress. She'd let it grow since she returned. Her hair was longer now than ever before. Seemed she brought a piece of the eighteenth century back with her.

Unable to wait a moment longer, his mouth captured hers in deep breath-stealing contact. He shifted her in his arms. She held her hands around his neck. Helped him deepen the kiss by opening for his entrance. Her fingers glided through his hair at the base of his neck. With his hand on her sweet butt, he pulled her closer. Sent his tongue exploring farther inside the dark hot recesses of her mouth. His tongue glided across her teeth, touched sensitive inner flesh. Her soft feminine whimper delighted him. After he pulled away from her, her lips were swollen just a trifle. Moisture glistened where he kissed her. She was ravishing. Gorgeous. He was famished for her. His body jumped to life with the first touch of his mouth on hers. She responded as if she was also in need.

Can you stand?

Yes.

A waiter handed them two glasses of French champagne. "Hold the crystal flute up to our audience." As the people around them lifted their flutes high in salute to them, another cheer ripped around the room. Plates of fruit were set on the table as well as vegetables and meats, along with various cheeses. Sliced bread appeared. The Scottish fare would come later in the evening.

They each sipped the bubbly drink. He touched his tongue to the dampness the champagne left. Held visions in his head of dribbling the bubbly drink on her bare skin then sipping. He put that thought to the side to concentrate on these moments in front of him. He had a purpose; he meant to see to it.

Rafe pulled out her chair for her to sit. She settled into it with a deep breath of air. She appeared both relieved as well as exhausted. Dallas would recover. She was strong. He would give her a few more minutes before he began seducing.

Looking down on her, Rafe grinned. "You are still weak," he murmured in a quiet voice. "Drink and eat. Your strength will return. We have as much time as you need." He sat down beside her. The bodice of the gown had slipped down a bit. He must not have fastened the laces tight enough. She didn't appear to notice. That was good. At least she wasn't falling out of her dress. Now, he received a nice view of the tops of her rounded breasts along with the valley between. He wished he could see the rose bud color of her nipples.

Rafe watched her sip on the drink then nibble on the appetizers in front of them. She followed his instruction. His conquest of her was next. Letting the charming of her sweet body go farther into the celebration didn't seem a good option. While people were eating, few would notice what they did together beneath the table. He set his hand on her knee. Felt her jerk. She understood he was beginning the seduction. He ran his finger up to her hip where he let it rest for the moment. Caressed. The table was covered with cloth from the floor to the top of the wooden structure. No one would be able to see what went on beneath the covering. He had *carte blanche* with her beautiful body. Over his adult life, while he'd enjoyed other sexual partners, everything was new to Dallas. She was new to him. He'd never given her a woman's pleasure even though he'd touched her secret places. Tonight, he would touch as well as taste. Pleasure her until she fragmented in his arms. He needed to hear her scream his name.

As if she understood what he was about, she scooted away from him. Rafe followed with a soft smile, one he hoped appeared sincere. His hand never left her. He explored her sweetness. Swept his hand upward to cup one breast, brushed his thumb across the top before he slid it below the level of the table. He splayed his fingers on her belly. She squirmed. He caressed. She was so soft.

She was breathless when she spoke to him. Her words a gentle whisper. He watched as she swallowed a deep breath of air. "You are not going to do what you told me you were going to do. I'm not going to let you do that. I won't. Oh!"

Touching tender, sensitive territory caused the response. She would understand better if he showed her. "Alright, I'm not." His hand moved along her thigh down to her ankle. As his fingers traveled back, he brought fabric of her gown with him. She would feel flesh against flesh. His fingers would find sensitive territory. Behind her knee. He wound his hand around the inside of her thigh. Smoothed. Caressed. His thumb along with his fingers created gentle circles on the sleek muscles he found.

"Rafe..." his name was a thin whisper. "You can't...you don't...really. You don't want to do this. Rafe..."

He brushed his lips against the nape of her neck. Nipped. Felt her body quiver. His thumb hooked around the waistband of her panties. He didn't need to remove them, but he meant to leave the evidence of their brief seeking of pleasure for those remaining behind to witness. Her little thong bikini panties were quite easy to get around. All he needed to do was slip the slender string to the side.

"I should have left these in the church." He was surprised when Dallas lifted her hips without being asked. Her passion staggered him. He slid them the length of her legs, letting them fall on the floor. Now, she was naked beneath the gown. A condition he meant to enjoy. "Sip the bubbly stuff. Eat whatever takes your fancy." Rafe placed a strawberry on her lips. She bit the tip. He finished by popping what was left into his mouth. Sought another kiss. She tasted of champagne coupled with strawberries. A delight to his senses. He caressed her upper thighs. Moving ever higher. He was enchanted when she parted her legs for him. *So soft.*

"You cannot do this." Even while she protested, she accepted him. Allowed him access to her beautiful feminine parts.

"No one is watching." He slipped his fingers along moist folds waiting for him. Seeking his attention, inviting him to do whatever he wished. "You're anticipating me, prepared to accept the invitation of me within you."

"Everyone knows. That's why they are not looking our way. If you do this, I'll never forgive you." Her objections would never stop him. Even if her mind said no her body cried out yes. Didn't she just part her legs for him?

"True. I'm not worried about your forgiveness. By the time we are finished here, you will beg for more. You will never wish to let me go. Tell me you want me inside you. Reassure me you want your pleasure." With his hand, he pressed her legs farther apart. Orchestrating a slow, lethargic pace he moved his fingers between the soft creases at the apex of her thighs. Discovered the most sensitive nub deep within the softest part of her. Delighted in the movement of her hips as she responded to his invasion of intimate territory. She couldn't control herself. Her head moved back and forth against his chest. Pushing her nose against him, she gasped for air. Rafe continued the exploration of the feminine petals he needed to travel. Wet. Hot. Her nectar flowed. This was heaven. He continued to massage the tiny pearl of pleasure. Manipulated until she arched again and again. Throaty soft sounds undulated from her lips.

"Rafe...yes, I want my pleasure," she moaned. Her climax would come soon. This was everything he ever wished for. "Rafe...please."

This time he didn't mean to hold back. "Put your face against me. You need to hide your expression from anyone who might dare to look on what we are doing. Don't make a sound. If you do, all eyes will focus on you." His fingers slid into her channel then out. His thumb worked the tiny treasure. Penetrate then retreat. Slow then fast. The feelings would build then build some more.

She turned her face into him. Her breaths were short as well as fast. She put her hand on his wrist, holding him as if she thought he might stop.

He found a grape to tempt her with. Stilled the motions of his fingers. Watched the disappointment in her eyes when she looked at him. He wasn't going to allow her to spin away from him until he was ready. After that, a piece of cheese resting on a slice of ham was put in front of her lips. He fed her. Handed her the champagne. Made certain she drank.

The magic beneath the table continued. Slow then fast. Hard then soft. Insistent with need. If he wasn't careful, this orgasm he orchestrated might be messy as well as loud. Didn't know if she could handle noisy and untidy. He found more tempting flesh, soft skin. Beneath his hands she was all silk and satin so soft. Her passage was velvet to his touch. Once more he brushed his lips along the column of her neck. Touched the tip of his tongue in the hollow between her collarbones. She looked at him. He couldn't resist her mouth. Kissed her long, deep, with sensual passion that had been in check for years. He ravished the inside of her mouth with both fierce thrusts then soft ones.

A breathy sigh gave him pleasure. When he settled his hand on her belly the flesh retracted. Quivered with urgent need. He wanted the magic to continue. Saw the slight glazing over of her eyes. Needed to speak with her where no one would hear their thoughts.

Do you like this, lass? Should I stop? Leave you needing more? Shall we finish what is started. A precursor to the night.

You should not be doing this here, during the feast. I protest.

As I told you before, it's an institution. If I failed in my part, we might have bad luck. That's it. Open your legs wider for me. Give me greater access to those parts of you that will go up in flames when I fondle them. Let me explore all of you. Touch all those wonderful erotic parts of you. There you go. You must remain open to all possibilities.

You are...you are making me feel so...

Good...yes, wonderful...more than magnificent.

Rafe continued his tender assault. A gasp. A breathy whisper. Broken splinters of disjointed words. Sighs of ecstasy. All floated in ribbons encircling them.

Look at me, sweetheart. I want to see you when your shatter into thousands of shards.

His kiss stole more of her breath. His tongue swept then rubbed. Danced. Played while she joined him. She responded by sliding her tongue along his, reaching into him. He sucked on hers, bringing her deeper inside his heat. She writhed. Her hips bucked, lifted, searching.

I'm on fire. I feel as if you've put fire breathing dragons inside me and they've unleashed the full force of their power. I...

The first pulses of her raw urgency set her hips moving. His roaming fingers took control. Her body quivered as she tried to hold back the explosion of her senses. Stopping what he created would be impossible. He would make ceasing impossible. He sent two fingers inside her. Felt the clenching of her muscles. The milking of her sheathe swept along his fingers. She pulled herself away from the kiss. Buried her nose in his shirt.

Don't cry out. I understand you will have to... Don't make a sound. Keep the noise inside you.

I can't...I...!

Her teeth sank into his shoulder. Through the fabric of his shirt, he felt the bite. She wasn't quite there yet. He would have to increase his efforts. *Good girl. Take a hunk out of me. Suppose I deserve the bite considering what we are doing here. You are a delight to my soul. My heart as well.*

Shocked when her hand pushed against his groin could never describe his emotions. Her hand traveled up his leg just as he did to her. She learned fast. She tugged on his drawers. Lifting his kilt. *Little witch. I wouldn't have this any other way. You're going to give to me what I gave to you. Maybe I will roar out my pleasure. It's not tradition for the bride to seduce the groom.*

Thought men didn't wear anything under their kilt. Believed you would be naked. I'm disappointed. Well...I never saw you when you dressed. Can I touch you?

God yes!

Her fingers closed around him just as she jerked, shattering into her own climax. She was shaking. Still tried to arouse him. Her hands moved up then down. Slow then fast. Good God, he was just about to spill his seed on himself. He should have more control. He pulled in a deep breath of air. Shattered. The seduction was over. She milked him for all he was worth. This moment was one he would remember for the rest of his life.

Limp, almost as much as she was when they were on the floor after the ceremony, Dallas lay against him. He heard the steady beat of her heart. The fast intake of breaths again then again as her body attempted to calm itself. He pulled a napkin from the table to wipe away the evidence of her conquest. It had not taken much for her to bring him to his release. For too many weeks, he'd been on a tightwire. Looking at her, talking to her, everything about her never failed to awaken him.

Is it over now? I don't think I can do this again; I'm shaking. Couldn't lift anything. Can't eat. You will need to wait for that dance you spoke of.

We should eat more. The waiters are serving dinner. All our favorites plus some normal food for those who would rather have...

I'm not hungry. How long will we need to wait for the first dance? Can I dance with Cole since he brought me to you? His role is the father of the bride. Would you mind?

I don't mind. Nonetheless, you should try to eat a little bit. The food is wonderful. We will be up most the night finding our pleasures. I believe the women will have decked out the room for us. We'll have plenty of food as well as drink. We won't starve. Do what is best for you.

The rest of the evening slid by. They danced. Cut the cake. Dallas danced with Cole once. She was still fatigued from the rigors of the ceremony. He wasn't sure how long it would take her to return to normal. Not much time passed before Ruby came for his bride and whisked her away. He received a slap on his shoulder from Cole. Some of the other Stuarts and McKenna's gathered around him to gest about the wait for his bride. In the McKenna fashion these celebrations never changed. Nothing was ever different.

Tradition.

No male comprehended what went on behind the closed bridal chamber with the women. The women didn't share, not even with their husbands. All the men asked at one time or the other about what was said…what was done. They were hushed then told that what happened was for women's ears, not theirs. Men all had their secrets. The women would keep theirs.

Cole brought him more champagne and he leaned against a pillar to watch the celebration. Impatient to be brought to his bride, the small talk went over his head. When Cole tapped him on the shoulder then pointed to the stairs, he jumped.

"I believe the moment has arrived."

Rafe swept his tongue across his parched mouth. His body strengthened with eagerness. He just had a small glimpse at the mercuric release of her passion. Now he would taste more. The men surrounded him before they lifted him high. Carried him on their shoulders up the long sweeping steps to the door. Stopped in front.

With his mother by his side, Cole opened the barrier. Inside, they set him on the ground. In seconds, he stood in front of his wife. He wore only his kilt. His feet bare, he wiggled his toes in the plush carpet.

His breath caught at the sight of her, clothed in silken lingerie of the palest blue. She was perfection. Words wouldn't form. The men along with the women slipped from the room.

We are alone.

At last.

~ * ~

"Dallas married that man, Rafe Frasier. After all the effort against such a thing, she's wed a shifter. What are we going to do about that? I'd like to know. What do you intend?" Helen paced the confines of their small living room. She was terrified for her daughter. Ever since John came into her life, he threatened her with the life of her only child. She'd been made to denigrate shifters. By her words, he took a part of Dallas from her. Took a part that should be held in reverence. She didn't know why Rafe came to her with the earrings. Was pleased that he did. That fact gave her a chance to speak to Dallas on her wedding day. To be just a small part of her life even though Dallas didn't wish for her to be there. Helen couldn't blame Dallas for her resistance to her.

John, the only parent Dallas had really known, was drinking whiskey. He sat back in a large, cushioned chair with a bland smile on his face. Unconcerned. "I don't give a god damn what she's done. She's always been a thorn in our side. Damn shifters," he muttered. "They are good for nothing. A blight on humankind. That's what they are. Your husband…first husband, ruined my life by taking you to wife. Wanted to have you from the first moment I saw you. I sent the man away so I could have you. He's not coming back. I understand you've prayed for his return. He can't return from where he's been." John held up his hands to stop her retort. "No, I didn't kill the freak. I promised you I didn't."

"I'm not admitting anything to you." Helen never said anything to the man who beat her if she disagreed with him. Of course, she prayed for her real husband's return. He would correct all the wrongs this man did to her along with Dallas. She loved her true husband. Despite the appearance, she loved her daughter. Her husband was her mate, not this man. Her first husband claimed her. Helen spoke through her teeth. "My husband is gone. I've accepted that for a long time. You took his place. No one realizes you are not my husband. We never married. Don't know how you did it. Made the transition with so much ease. Even my parents never knew who you weren't."

"I despise those damn claw marks on your shoulders. What the hell do they mean? I'd like to know." He was sitting up now, his drink on the table.

For Helen that was a bad sign. If she didn't act fast, she'd feel the back of his hand. "They don't mean anything," Helen was quick to say. She felt certain Ian would return as soon as he could find a way home. He was her savior, the man she loved. He'd been gone so long now. Even with all the faith she could stuff into her head, she feared he would never return to right the wrong done to both of them.

John was correct in his assumption. Every night, she did pray for Ian's return. She despised this man. This despicable person who called himself her husband as well as Dallas' father. He wasn't either. She loathed everything he made her do where Dallas was concerned. He'd stood over her time and again when Dallas, with the innocence of a toddler, changed form. Insisted, she make certain Dallas realized she should never change her shape. Altering who she was, was evil. The devil made shifters for his use. Drummed the notion into her little innocent mind.

"Liar. I understand claiming. Heard enough talk. So the man, my near twin, has claimed you. That means the two of you will meet again in another life. Not if I have anything to say about that occurrence." He stood, his hands fisted at his sides.

She backed away, afraid he meant to use them on her. He would strike her given any opportunity. He told her he loved her. In truth the man hated her. "What did you do with Ian? You led me to believe he didn't die. That you didn't kill him. Why can't he return home?" She was pacing again, stopping long enough to pour herself a glass of wine. She wanted to be at the wedding as well as in the bridal chamber. Needed to be with her daughter when the women brought her to the room she would share with Rafe during their first night as a couple. Remembered that day so long ago, when they brought her to the same room Dallas would share with Rafe tonight. Ruby guessed there was something amiss. Had the forethought to invite her to the wedding when her daughter didn't want her there. She couldn't tell either Ruby or Dallas the truth. If John ever found out, he would beat her until she couldn't move for a week. Would never allow her to seek medical attention. There would be too many questions. Either that or he would find a means to hurt Dallas.

Ruby McKenna might be someone she could confide in. The woman might not keep the secret. Her husband Aaron was gone too. Cole was also a determined man, the head of the clan now. They kept the clan together. Solved problems that were family difficulties. Sometimes acted as both judge as well as jury. That was the way of the Clan Chattan. What then? John would kill Dallas. He threatened her life so many times she lost count. Threatened her if she didn't demean her daughter. It was because of this horrible man Dallas despised her. Didn't want anything to do with her. Dallas didn't even want her at her wedding. Moisture clogged her throat. She pushed the tears back where they belonged. If John saw her tears…

For Helen, there had been no choice except to go along with John's wishes. She had no one to help her, no one to turn to. Ian always told her she was stronger than she thought. That was a long time ago when he'd been around to give her strength. His words weren't true. She tried to heed them. Tried so hard. Fear encapsulated her. Anxiety for Dallas drove her to be John's pawn.

She was weak.

Her daughter was strong. Dallas was in love. Her daughter found her mate. That fact would bolster her. Helen had never been so relieved to discover some of what happened to her sweet one. The baby she rocked in her arms would be happy. She understood that now. Wished with all her heart for Dallas' happiness.

She would need to take solace in that knowledge.

Chapter Seven

Dallas looked to the floor. Saw her bare toes peeking out from between the sheerest material she'd ever seen. The fabric of her robe fluttered around her feet. She recalled all the wonderful sensations Rafe orchestrated less than an hour past. Just thinking of them caused her body to thrum to life. When she looked up, he was grinning. Swallowing the lump in her throat, Dallas tried to smile back. She didn't have to hear the words to understand Rafe heard her thoughts. Heat rushed to her cheeks. She brought her hands up to cool her face. His soft chuckle sent more heat flowing. She knew her cheeks got redder.

Without speaking, Rafe stepped forward and splashed wine into two large crystal goblets. "Shall we sit?" he asked while he handed her a glass. "I'm exhausted from pacing while I waited for Ruby to show herself at the bottom of the stairs. How about you? Are you still weak from the clan ritual?"

Nerves rifled through her. Stretched to the snapping point. Her stomach churned from sensations stripping her. She upended the glass. Some went down the wrong way. Her cough sent a few drops of wine into the air. She sputtered, trying to collect her thoughts. Embarrassment heated her more. Rafe set his hand on her shoulder. She felt the warmth of his hand through the delicate fabric of her lingerie.

"Nerves are fine. I'll do all I can to help you through the first part of the night. After that, there will be no more fears." He sipped the tiny drops of Bordeaux from her lips, her chin, then along her chest.

"I don't want to be nervous," she told him in all truth. She wished she could be brave through this first joining along with the claiming. "I've never…"

She started for a chair thinking to sit. Rafe must want to talk. She didn't know what about. Being a bundle of nerves after the interchange with the women, who didn't tell her anything, she couldn't think straight. She'd thought they would explain the claiming. Instead of clarifying anything, they told her Rafe would be the person to inform her.

Before she could sit down, Rafe took her hand then tugged, pulling her toward him. "I wish to sit with my wife. Together. As one. Not apart, in any way. I need to feel you." He looked to the large, overstuffed chair. "On that chair. I need to hold you again."

"I see…," she said but she didn't see anything at all. "What do you want to do? I thought…" She thought she would get this ritual over with as soon as possible. Believed she didn't want to worry about the claiming or the first time with him. True, he gave her pleasure. True, he would do so again. Fact, he would cause pain.

She didn't like pain. Ever since she could remember, pain had been her nemesis. She held a vague recollection of her father hurting her. The thought surged into her head. Remembered her mother's tears as she pleaded with him to stop spanking her. Heard her father say that every time she shifted, he would punish both of them. No that couldn't be right. She pushed the bizarre image from her head. The memory faded. Her frown didn't.

"Let's relax," Rafe said, his voice soft. "I want to tell you a few things you should understand before we do anything else."

Rafe was sitting, patting his thighs as if he expected her to sit on his lap. She did want to be closer to him. Sit with him holding her. She swallowed the lump in her throat while she debated the pros and cons of doing what he asked. He wasn't going to toss her on the bed and do whatever it was he was going to do. Oh, she understood part of what he intended. Classes at school taught her the basics about sex. Movies taught her a bit more. Her mother never told her anything. Of course, her mother didn't talk to her. Helen didn't have use for her. Maybe it was her father who hated her. Might be both.

"A few things about what?" Dallas did step closer to him. She found herself between his legs. His hands rested on her hips. They were warm. His hands were always warm. Tender. Creative hands. Hers were cold all the time, as were her feet.

"Sit." He encouraged with a soft voice. His hands roamed higher.

Encircled her waist. This wasn't a command, but a suggestion that held merit.

Dallas could see the glimmer of his steel-gray eyes. When he turned her, his hand curved around her butt. Rubbed. The ache he created with every caress grew. Deepened. Her knees felt weak.

"Delicious, I need to taste you here where my fingers are," he murmured with exquisite softness. "Babe, we aren't going to do anything right away. I'm not going to ravish you, toss you on the bed or rip off your gown. I need to give you pleasure first. This time I want to see your eyes when you shatter into hundreds of tiny pieces. I don't wish for your face to be buried on my chest."

The gasp of air startled her. Rafe chose not to return her thoughts when she was thinking them. Now, he did. In her mind, she didn't get as far as the ripping off her gown part. Nor did she think ravishing, though the word was a close second.

"What did you want to talk to me about?" She did sit. Felt the hardness of his thighs. Drank her wine as if that would give her comfort.

Rafe handed her a strawberry. "Take a bite. Eat a couple. You didn't eat much at the celebration."

"Too nervous, still anxious, close to panicked. I will be anxious until all is finished here," she murmured while she chewed. The berry was sweet, delectable. Juicy. Maybe she should do as he said. Eat. "I want to do this claiming business and after that be done with all the so-called duties. I need to forget the notion of pain. I'm afraid of pain." She ate another berry. After that another one. Drank more wine. Rafe refilled her glass. Her stomach rolled over. He placed his hand on her thigh.

"When I walked into the room tonight, your thoughts were clear," Rafe murmured in a low voice. "Now, they've spiraled in a different direction. Not pleased with the tenor now. What will it be? Should we just get the formalities over with? I, for one, would rather proceed with slow caution. I don't like the idea of 'just getting it over.' Your pleasure is important to me. How we proceed this evening will set the stage for our future."

"That's because you won't be the recipient of the pain," Dallas shot out, angry with the situation, yet furious with herself for being so petrified of something that all wives of shifters go through. On some level the terror seemed over the top.

"If it's any consolation, rumors have it that if the woman is also a shifter, the pain is never so intense. I do believe you are a shifter, Dallas. That is the reason your mother has tainted the way you think about us. Helen has orchestrated this irrational apprehension."

He confirmed her fear. There would be pain. Dallas cringed. "I'm afraid of pain. This entire night I'm afraid of. That's why…"

"I find I'm beginning to change my mind. The sooner we get this accomplished the better you'll feel. Until that happens, you won't be able to enjoy the evening. Besides, I wish to know what you saw during the ritual. Rumor has it when I claim you, you will also revisit parts of our past lives. There will be more for you to tell me." Rafe smoothed his hand along her back. Touched upon each vertebra with a fingertip. The tender caress sent vibrations to all of her. Shivering, she hunched her shoulders. Her neck ached. She was stiff from the tension surrounding these moments with Rafe.

"Yes, to the deed…" She caught her lip with her teeth before staring into his eyes. "I…that's not what you meant. Is it?"

"Not quite. You want to make this into a race. I'm not willing to do that. Enjoyment is what we should be after. Still, to take time discussing this, will only prolong the event. Lengthen the time your nerves will be spinning out of control, snapping with fear."

"Easy for you to say. Enjoyment. I would like the enjoyment too." If he continued in the delightful way he did earlier, she would relish the sensations. There would be pain too. She also wished to see them in their past forms.

He didn't hoot though he did laugh at her words. "Do you imagine I like giving you pain? You are my life mate. Mine from now till eternity. We've done this in the past. Will certainly do so again in the future. Perhaps in the future you will not be so afraid. Perhaps tonight if you're willing, we can work on your shifting. You can play with the notion. Try to shift. I'll give you pointers."

"I…no you would never like your role if it caused pain. I do know you, Rafe Frasier. Almost as well as I know myself. If you wish, I will try to shift. For some reason I don't understand, I'm beginning to believe you about my heritage."

"…and I know you, Dallas Frasier. You are brave."

"I have no courage."

"Strong."

"Weak when it comes to thinking about pain."

"Seems we've come full circle. Now, we're back to pain. Not strong or courageous." He cupped her head, drawing her close. Her shaking hand curved over his shoulder. He closed his hand over hers, giving the fingers a gentle squeeze. "I don't want you to dwell on that aspect of the evening."

Dallas understood by the expression in his eyes he meant to kiss her. His lips touched upon hers. She gave him entrance, knowing the pleasure his kiss would give her. They played together. She delighted in the magic created by the shared, intimate contact. Wished all they did tonight would be this pleasant. Closed her eyes while he held her breast in his hand, seeming to weigh the globe. Slid his hand along the ladder of her ribs then back to continue the tender glide of his fingers around her breasts. With the sensual attention, she couldn't think.

When he pulled back to study her, his eyes were dark pewter. The expression hot. Demanding. He'd told her he wished to savor her. Devour all of her. Said he was hungry for her. From his kiss, her lips were moist. Tender where he caressed. She was hot. A breath of air staggered into her lungs. She was back to that weak state he created with the gentle assault of his lips on her mouth.

"Did that cause pain?" he asked, his voice husky with what she assumed was hunger for her. His thumb brushed across her damp mouth then beneath her chin to lift it. She could hide her eyes. "I… would have you tell the truth."

"You know the answer. There was no pain." He did understand what he was about. Though the kiss was hot, evocative, he touched her with gentleness. "A shared willing kiss does not cause pain," Dallas blurted a truth she'd never intended to tell him. He would react to the words. She would need to explain. That was something she was loathe to do. He'd told her shifters were always gentle with their mates.

"Willing?" One eyebrow rose a fraction as he seemed to digest her words. The question was stark. Hard. Rafe expected an answer to that last part. "Who have you shared a kiss with that caused you pain?" His eyes blazed while his brows drew together. He didn't mean to let her get away with an evasion of the question. "I don't like to think of you kissing another. I want to have you all to myself."

Dallas knew him. She saw the anger in his expression. Telling him was something she never intended did not suit well. This man she loved with all her heart knew everything about her. He understood she'd found no one to consider as a date, let alone anything else. Men kissing her had been rare. To no avail, he would seek revenge. She caught her lip between her teeth, searching her mind for a feasible answer. She could tell him this information was not his business. Would do so if she didn't expect him to pursue an answer.

"Who, is not important. Not now, not ever." She set her gaze firm upon his, determined to convince him there was no need to pursue the answer. "It happened. I don't wish to speak of that event. It's in the past."

"To me it's important. I didn't know…" He was thinking. She understood he was trying to get the answer from her thoughts. She had no means of blocking him except perhaps to jumble hers to such an extent he wouldn't be able to pinpoint anything.

His mind was spinning, sorting out different scenarios. Whether she volunteered the information or not, he would discover the answer to his question. She gave up, deciding this would be easier if she told him. She could back pedal afterward. "Gordon…kissed me. I didn't like the feel. I was willing at first. After he touched me, my mind changed. Yes, he was rough. He bit me; drew blood. That all happened after I told him to stop," she blurted before she choked on her words. "He…it was after I hitchhiked. After I came here to see you. To tell you I was fine. He thought I lied. Thought you… So, he felt he could do what he wanted."

"I'll kill the man." His fists tightened on her hips. "Did he do anything else? Should I be more concerned?"

"I left the apartment we shared for the few days after he gave me the ride. I was stupid. What happened months ago is no longer of any importance. As you know, I've moved on…we've found each other."

"It was a willing kiss?" His anger didn't ebb.

"Yes, at first…until it wasn't," she bristled. Rafe didn't have the right to interrogate her this way. "I didn't tell you because nothing else happened. Didn't intend to ever see Gordon again. As you recall, we didn't know yet if what we felt that night meant anything. One kiss. A spark. I wondered if the rise of temperature I felt was a one-time occurrence. If I admit the truth, for me, the kiss with Gordon was a one-of-a-kind experiment. I wondered if I would feel that spark that was missing with us. At the time, I was insecure. Didn't understand what happened to me over the weeks I was gone. I had memories that were fading. Others that appeared so vivid and clear it seemed I experienced them. Some of those memories I decided were dreams."

Nerves stretching her thin, Dallas drank down the rest of her wine in a long gulp of need. Damn, she needed the wine. Had to have the fortification if they were to go on with this night. She didn't want to talk about Gordon. There was too much said already. When she set the glass on the table, her hands were shaking.

"I can't do this, Rafe. Not now. Can't think about those two horrible creatures. Not on my wedding night. What else did you want to talk to me about?" She hoped they would not find themselves sidetracked again. Thoughts of Gordon along with Tinley horrified her. "We need to find something pleasant to talk about or…"

Rafe held her. Set her head against his chest. Inhaled long and deep. *Don't wish to upset you ever. Especially not tonight of all nights.* She listened to the sounds from his body. The words he thought to send her way. Reassuring sounds. The beat of his heart. The steady breaths of air into then out of his lungs. His scent was spicey. His kisses tasted of the wine they'd been drinking. She wanted more of the same. Knew he listened.

The smooth caress of his hands reassured. They glided across her back, then the curve of her hip. "I wished to speak of the claiming. Need to explain to you what will happen. Will that be a good or a bad idea? Again, I don't wish to upset you."

"Do I want to learn what will go on before it happens? No. Neither do I wish to understand when. The claiming can be an unwanted surprise, not fearful moments awaiting the pain." The breath she drew into her lungs wobbled. She let the oxygen out in a rush of air.

"Let's just forget about what is going to happen. Think only of the ecstasy I will give as well as receive. There will be pleasure for both of us. Pain for both of us as well. You experienced some of that ecstasy at dinner." Rafe brushed hair away from her neck. Set his lips there. His tongue found tender places to explore, sensitive spots that sent her body pulsing with need. She ached. Her desire rose. Passion flamed. He pressed light teasing kisses down the column of her throat then back to mold her lips with his.

She felt his mercuric touch. The sensual press of his hands. The magic his lips along with his fingers created. Rafe was an artist. Drew pictures on her body with his hands. Sent heat along with the rush of her thirst for him. She needed more and more after that. She closed her eyes to allow all the wonderful sensations to course over her, through her. His hands, along with his mouth, orchestrated a tempest of raw hungry desire she couldn't deny. Need erupted. Flames ignited. Her sigh into his mouth seemed to be caught within his tender hold. He captured the air. Held on to the moan of hunger as if it was his. With gentleness he held her. Swept his hands along her body across sensitive places. Passion rose to a crescendo as his caresses found more evocative places to explore. He ignited her. Created a tempest of fire. A dance of passion. He played her, knowing her body, understanding what would draw the most response from her.

Running her hands across his chest, Dallas reveled in the crisp dark hair teasing her fingers. Followed the trail down his whipcord lean abdomen to where the fabric of his kilt met his flesh. Toyed with the idea of touching his sex. Earlier she touched him. Excited him. Held his sex in her hand. Felt the expulsion of his climax when she teased him. He'd been so hard. So big. She shuddered, frightened of the first time. He would thrust inside her. They would become as one. Wishing she understood more of what would happen, Dallas delved into her limited knowledge. Sought answers to her question. There were none.

"Don't be afraid." It appeared he sensed her apprehension as well as understood her fears. Rafe didn't have to sense anything. He knew her thoughts. All of them. For her, between them, secrets would never exist.

"I'm not afraid of you. It's just…there is so much I don't know. You are so big. Wish we would have…wish this wasn't my first time for everything." That was true. Any number of times opportunities presented themselves. They could have joined. He wanted to save their first union for the wedding night. She should have protested more.

"I'm beginning to understand some of your reasons for the 'let's get this over.' The evening will be so much better when we have accomplished the first time together along with the claiming. Father told me the pain at claiming vanishes. It's brief. Will hold only a flicker of time in your mind tonight. Any pain you feel this first mating, will also vanish. The pain will be as if it never existed."

Easy for you to say.

She caught his tender chuckle. Seemed they'd been over that road before. He said nothing more either in his mind or with his voice.

The delicate robe covering the sheer nightgown slipped from her arms. Dallas wasn't certain how that happened or when. What she understood now was that his fingers played with the straps that kept the fragile gown on her shoulders. The palms of his hands whispered across her collarbone then along her shoulders. Just as the robe was removed, the straps fell away then down her arms. The bodice tumbled to her waist. Revealed her soft rounded globes. The sway as she moved. Air floated across her breasts. The tips hardened. While he watched what he uncovered, Rafe swept his tongue across her mouth. Entered deep into her. Teased. Frolicked within the warmth. He became one with her. One hand cupped her breast.

"Starving," Rafe told her as he pulled back to take another long look at her. The raw huskiness of his voice startled Dallas. His palm floated across the tips of her breasts. "Famished for you. That one time at the celebration of our marriage was not enough. I did not expect what you did. Thought the only climax at the feast would be yours."

She moaned with the pleasure of it all when his mouthed closed over her nipple. Sucked hard. Brought the globe deep within his mouth. Nipped with a tender bite. Laved with a gentle caress. Shivers vibrated, sending signals she couldn't ignore. Signs she didn't want to discount. She hoped to feel all the amazing sensations he gifted her with earlier. The shattering of her body. The feelings that left her breathless as well as weak and shaking. She ached in ways she never felt before this evening.

"I need to feel the soft velvet of your channel enclose my sex. Wish to have your heat surround me; feel you pulse along my length. I must send you to that place where all contemplations evaporate. Where all one can appreciate are the sensations that take over all rational thought. I want to hear you cry out my name with the pleasure I gift you with."

"Rafe?"

"What?"

"Please… I want that too. Don't wait any longer." She wiggled to help him remove what was left of her gown. She helped him discard his kilt.

Rafe gave into her wishes. Proceeded on that course she invited. In seconds she was as naked as he was. Pressed against his hard frame, Rafe carried her to the big bed. The covers were turned down waiting for them. He came down on top of her. She felt his weight covering her. Loved the feel of his big body on top of hers, pressing her against the mattress, blanketing her. For the first time in her life, Dallas felt secure. Protected. Between her legs, she cradled him. Noticed his sex resting against her soft belly. Hard. Hot. Waiting to enter within. She understood some of what would go on between them. Breathless with her need, she arched, writhed. Spread her legs wider with silent invitation.

His tongue bathed her. Licked. Relished. His teeth nipped. Bit with gentleness. She whimpered then reached for him. Magic stirred. Tempest raged. The fascination of this all-inclusive. Arching against him, she gave the message he would receive. She needed him. Wanted him with all her being.

Enchantment.

Magic.

Sensual delight.

Panting need coupled with painful, pleasureful…hunger so overwhelming she cried out. Moaned with her need.

"Now?" he asked, as her body began to splinter into thousands of crystal shards. She shook. Twisted with need so great she could never refuse him anything. Her head thrashed on the pillow.

"Yes…"

His gentleness surprised. Shocked. He entered her inch by inch. With slow meticulousness he moved farther into uncharted territory. Her body stretched to accommodate. After tonight, she would no longer be a virgin. She would no longer be chaste. She was prepared for the next stage of her life. For a brief moment, he stopped.

"Now," he said the word.

The hard thrust shocked Dallas. She cried out, not with the breaching of her innocence but with the pain on her shoulders. Just before Rafe scored her shoulders, she saw his nails change to claws. Pain claimed her senses. Gulping pants of air cascaded into her lungs. Tears formed in her eyes then trickled downward to soak the pillow. When he tried to kiss her again, she turned her head away unwilling to give him respite.

Holding himself above her, Rafe held still. Lines of strain formed around his eyes. "I'm sorry." She felt the drop of a tear on her cheek. Rafe cried.

As he told her, the pain would vanish. She'd felt what seemed to be the significance of a small scratch when he broke through her maidenhead. Her shoulders stung. Still ached with the piercing of her skin. She reached out to touch his cheek. Caught one of his tears on the tip of her finger. He set his forehead against hers. More moisture fell against her cheeks.

"I want you to know…" Another tear fell to slide across her lips.

She tasted the salt from his tear. "I understand. I think so anyway. You're not the type of man who would enjoy inflicting pain. As you told me, this was something that needed to be done, to secure our future together." She was starting to elaborate when Rafe interrupted.

"Especially on my mate. Given any kind of choice, I would never hurt you, or give you pain of any kind." He braced himself above her. Touched each of the ten marks on her shoulders with his lips.

"Your claws are gone. I don't believe I would have screamed so loud if I didn't see them just before…" This time she couldn't finish. Her voice cracked.

"You feel no more pain?" Rafe brushed his lips on hers. Touched upon each side of her mouth. Tender brushes. "I will get the soft cloth we use for…"

"Washing away the blood. The marks no longer hurt though they might be sore." She turned to look at what she could see. Except for two marks on the front of her shoulders the others were on her back.

"What about…?"

"Didn't feel but a moment of hurt then nothing. You are right, there was pleasure too."

Dallas watched him walk from her. He was tall, lean. His muscles flexed with each stride. Broad of shoulder, lean of hip, he was a rare specimen of a man. He was hers. She sat up. Leaned against the headboard while she waited. She too, touched each mark he left behind. Thought about the visions she witnessed this evening. He told her he would want to hear everything about them.

Kneeling on the bed, he touched her side and bent over. Cleaning the marks left behind. She was claimed; was his through this life then on to the next. Thoughts of Aaron coupled with Ruby sent chills throughout. Their lives in this time had been cut short. At least they had the next one to look forward to living, as would she and Rafe. When he finished cleansing the blood, he handed her a second damp cloth.

"What?" After her question, she realized why. Heat flushed her cheeks then along the tops of her breasts turning them red. Embarrassment shot through her. Touched her in ways she didn't understand.

"They are a delightful shade…your breasts." Without asking, he strode through the chamber to the bathroom, leaving her alone to wipe away the blood from her lost innocence. She tossed the cloth into the basin. The women had left it there for that use. They'd know the blood from the claiming would need washing away. They wouldn't know the second part. Rumor had it that most of the men in the clan made love to their partners before the wedding night. Rafe had not.

When he returned, she found heat still stained her face along with the tops of her breasts. Rafe poured more wine before sitting next to her on the bed. He leaned back, his head against the wood behind him.

"How are you feeling? Sore?" Silence followed his question. "No more fears? I believe you were right in getting the deeds done. The rest of the evening will be all pleasure. We will satisfy our bellies as well all our other needs. Are you hungry yet?"

The big clock that stood sentinel in the room must be a replica of a time past. It ticked. Hummed with life. How many matings had come and gone listening to the clock tick. The time neared midnight. Dallas understood he waited for her to begin the conversation and comprehended what he wished to learn. All she witnessed had not been pleasant. She could tell him only the good things. Times in the past were not easy. Not like they were here. Still, men like Aaron did not live long enough.

"Guess I'm tired. No, yes, sore only a trifle. As you've told me the pain will fade. The claw marks no longer cause pain. You said they would be with me forever."

"Yes, my marks are significant in that you will carry them the rest of your life."

"You can ask me what's on the forefront of your mind. I did see us in our past. There were other things I saw too. Disturbing things I don't understand."

"Like what? No…talk to me first about us. Tell me what you saw. When…." His voice was eager. Curious.

"This is serious. While I was spinning in a world of dreams, I realized the elements of this world were in play. The earth moved beneath my feet, trembled with the chanting of the priest. Father Richard or some higher being created the world I found myself observing."

"Earth, wind, fire, water…?" Rafe asked. His eyes were closed as if he tried to picture everything she told him.

"Yes, the first time I saw you…" She tried to think of how to explain. "You seemed to erupt from the earth. Cresting a hill as if exploding from the craigs around you. You ran hard. Your cat was huge. Almost as big as when you showed me yours. By the time you were panting you reached another black panther. The cat was me. I waited for you. The anger in your eyes was vibrant. Simmered. Talking to me in your head you lectured me for not hiding. Told me you would have to punish me for disobeying you. Is that done now? I would not find myself punished for asserting my opinion. For helping when needed. I knew the cat didn't hide because she protected her mate. She made herself a diversion. Saved his life. He held no respect for her courage."

"You disobeyed me." Rafe seemed to turn that thought over in his head. "I believe in the past when there was more danger to our kind, the female was expected to obey the male. The male's role is to protect. There must have been some kind of hazard. It was the male's job to keep the female safe. You made that more difficult for me. Of course, I was furious with you. I imagine there might have been some form of punishment. Wouldn't have any idea as to what that might have been."

"He said he would punish me for my willfulness. That doesn't sound like you. Neither does the thought of punishing. What would that entail?" Dallas shuddered at the idea. More questions formed in her mind. She didn't appreciate the notion of punishment when all she did was think for herself. From instinct, Dallas knew the female cat saved her mate's life. "I led the danger away from you. Was not appreciated for what I did. You might have been hurt, even killed." It seemed as if she spoke to the people in a different century. The words didn't apply to Rafe.

"Ah, no, I can see why you did as you said. You put yourself in jeopardy. That would serve to deflate a male ego real fast. In this world there are few situations that might be considered life or death."

"Suppose so." Dallas was still perturbed at the barbaric notion of the first shifters she witnessed in her past.

"You were willful back then too," Rafe murmured, the amusement clear in the tone of his voice.

"Yes, it wasn't the only evidence of my nature. Never thought of myself as willful. That wasn't it at all. Am I stubborn? Is that how you see me?" Dallas understood she would never obey an edict she considered wrong. Would that garner her punishment? She didn't know. Didn't wish to dwell on that subject any longer.

"Yes, about things that are important to you. Your stubbornness comes to light. I appreciate that willful streak in you."

"Oh…"

"What else… We still have the wind, the fire along with the water to consider. Did you ever see what that danger was?" He played with her hair. Let the long strands shift through his fingers. Curled one end around one then pulled her close. Kissed her. Swept his lips along the firm set of her mouth.

Dallas sighed into his. She understood she could not let her body respond to his sweet-talking. Clearing her mind, she replied, "Not that time. I thought I might see the pair in their human form. That didn't happen either. I realize Roc and Lainie resemble us. I wondered if the other times we would be so similar it would be hard to distinguish between us."

Rafe set his hands behind his head, seeming to wait for her to continue. As if he needed to hear everything, he ended the seduction he'd just begun to orchestrate. "So, was wind next or fire? Water?"

"Fire came next. What I saw surprised me. I watched Lainie and Roc at the bonfire. They were chatting. She sat in front of him, just as we do. He had his arms around her. I think the man was doing more than just holding her. He was seducing her. Touching her in places that would ignite heat. Would bring her to his way of thinking. Flames licked the sky. Sparks jumped out. Lainie had her head set against Roc's chest. She was smiling. I think she was with child. Couldn't see her belly to know for certain. The thought was just an impression. We knew before then that we appear the same. Almost twins."

~ * ~

So far, Dallas' accounting of the past was a disappointment. He hoped she would reveal more. Still, this was just one sighting. There were three more to go. Somehow Rafe understood there might be accounts she didn't intend to tell him. That was her right…her prerogative. She could keep encounters secret. Patience was what he needed. She'd been through a lot today. From reading her body language, he realized she was exhausted. He'd seduced her. Made love to his mate. What more could he expect from her?

"The wind?"

Dallas took this opportunity to nestle next to him. Fitted herself to him. Her cheek in the hollow of his shoulder. Ran her hands along his chest. Touched him with the tip of her tongue. He felt the whisper of each breath she inhaled then exhaled. The touch of her lips on his flesh traveled straight to his groin. Doing nothing except lay against him, she aroused.

Stimulated in ways he could have never comprehended. He wanted her again. Needed to give her more time. This was not the moment to seduce. She had more to say. He had more to listen to. Until a few minutes ago, she'd been a virgin.

A soft sigh told him she was ready to speak again. Her lashes fluttered against his chest. He enjoyed the way that felt. She cleared her throat before she began. "The wind fanned the flames of the bonfire.

It seemed the fire rose higher and higher still, until there was no end in sight. Night turned to day. Clouds darkened the sky above the cat, along with his mate. This time, the male cat flew along the craigs, racing the wind. A stream far below wound its way to the sea. The barren craigs turned to wooded forest. Still, the black panther ran with the storm surge along a dark path. Unlike the nature of the panther, he didn't seem to tire. Seemed he ran forever."

Fascinated, Rafe listened to her story. As she continued to speak, she painted an explicit picture for him. He wished he dared jump into her head. Without speaking out, she could continue the narrative. Doing so would not be as exhausting. They could continue in that vein until her energy returned.

"The male cat stopped. In front of the great panther was a house made of stones. Smoke from a fire inside traveled out the chimney. The scent of new baked bread filled the air. Dinner was on the table. I don't believe this meal will ever be eaten. Why, I don't know. A woman stood at the doorway, her arms outstretched as if greeting her mate. Her smile was tentative and the deepest darkest blue imaginable. She was pleased to see him, yet she understood she'd done something he would take umbrage with. This woman understood she would find herself punished."

"This was their home? He would also punish her?" Rafe said, his feelings on that matter were easy for Dallas to understand. This notion was archaic.

"Would imagine so. The two gazed at each other for what seemed to be the longest time. He in his cat form. She winding her fingers though her skirt. Her apprehension tangible. She didn't wish to be punished. Seconds turned into minutes. If they spoke to each other, it was through their minds. Then it seemed they argued. Her face turned red while her brows drew together in anger. He roared, the sound reverberating through the small clearing. Have no idea what the quarrel could be over. The woman stripped after that, she shifted. She was in her cat form."

"Did she look like you?"

"A little but no, her hair was brilliant red. She was thin almost to the point of appearing frail. Nothing like me. Her breasts were not large. Small tipped with soft pink. Her belly was flat, concave. Nothing like me."

"What happened next?"

"Together they ran. Ran until she stopped, sat on her haunches in silent protest. She was having trouble catching air. Though we both understand she could be giving the arrogant beast an ear full of her thoughts. I sensed the woman was furious with the man. She didn't intend to go one more step at the rigorous pace he set."

He couldn't help the sharp bark of laughter. "I'm certain she is furious. Annoyed. Irritated. Just as you would be if I ran you to the ground. You would tell me what you thought. You would never mince words. For that I'm grateful. I don't believe a person should keep their feelings bottled up." With gentle fingers, he moved hair from her face before running his knuckles along the roundness of her cheek then down the silken column of her neck. Making love to her again would be too soon. Later tonight they would join together. Perhaps as she became more comfortable with him, he would change to his cat. He could teach her how she could do the same.

Dallas cleared her throat, intending to continue with her story. "The male stopped. Waited for her. She walked to him, rubbed against him. He licked her face. His actions gentle. Tender in the extreme. I heard the purr rumble deep in his chest. Side by side they walked until they reached another home. This one stood two stories tall. It was made of wood. On the porch, before they entered into the home, they both changed to their human form. He swept her into his arms." Dallas lifted her shoulders high. "He looked just like you. Dark. Handsome. His eyes blazed silver-blue when his silver gaze met his mates. He wanted her. Was hungry to taste her. He'd been afraid for her life."

"Ah, did all the women you saw…were they all able to shift?" He tried to make a point. Neither believed that Lainie could change form. He wondered, just as Dallas didn't realize her abilities, neither did Lainie. Now, at this juncture, there was no way to learn the truth. Roc would have sensed her ability if it was there. He would have seen to her instruction.

"I don't know. Suppose the truth of that…anyway…" Dallas paused for a few seconds. "Are you certain I can shift?"

"Yes."

"Very well… After that was when the water tore from the sky. Rivulets poured down on the ground. I was thrust up then above the highlands as if I was in a plane. Everything was small…a dream of sorts. Saw rivers all over Scotland rise. Overflow their banks. Wondered what possible reason there could be for something such as this to happen."

Fear spiraled within Rafe because he felt her terror. Wondered if there was something she wasn't telling him. Some unknown force that would threaten them. "There is no reason for you to fear this scene you watched. That was centuries ago. I'll wager if we do some research, we will learn there were floods then. Nothing will happen to you…to us. The little streams we live by would never become raging torrents. Never grow so large they would flood this area." Rafe wasn't all that certain. Yes, they were safe in Carnoch. There were still photo shoots Dallas would be assigned to cover. If caught in a storm of that magnitude, her life could be in danger.

"I'm not afraid for us. Don't know where the fear should…just don't know anything. Maybe I was afraid for the two I left behind. I think you might have expected more from me. All I can relate to you is what I witnessed."

Rafe accepted her hands into his. They trembled. She wasn't telling the absolute truth about the terror she felt. He tried to soothe her fears with the gentleness of his touch. Brought the back of her hand to his lips to brush a tender kiss. Didn't seem anything would undo the fears in her head.

"Do you want to stop?" Everything didn't need to be said this instant. He rose, topped off their glasses of wine. "We can finish with this later. We do have the rest of our lives to talk. I would that you were more comfortable."

"Not yet."

"Good." He felt both relieved as well as terrified for her. She'd been through so much these last few weeks. Today, more than any of her life, she'd been put through things she had no comprehension of.

They both took a few seconds to think, to sip the wine. He held out food for her. She accepted the nourishment.

"I do need to go on. Would like to finish with the telling so I can put all behind me. Next," she paused for several seconds keeping her eyes closed, "I saw a man jumping into a raging swollen river. That vision failed to make sense. The river was dangerous. The hazards immense. The flood threatened his life. I knew there had to be a good reason for his foolishness. Turns out his deed wasn't foolish at all."

"How so?" To say he was fascinated as well as curious would never come close to how he felt. All his cat senses were inflamed. Rafe realized the only reason the man would do something so incredibly dangerous was to save his mate. A shifter would risk everything for the most important person in his life.

"His mate was in the raging waters. The man swam hard. A reddish-blond head bobbed up then down in the river ahead of him. Thrashing her arms, she cried out just before her heavy skirts pulled her down."

"She was drowning."

"Yes. He dove. Swam beneath the water for what seemed an eternity to me. While I watched, I said a prayer for him. Held my breath until I could no longer hold the oxygen in my lungs. Seconds then a minute passed…maybe more. He couldn't keep from breathing that long. He was going to drown along with the woman, his mate. I jerked with relief when he surfaced, I lost the breath I held. The man held her in his arms. Keeping her head above the surface he swam to the edge. Pushed her toward the bank while he kicked hard.

"The man saved her?"

"Not yet. He was winded when he reached land, then pulled her onto the wet moss along the banks. Her breaths…she wasn't breathing. Her lips had turned blue. He didn't know what to do. I called out to him. Tried to reach him. Failed. He turned her over. Hit her between the shoulder blades, once then twice. I heard her gasp for air. The following breath was ragged. She stopped breathing again. Desperate now, he rolled her over. Set his lips on hers as if he meant to breathe air into her lungs."

"Artificial respiration. Her heart never stopped."

"Yes and no. Seemed he tuned into my advice after all. More than once he breathed air into her lungs. Again, she sputtered. Moaned. Her head lolled. He sat back watching. Smiling. Her eyes flickered open. She reached up to touch, but she wasn't strong enough. Her hand fell to the earth."

"The man saved her."

Dallas buried her face in his chest. He felt her tears against him. After she pushed away from him to speak, she brushed moisture from her face. "Yes. God, she, that woman, looked just like me. She could have been my twin. Might have been Lainie. The man could have been your twin. Roc. The scene unraveled as if I watched something that would happen to me…happen to you. Only…"

"Only?"

"She was dressed in clothing of the eighteenth century. The woman wasn't me. Couldn't be me. The man wasn't you. Those two people might have been Roc and Laine. Though…I don't think they were." Dallas breathed in deeply, once, then one more time, as if she couldn't get enough air. "I can't do this anymore. What I saw later, the telling will need to wait. My mind is drained. I need respite."

"You're exhausted. All of you."

"Yes."

When he woke, she lay sprawled on top of him. Her legs were cradled between his. Rafe enjoyed the feel of her draped all over him. All her lush curves were pressed to his hard body. He brought her awake, kissing her, exploring all the sweet tender spots he was beginning to adore more now that he tasted. He knew her most sensitive places. Her soft moans of pleasure sent heatwaves in a flaming caress to his groin. If she wanted, he would make love to her again. If not, he would hold her just as she was now.

"Do you wish to make love again?" He nipped the long column of her neck. Found the throbbing pulse at the base of her throat. "…or… eat? Drink more wine? Tell me more about what you've seen? Whatever we do is up to you. Only you."

Her small hands flattened on his chest and pushed against him. She rose above. The tight hard crests of her breasts sashayed across his chest. He groaned, knowing if she said no to his question, he would have a devil of a time stopping his mounting hunger. His body was alive with raw passion, urgent desire.

"I don't wish to make love right now. Show me your cat. After that, if you truly believe I'm a shifter, teach me how to change my form. I would make you happy by trying. I don't know how this imaginable transformation could be possible...this ability you seem to think I possess."

"Ruby no longer believes the ability to shift jumped a generation. Her mind has reviewed what she knew of your mother over twenty years ago, along with the changes in her personality we see now. Cole's mother thinks there is something else at play here...some evil force. She believes something happened...something underhanded. What that could be is anyone's guess. We are both of the opinion, for some reason, your mother was behind your inability to alter your shape. We don't understand why. We think she was the shifter. For some reason she might have been ridiculed by a person who was important to her. Maybe taunted about being a freak of nature. We all need to stand firm with our heritage. If she had no support...if her husband was the person undermining her..." In a deep shrug, coupled with a sigh, "Who knows what could have happened? You, however, were the one hurt."

"That's a lot of information for me to absorb. My mother dissuaded me from shifting? She called me names when I did so?" Dallas was shaking her head, disbelieving how that could be possible. "She despised what I am so much? Hated everything about me."

"Most likely. Toddlers don't understand about shifting. They do it with ease. It's a game to them. What they need to be taught is precaution. Somehow your mother turned you against everything we believe in."

"My father? How did he...would he have encouraged her?"

"He did nothing to change how Helen reacted to you. They are both despicable humans. How could a parent treat their child with such little regard?" Rafe felt anger boiling, simmering just below the surface. He tried to tamp the rage to a low rumble. What he didn't know was how to go about discovering the truth. If what they were thinking was true, Helen would deny involvement. She would never admit to something so underhanded.

"Maybe my father is the shifter. How could you know… Mother… I don't know. What you're suggesting is even more unmotherly than what we know for a fact she's done. The way she has made me think about myself. Let's not talk about this. In the morning, I'd like to see Ruby. Talk to her with you. Find out what she recalls from the past about my mother. You said there were discrepancies."

"Your father should have known better. Helen should have apprised him of what was to come. If they are true mates, honesty between them is most important." He ran his fingers through his hair, unable to come to terms with this discussion. "We are off…this is not…what we are thinking can't be truth."

"You say Mother has the ability to shift. Father does not. Could my father…? Never mind. I'm grasping at straws. This is all so messy. So hard to believe or discern the truth. While my childhood was never idyllic, my father never seemed to care about me one way or the other. Would never have made the effort to make me feel bad about myself or defend me."

"Do you still wish to try out your cat? Let me shift first. Watch close. All it takes is a bit of concentration."

"Concentration?" she asked with a small laugh. "Imagine you can probe my mind. Help me with what I get wrong. This night has been taxing. Don't expect a miracle if attentiveness is what is in order."

"So…you do believe," Rafe stated, not bothering to turn his words into a question. "That's most of what is necessary to be successful. You must believe in yourself as well as your capabilities. Your aptitude is there waiting for the opportunity." He grinned at her, looking forward to this new phase of their lives. "I would like to take you to the summer home in the highlands. We can have the place all to ourselves. We'll be able to run together in our cat forms. Swim in the loch. Sun ourselves on the ledge. I'll clear my schedule. You can clear yours. We'll have all the privacy to play that we need. We will be able to discover more about each other. Our dreams."

"I'd like that. I love being everywhere with you." Dallas sat back, watching him. She studied the expression on his face. Rafe understood what she was doing. Was pleased by the notion. "Now…it's your turn to show off your skills. After all, you're already naked. Won't be tearing through clothing."

Pride filled him at her courage. Rafe was proud of the fact Dallas seemed to be accepting who she was, along with her new talents. He hoped this time she would not be terrified of his cat. She'd had time to adjust to the notion people could change form. The man she was destined to be with for the rest of her life could do so. Soon she would also reveal her once hidden talents.

"I'm going to let you into my thoughts while we both concentrate on the idea of altering our shapes. Are you ready?" He stepped from the bed. Stood in front of her, watching, waiting for her to give him the go ahead. Rafe focused on her eyes. Knew the moment she was in his head, listening to him. Watching his mind go through the changes too. Before this he'd never thought about the how…now that was all he could think about.

"I'm ready," The sound of her voice was soft. Insecure. He heard apprehension. His heart went out to her.

Rafe wanted to reassure her through his mind. He reached out with thoughts then instructions. "You should stand up. You might be a quick learner. Who knows, while I adjust to my different form, I might be able to bring you right along with me."

Dallas followed him. They stood in the center of the room. Rafe held her hands in his, thinking the warmth from his touch might help with the process. She stood in front of him, naked. Much the way he remembered from the claiming ceremony. Just as then, she still relied on him. Would lean on him for help.

Her small pink tongue roamed across her mouth. She was nervous. That small gesture coupled with the trembling of her hands told him as much. He smiled at her, nodding his head as if the simple gesture would give the needed encouragement.

"What if I fail? Now that we've talked so much about this, I don't…I want to be able to do this. Now that I've seen some of our other lives together, I understand how we could be if I've the same proficiencies as you."

"You won't fail."

"You can't know that for a fact."

The grin he was feeling on his face grew. He squeezed her hands. "I sense it. Just as my other instincts have kicked in where you are concerned. Something deep in the pit of my belly tells me you are capable. If not tonight, the next time or the one after that. We can't expect immediate results. You've had such negativity thrown at you. This might take time to erase the blockage in your head."

Her breasts moved enticingly when she tugged in a deep breath of air. The tips were hard, begging for his devotion. He ignored that stimulus to concentrate on the task at hand.

"Lead the way."

"You can do this," he encouraged. "Follow my example. This won't be a quick change. I'll take the altering slow." Rafe was pleased she was at ease with her nudity. When she posed for him, she was never bashful. Her innate confidence along with familiarity helped in this situation.

She nodded. "Do what you do. I'll try. Rafe, I want this to happen. I'm no longer conflicted. You should understand that fact. I'm not going to be afraid of your cat. I've learned how gentle as well as tender you can be."

He did understand this might not be as easy as he hoped. If she remembered her toddler years when she shifted with ease, they would have no problems. Those first few times were always instinctive. It also depended on how deep her mother ingrained in her that shifting was depraved. She might have punished her for shifting. His gut tightened at the thought of a small girl being disciplined for a talent that was so amazing. Dallas might have a great deal to overcome in order to realize her true potential.

"Close your eyes then think about your cat. What you believe you will look like. Think of the female cats you saw during the ritual. Pattern yourself after them." He did the same while he attempted to channel his thoughts into her. He brought in a deep breath of air. This was the first time. They would deal with whatever would come to pass.

Concentrate on your cat. Only your cat. Remember the color, the form, the power. You've seen your cat during the ceremony. You understand how you look. Think about that. Know that this ability has been given to you for a reason.

Rafe repeated himself, then repeated again. He turned his mind upside down trying to think of something to help her with the task. He felt his body vibrate with the need to adjust while he held back. Dallas was stalling him. Didn't understand the hesitancy. Obstructions were vivid in her mind. Firsthand, he heard her mother reprimanding her when she shifted before bath time. Heard the father call out his opinion of the nasty little girl. His head thundered in revulsion. His heart splintered into thousands of pieces for her. Rafe felt desperation in all her thoughts. The confusion.

Your paws. Your tail. Remember how you feel when you run. You are a small girl getting ready for your bath. You are naked. your body is twitching. Trembling with anticipation. Vibrating with happiness. You've become a cat and are amazed and thrilled at your skill. You want to show off to all who will look. You are proud of yourself. You strut around the bathtub. Arch your back. Preen.

Mama? No?

Change back now! Now! I say now. Fast!

Why? It's fun to be a cat.

You are a horrible, despicable child to disobey me. Change so you are normal, an ordinary person. You must mind me along with your father. You've been told this is not acceptable. Told that changing will ruin your life.

Make that child of yours stop! So help me if she stays in that cat shape of hers, I'll wring her little neck! She's repugnant. She's no daughter of mine!

Papa!

Rafe felt the rejection of her mind. As if he was part of her, he understood this was over for the day. She no longer listened to him. Dallas no longer tried to change to her cat. What that man who yelled at her did was send her mind tumbling back until she recalled what happened to her so long ago. Remembered how she'd been chastised. Denigrated. The memory of the spanking afterward left welts on her tiny bottom. Rafe heard the sobs Dallas was reliving. No wonder she was afraid of pain. His stomach churned. He held the distinct feeling this scene played out more than once. Her mind kept her from changing…from remembering. She'd been censured then brutalized so many times she wasn't going to risk another encounter. Her inability was in her mind. Somehow over time he needed to discover a way to reach her.

He stayed in his cat even though she was unable to become her cat. While he watched, she sat on the edge of the bed, shivering with fear. When she focused on him, there was terror in her eyes. This would take effort on both their parts. Dallas had a great deal to overcome. He wasn't certain how to erase the horrid past from her head and move on to her future. There had to be a way.

Confused, Dallas stood, then sat on the bed again. She reached out to him as if she needed to touch, then retracted her hand. Tears left her eyes, sliding down her cheeks in silver ribbons of despair. A sob caught in the back of her throat.

Don't worry. We'll find a way to jerk all that nonsense your mother and father have created out of your head. You will believe in yourself. Will never again think you are repulsive, a freak of nature. I promise you, Dallas. I'll never hurt you. Will never scorn you or thrust insults your way for something so precious. You are treasured. Trust in me. Whenever you feel up to trying again, I will be there to help. If it's tonight, tomorrow or next year, I'll be there to help guide you. For now…will you pet me? I need to feel your hands running through my fur. You can scratch me behind the ears. I enjoy that too.

To his delight she giggled.

He set his head on her legs. Rubbed his face on her belly. Heard her gasp of surprise. Saw the tiny quiver of a half-smile form on her mouth. After that another small giggle erupted. She was not afraid of him. He licked her hand, slid his tongue between her fingers. He lay down next to her on the bed. Grasped her fingers within his teeth to lead her hand to his back. He arched trying to show her what he wanted.

Caress me, love. Rub your hands through my fur. Get to know me this way. In time, we will play together as cats. Romp through the highlands. Swim in the lochs. I will erase all the fears that your subconscious holds at bay. You'll find happiness with this man.

It was my mother who did this to me. Who made my life...she was horrible to me. I loathe her even more now than I did before. Will never forgive the meanness in her. She chose my father over me. Chose to demean me because he ordered her to humiliate me.

I'm not so certain. Did you hear what your father told her? Helen might also be a victim of your father. Maybe both of you are shifters. It's possible he despises her for being something she can't change. She obeys him perhaps because she is also afraid of what he will do to you. When you didn't do as he ordered, you were beaten. He beat you. The man might have done the same to your mother. I would confront him. Teach him he can't treat children as well as women that way.

I don't care. She is hateful. My father is worse. I despise them both. Will never forgive them. Can't believe I lost all memory of what they did to me. Those years are gone from my life. I will never be able to retrieve them.

Don't you wish to discover the truth about your parents? By some miracle, they have created the most beautiful woman I've ever known. She is kind as well as gentle. Nurturing, even though her role models were contemptable. True, they've given you fears. Those fears will be dealt with. They have played havoc with your mind. You will overcome everything. I promise you that. Together. We are as one now. You are my life mate.

Purring, he tried to show her how he felt. He loved the feel of her fingers sifting through his fur. Understood he should become human again; take her into his arms. Hold her until she vanquished some of the terrors in her mind that were holding her prisoner. He wondered how much time would pass before she decided to try again. He would encourage in the only way he could think of...support her. Now, after this first trial, he knew for a fact Dallas was indeed able to alter her human form. He comprehended one more reason why they were always able to understand each other. It wasn't just a sixth sense. He'd been able to hear her pain. Thought if he understood the scope of what Dallas endured when he first met her, he might have helped more.

Rafe stepped away from her. In an instant he was once more in his human shape. Dallas rushed into his arms. Pressed herself against him. In the next moment he was aroused. Stimulated to the point of no return. He hoped she would feel the same.

"Do you want me? I don't…"

"Please, yes. I need you so much."

They made love. He reassured her that in time she would be able to shift. Reassured that he would do all in his power to find out the truth about her mother and father. As planned, he would go with her tomorrow morning to speak with Ruby.

~ * ~

It was mid-afternoon. Ruby received the message from Rafe in the early morning. He and Dallas wanted to meet with her. Off and on during the day, she wrote down tid-bits of information she recalled from over twenty-two years ago. There were many discrepancies between then and now. The Shaw's became reclusive, keeping to themselves. They never went out other than for work. That wasn't what she recalled about Helen or John. The two loved to entertain; to socialize. The first year of their marriage they had several dinner parties. She and Aaron had been invited. The two were a happy fun-loving couple. Something along the way changed that fact.

After she thought long and hard, she remembered John was not the name of the man Helen married. Nor was Shaw their last name. The name of the man Helen wed was Ian McDonell. That single memory gave her pause. Seemed she'd forgotten so much. Maybe took things for granted she shouldn't. The more she reflected on the past, the more she realized the differences between then and now. If Aaron had been alive, she would have spoken to him about the man Ian McDonell. The two men were close. At some point, Ian had changed. As head of the clan, it was Aaron's business to know who the shifters were. She never paid much attention to anything that did not affect her in the present.

She thought the shifter was Helen. Now she wasn't certain. Something…hell…nothing rang true about that pair. Ruby sent Cole to

Father Richard to learn everything he could. Hoped Father Richard would remember the ceremony as well as who the shifter in the family was. He would have performed the ceremony for the McDonells or the Shaws.

The birth certificate should have the father's name recorded on the document, as well as the certificate of marriage. A birth record could not be changed; neither could the marriage record. This situation was stranger than she thought possible.

Her first visitor was Cole. "Hello…" Cole beamed when he walked through the door. He kissed her cheek before pouring himself a cup of coffee. "When will Rafe and Dallas be here? I've a few pieces of information to discuss before they arrive."

"Another half hour. What did you find out?" She found herself wringing her hands while nerves spiraled through her. Ruby wasn't all that certain she wanted to discover the truth, though she understood this was her duty as well as her son's. If some wrong was committed, fixing that mistake needed to be done.

"Not enough and more than I wanted." Cole held his cup in both hands while he sat down. "There is something mysterious about the Shaw couple. Something isn't quite right. Father Richard told me Ian was the shifter. He now goes by the name of John. My major question is why?"

"Dallas' birth certificate reads Dallas Elaine McDonell. Could Helen and John have decided they didn't like their last name? A person can change names. There is nothing illegal here. They made a choice."

"Yes, that's true enough. But why?" Cole asked, sitting back to study his mother. "You have this interesting look on your face. I would like to know what it means."

"We both understand that Dallas traveled through time in order to set something right. Could one or both of them have traveled from some place to make something wrong? Could that be possible? Whatever has happened here with Dallas is wrong. Dead wrong. We must correct that something, whatever it might be. I'm beginning to think we don't know the half of this scene. It's up to you as head of the Clan Chattan to figure this out. To make whatever went haywire become functional once more."

"That's a tall order," Cole mumbled. "I like those two. Let's wait and see what they have to say today. I think Rafe wanted her to try to shift.

Maybe last night…" Cole let the thought trail off with the knock on the door.

"That must be the two of them," Ruby said, standing up to get the door. "What do you think? Will they be able to shed more light on this conundrum?"

"Let's hope so."

"Rafe…Dallas…welcome. Cole is here too. We've, or I've been trying to think back more than twenty years in the past. Cole visited Father Richard in hopes of learning more details about your life before. We wanted to find which parent was the shifter."

"I believe you are right in assuming the problems with Dallas go back to the beginning," Rafe agreed as they stepped into the room.

"Coffee?" Cole asked as he was already pouring two cups. "There are brownies on the tray if you're hungry."

Ruby circled the room. She searched for the right words. Creating more fears wouldn't do. Drowning herself in a large dose of oxygen, she began, "Because, in my mind, things are not adding up. There are many gaps in my head. Things I thought I knew about Helen and John coupled with the way things are now don't add up to make a whole. They aren't the same as they were more than twenty years ago." Ruby held up her hands at the expression in Rafe's eyes. She knew what that meant. Aaron used to look at her in the same light when he needed more information. When she stimulated his mind with her prattle. "There is nothing concrete or definitive in what I recall. Just some oddities. That's all. This is too frustrating. I need answers."

"Maybe we can add to the story or the memories. I tried to shift last night. Couldn't. I blocked myself. I witnessed my two-year-old self change," Dallas said as she added cream to her coffee. "I…"

"It's difficult for Dallas to speak of that memory. She learned some things that are disturbing. Nothing that makes sense or sends us into a conclusion that we can defend, or even understand what remains in the mind over time. Those events all happened so long ago. Dallas is confused. Frustrated. Doesn't know what to think."

"I imagine so…" Cole said with a bland tone. "If she tried to shift but was stopped for some reason that would be disconcerting. If she found herself belittled or harmed at every turn, she would put her ability from her mind. You both believe Dallas is a shifter."

"Yes," they spoke in unison.

Ruby smiled, the two were indeed mates. They presented a united front. Something wonderful in this world was happening here despite all the difficulties this young couple had been put through to make it this far. These two would love each other forever. She sensed their love. Felt the love bone deep.

"If you're comfortable, tell us what happened when you tried to shift," Ruby encouraged with her soft voice. She didn't want to infringe on the privacy of this newly married couple. The information was important. If this pair would relate their experience, the knowledge would help Dallas recover from her abuse. "Whatever you relate to us won't leave this room."

Dallas and Rafe looked at each other. He picked up her hand. Held it with the same possession all male shifters had for their mates. Before he began, he looked into Dallas' eyes. After she nodded, Rafe began to speak. "I'll talk. I believe this will be too difficult for Dallas. She is in a fragile state today. Still exhausted from the trauma of the ceremony as well as the wedding night."

Ruby expected as much. Dallas was pale. Purple shadows smudged her eyes. After the wedding night, these two should be vibrant. Ecstatic. Dallas didn't display her usual vitality. "We'll listen. Won't pass judgement on anyone involved. The object of this time together is to attempt to put the puzzle pieces into a solidified whole. To do that, we must understand the circumstances surrounding her younger years. We all know Dallas withdrew from her parents upon meeting you."

Rafe nodded while he pulled in a breath of air. His eyes focused on Dallas, he began, seeming to pause over each word. "When we attempted to shift together, she could not. I tried to reach into her mind to better understand the problem she was having. Heard her memories from her childhood. They raffled through her mind at blinding speed. One after the other brought terror to her. Stopped her from achieving the goal."

"Bad memories, I wish we knew why," Ruby said with thought, as she waited for something tangible. Definitive words she could grasp.

"Very bad. As a toddler when she played with shifting, she was denounced by her mother then brutalized by her father. He beat her under the guise of a spanking. I saw her reddened bottom. The welts. He couldn't have used his hand. Must have used a board or a leather strap. No one, man or woman, has the right to beat a child." Rafe's fury was apparent to Ruby with every word he spoke.

"Were you able to figure out which one of the two is the shifter?" Cole asked, posing one of the other questions on everyone's mind.

Rafe cleared his throat. His intentions to speak for Dallas still apparent. "No, however in my mind the mother must be the shifter. Even though Father Richard told us the shifter was the father. By her father's reaction to her, he couldn't have the skill. From her memories, it's obvious the man despises shifters. For whatever reason I would begin to give, he took all his hate out on Dallas. He meant to make certain she would never shift. In order to protect herself, Dallas put the concept to the back of her head. After that last spanking, I doubt if she ever tried again."

Ruby sucked in air. From the beginning, she'd been afraid of this. "If Aaron were here, he would be able to tell us the truth. What you've said makes the most sense of any of the scenarios I've constructed in my mind. Still, none of this falls into a logical seam that could be sewn together." She couldn't put a finger on what wasn't in order or out of order. Some of their logic was messed up. All their conclusions were not correct.

Rafe went on to explain all that he learned last evening. Dallas said nothing. Her face remained pale, she clung to Rafe. They too learned what Cole discovered.

"Her father's name on the birth certificate is Ian McDonell?" Rafe asked. "How can that be when her last name is Shaw? This is something I don't understand."

"Dallas is a McDonell, not a Shaw," Ruby said with a matter-of-fact tone. "I've known Ian since we were children. Ian was always kind as well as gentle. He was not a man who would beat a child. This part is one of the pieces of information that doesn't ring true. For an unknown reason, Ian changed his name. We would need to ask him to discover why. They were gone from the village for a few years. Right after Dallas was born."

"Can you ask him to meet with us?" Rafe asked. "We need

answers. Seems only John and Helen can give them."

"The two would need to be willing."

Dallas jumped from her seat then sunk back, grabbing Rafe as if he was her lifeline. "No! No, I don't want to see my father again." Dallas' fingers looked to be biting into Rafe's arm. "He will hurt someone. Maybe Mother. Even though I detest the woman, I would not wish harm to come to her."

"As head of the clan, it's up to me to sort through this mess. You don't have to be at the meeting. Though I would ask Rafe to represent you. If that's acceptable, I'll send a message to John Shaw that a meeting is necessary. I would see him tonight if that is possible."

"We will proceed with haste. The sooner this is sorted out, the better," Ruby said, as she sat down at her desk to pen the words that would bring John and Helen to see her. They would not be given a choice in the matter.

Chapter Eight

Dallas understood Rafe was concerned about her. She was fine. After the meeting with Cole and Ruby, she'd been tired. Tried to tell him both with words as well as her thoughts that he didn't need to treat her as if she was on her deathbed. After the meeting with Ruby and Cole, he'd been solicitous. Careful as well as guarded about her feelings. He meant to take care of her, waiting on her. In some ways she appreciated the gesture, in others not so much.

Her laughter before she spoke to him was soft. "I'm not fragile, Rafe Frasier. I'm not going to break nor faint nor shatter into a million tiny pieces," Dallas told him as he escorted her into their home. She was surprised he wasn't carrying her. "Don't dwell on what happened last night, as well as this afternoon at the meeting. As the minutes tick by, I'm recovering. By dinner time I'll be as good as new." She wanted to tell him the memories were fading. Didn't wish to be a person to hold onto the past at the detriment of her future.

From behind, Rafe wrapped his arms around her, holding her close. The warmth of his body heated her chilled bones. For a few seconds, his chin rested on the top of her head. She listened to the evenness of each breath. Wished he would kiss her. Maybe she should think so hard on that notion he would hear.

Rafe turned her around. "I know you aren't a delicate swooning type of girl. Does it matter so much that I'm concerned for you? Getting to the bottom of this is important to both of us."

"Yes, very much so. Now, however, I wish to fix dinner for you. Before the wedding, I shopped. I've all the ingredients for fish tacos. Would you like lemon pie for dessert? We can have rice with the meal. Maybe…" She set her finger on her chin. "I've both beans and corn. Which would you prefer?" Dallas understood she was hiding from her fears. Dwelling on her parents wasn't conducive to her peace of mind. Always a bit flighty, she needed to keep moving. Cooking soothed her.

"Think we should order pizza. Go upstairs to the studio. You can pose for me. I've this inkling to paint you naked. Love looking at your magnificent body. What do you think?"

"You just want to be able to ogle me when I'm without clothing. I'll pose nude if you'll paint nude." She laughed at his look of chagrin. Rafe never failed to surprise her. Now that they'd made love, she didn't understand the shyness he exhibited. Many times before when she'd made that same request he never delighted her with a yes answer.

Changing the subject, Rafe began with a different notion, "We should order pizza then take the meal to the bonfire. A soft drink would be nice too."

"We could stay here with a bottle of wine. I could try to shift again. Now that I understand what was keeping me from changing my form, I'll succeed. I no longer have the fear of reprimand in my head. You've changed everything in my mind."

"You want to try again, today?" Rafe sounded incredulous. "Didn't expect you to attempt so soon. Would have thought..."

"You look surprised. I'm no coward. This is something I want for myself. You gave me the confidence I needed to overstep the fears inflicted too many years ago to heed."

"I just..." Again he broke off his thought. Seeming to marvel at the resiliency her statement ignited. "Never wanted to pressure you."

"Didn't think I would give up, did you?" She thought that was strange. Believed he would have asked her if she wanted to try several times by now. He hadn't. Seemed he was acting patient with her feelings. "You truly meant to wait until I broached the subject. I told you, Rafe, I'm fine. Just dandy. Yes, parts of last night were difficult. Yes, I'm tired." She stopped when she saw him wince. "Parts were wonderful too. The things that stopped me last night are in my mind. Those ridiculous notions were put there a long time ago."

"True, it has been at least twenty years since the event happened. Maybe a bit longer," Rafe agreed, his voice laced with caution. "After he blistered your bottom because of his rage, you probably never tried again after that."

Dallas couldn't help but cringe when he mentioned the spanking. To get welts, he didn't use his hand. A board came to her mind. When she tried to recall more, her mind was a blank slate. The fact her father beat her was horrifying.

"Pizza would be nice, although cooking calms me. Since we've spoken to Ruby and Cole, I've been a bundle of nerves. During parts of the interview, I thought they would rip me apart. Would rather cook than do anything else. If you don't want fish tacos, I can make pizza. With the dough needing to rise that would take longer. We've got a lot of toppings in the fridge to choose from. How hungry are you?"

"Cook," he encouraged her, understanding that was the answer she wanted to hear. "I'll help."

She laughed, feeling lighthearted for the first time since she tried to shift, having then discovered more about herself than she'd ever thought possible. She held up her hands to place further emphasis on her answer.

"No, you won't. You can clean up the mess I make. That would be nice. The cleanup is the only part of cooking I abhor."

Rafe made a disgusted snort of a sound. "That's hardly fair. You get to do something you enjoy, while I…" He captured her in his arms. Kissed her hard. When he looked up, "I'll leave you alone to ease your nerves. I'll be happy to clean up whatever mess you make. I believe I'll go for a walk. I need time to think about all you've told me."

"Me too. That's why I need to be alone in the kitchen. Dinner at six." Despite her best efforts, moisture clogged her throat. Feeling both pleased as well as disturbed with all that was going on around her, she watched him start for the door. While the need to know was strong, the need to ignore her past was just as prevalent.

"Six it is. I'll be back before then. I'll chop anything you need chopped." He gave her a brief kiss to her forehead before turning on his heel.

Holding her breath, hands clasped in front of her, Dallas watched Rafe leave the room. When she heard the front door bang shut, she made her final decision. Hurrying up the stairs to their bedroom, she pulled her shirt over her head, unfastened her bra then did the same with her jeans.

Inside the room, with the door closed, she hopped on one foot then the other to rid herself of the rest of her clothing.

Rafe must know what she intended. He could read every thought in her head. Still, he left her to fend for herself. When he wanted, the man could be a saint. She hoped to have something to show him when he returned. Her new husband understood she needed to do this by herself. He would never interfere with her wishes. In front of him last night, she failed to shift. Something that should have been easy for her. Today, she meant to succeed.

Dallas stood beside the bed naked. She thought of all Rafe spoke of before the failed attempt. Channeled his words. Chanted them just as age old words had been vocalized in the ritual. Recalled the feeling coursing through her. Recalled the way her mind intimidated her to the point where she couldn't think. To a point where she couldn't be herself. She wanted all he wished for then more. Needed to be able to play with Rafe when they were both cats.

She gulped air…once then twice. Closed her eyes with another big gulp of air. Remembered the cats she saw during the ceremony. She watched one shift in front of her eyes. That was the way it should be done. Her arms as well her legs tingled with seeming anticipation. She was going to do this. This time her attempt would be successful.

While she channeled the cats she saw, her body trembled. Quivered. A blast of energy sped up her back. Surged. Electrified, half explained the sensations coursing within her. She was afraid this was taking longer than it should. Terrified she would fail. No. No, she didn't intend to fail. This was happening.

Relax. You're trying too hard. Breathe in then out. Unwind. Let your body do the work for you. Yes, you were right. I understand your need for privacy. Think about becoming a cat. Forget the nastiness. Pretend I'm with you, encouraging you. I'll be so proud of you when it's done. Don't try so hard. Just let this happen.

As if Rafe stood in the room with her, she nodded. Her eyes still closed. Her body calmed. With shock, startled by the suddenness, she was a cat. It happened. She did it.

Rafe! His name exploded from her head. *I did it! I did it!* She found herself jumping up and down. If she could have clapped her hands together, she would have.

Can I come home now? He was laughing. Seemed he felt her joy. Wanted to be part of that happiness.

She was certain he would sense the answer. She didn't want to tell him no. Nonetheless, that was what she intended. *No, I still have to cook. Don't want you to get in my way. You have this habit of stealing food I've prepared before it's finished. I'm going to become human again. We can play tonight after we eat. Not going to talk to you any longer. Goodbye.*

Dallas understood she could never tune him out nor could she keep him from listening to all her thoughts. She hoped he would give her the private time to absorb her newfound skill. Changing had been easier than she expected.

Don't put your clothes on.

Dallas jerked at the unexpected intrusion to her thoughts. Heat rose with his suggestion. *What? Rafe, I can't be in the kitchen naked. What if someone stopped by, I'd…*

Please.

No.

Didn't think you would do what I asked. I'm disappointed. Thought you were more adventurous than that. Wished…

I'm not someone who enjoys taking chances. You know that about me. While I don't mind posing nude in your upstairs studio. I'm not…will never cook, wearing no clothing. I won't.

We'll see.

Rafe didn't say anything more in return. In a way, she was a bit disappointed. After changing back to human form then dressing, she raced to the kitchen, half expecting that Rafe would be sitting on one of the kitchen chairs, prepared to disrobe her if she dared show herself wearing clothes. He wasn't. A relieved breath of air left her lungs. She sensed he had something else to do or he would do just as she suspected. Feared he would confront her father. Didn't want that either. He'd been so angry when he discovered her father blistered her bottom, she didn't know what Rafe intended.

If dinner was going to be on the table at six, she needed to get busy.

Humming, she went to work. She knew the recipe she was about to choose by heart, changing her mind about all the scenarios that were brought up.

She didn't make pizza. In the mood for something high calorie, she put together one of her favorite meals, chicken alfredo. The cream sauce turned out spectacular. She had a secret ingredient which set her recipe far and above anything she'd ever tasted. The presentation was beautiful. In anticipation of the mouthwatering dinner, her stomach rumbled. The screen door opening caught her attention.

Dallas wasn't surprised when Rafe sauntered into the kitchen, a bright smile on his face. As was his habit he wrapped her in his arms then kissed her hard. His tongue divided her lips, seeking entrance. His hands on her butt brought her against the proof of his need. She touched her tongue to his as his plundered inside her mouth.

Ahh…

You liked that, did you? We can take this one step farther before dinner. Maybe two or three steps farther. I spy a place I'd like to have you.

What?

It was so much easier to kiss you when we couldn't also read each other's thoughts.

After he ended the kiss, he spoke softly. Touched the tip of her nose with his finger. "I'm proud of you. Wished you would have waited for me. I wanted to be there…with you when you triumphed, but I understand your hesitancy. Want to do it again right now?"

No, not this instant. Dinner is ready. You just want me naked. Not going to fall into your wicked plans.

Wicked?

Yes. Wicked.

Dallas cleared her throat to speak. That kiss muddled her head. Sent heat spiraling into a cataclysmic abyss. "I know you wanted to be part of my shifting. I'm a coward. I was afraid to fail again in front of you. Needed the privacy. With you in the same room, I didn't want to… If you weren't with me when I botched it, the disappointment would not have been as bad. I needed the privacy to experiment on my own." Except for Rafe, it seemed she'd always been alone. He completed her. Made her whole. Why didn't she want him with her in such an important time?

Dallas had no further answer to that question. Nothing that would assuage his wounded senses. Rafe knew her so well; he probably would have an idea.

Rafe still held her. One hand roamed her back beneath her shirt. When he spoke, his voice was tender. "I didn't know how I would get all those negative vibes out of your head. You did that all by yourself. Thought at one time you might need hypnosis. Glad we didn't need to find someone who could do that for you."

The thought of lying on a couch while being hypnotized didn't suit her. He brushed soft kisses down her neck then back to touch her mouth again. "Me too. Are you hungry?"

"Famished." His gaze was focused on her and swept down the front of her, lingering on her breasts. "For you. I'm hungry for you." His hands tightened around her waist and slipped beneath the hem of her skirt. His thumbs hooked at the top of her panties.

She tried to ignore the ardent gaze, the avid sweep of his eyes down her body. When she spoke, her voice was weak. God, she wanted him too. Starved for him. He was pushing her backward. She clung to his shoulders. Seemed it had been so long since they last made love. "I've made one of your favorite dishes. We should eat first. Hmm…" At the new placement of his hands, she had no more words.

Rafe's laughter hooted from his lips. He looked at her as if he was already devouring her. "You and I are of the same mind. Don't know why we need to wait to make love. The food will still be there when we're finished. I can have you before as well as after dinner. Maybe even during." He picked her up as if she weighed nothing. Set her on the table. Came to stand between her legs. "I'm going to make love to my wife. To the best friend I have in the world."

She gasped at his outrageous words. Shocked by the thought of becoming intimate on a table in the kitchen. "No. No, Rafe, you're not. Not here!" She heard the panic in her voice.

"Seems lately no is all you've been telling me. Need a yes from my woman. If I don't get one, my ego will be bruised. You wouldn't want to injure my self-esteem. I know you, Dallas. Better than anyone else on earth."

She put her hands on his shoulders. "Not in here, Rafe Frasier. Can't. What if…" Her question was halted by the play of his mouth on hers. The sweep of his tongue across hers. His fingers exploring dark, intimate territory.

No more protests, love. Just go with the flow. When I bring you to your pleasure, you will be more than pleased.

He continued the dance of their tongues between her parted mouth. Slipped his hands beneath her shirt. He didn't need to ask. Dazed, she raised her arms. He found the clasp on her bra. A moment later he swept the garment from her arms. Her shirt over her head. Both tumbled to the floor. Her breasts fell free. The nipples tightened from the crisp air wafting through the open window. He cupped the rounded globes in his hands while he continued to kiss. Tugged her bottom lip. Bit with delicate care. Placed tiny biting kisses down the column of her neck then across her collarbone. He found the hollow between. Laved. Sucked hard. Moved back to her mouth. Kissed her sweetly. Kissed her hard. Explored the inner recesses.

His caresses on every part of her were sensual. Mercuric. Her body flamed to life. She sought more from him. Her hands wandered down his back. She forgot about her protest. Forgot about everything except what Rafe did to her. Stunned by rippling sensations, she couldn't think. No longer cared if they made love in the kitchen…on the table. What she understood was the primal need orchestrated within.

"Lift your hips, love. Need to get rid of the rest of your clothing." After those few words, he returned his attention to her throat. Across her collarbone again. He sipped on one hard crest then the other. Tugged her skirt along with her panties down her legs. Her legs were parted. She was open to him in every way.

Stepping back, staring at her as she sat on the kitchen table, her legs spread wide, he disrobed, tossing his clothing on the floor to join hers. He was everything to her. She might protest but she never wanted to deny him. The kitchen scenario was novel. Daring.

"Ever since I left you, I've been thinking about this. I want you now. Don't like to wait for the woman I need." His fingers brushed her moist dark secrets. Touched her with slow precision. Moved on her most sensitive flesh. Ignited. He grinned at her mercuric mewls of pleasure.

Because of the slight distance created when his gaze romanced over her, Dallas' thoughts returned to the 'what if someone came along?' scenario. Looked in the window? Opened a door? She saw Rafe shaking his head, grinning. His expression reminded her of a little boy in the candy store picking out his favorite chocolates.

One more time he read her mind. "No one would dare visit us this instant." He still stood between her legs. His hand on the curve of her hip. "Wrap your legs around my hips, sweet. This is going to be fast, hard and chaotic. Scream if you want. No one except me will hear you."

She did. He entered her in one powerful thrust. Her body arched to meet his. He plunged again then again into her channel. Deeper each time. Harder. So solid she moved on the table. The burst of energy filled her, sent all her senses into a whirl, fragmenting, shattering. The world seemed to implode as all control left her body.

With his climax he roared. Two more thrusts then he stilled. His next breath was deep. He set his forehead against hers. His breathing harsh. Their gazes met. "I'm sorry. Next time we'll go slow. The pleasure will be exquisite. I'll have a slow hand. Make you writhe with your need. Ease my way."

Dallas didn't care about slow. The climax he orchestrated was everything she could have ever wished for. Her breathing calmed as did Rafe's. The scent of the meal filled the air mingling with the spicey scent of Rafe.

"Should we eat now?" Dallas didn't know what to say. She was still shaking from the powerful end to their loving. Everything she thought about sounded stupid to her after what they just did on the kitchen table. Oh, God, they made love on the kitchen table. Before this instant, she'd never thought anyone would do something such as this. What else would Rafe do to surprise her?

He pulled her back, so she sat. Her breasts bounced with the movement. He grinned again. Seemed he couldn't stop smiling. Stepping back, Rafe watched her while he continued to beam at her. His gave traveled over her. "Love the way you look after we make love. Haven't seen you many times like this. Flushed. Sated. Parts of your body swollen from my loving attention. Your breasts moving softly as you try to breathe again. When we finish eating, we can take this to the living room. Make love in front of the fire or we can go upstairs. Oh, I forgot about your cat. I need to see your cat. We'll do that first."

"Will you hand me my clothes. Please." Once more, Dallas was at a loss for something appropriate to say. She needed armor to protect her from his gaze. She felt both shy as well as vulnerable.

"No. You're just the way I want you. No changes. If you recall, we ate naked last night after we loved each other. We can do that again. Tonight is only our second night together." He kicked their clothing aside.

"Last night, we weren't in the kitchen of your house. I wasn't sitting on the table naked while you stared at me." She tried for stern; couldn't accomplish that particular note with him staring at her.

"Forget it, Dallas. The clothing is off limits tonight. No one is going to come by the house. Let alone walk in on us without knocking. There is no one who would spy on us by staring in the window."

"I can't."

"We'll move into the dining room. There are no windows."

"Rafe!"

"I'll close the curtains then lock the door if that will make you feel better." He headed for the door.

It would. She didn't want to tell him that. A tiny giggle rose from the back of her throat. "Your incorrigible."

"I want to look at you. If you'd chosen to go out, you wouldn't be in this predicament. If we ordered pizza and walked to the bonfire, you wouldn't be sitting on the kitchen table naked, your legs parted for me, searching for the words necessary to gain your clothing. If—"

Dallas interrupted as she turned to watch him do as he told her he would do. She liked to look at him too. His butt was tight, firm. His shoulders so broad. Even though it was only May, he was bronzed from the sun. She could never spend enough time looking at him. He was so different from her.

"I'll dish up." Dallas scooted from the table. She felt self-conscious as well as shy. Wished she dared put something on her body. Even a robe would be nice. Rafe would know she was naked beneath. That knowledge should be enough to satisfy him. In his present mood, she understood he would object. Trying to talk him into it would be a waste of energy. Once Rafe's mind was made up, nothing could move him to a different tact.

She piled both plates high. He poured wine. They sat in the dining room. Ate. Drank. She felt awkward. "This was different when we were in bed," she blurted.

He ignored her comment. Forked a piece of his meat. "When we're done with this, should we retire to the room upstairs? We are in the perfect outfits to shift…wearing nothing at all. I need to watch you change to your cat."

"If you intend to do the dishes naked, I would watch." She felt a bit of vindication at her suggestion when he frowned. She would be surprised if he accepted the small challenge. On the other hand, if he did as she asked, they would never make it upstairs. They would make love again. More than likely in the kitchen. On the table.

"You would put off the shifting for the dishes? I guarantee you that if you watch me, you'll find yourself back on the kitchen table. If that's what you want…" Rafe waggled his eyebrows at her, all the while grinning.

"Rinse them now. We can do the dishes later." Dallas didn't want to walk to the sink naked in front of the man. She knew he'd focus on her breasts, their movement. He told her often how much he enjoyed watching them, the way they bounced. If she could stop her breasts from jiggling, she would.

His ensuing smile told her he was getting everything he wanted. When she started rinsing, he set his hand against her backside. Ran his fingers along the ladder of her ribs to reach in front so he could hold one breast. She sucked in air. He allowed his other hand to smooth across the curve of her hip then behind to claim her backside.

"Listen, buster!" She turned to him. He watched her breasts slide along his chest. She wanted to put her hand across them to stop the bounce. He held them to her sides.

"Before you start, I know what you're going to say. Behaving is impossible when you're standing beside me not wearing one stitch. I will never get enough of your body. Love all of it. Every precious inch. Later, I intend to show you how much."

She turned. Shoved a plate into his belly. "Here. Make yourself useful. Put this into the dishwasher."

They finished the dishes. Despite her protests, he swooped her into his arms to carry her to the bedroom upstairs. After he set her beside the bed, he stepped back. Leaned against the bedpost with his arms crossed. He appeared to be a man with no concerns.

"Show me what you can do."

The pride Rafe felt in her carried through in his words, coupled with the tenderness. She needed the emotions he generated. All her life, except for with Rafe, she'd felt inadequate, lacking in so many different ways. She was silent a bit longer. Shy. Dallas imagined a lot of her feelings had to do with those first few times she was denigrated for shifting.

"Will you shift along with me? Like last night when we tried?" Dallas didn't know if she wanted him to watch her. Once again, she felt uncomfortable. Out of place. "What if I fail?" Her biggest fears seemed to be of failure.

"You won't. Now you've reacquainted yourself with the process, nothing will hold you back." He lifted his broad shoulders. "Shifting is equated to riding a horse or a bicycle. Once you learn, you will always remember how it's done. Just an hour or so ago you changed to your cat. You recalled doing so as a little girl. Now that you've repeated the process, you won't ever forget."

"I'm awkward. I know it took me longer than you to change forms. I'm…" she didn't wish to tell him she was embarrassed or felt inadequate. She was both.

He sauntered over to her. Kissed her quick before stepping back. "I want to watch. You know I won't change my mind."

She was resigned. As he told her, he wouldn't differentiate from his stated purpose. "If that's what will please you. Who am I to change your opinion?" she told him, a bit sharp at having her wishes ignored.

"Now…don't get bent out of shape. Just this one time. I'll be with you as soon as I see your cat. Alright? Humor me in this."

"Fine." She threw up her hands in frustration. Gave up to his whim as she'd known she would do all along.

Rafe stepped forward, reaching for her. "Let me hold your hands. I need to feel the surge of energy that will race into you when the moment comes. Adrenalin rush is something unprecedented."

His words made her feel better. She did want him to hold her hands. Did need the security. "That would be nice."

"Thought you might say as much." The warmth of his hand surrounding hers created confidence.

She swallowed down her fear of failure. "Yes, I don't think I can refuse you anything."

As if he understood it was now time to put herself on the line, he smiled then nodded. Dallas closed her eyes. Thought about her cat. This afternoon she looked at herself in the mirror. Strutted her stuff for a few seconds after the final excitement calmed.

Adrenalin pumped. Power flowed in unending waves. Her body vibrated with sensual anticipation. Arms along with legs trembled. She was in her cat. Rafe stood next to her. Dallas felt dwarfed by his great size. He touched his nose to hers.

You're beautiful. I want to play.

How do cat's play?

They wrestle. Swat their paws at each other. Tumble on the ground. Without warning, he pulled her down to the floor. He was on top of her. He switched position so now she sprawled on top of his huge body.

Rafe! I don't know how to play.

I can see that. His voice was tinged with amusement. *As a human you also have difficulty with playtime. It's something I'm going to have to teach you. Now, step back. Walk around the room. Strut your stuff. I wish to be able to recognize your cat.*

Dallas did as he asked.

You do have a bit of swagger on you.

~ * ~

As it turned out, John Shaw didn't accept Ruby's invitation, which wasn't an invitation but more of a command to see her the next day. He ignored the request, refusing to give the order credit. While Rafe was frustrated by the delay, he wasn't surprised. The man didn't understand that one didn't refuse the McKennas.

Ruby swore. At least that was what Cole told him when they met later in the day. Cole drove to their home. Knocked on the door. When Helen answered, it was to open the door a crack. After what he related to the McKennas the morning after the wedding, Cole wasn't surprised to see the blackeye. This man, John Shaw, was violent. From what Rafe understood, Dallas' father, the one all remembered when the two were first married, was not a violent man.

This new revelation put more of a spin on what they understood about the family. While Dallas told him there were times she thought her father hurt her mother, he'd believed it to be a child's memory. Until this moment, he wasn't certain Dallas recalled events correctly. Possibly, what she remembered was about something else. Perhaps something she didn't understand.

"What are you going to do if John Shaw refuses to come to you?" Rafe understood the question to be fair. Long ago, someone would have been made to sit for an interview. Force was not a tactic that could be used in the present.

Cole swept his fingers through his hair, leaving some strands standing on end. "I've been thinking about that. Guess we'll have to go to him. The interview cannot be put off. This afternoon would be as good a time as any."

"The man doesn't have to open his door to you," Rafe reminded him of a fact Cole was certain to have thought of. John could remain inside for an indefinite amount of time.

"I'm going to his job. Confront him at work. If he knows I'm there, which I hope he won't, he won't be able to hightail it out the back door. His boss will give me a room where we can speak in private. Ruby will wait there while I strong arm the man so he makes it to the private room his boss will have ready for our use."

"A surprise tactic," Rafe suggested, thinking about Dallas along with everything that man put her through. This afternoon, if they were lucky, there would be answers to some of the questions, if not all.

"A surprise tactic," Cole agreed with a chuckle. "I will expect you to be at the back door waiting for the runner. You have permission to tackle the man, to use any means at your disposal to bring him with you to that isolated space we will have at our disposal waiting for us to use."

"What do I do then?" Rafe began to enjoy thoughts of John finding himself brought to task. He hoped Dallas' father would try to run. A good scuffle seemed to be in order at this time.

"Catch a cat. I believe John will try to escape me. He won't. Not with both of us on to him."

"Haven't we decided that Helen is the shifter, not John?" Rafe asked, bemused at the conversation. Both he and Dallas needed to get to the bottom of this affair in order to move on with their lives together.

"That is a definite possibility. Something mother remembers from the past points the finger toward John. Don't understand why he would punish Dallas for shifting if he could change to his cat. Wish father was still alive. Mother says at one time they were good friends. He would be able to tell us the truth. Suppose I haven't spent enough time getting to know, as well as understand, the clan. From this point forward, I plan on changing that. Been too caught up with my life to pay attention to those who need me."

"Don't be too hard on yourself. When your father died you were young. What were you? Ten? Twelve?"

"I was eight. Didn't understand why he was gone. Mother kept secrets from me. Secrets I now know."

"What happened to your father? Ruby told Dallas' he died of cancer. That's not true. Is it?" Rafe was afraid he was overstepping. The need to understand overpowered politeness. There were too many questions to leave anything to chance. He found himself tapping his fingers with impatience while he watched the play of emotions on Cole's face. The McKenna was in the process of debating what he could and could not tell him. Rafe held the distinct feeling, Aaron didn't die. In that case, what happened to Cole's father? Understanding the nature of shifters, Aaron McKenna would not have run away.

Cole was shaking his head, his brows drawn together in a deep frown. "This doesn't go farther than this room. Mother and I, along with the rest of the McKennas, have kept this secret for more than twenty years."

"You don't believe he is dead." There was a wealth of scenarios to follow that statement. Dallas was gone and she reappeared, though not after twenty years passed. He'd heard of the Kinnel Stones. Rumor had it that if a person entered into them, they would be transported somewhere. No one knew where.

"My father didn't die of cancer. You're right on that score. Mother thought it best to spread that story instead of the fact he disappeared. Father didn't run out on us. He was faithful. He loved his family with all his heart. Hell, Mother was his mate. Shifters don't do that. Don't leave their mates for any reason."

"Aaron disappeared." Rafe snapped his fingers. "Just like that, vanished. Sounds too much like Dallas' story. That's what happened to her. The difference is, she came back to us. So…where the hell is your father?"

"Dallas' return is what has my mother hoping Aaron will return from the dead. If at all possible, my father would figure out a way to come home. He would move heaven and earth to do so. The McKenna would never stop trying."

"Damn," Rafe rose. Paced. "I can relate to your mother. At the time, I didn't know Dallas was my mate. When she disappeared, she was my best friend. I missed her. When I couldn't find her, I felt as if my heart shattered."

"I understand you can relate."

Rafe stopped. Turning his attention back to Cole, his gaze pierced into his friend's eyes as if reading his mind. "The two of you, you along with your mother, don't think John Shaw is Dallas' father. Who is that man? Do you have some idea?" Every piece of information sent Rafe's thoughts spiraling in different directions.

Cole paused for a few seconds while he stared out the window. "We have some thoughts on that subject. Nothing concrete, mind you."

Rafe sucked in a deep breath of air, coming to a conclusion. "John Shaw isn't Ian McConnell. Dallas' father might have disappeared around the same time as Aaron. Ian along with Aaron have gone missing. Do you suppose they are together? If they were, that would put your mother's mind at ease. Do I have anything about that right?"

"There's a thought. Can't tell you if your summation is correct."

"You're guessing at everything."

"Yes, the two went missing at the same time, give or take a few hours. Are they together?" One dark eyebrow slanted upward. "Imagine they could be. Suppose they might be in different centuries. Now you understand our predicament a bit better. We can't accuse John Shaw of something we are not certain about. The only way Mr. Shaw can be brought to justice is if either my father or Dallas' father return from wherever they've been for the past twenty years. If I was a betting man, at this point, I'd say that's not going to happen, even though Mother prays for that with all her heart. All these years she has kept Father in her heart, refusing to accept the fact he might never return to her."

"I can't tell Dallas any of this. How can I not?" Rafe was beside himself with confusion along with frustration. "She deserves to learn the truth as we are uncovering the facts. Doesn't she? She should understand the man who beat her, put welts on her tiny bottom is not or never has been her father or a father to her."

Cole almost smiled. The gesture didn't quite reach his eyes. He coughed as if to clear his throat before he spoke. "You're the only person who can answer that. The only one who can decide what Dallas is capable of dealing with. Mother and I discussed the situation. We both agree the telling of the story is up to you. If it were me, I'd want to learn the man who abused me physically as well as mentally was not my father. My mother and I are certain that John Shaw is an imposter. For some reason, he orchestrated two men's disappearance then he took over Ian McDonnell's life."

"Do you think Helen knows about any of this? Could she be culpable? Part of a conspiracy?" That was a notion Rafe didn't want to conceive. Dallas' mother was not a role model anyone would simulate. Still, Helen was her mother. She was supposed to have loved her husband. Helen would bear the scars from her claiming.

Nothing made sense.

"Yes. How could she not be part of his plans? She lives with the man. Has done so for over twenty years." He paused in thought, tapping his chin. "Helen would have been able to tell the difference between Ian and John. Don't you think? While they do appear the same on the surface, they couldn't be identical. There would have to be some differences in the two men."

"Makes sense to me. If what you say is true, what could the man hold over Helen's head to keep her from speaking out?"

"Isn't it obvious?" That dark eyebrow flew up again. They appeared to have the same mind set now.

"Dallas!" Both seemed to say her name together.

"John held Dallas over Helen's head to keep her in line. To keep her from announcing to the world who he was…more important…who he was not. You know, I don't believe either Helen or John are shifters." Rafe found himself sifting through the data given to him. Trying to recall everything Dallas ever told him about the two people she assumed were her parents. He felt both relief as well as fury knowing John Shaw was not the biological father to Dallas. After that, sadness for Dallas' childhood swept through him. His emotions waged war inside him. He needed to control those simmering passions during the upcoming interview. Shifters were known for their patience along with their control. Now, he needed to use all of those characteristics to Dallas' best interest.

"Ian was the shifter," Cole mused with some thought. For a few seconds he stared at the billowing clouds above. "Mother and I never discussed that as a possibility. I'm more than eager for the interview."

"That's why John doesn't like shifters. He understands that Helen will never give herself, heart as well as soul, to him. Might despise all shifters for reasons we can have no idea about. I'm eager to learn."

The two stood in front of the factory where John Shaw worked. Ruby was there waiting for them, looking determined. Rafe's heart went out to both her as well as Dallas. He prayed there would be a few answers waiting for them when they finished speaking with the fraud. Nevertheless, no one expected John Shaw to admit to anything. Rafe imagined this was perhaps a waste of time for all of them. If any truth was to be had, those facts would come from Helen. That was also doubtful. She would be too afraid to shed light on her true husband's disappearance. Helen kept quiet for so long.

Earlier, Cole spoke to the owner of the factory. He arranged a private room for the interview. Rafe was no longer delegated to the back door, since the place for the discussion was secure. John's boss corralled John then brought him to the empty room to await his questioning, never telling him specific details.

As the three entered the room, John was pacing around the perimeter. When John saw them, his face blanched. His eyes appeared wild and dark. He flinched. Tried to turn away. If he could have reached the door then disappeared, Rafe didn't have one doubt he would try. The door was blocked to him.

"Have a seat, John," Cole said, his voice void of emotions. One would never be able to tell how moved he was or the anger simmering deep inside. Cole had more than one job to do. For everyone's benefit he needed to discover the truth. "We only have a couple of questions for you, John. The first of which, is why didn't you come to the keep when you were summoned. You must understand the laws of the Clan Chattan."

Silence greeted the first question. Cole might never receive the resolutions he looked for. Time would tell the tale.

Rafe took a seat around the table as did Ruby. John remained standing, moving from one foot to the other, clearly nervous. He raked his hands through his hair. Ruby's hands were folded in her lap. Rafe leaned his forearms on the table, running his hands across the smoothness of the cherrywood. Cole stood a few feet inside the closed door.

Tension crackled in the small room while Cole waited. Slow, jerky movements brought John to the table to sit. He set his hands on the wood before leaning back in his chair. His chin was up. The man's hair was the same color as Dallas'. As, he was told, was Ian's. His eyes blue. Many of his physical characteristics were passed down to Dallas. The eyes, the hair...perhaps the body build. Helen was slender, frail. Her hair was brown, and her eyes were a soft color of blue; they held no vibrancy. Perhaps that was something that was stolen from her when Ian McDonell vanished so many years in the past.

"What's this all about?" John sounded annoyed, even impatient. "I'm losing pay while we idle away the day. Can't afford to lose pay. Have a family to support. If the McKennas weren't so arrogant, they would

262

understand the needs of the common laborers."

Cole nodded to the man. "Why didn't you answer the summons? I would learn why the McKenna was ignored." His expression still showed little to no sign of the fury Rafe knew boiled beneath the calm façade he presented.

It was obvious John wasn't going to be forthcoming. They already understood that much. If he knew what happened to Aaron along with Ian, he would never convict himself by saying as much. Would never explain away the disappearances. A new tact would need to be taken. Even minutes into the interview, Rafe understood the futility of the summons. All they could hope to gain by this order would be to detain him so they could talk to Helen. That interview might well be just as futile.

The man who pretended to be Dallas' father lifted his shoulders with an insolent gesture. The sneer on his face told a story all its own. "This isn't the medieval ages. Didn't see a reason to answer your summons. Not against the law to ignore the mighty McKennas."

Cole inhaled a long deep breath of air, seeming to think on a reply. "No, it's not. Coming to speak with me is a sign of respect. From your apparent attitude, I will draw conclusions then deal with you as I deem appropriate."

"Deal with me..." John jumped to his feet. At the expression on Cole's face, he sat down again. "You can't be dealin' with me. You're not the law. The only rights here that you have are archaic."

"You're correct. I'm not the law. I do have power in this part of the highlands. That reason is precisely why I can do whatever I want. I have the means to put you anywhere I wish. Could imprison you for the rest of your life. There are still dungeons in the keep." Cole bent over; his hands braced on the table to stare into John's eyes. "I would be careful here. The conclusions I've come to are far from flattering for you. Sometimes in the highlands a man creates his own laws. Laws that apply to a deed we all take exception to. A man can disappear without a trace in the remote highlands if he isn't careful. There are places where no one would find them for say twenty, perhaps twenty-two years, even longer. I believe you accepted that power as your own, to serve only your purpose. That is not the way we do things in the highlands."

"Now see here!" He shook his finger at Cole. "You can't!" One more time John started to rise and was stopped by Cole's piercing glare. "You have no authority to do anything. I'm leaving. You can't hold me here in this room without my consent. I'm not giving my permission." Even after his outburst John remained seated.

"By the power of the Clan Chattan, I can."

Shocked by Cole's calm demeanor, Rafe almost thought Cole believed his words. Maybe he did. The McKennas ruled over the Clan Chattan for centuries. In their strong hands, they held the power of life as well as death. Beneath their capable hands, the clan flourished over all those centuries.

Rafe could almost believe.

Cole stood. Walked around the table to stop behind John. If he meant to intimidate, the plan appeared to work. "Why do you beat your wife? I know for a fact that Helen married her mate, a shifter. Mates don't beat their wives no matter what."

"Where do you get that crazy notion? Never laid a hand on Helen. Would never beat her. I love her. Have always loved her. Needed her. Wanted her. I meant to have her." After those words, his face reddened. Seemed unwillingly he gave something of his emotions away.

"Yesterday she had a black eye. Was afraid to open the door. Kept the barrier slitted a crack while she talked to me. The light was enough for me to see her eyes," Cole reiterated what had been witnessed. "You beat her, didn't you?"

"No! Helen ran into a door. She's clumsy like that. Always has been. One of the traits I enjoyed about the woman. She does have two left feet. Can't dance worth a damn," John was trying to defend himself with a flimsy argument. There was no argument that could protect a wife and child beater. John Shaw had a great deal to account for.

"You used to beat your daughter, Dallas. She was around two years old at the time." Cole turned his attention to Rafe, asking permission to go on. Rafe shook his head. This was not the time. He had to talk to Dallas first. Only she could give this type of permission. Dallas wasn't in the room with them.

"Falsehoods everyone. Dallas hates me! She would lie to see me punished. The girl has always despised me. Never trusted me like she should her father."

He found her in his head. *We are confronting John Shaw. Do you have objections to my sharing your story with him.*

Which part?

The times when he beat you for shifting. Would mention the welts he gave you.

Do whatever it takes.

Rafe cleared his throat, jumping into the discussion after looking to Cole for permission. "I saw them. The welts you put on Dallas when she was so tiny she couldn't do anything to shield herself. She had no one to protect her. The damage to her little bottom wasn't something that could be accomplished with a man's hand. What did you use, John? A board? A whip? Something else? My God, she was only two. I don't need proof. I saw the damage through Dallas' eyes. A shifter never resorts to violence against women and children. Is only violent to protect those he loves…his family."

"You've no proof! You can't prosecute a person without a trial." John drummed his fists on the table. Anger overcame him. His fury skyrocketed.

"Haven't you been listening to me, John?" Cole asked. "Here in this village of Carnoch, I've authority no one would dare dismiss."

"I'm leaving."

"You're welcome to try," Cole said agreeably as he watched with a shuttered expression.

John sat down, seeming to understand leaving was not an option. He didn't say anything more. Appeared to be waiting for Cole to issue a verdict. Cole wouldn't do that without discussing the options with his mother. Together, they would decide with great care what to do about the man. John had a point though. Without proof of Ian's demise, they couldn't claim any foul play on his part. They didn't even have a body.

"You will remain here until further notice." Cole's command seemed to surprise John. "The door will be secured. I will send someone to make sure your needs are attended to. It will do no good to attempt running. You have nowhere to hide from the clan."

With John confined to this room for an indefinite amount of time, Helen might speak some of her truths. Might enlighten them about her treatment of her daughter. Dallas' mother might indeed be this man's victim. A victim of over twenty years in the making. Helen never reached out to anyone. Never asked for help. There must have been people she was close to who would have helped her.

Rafe found himself shaking with his frustration. Angry as well. Confronting Dallas with these truths would never be pleasant. She deserved to know that nothing was accomplished. John would remain a free man. No one would believe she recalled a beating when she was a toddler. She would be shocked to discover the man wasn't her biological father. Though there was also no confirmation of that singular fact.

Together the three walked from the room, leaving John behind. Their footsteps echoed in the long corridor. Cole stopped to speak with the owner of the business.

Outside, they paused. The air smelled of the coming rainstorm. Rafe thought the weather mirrored his mood. Dark clouds sat on the horizon. A brisk wind whipped around the buildings, turning up fallen leaves.

"What do you make of the man?" Ruby asked as they continued toward the car. In deference to her son, the McKenna, Ruby didn't speak during the questioning. Now she did. Her need to know apparent. She cleared her throat before making her feelings known, "I want the two of you to bring Helen to me. While her husband is locked up, I'll be able to question Helen as well as give her some reassurance as to her safety. From this discussion coupled with what I remember of Helen and Ian, I've come to a few conclusions on my own."

Rafe looked back to the secure room where John was imprisoned. His heart skipped a beat while he thought about his wife. Wives were a new experience for him. Thinking about Dallas' needs was not. "I must be at the questioning also. For Dallas' sake, she needs a spokesperson. Someone to see to her needs. She won't wish to see or speak with her mother. Experiencing Helen at the wedding was one time too many for Dallas. I'm not going to put her through that trauma again."

"We still don't have answers," Cole reminded everyone. "We have ideas with nothing substantial to backup those thoughts. Maybe Helen will be able to give us some relief."

"This all seems as if it's a dead-end."

"Let's visit Helen. See what she has to say," Cole suggested. "What harm can talking to her do? Nothing. We'll bring her to your rooms at the keep, Mother."

~ * ~

Helen sat on the edge of the straight back chair, teacup along with saucer in her hands as she looked around the room. Ruby watched Helen's hands shake. Saw the thin line of her mouth as if she didn't intend to say one word. Her back was stiff with apprehension. The woman was terrified. That much was obvious to any observer. Helen kept looking over her shoulder. Almost as if she expected John to burst into the room unannounced.

"Why don't you relax? I could get you a glass of sherry if you like. The alcohol might ease your nerves better than that cup of tea," Ruby suggested. If she wasn't so upset with the woman for the abuse she heaped on her daughter, she might feel sorry for the lady. After speaking with John, Helen might be innocent. She understood keeping that thought in mind was important. If Helen found herself intimidated into doing things against her nature, they would need to deal with the situation with more caution. When Ruby drew on past memories, she leaned in that direction. Helen also was John Shaw's victim.

"How can I relax? You have my husband held within a locked room. I know you do. He would be here if he didn't find himself detained. He would defend himself along with me." With a shaking hand, she brought the cup to her lips. Sipped. Set the cup on the nearby table. "I believe I'd like that sherry you offered."

"Your husband has been questioned, yes. He's been given the opportunity to defend himself. True, the McKenna detained the man as is his right by the laws of the Clan Chattan. When we learn what is going on here, John might be released. He might find himself punished. Held accountable for crimes committed. The clan laws are specific about certain offences against other people. From what we've learned, John Shaw has committed wrongdoings against both you as well as your daughter. There are other accusations he needs to explain."

"He has done nothing wrong." Helen exchanged the tea for the crystal glass of sherry that was brought to her. She sipped until most of the liquid was drained from the container. She set that next to the teacup. "I've heard enough. I'm going home if it's all the same to you. I have no reason to remain here. Unless I am also a suspect."

Ruby was surprised Helen challenged her. She would meet the challenge with one of her own. "Dallas, your daughter, was abused as a baby both physically as well as mentally. We know that for a fact. When she shifted for the first time in twenty years, she recalled a number of things. You abused her verbally. John abused her physically as well as verbally. My God, how could you have allowed that horrible man to beat your toddler until there were welts on her bottom? That fact is unconscionable."

Helen wilted back into the chair. Her face paled except for the purple and dark blue bruises around her eye. "No…I didn't…love…" Obvious she was having trouble speaking. "I love Dallas. Your accusation is unfair. I would never hurt her with words…" her voice trailed off as if she realized she lied. Helen did that very thing for most of Dallas' life.

"You belittled her. Made her feel less than what she was. Berated her to a man who detested her for shifting. Something all shifters experiment with. Taunted her with the beautiful womanly curves she possesses. Curves her husband adores, by the way."

"I didn't want to…" Again, Helen's voice faded with the realization she said words that should have been kept secret. Had been kept secret for years. Looking at her lap, she ran her hands along the jeans she wore.

"Sweating hands? Nervous hands? Of course you are, Helen. You're lying through your teeth. When are you going to become a real mother? Defend your daughter. Love her unconditionally. If you could do that, she would forgive you all those years you kept her at arm's length."

"I did. I did love Dallas. I do. John…he…" Helen sounded desperate to speak the truth. Still, the woman hesitated.

The threats her husband held against her must be very real. "John made you? Does he hate shifters so much then?" Ruby continued as if there was no end to her accusations. She didn't intend to let up. If she pushed hard enough, Helen would give something away. Helen was weak. She'd been beaten down. "How could he do that to his daughter? To you? Shifters aren't violent to the ones they love. He claimed you. You're his mate. Can I see the scars left from the claiming?"

Helen gasped. Stiffened. She bit out without thinking. "I have no scars. Don't know what you're speaking about."

"Of course you understand. I witnessed your marriage. You and your husband spent the night in this keep in the tower room designated for the happy couple. Ian would have claimed you that night. All shifters claim their mate as soon as possible. It's the only way to ensure the two will see each other in another life. I'm also certain the women around you would have explained certain events to you. You're lying. The question is why? Why would you disclaim something that is a known fact to more people than just me?"

"Ian...? It's John Shaw I married. He's not a shifter. We didn't spend the night here at the keep. You must be mistaken. You're thinking of some other couple. Your memory..."

"You've been married twice? When did that happen, Helen? I'm not mistaken in this. I remember the event as if it was yesterday. The last name on Dallas' birth certificate is McDonell. Why don't you tell the truth? You will feel better once this is all out in the open." Ruby was thoughtful at that moment. She realized Helen had been maneuvered into a corner. Her face was now void of all color.

"I..." Helen swept her tongue across her lips. "I..."

Ruby thought she might as well jump in with both feet. Needed to lay everything she suspected on the line. This wasn't what she hoped would happen, though it was what she expected. In every movement that Helen made, Ruby understood she wanted to speak the truth. For more than twenty years, she kept secrets. Now was the time to free her mind of all the pain those secrets caused.

Ruby began to speak. "John is Ian's twin. Am I right? By birth or by accident? Was it just a coincidence that the two looked so much alike people would think they were the same person? Are they true twins?" Ruby didn't intend to back down now that the real questioning began. This session was as much for Helen to tell the truth as for her to learn about Aaron. Ruby suspected the two disappearances went hand in hand.

Helen was nodding. She moistened her lips. Swallowed more liquid courage. "I…" After that she was shaking her head. "John just looks a lot like Ian. He took advantage of that fact… Oh! I said too much. Don't believe anything I've told you. There weren't two marriages. Just one." Her hands shook. Sherry spilled from the glass she held. Dripped down the sides. "He might kill..."

Obviously, there was more going on here than Helen was willing to speak about. Somehow, she had to pull the words from her. Keeping her voice as calm as possible, Ruby continued the questioning, "By my point of view, you haven't said enough. Not even close. What happened to Ian?" Ruby found herself holding her breath, waiting for a reply. She needed the truth more than she needed to breathe. Though she prided herself with her patience, that commodity was fading fast. Perhaps there had been only one marriage. In that case, Helen and John Shaw lived in sin.

Helen gasped in a breath of air. "I can't say anything more. He will hurt me for being here. If he found out, I… No…" Helen was shaking her head. After she tried to stand, she sank back into her chair.

"Who will hurt you?" Ruby stepped out on a limb with this question. She needed the confirmation. Seemed Helen needed to confide.

"John… Yes, he gave me the black eye. Didn't run into a door as I *ken* he told you. My clumsiness is always his excuse for my bruises. I…" Tears poured down her cheeks. Her sobs made her small body shudder. "I hate the man. Despise him… It doesn't matter anymore. After he hears of this, we, Dallas and I, are both dead. I can no longer protect my daughter. He despises her because she is Ian's daughter. Because she can shift just like Ian. Nothing matters anymore." She looked up. With the backs of her hands, wiped tears from her cheeks. "Ian is gone…"

"Your husband is confined to a private room in the factory where he works. If you tell the truth of what happened to you, he won't be able to get to you or Dallas. The clan will keep you safe."

"You can't believe that. He is cunning. John will find a means to get past whatever guards you might have at the door. We are all in danger. You too, now that I've told you my truth."

Ruby needed to stand firm in her beliefs. Needed to convince Helen the clan would keep her and her daughter safe. Convince her she had nothing to fear. Ruby had no doubt that Rafe could protect Dallas. "I don't think so. What happened to Ian McDonell? Do you know? Did John kill him?" Ruby hoped with this revelation, she might discover some truth about her husband. Hoped Helen would deny the death.

Sobs still wracking her slender body, it took some time for Helen to reply. When she looked up to speak, her face was wracked with unhappiness. "I don't know what John did. Ian disappeared. I miss him so much. Every night I pray for him. Hope he will someday come home to me, even though in my heart I realize he won't. Ian has been gone far too long. If I think with logic, I believe he is dead. When my heart steps into the act, I know he is alive. If my mate died, I believe I would feel the death. Would know in the deepest part of my heart that he is gone." Helen stopped talking to wipe a new onslaught of tears from her eyes. "I've waited for Ian to come back to me. To fix what John has done. Nothing has happened." When she looked up, silver tears streaked down her face. "No one found his body. Ian would never walk out on me. I don't know what happened," she hiccupped. Her hands in her face, she cried out all her fears.

Ruby sat down beside her, feeling many of the same emotions. She placed her hand on Helen's back, rubbing with gentle strokes as if trying to sooth a small child. "Hush…we are trying to figure all this out. There is so much we don't know. Ideas we have guessed at yet have no answers. The same can be said about my Aaron. He disappeared. No one found his body. One day he was with me, the next…gone. I made up a story about his death. Though…I know he is not gone from this earth." She moved away from Helen. Repeating herself as if she didn't believe the facts in front of her. "The next day he wasn't anywhere to be found. Aaron would have never left me either. As with you, I know in my heart Aaron is alive somewhere trying to return to me. We need to do everything possible to find these two men."

When Helen looked up, her brows furrowed together. The crease line in the middle of her forehead deep. "John will kill both of us. Dallas won't live and neither will I. He threatened me with her life more times than I can remember. Because of that, because of all the things he made me do and say, my daughter…my own daughter despises me with every breath she takes. I love her so much. This situation tears my heart into shreds. Short of sentencing Dallas to death, there was nothing I could do."

"She will learn different feelings when all this is brought to light. I'm certain she will forgive you. Dallas won't hold a vendetta against her mother once she knows the truth. Perhaps your future is brighter now."

"You think so?" A small smile flitted across Helen's mouth. "I hope so."

"Know so. Right now, as I said earlier, John is being held in a room where he works. He cannot get to either you or Dallas. With this new information, Cole will make certain John is detained. We have places in the keep where we can secure those who have committed crimes against the clan. While we are not above Scottish law, we do have clan laws that must be upheld."

"How will we ever prove the truth? I believe John did something with Ian. Don't know what. If he killed him, where is the body? He will never admit to anything. John will never shed light on what happened."

"I shouldn't have to remind you that your daughter disappeared for several months. Do you think John had anything to do with that? I don't. That was a crazy quirk of fate to bring two shifters together who had been torn apart before the claiming. However, the fact remains that in the highlands unexplainable things happen. We can be a superstitious lot. We believe in myths as well as fairy tales. If need be, we could send John Shaw someplace out of our lives. There are rumors about the Kinnel Stones. Cole along with Rafe could see that he enters into them."

"You don't think Ian or Aaron are dead? According to rumor, no one can return to his or her time once they enter into the stones." Helen pulled her lower lip beneath her teeth. Worried it while she thought about what had been said. "I don't believe Ian is dead either. Sometimes he talks to me. Tells me to stay strong. He's told me he is trying to come home to me."

"With all my heart, I believe my husband is alive. We've always been connected through our minds. Our hearts beat as one while our souls are united, even with the distance between us. There are times at night, that I'm certain he is talking to me. Telling me to take care. He's told me as soon as possible he will return. I have to believe. As to no one returning from the stones, seems there was an account of a man finding his way back to his time. He was a Stuart, Kit Stuart. That happened hundreds of years ago. So…we know coming home is possible."

Ruby never told Cole about those evening encounters. She didn't want to get his hopes up. Perhaps she shouldn't say such things to Helen. Maybe all this was better left private. She needed to confide in someone. Who better than a woman with a similar experience?

"I've had similar nights with Ian…not every night. Since Dallas' return from the past, I've spoken with Ian more often. He knows about Dallas tumbling through that strange void to a different century. I don't know how he knows. Since they are both shifters, perhaps there is a connection between them I can't possibly understand. What do you think?" Helen looked at her, hope shining in her eyes. "Do you believe they are alive?"

"Yes." What more was there for her to say? With all her heart, she believed Aaron was not dead. What she could say beyond a doubt was that he might never come back to her. She missed so many years with her mate. If he managed to return, Ruby would never allow him out of her sight. Unfortunately, her man would feel smothered. That sentiment wouldn't last more than a day if she was lucky.

Chapter Nine

The kitchen was blanketed in dirty pots and pans. The dishwasher was running. Aromas of fresh baked bread filled the room. Dallas' hands were buried in another batch of bread dough. With the back of her arm, she tried to push an errant strand of hair from her sweaty face. The flour on her nose itched. Turning her head, she sneezed then sneezed again. Fine strands of her hair tickled.

"Allergies…" she muttered, disgusted with the horrible pollen in the air. She knew she could take a pill to ease the symptoms. Hated pills. One pill always led to creating a side effect that would need a second pill.

Damn things.

She heard Rafe's laughter at her swearing. He always thought it amusing when she swore. For her that was a rarity.

If you don't stop laughing at me, you won't get dinner.

Happen to know there is more food in our kitchen than we could eat in a week. Rafe shot back at her.

She needed to finish with the dough so she could wash her hands. The dishwasher would stop soon. The dishes would need unloading. So worried about the interviews, she needed to keep busy. This was the best possible way. Putting the final touch on the dough, she set the bread to rise in a large bowl that had been smeared with butter. Covered it. Set the dough in a warm place to rise.

Because of her restlessness, dinner turned into an extravaganza of food. On the countertops were enough dishes to feed a small army. She made two vegetable dishes. Two types of potatoes. A roast was ready to go into the oven when the oven was empty. There was rice as well as noodles.

Dallas debated inviting Cole along with Phoebe to the house to share a meal. They could invite Ruby too. Heaven alone knew they had more than enough food. She decided against doing so. Cole was busy. The questioning might be over now. It might not. Could last into the evening. Rafe wasn't reaching out to her except to laugh at her swearing. That fact led her to believe his mind was busy. She didn't think that was a good excuse to ignore her.

She wondered at the lack of communication between them the last few hours. She didn't believe he'd ever been silent so long. Maybe he found some piece of information he couldn't divulge. She shuddered. Rafe would believe she deserved to learn everything about her mother as well as her father. She fidgeted. Did she want to know? Yes and no.

The timer dinged. The potatoes were done. They came out of the oven to be set in the microwave to stay warm. The chicken frying in the pan on the stove needed turning. She thought about making a pasta salad. There might be time. She had no clue as to when Rafe would return. Looking at the clock on the oven, she saw the time was four thirty. Plenty of time for a pasta salad. She decided no. If she succumbed there would be more dirty dishes. She hated doing the dishes.

She grinned. With a huge sigh of contentment, she continued with the dinner menu. Rice simmered on the stove. The recipe contained a special blend of spices including turmeric, she put together as an experiment one day when she felt lonely. She'd loved the taste. Until she returned from the past, she often felt lonely. Never knew what to do with herself. So, she cooked. The lonelier she was the more she cooked. The more at odds with her feelings, the more she cooked.

The sight of the kitchen table reminded her of the past evening. What they did there. Her cheeks heated with memory. Embarrassed to the tips of her toes wouldn't come close to describing how she felt. He undressed her. In this same room she was naked, as was he. After he started kissing her, she forgot her mortification at her state of deshabille. Now, the top of the table was covered with various dishes. Not her body with her legs wrapped around his lean hips. The apple spice cake she baked earlier sat on top. A salad of fresh greens filled a bowl sitting next to the desert. She washed strawberries. Cut up an apple. Grapes were piled into a bowl along with a banana. The fruit salad could wait until the morning. The dish would be great for breakfast. She wiped her hands on her apron. Fanned her hot face. The kitchen was too warm.

Maybe she should give both Ruby as well as Phoebe a call…an invitation for dinner. After the meal the fridge would be filled with leftovers. Well, what did Rafe expect when he left her alone all day with nothing to keep her occupied but cooking. All her photos for the magazine had been taken care of then sent. The photos she wanted to use for her exhibit were printed and taken to the framers. Rafe had known for years, when she was anxious, she cooked or baked. Many times, he'd been the recipient of homemade meals along with an assortment of baked goods coupled with deserts that took her fancy.

The timer dinged again. The trouble was she didn't remember what was ready to take off the stove or change to a simmer. Maybe the cinnamon rolls she put in the oven about twenty minutes ago were done. She needed to test them. She pulled open the oven door and tapped her finger on the top of several rolls.

Bent over at the oven, checking the rolls, she jumped; startled by the hands on her person. She knew it was Rafe's hands caressing her backside. She would recognize the caress anywhere. His scent…manly yet spicey. The feel of his strong hands sending an electrifying surge of ecstasy through her to the tips of her toes, then back to become an ache in her core.

She sensed him smiling.

"Hush, love. It's only me. I want you. Seems you've covered the kitchen table with dishes of food. All that for dinner? Your eyes must be larger than your stomach." Rafe's hands were on her rear, fondling. Squeezing. Sending heat spinning into her or…was the heat she felt from the oven? A little of both.

I know it's you. Who else would be caressing my butt? Besides, there is no one else who could be in my head.

You cooked.

What did you expect? Dallas wasn't surprised he didn't answer her question even though he didn't stop exploring her backside. She didn't ask him to stop. The sensations Rafe created with his touch were all too nice.

Not this much food. You made all these dishes so I couldn't put you on the table again. Need your legs wrapped around my flanks. What do you say? Should we find a different room to seek our pleasures? You don't need to answer. I'll find somewhere else, love. I've missed you. Haven't seen you all day. Need to feel you beneath me or on top of me, even in front of me. We could try something different.

He moved his hands again, embraced her. Ignited her. Oh yes, the hot caress on her rear caused by his hands was calculated. Meant to disturb her peace of mind. Make her forget the problems facing them all. He intended to seduce. Charm his way. Sweet-talk her into oblivion. While she had her hands inside a hot oven, she needed to keep her mind on what she was doing. She pulled out the rolls. He backed up, his grin plastered across his face. The man did like to find her in positions where he could take advantage of her.

I need to put icing on the buns.

Not while they are still hot. You're mine until the rolls cool off. Icing buns. Hmm... I could ice yours. You could ice mine. We could taste.

You're incorrigible.

Those words have been said before.

That much was true. She thought of the kitchen table. After he heard her thoughts, she heard the silent laughter. After that memory, he didn't keep his humor from echoing in the kitchen.

Not today, buster...too busy. You've got to tell me all that happened. I'm a nervous wreck waiting to know what was going on just down the road. She found herself laughing too when he lifted her off her feet. Carried her to the living room. The blinds were all pulled. She assumed they would not be showing their neighbors what he intended to do with her buns.

The doors are locked. The shades drawn as you can see. Wanted to make love with my wife in a different room today. This one will do for now. He nipped her ear. Sucked on the sensitive lobe. *The kitchen table was full of food. Did you bake so much so I couldn't love my wife on the table? You should know by now; I'll always find a place to give you pleasure. Need to hear you moan, call out my name. I love the sexy little whimpers rippling from the back of your throat when I pay attention to your lovely breasts.*

I don't mind. I've missed you. Want you more than you want me. I'm certain of that. The living room is just fine. No one is coming...

Doubt it about the missing you part. You couldn't miss me more than I miss you. Thought about you all the time I was gone. Thought about all your lovely curves I need to rediscover.

That's confusing. I'm all yours. Thought about those different parts of you I need to sightsee.

True to the confusing part. You can stroll around my body any time you wish.

Just like the first-time last evening, the loving was hard and fast. Disordered. They needed each other too much to wait. Rafe groaned when they finished, his forehead against hers. He was breathing hard. "Next time I'll make this right. I'll love you with a slow hand. Won't be messy. Need to make the loving last. Want you to beg for your pleasure."

She was sitting up, trying to pull her shirt over her head while searching for her cutoffs. He was sipping on one breast. She was certain he meant the next time was now. Pushing away from him she drew her brows together. He ran his finger along them, smoothing the fullness. "Feathery soft."

"Rafe, stop! I need to finish dinner. Food will burn. Come into the kitchen. Pour me a glass of wine. When that's done you can tell me what happened today. I need to hear all about it. Every important word that was spoken. What did John Shaw tell you? Did he do all those awful things you were thinking about?"

"Did you buy out all the stores?" He looked over the entire kitchen. His perusal not just the kitchen table. "I don't think you have ever made this much food. Are we expecting company? You should tell me," he said, with a quick bark of laughter. "We've enough here to feed a few hundred people. Is someone we know getting married? Are we taking this to the keep for the celebration?"

"No, to both," she muttered, irritated with his comment as well as his laughter. He should know her well enough by now to guess at her state of emotions during the day. She huffed, sent her breath of air skittering from her lungs, "I was nervous, as you should guess. You know me and how I get. We can take some food down to one of the homeless camps by the bridge. The people there might appreciate what you don't." Her grumpiness was not warranted. She understood why he frowned at her.

He leaned his backside against the counter. Crossed his arms over his chest while he watched her putter around the kitchen to finish what she began. "In case you haven't realized this yet, everything you do I appreciate. Don't ever doubt my thankfulness. I love all the food you cook. Nonetheless, there is only so much this man can eat before the food spoils. I believe your idea about the homeless camp has merit. We can take care of your proposition tomorrow when there is more time."

"You do?" She rose on the tips of her toes to give him a quick kiss on his cheek. He tried to deepen the kiss. She danced away shaking a finger at him. "Irredeemable. You've only one idea in your head. Tell me what happened while I tidy things up here enough so we can eat. I'll wrap up the food that will save the best. Figure we can keep most of the dishes for up to a week."

He'd set his hands on his narrow hips. His grin widened while his eyes sparkled. "We can't eat until our guests arrive. That wouldn't be polite. I am starving," he told her deadpan. "Do you want me to set the dining room table?"

"What?" She whirled to stare open mouthed at him. She felt as if she dropped through a hole in the floor. "What did you just say?" Dallas wiped her hands on the dishcloth she held. "You invited guests without asking? What if we don't have enough…" She stopped the question before she could finish. The ludicrous thought didn't bare repeating.

He lifted those broad shoulders of his she loved to touch. The grin on his face broadened. She wanted to trace the smile on his lips with her finger or her mouth. Either would suit just fine. She wasn't upset he invited people. After looking at all this food, she'd thought the same way earlier in the day. He took the decision out of her hands.

"I do recall what you're like when you're waiting for news as well as when your nerves are stretched to the snapping point. I've known you for how many years?" The question was rhetorical. He didn't need an answer. "Understand the only way you know how to relieve your stress is by cooking. Ruby, Cole and Phoebe should be here in about twenty minutes. Needed time to make love to my wife before the guests arrived. I'll set the table. Good dishes?" He quirked an eyebrow her way. "You do understand, both Ruby and Cole will have things to tell you. Neither Cole nor I were with Ruby when she spoke with your mother. Perhaps we should have invited your mother to dine with us also. Helen might have some interesting facts to shed about John Shaw."

"No!" Her heart lurched. The beat stopped for a moment. "You can't do that. I don't want to be around my mother. Ever!"

"Adamant, are you? Are the dishes in the dishwasher clean? I'll unload them. Believe you might change your mind." Rafe backed away from that statement to his question.

"You do that. Set the table…unload the dishwasher. Make yourself useful. Anything you want but that. Just don't bring Mother here. Promise. Don't call her with an invitation. I need time to come to terms with whatever I learn tonight before I see Mother ever again." Dallas wasn't certain how to feel about the interference. She didn't know if she wanted to be with company when she received news of today's events. Privacy had its advantages.

"What's wrong? You look as if you've seen a ghost." Rafe wrapped her in his arms, pulling her close so she fit against his body. "Do you not want company? I would think all the news you could inhale would set your nerves to calm. We cannot have you cooking all day tomorrow."

"I do want company. It's just that I'm not certain I wish for you to share the news with me right now. I might want some private minutes to come to terms with possible disappointment. You're the only one I can share such things with." Feeling both excited as well as uncertain, she touched Rafe's chin.

He held her finger. Kissed the tip. "You won't be disappointed with what you hear. Know that for a fact. I'll give you a tiny hint, after that we can finish preparing for our guests. Your father is not your father."

"Don't tease. What you say makes no sense." Dallas turned in his arms. "You're speaking in riddles. Plain talking is what I need." Yet the truth of what he told her entered her mind hundreds of times during the past years. She never wanted that man to be her father. Sometimes hoped and prayed he couldn't be the man who sired her. The fact should relieve her mind. "If John Shaw is not my father, who is?"

From above her Rafe grinned. Kissed her hard then set her aside. "John Shaw is not your birth father. By the way he treated you while you were under his roof as well as his protection, he is also no father to you in any way. As to your real father, the man's name is Ian McDonell."

"I'm confused. Who is my birth father? This man you call Ian McDonell?" Dallas felt a giddy rise of excitement enter into her. She didn't know why. It was Helen who abused her through the years as well as her father…John. John wasn't her father. John never gave her any consideration to her once she stopped shifting. To him it was as if she didn't exist.

Unless I shifted, I didn't exist.

True, that's when the man who is no father of yours put welts on your little bottom. Forget about John. He won't ever be able to hurt you again. He is under confinement at the McKenna keep.

Are you certain?

Yes.

Rafe cleared his throat. "What I told you before. The man by the name of Ian McDonell is your birth father. He is a shifter too. Helen cannot shift as we guessed. Neither can John Shaw, the man who raised you."

"Ian McDonell." She rolled the name around in her head. "He is a shifter. My mother's mate or a man who seduced my mother?"

"Both." One more time Rafe was laughing. His chuckle sent heat coursing through her. She felt the sensual gaze of his eyes cover her. "Just as I have seduced you any number of times. Don't you think it was fun?"

"What happened to my father? To Ian McDonell? The man wouldn't just up and leave his mate along with his daughter." Dallas tried to ignore his thoughts. He was having too much fun teasing her. She was having the devil of a time shutting him out of her head.

"Good question. No one knows the answer to that one. Just as you disappeared so did your father. The difference being you returned. He hasn't. It's been more than twenty years. Ruby never told me the exact date of Aaron's disappearance. Helen hasn't mentioned the date that Ian left her. The two men might have been caught up in the same vortex."

"Do you think Helen loves John? Would they have been in a conspiracy?" In her heart, Dallas prayed her mother felt nothing for the horrid man she'd called Father for all her life. If Helen didn't love him or care, why did she stay with him? Why didn't she leave him? John masqueraded as her father. Dallas hated to think the man threatened her mother. That thought put a new spin on her story, on their story.

"I need to freshen up. Can you look after the rest of the meal?" What she needed was time alone to digest this news before the others came and she learned more. Dallas hurried up the steps to their room. For several long seconds, she leaned against the closed door. Closed her eyes. Assimilated information. Taking deep breaths, she let the silence surround her. She was right. With company, there would be no privacy to her thoughts.

Ian McDonell was her father, not John Shaw. That fact would mean her name was Dallas McDonell. Dallas liked the way her name sounded. As soon as possible, she meant to do something about that. Maybe tomorrow she would look into getting the papers that would change her name back to what it was supposed to be. Did she need to do that? Wouldn't her birth certificate have the correct name typed on it? Wait…she was Dallas Frasier now. No need to change her last name.

Looking at her watch, she realized she had ten minutes before their guests arrived. A quick rinse in the shower would have to suffice for now. Dallas left her clothing scattered on the floor from the bedroom into the bathroom. Soon, hot water poured across her back and shoulders. The heat soothed her tense muscles. Because she spent the day cooking, she didn't realize how stressed she'd been. The array of food on her counters should have told her the extent of her turmoil.

Naked in the bathroom, Dallas sprayed a light perfume over her. Used lotion on her arms and legs. She picked out a never before worn long gown that would give her comfort. When they finished with their meal and retired to the living room, she'd be able to tuck the fabric around her when she pulled up her legs beneath her.

A few minutes later, she walked into the kitchen through the dining room. True to Rafe's word, the table was set. He picked out the dishes he thought would be best to serve for the evening meal, selecting one of her salads, the fried chicken, coupled with a potato casserole.

There were two bottles of wine. Cole and Phoebe brought one as did Ruby. Rafe uncorked them before she arrived and poured glasses for everyone.

"You look beautiful," Rafe said as he handed her a glass then bent toward her to give her a quick kiss. "Whatever happens, know that I'm here for you. Always will be."

"Thank you." she turned to her guests, held up her glass. "Ruby, Cole and Phoebe. Welcome to our home."

"We won't speak of anything until we finish dinner. Promise," Cole said, seeming to see the stress lines around her eyes. "Don't wish to talk about anything that might upset you or keep anyone of us from enjoying this magnificent meal you've created here. Rafe told us you've been cooking all day."

The chatter at the dinner table was nonsensical, given the intensity of the upcoming conversation. Weather seemed to be the main topic of discussion. Dallas wasn't certain about the prospect of waiting. Unable to eat, she pushed food around on her plate. Her stomach churned and she decided she needed the nourishment. She sipped the wine.

Rafe noticed. He splashed more chianti into her glass. She didn't want to drink so much that she became tipsy but couldn't help herself. Rafe smiled at her. It was an encouraging gesture. The table was cleared. Phoebe helped Ruby fill the dishwasher. She set pieces of apple spice cake on plates and Rafe made coffee to go with the sweet dessert.

They met in the living room. Dallas curled her legs under her while she sipped on the next glass of wine. Rafe stood behind her, his hands on her shoulders. He used the ensuing minutes to give her a light massage. He understood the tension had not ended for her.

"Where do we begin?" Cole asked while his gaze traveled from Cole to Ruby then back to her. "Dallas, what would you like to know? I imagine that is the best place to start since there is so much that needs to be revealed."

Dallas didn't hesitate. She turned her attention to Cole's mother. "I want to know as much as you can tell me about my father, Ian McDonell. I don't understand how this imposter could deceive Helen. Doesn't make sense to me."

Ruby cleared her throat, directing everyone's attention her way. "This is my part. By the time Helen left my home this afternoon, she divulged much of the story. More than I suspected by the time we met. John didn't deceive Helen. She knew who he was the moment he stepped into her home wearing a smug, satisfied grin."

"There is a story?" Dallas didn't understand her surprise. From what Rafe told her earlier, there had to be a tale to tell. If John didn't mislead Helen, then how did the man come to be in their lives?

Ruby began her story. "Ian McDonnell, to begin with, is a shifter. He was proud of you. Knew you had the ability to change form when you were in the womb. When the truth was divulged to her, Helen was pleased too. She loves Ian with all her heart. Ian McDonell is her mate not John Shaw."

"What happened?" Dallas' heart felt ripped in shreds. All the years of abuse, of hate, tore at her insides. If her father had lived, none of that would have happened. "Mother shouldn't have been—"

Ruby shook her head, holding up her hands. "Wait. You've got to allow me to finish. Helen didn't have a choice."

"There is always a choice."

"Sometimes there are no viable choices. Not for your mother anyway. I'll get to that in time. Helen doesn't know what John did with your father. Helen swears the man is not dead. Says she talks to him in the evenings when the house is quiet. Most of the time he comes into her head when John isn't home." Ruby turned to Cole. "Just as I speak with Aaron."

Cole's eyes widened. He appeared as if he was blindsided by his mother's statement. "You've never said anything like that before."

"Didn't want to get your hopes up. I believe with all my heart that your father, my husband, is alive. Must believe it in order to maintain my sanity."

"Ian? You said Helen thinks he is alive?" Dallas' heart caught in her throat. Her hands twisted in the fabric of her gown. "I don't know him. Wouldn't recognize my father if I saw him."

"You would," Ruby told her. "Your father and John could be twins. It was by coincidence not birth. John wanted Helen from the moment he met her. The two were in high school together. He couldn't have her because she'd never wanted to be with anyone except Ian. John devised a plan to get rid of Ian. Seems to have worked."

"How? What?" Confusion rifled through her head.

"We don't know. Could be some type of vortex like the one you fell into. John swore to Helen he didn't kill your father. Told her the last time he saw him, he was alive. Also swore he would never return from wherever he sent him. I don't know why but I think Aaron became part of that scenario. He might have been in the wrong place. John won't admit anything. Helen doesn't know. Might have been trying to save Ian."

"I returned from the past," Dallas said, calmer than she felt. "Doubt if there wasn't some way my father, as well as Cole's, wouldn't be able to return. Maybe it just takes determination to return to the woman he loves."

Rafe pinched the bridge of his nose before running his hand along his neck. "Different places act in different ways. Except for one case as far as we know, the Kinnel Stones have never returned a person to the time they left…except for Kit. In his case it wasn't the exact same time. Months later in his case."

"If that happened, the men could be trying to return closer to the point where they were forced into the power of the stones. Don't you think?" Dallas asked as she sifted through the wealth of information she'd been given to think about.

"They could be following the course of our lives trying to reunite as soon as possible," Cole pointed out. "They might not have been able to return right away so…" He left the rest of the sentence unsaid. "There is so much we can't understand about traveling through time."

"We've no idea," Ruby said, her voice weak, a whisper in the room. "Maybe something traumatic has to happen to make an opening." Obviously, she was affected by the turn of events. "However, the conversations I've had with Aaron are in the here and now, the present not the past. I've told him about Cole along with our daughter. While I would love to have him back the second after he disappeared, doing so might change history. Since he didn't step back into our lives so many years ago, he would have come to us now if it was possible."

"Dallas didn't return the same day she disappeared. Her reappearance occurred several months after the fact," Rafe pointed out to the assembly. "Maybe that's the way of traveling through time."

Ruby leaned over to pat Dallas on the hand. "You should hear more about your mother. She's not what you've thought your entire life. She's a kind, dear person. A woman who hated what John made her do."

Dallas' back stiffened, still unable to forgive. "I don't know why. Helen abandoned me to John Shaw. She did nothing to help me. Humiliated me at every opportunity. Why should I listen? If you're trying to tell me the woman was a good mother, there is nothing you can tell me that would convince me."

"On the contrary, she was the best mother she knew how to be given the circumstance. Helen did all she could to protect you. She kept you alive." Ruby tucked a breath of air into her lungs before she repeated, "She was the best mother you could have. John threatened your life at every turn. All Helen's actions were orchestrated by that horrible man. She suffered to protect you. She cried when her words hurt you."

Ruby continued with her story. Filled the room with knowledge. When the tears began, Rafe picked Dallas up in his arms. Held her close while she cried out her sorrow. She soaked his shirt with her tears.

"What are we going to do?" Cole directed his question to his mother. "I've John imprisoned at the keep. We can enforce whatever punishment is justified."

"We should use the Kinnel Stones to send him away from here. After that, pray he doesn't find a way back to this time. If he did, we would have to punish him some other way," Ruby seemed to be searching for agreement from the people involved with Shaw's scheme.

"We could take him in the morning," Cole suggested. "Watch him walk into the stones. Make certain he doesn't leave. I would stay there until I was certain."

"No, I'd rather wait. I don't understand why, but I believe both Aaron along with Ian will be with us soon. If, and I mean if, we are able to meet our men again, we will have the proof we search for."

All Dallas wanted was to never see John Shaw again. Needed to put the past behind her in a way she would never be hurt another time. If what she was told about her mother was true, she should reconsider her thoughts. Doing so would be difficult. She'd loathed her mother for so long. "How does Helen feel?"

"About John, much the same as you. Helen despises John. Always has. For you, she hopes you will find it in your heart to someday forgive her. Helen told me if you can't, she will understand. She knows she tormented you."

"I would meet her tomorrow morning. Here. If Rafe can stay, that would be the only way I could talk to her. I don't wish to be alone with Helen." Dallas didn't understand how her life could turn around the way it had. All she thought was fact was no longer truth. Except for Rafe, she had no truths. Rafe was her rock. The only person whom she could depend on.

"Tomorrow then…" Rafe gave his agreement.

"After I get back to the keep this evening, I'll send a message to Helen. Do you want anyone else there?" Cole asked.

"No," Dallas murmured. "Just Rafe. He is all I need."

Minutes later, after all left, Rafe still held her. Dallas nestled her head in the hollow of his shoulder. "Do you think Ruby is right? That my true father is out there somewhere trying to find his way home?"

"Yes," he murmured, his chin resting on the top of her head. "One must have faith to believe in miracles. All this time has passed. There is much I don't know or understand. The universe is an interesting, as well as surprising, place. What I do comprehend…" he paused. "If I was displaced, taken from my wife as well as my child, I would spend my entire life attempting to return to you."

"That's sweet."

"My words are the truth."

What Rafe told her was a certainty. Given what she knew about the nature of shifters, she suspected both Ian along with Aaron were doing the same, searching for a way to return home. They would be driven to find their mates. The need to protect within them was strong.

Rafe slid his hands along her arms. "It's late. We should go to bed. Tomorrow will come too soon."

"Dallas! Dallas…Rafe open the door!"

"Who?"

~ * ~

When Rafe opened the door, Cole was there. Phoebe stood beside him, holding his hand. Her body pressed against his as if she needed support. Cole's expression was hard to define. He and Ruby had enough time to get home then for Cole to return here. Perhaps more, he wasn't certain of the number of minutes ticking along. Seems he lost track while speaking with Dallas. Rafe felt stunned by the expression on Cole's face.

"Did you forget something?" Rafe asked, understanding there was more to this surprise visit than met the eye. He looked into the living room as if searching for someone. Dallas joined them at the door. She walked to them; curiosity written in her expression. Cole didn't say anything more. Rafe placed Dallas' hand in his. Waited.

"Everything we anticipated, hoped for, has come true." Cole was breathing hard. His face was flushed with excitement. He brought Phoebe's hand up to kiss the back.

"We spoke of a lot of things," Rafe pointed out with a bland tone. "What is it you're talking about?"

"Aaron, accompanied by Ian, has returned. The two men, my father along with Dallas' father are at the keep. Exhausted from their ordeals, Ian is asking for his wife and daughter. Aaron is with Ruby. She sent me to tell you the good news.

"I'll get Helen as soon as I know the two of you are on your way to the keep. Mother called her before I left. On speaker, I heard her sobs of joy. We'll meet you in mother's suite of rooms." Cole wrapped an arm around Phoebe. His grin of pleasure never left his lips.

After the door closed, Dallas threw her arms around Rafe. Pressed close against him, Rafe felt the beating of her heart. One more time, Dallas buried her face against his chest. More tears streaked her lovely face. Rafe understood her terror coupled with what had to be happiness. She was about to come face to face with her father, a man she didn't know. Ian was a father she couldn't recall.

How do you feel? Having your father return this unexpectedly is a lot to absorb. If you'd rather not go, we can meet them in the morning. We can wait as long as you need. There is nothing that says you have to see your father now or even tomorrow even though he requested your presence. I'll stand by whatever you decide. Be there for you. Come let's sit. You can think.

Thank you… With her knuckles, she rubbed her eyes. *Don't know what would be best for me. Can't decide if I want to meet the man who fathered me. Right now, I'm trying to take in all the other information. Trying to come to terms with the fact John Shaw is not my father. That Helen didn't abuse me because she was a horrible person.*

"Your father might want time alone with his wife, his mate. The two of us could intrude on something more private. Giving them time to adjust might be the right step. What do you think? You could make up your mind in the morning."

"You're right on all counts. I would rather wait until the morning to see Father then confront Helen. Not certain I'll feel ready even then. This day…these events have overwhelmed all of me. My head aches. Can't seem to…"

"Hush," Rafe pulled her close. "I can't imagine how you must feel with all this new knowledge swirling in your head. I'll call Cole. Tell him we are staying home tonight. We'll let him know tomorrow if you're ready to meet with your parents. I'm certain Helen and Ian have a great deal of catching up to do.

"We'll see your mother along with your father in the morning, almost as we planned, if that's what you want." Rafe smiled at her, brushed long strands of hair away from her face. When he tilted her head so he could look into her eyes, they shimmered with moisture.

"Almost as we planned…," Dallas murmured. "Nothing these last few months has been almost as we planned."

The two were sitting together. He held her on his lap. She nestled into him. Rafe wound a length of silken hair around one finger. His voice close to her ear, he murmured. "What are you thinking? Would love to know. You are blocking me. You've learned something new."

She curled into him. Pressing against him. Seeking the warmth of his body. She whispered her answer. "I'm wondering what Ian is like. Is he nice? Cruel? Does he have the same arrogance much of the clan have? Will I ever be able to call him Father? Now, he is just Ian to me. Though I'm forever grateful John Shaw is not my father."

"I'm certain you will discover most of the answers to your questions tomorrow." Rafe's knuckles grazed her chin then down her throat.

"Are his eyes blue like mine? John's eyes were blue, but they were pale. Mine are dark blue. Most shifters have that same silver blue as you have."

"Not quite true. That silver blue you are thinking about are characteristics of the McKennas, Stuarts, and the Frasiers. I would guess Ian's eyes are very similar to John's. I don't know though. John was able to pass himself off as Ian. There must be marked similarities."

"John's hair is a tawny color."

Rafe smiled. While they talked, she managed to undo the buttons on his shirt. Now her hands splayed across his chest. Seemed she invited him to play. He had no objections to making love to his wife. Doing so might keep her mind off the developments she had no means to change.

"Are you sending me a hint?" His soft chuckle had her looking at him again. Her eyes were wide. Huge pools of blue. Her roaming fingers had a way of heating him, setting an inferno to burn. "I'm up for anything you wish. Hard as steel."

Her hand pressed against his sex. Even through the fabric of his jeans, he leapt to life. All it took from Dallas was the smallest hint, a suggestion that she wanted him.

"Not here in the living room. Need to find the bed this time." She pressed kisses along his torso. Nipped down the middle of his chest to stop at his waist. After unfastening his pants, her hand slipped beneath to caress him. His teeth grit together. She enticed every nerve ending he possessed. He couldn't have told her no if his life depended on that very thing. Adrenalin flared.

Rafe couldn't stop the groan of pleasure from rumbling from the back of his throat. His mouth found hers, hot and sultry. He feathered soft kisses. Deepened hungry kisses until a tiny whimper of pleasure floated from her mouth into his. He looked up. Touched the tip of her nose with his, his voice was soft. "While I love you touching me, I don't wish to explode this instant. Don't wish to embarrass myself. Promised you slow next time. This is next time." He tugged on her hand. Brought her fingers to his lips. "Call Cole…have to…" was all he could say as she straddled him. Her legs were on either side of him. Even with the fabric between them, he felt the dampness along with the heat that was hers.

Her long dress settled around her thighs. She bent over to touch his mouth with her tongue. The stroke gentle. "Call Cole when we're done here," she murmured as she slipped soft kisses along his neck. The hollow across his collarbone. Lower to nip with sensual touches on his chest. Strategic places meant to send him to the sun.

Rafe sent his hand into her hair. The long silken strands glided through the insides of his fingers and tantalized each nerve ending. In a million lifetimes, he would never get enough of Dallas. It seemed so much happened since their wedding. Her life was in turmoil. She still wanted him. Needed him as much as he did her. He relied on her. She taught him about patience. Showed him how to adapt to trying situations. Dallas was his everything.

"Thought you said the bedroom," Rafe murmured, though he wasn't disappointed. He would oblige his wife. If she didn't wish to wait until they could walk up the stairs to their soft bed, so be it.

"Takes too long to get to the bedroom. I need you now." Her fingers fumbled with the fastening of his pants. He didn't think she would ever get them undone as he resisted the urgent need to give her assistance in her endeavor. She might not welcome his help.

"You know I'd never complain about having sex with my wife in the moment. I like trying new ways along with new places to make love. Don't believe you've ever sat on me. Have you?" Rafe asked the question even though he knew the answer. He lifted his hips when she pushed at his jeans. They were around his ankles. He kicked them off. Pulled her dress higher. Her long white legs nestled against him. Direct heat at the apex of her legs tightened him more. She moved across his sex. The wetness of her sent more heat throbbing.

When his fingers slid between her legs, she was ready for him. He pushed aside the tiny strap of her panties then thrust inside. The tight channel heated and pulsed, milked him as he held still waiting to see into her eyes. For a moment her head fell against his chest. When she sat again, her ripe breasts held him in thrall. His hands covered her breasts. He palmed the hard tips through the fabric. He needed to taste. He could never taste Dallas enough to suit him. He tugged the bodice so her breasts would fall free. His mouth framed hers. Whimpers rippled from her into him.

He felt the shiver that was Dallas wrap around him, glide around his sex. Pulse. Enchant. Tempt. Together they were explosive. In seconds she cried out her pleasure. His growl drowned her cry. His heart raged. Her breaths were little sips of air as she tried to stop the shaking that encompassed her. That was too fast. Too needy. Would sex between them ever change?

"Rafe…"

"Hmm…"

"Can we go to the bedroom now? I need to sleep." Her breasts pushed against his chest. The nipples hard buds that he didn't want to ignore. Even if he wanted to forget, Dallas was making it damn hard to overlook.

Rafe felt the hardened tips sashay across his skin. He would have enjoyed tasting her, giving her more pleasure. He kept saying he needed for her to beg. A few seconds ago, he was replete. Satisfied. Now he wanted her again. "Why can't we do this slow? I'd…"

Dallas pushed away from him, laughing. He was mesmerized by the sight she presented. A little bit sweet and quite a bit naughty.

"You're still inside me."

"Hmm… should we do it again just like last time? Fast…untidy…" The constriction of her muscles sent an inferno of blood pulsing into his sex. One tiny movement and he could explode. Holding his breath, he grit his teeth.

"If we do, doubt if I'll be able to breathe. You're going to be the death of me." Dallas nipped his chin. Bit. Licked the small hurt.

"Who are you kidding? You've more stamina than me." Deep inside, he was laughing, enjoying the seductive Dallas. "What will you think of next? Should…" She touched her top lip with the tip of her tongue.

"Should we what?" He saw inside her head. Found himself chuckling. His Dallas was getting innovative.

You're right. The shower would be fun.

Hmpf…

"No one, I'm not kidding anyone, especially you. I wish you would stay out of my head. You take all the surprise out of my life." Dallas licked the spot where she nipped. Sat back, her breasts moving just to provoke him. All this suited some purpose. "If you're going to be that way, I want something to eat. Another glass of wine."

What way? He groaned, not about to wait until she consumed food and had another glass of wine. Dallas could make the next minutes last an eternity if she had a mind to do so. "You're a tease." His hands on her narrow waist, he thrust hard. Sucked one breast into his mouth. Laved and bit, provoked as well as tantalized.

One more time, she cried out and his seed filled her. She leaned against him, her head on his chest, breathing hard. He was stroking her back when she asked, "Do you think I've conceived?"

Startled, he set his hand on her belly. Felt no movement or heat that would indicate conception. "I'd not thought of that. No…don't feel a little shifter there. Not yet. Did you stop your protection?" He wanted to be apprised if she did. Seemed… she must have since she asked the question.

"You can tell by touching me? Tell if there is a little Rafe in my womb?" She sounded astonished by his statement.

"Or…a miniature Dallas? I'd like that. A little girl I can spoil. One who I will teach from the beginning that the ability to shift is a gift, not a horror to hide from." The thought pleased him. A little girl to spoil, to teach all he knew, sounded delightful to his ears.

"Can that be possible? Wouldn't we need to get a kit to know? You know, a pregnancy kit? You can't just touch me and know." Dallas ran her little pink tongue across her lips. Enticed. Tempted all his male endowments. The trail of moisture gave him reason to kiss her again. If he kissed her, they wouldn't leave this spot for another five minutes or more. She wouldn't get her glass of wine or more food. He needed to feed her. Maybe the next time should be in the shower. He was hot, sweaty. The sheen of moisture on her beautiful skin told him she was in the same condition. He'd never made love in the shower. They were all about new experiences.

"Yes, I will know when conception happens. Don't know if I would comprehend the fact the very instant, but soon after. So perhaps you have conceived tonight. We've a need to put something in your stomach. Come on." He set her off his lap then held out his hand. He wasn't going to allow her to dress. They would go to the kitchen for the needed nourishment then to the bedroom. "You said you needed food along with drink. If we're going to have another wedding night this evening, we best have fortification to last us into the *wee* hours of the morning. A bottle of wine on the bedside table along with a tray of snacks. Would you like an assortment of cheese and crackers or something more filling. We can raid the fridge. Find one of those deserts that will feed your sweet tooth."

"I would rather be in bed. Though a shower sounds divine. Can we take the wine in the shower? We could use those tin mugs we take to the bonfire in case one of us dropped the cup. We could just drink from the bottle." she murmured, moving away from him. When she started to bring her bodice to cover her, he stopped her, his hand on her wrist. His gaze roamed the length of her from top to bottom then back again.

"Don't, leave the bodice down so I can watch. In fact, why don't you take everything off. Leave the clothing behind. The floor is a great place for unwanted clothing. Gives testimony to our pleasure." Rafe was having visions of watching her walk naked up the steps. His imagination worked overtime. "We should go to the studio. Sit in that big chair. I'll hold you on my lap. We can see what comes next."

"I want to be in the bed…after we take a shower together. We can do that tomorrow night. The big chair, you know, it will bring back memories." She winked at him. Tossed her hair over one shoulder. After she stood, her dress slid down her body. He hooked his fingers around her panties encouraging them to follow her gown. The unwanted clothing pooled on the floor around her feet. With dainty steps she moved away.

When she stood in front of him with nothing on, he felt a self-satisfied smile form on his mouth. "That's perfect. You're perfect. Ravishing. Gorgeous."

Her face colored. He loved the fact she still felt uncomfortable being naked with him. Loved to see heat flame on her cheeks. Such a difference from when all he did was paint her. "We should get…hmm…what we need."

"The wine."

"Cheese and crackers."

"You get the wine along with the cheese and crackers. I'll bring up some of those lemon bars I saw cooling on the counter a couple of hours ago."

He did enjoy watching her carry the wine along with the glasses. Loved watching the curves of her hips entice him with their gentle swing. Liked her butt almost as much as he adored her breasts. Decided then and there he would give her rump more attention. He thought kissing both sides would be an enjoyable experience for them both. Wished to see her cheeks quiver when he kissed her soft skin, licked the small dimples she so detested. After they had that glass of wine along with something to keep the stomach from growling, he would explore more sensitive territory. Maybe carry her to that shower she spoke of with only the slide of water between them.

Sitting on the bed, each with a glass of wine in hand, he heard the soft sigh part her lips. He waited for the statement or question he knew would have something to do with her mother along with her father. Rafe supposed he couldn't avoid the topic forever. If she needed to talk, he needed to be there for her, a sounding board for her thoughts coupled with her fears. At the thought of meeting her biological father, she might also feel some excitement. She would have to bounce thoughts off him. Hear his viewpoint.

The base of his glass sat on his abs. He smiled at her. Saw the tension strains around her eyes. Wished he knew the words that would give her more encouragement. He didn't stop her when she drew the quilt up to cover her, then secured the fabric beneath her arms. Instead, his heart went out to her. "You're nervous again? Don't tell me you're thinking of going back to the kitchen to start another cooking spree. Are there even ingredients left in the house from the last one? At this late hour, would you be sending me to the store for supplies?" His teasing failed to spark a smile, not even a watery one.

Dallas held out her hand. True enough the fingers shook. "That's not from making love. The shaking is because of the thought of seeing my parents for the first time. I feel as if I've never known my mother. I have no recollection of my true father. Do I now have parents who care about me? What do I do with them? How do I deal with a mother and father who are going to ask questions? Once I left for college mother never said anything to me. Was that John's doing?"

"You're starting over…from scratch, so it seems. Your mother will be different if everything Ruby told us is true. Your true father is a singular man. You will have to discover who he is, as well as what he will come to mean to you. Does that scare you?" Rafe held her small hand in his. Rubbed his thumb along her knuckles. Saying the right words was important.

"I know. Yes, the fact they are both going to react to me in a different manner terrifies me."

"It's almost as if you've been born a second time. This go around is with the right parents. You will love them if they give you reason." What if those two took advantage of her a second time? He didn't wish to see her hurt. If that happened, Dallas would have him to help her through any difficult times. He would always be there for her. She called him her rock.

"Seems I'm always beginning my life from start." The long sigh she emitted ripped at his heart. He needed to fix everything for her. "I've had too many new beginnings in the last few months."

"Are you sorry? Any regrets? Do you wish all was as your life used to be? You would understand what is expected of you. As it stands now you've no idea what either of your parents would like from you. No idea if either of them cares."

"Yes, tons of regrets. How could I not? Life used to be simple. My parents didn't care for me. So, I didn't need to care about them. Now…" She leaned against the headboard, sipping her wine. Her face assuming a strange expression. "Do you ever wonder what happened to Gordon and Tinley?"

That thought rushed at him from out of nowhere. Since the time in Inverness when he saw the pair, he'd not given either of the men a second thought. "No. I'm just pleased the two haven't shown up here on our doorstep again searching for you. Can't write them off either. Not unless…" Rafe wondered if the two were alive. They were down on their luck. Living in a homeless camp. That's what he thought the place was when he saw them. "Maybe they were sent back to the time more suitable to those two. One could hope. Though, if they were, Lainie might find herself threatened again. That would never do. We don't want them to return to that time nor do we wish for them to stay in the here and now."

"Maybe not. You said you saw them by the docks?" Holding on to the comforter beneath her arms, she turned to him. Her eyes darkening as she gazed at him. Hope filled her expression.

"Yeah…" He rubbed the back of his neck, massaging tense muscles. "When we were there shopping for your dress. Something was off kilter about them." Rafe was thinking about the sighting on the wharf. If he wasn't mistaken, the pair were involved in a drug deal. Probably some drug they would know nothing about. There were lots of pills that could be bought that the pair would have never heard about. They did like their whiskey along with their women. The men could be easily taken advantage of. What Rafe didn't understand was why he cared.

Dallas didn't need to think about those two. She brought them up. Maybe talking about Gordon and Tinley kept her mind off her parents. If this was a diversion, he would humor her.

"How so? Not that I care too much. They are in a world they know nothing about." She'd set her glass on the bedside table. Now, she ran her hand across his chest. Seemed Dallas wanted him again. His little sex monster wanted him to be inside her. She intended to seduce him. He would never stop her.

"You ready for round three?" he asked, holding her hand with his. His tug on her quilt raised a smile. The beautiful firm globes he venerated fell free. He cupped one in his hand while he met her gaze with his. "This time we are going to do this slow and easy. Want you to beg me to bring you your pleasure."

"Hmm…" she sighed. Her hand stilled. "I believe I would like to beg. You can make love to me any way you like. Probably anytime you smile at me," she murmured with a soft sound. Her eyes closed.

"Dallas?" he asked, letting his knuckles travel across her cheek then down her neck. Rafe paused for a few seconds while he studied her.

She didn't answer. "Seems I wore you out."

Dallas was sound asleep. Rafe closed his eyes. He was far from able to go to sleep. Nerves strung tight after the last conversation would be an apt description of his concerns. Cooking would do nothing for him except make a mess that needed to be cleaned up in the morning. He thought of the return of the men, Aaron along with Ian. If John Shaw tried to do away with them, he could be brought in front of a regular court. However, if all he did was force two men into the Kinnel Stones, who would believe that was why they disappeared? Few knew of the superstitions revolving around those stones. Even so, most people stayed clear of the place.

He would have just as soon gone to the keep tonight. It seemed Dallas might be running from reality. Hiding behind her fears. He couldn't blame her. In his mind, reuniting Dallas with her father and mother needed to be accomplished as soon as possible. Dallas wanted to put the reunion off for as long as possible. Rafe didn't believe doing this would be easy or smooth. His mate would remain resistant to her mother. Forgiving her would be difficult, if not impossible. There was a great deal of hurt inflicted over her twenty-two years. Some of Helen's words would be hard to justify even if Dallas could learn to believe Helen had been forced to do and say the hurtful words and actions.

Leaning back, Rafe closed his eyes to the sound of the night. The time was growing late. Few cars traveled their street during the day let alone the late evenings. He heard the tiny frogs outside who liked the pond near their house. An owl hooted from some distance. Dogs barked, seeming to talk to each other. The evening was peaceful outside. Inside Dallas' mind, the night was a bombardment of stressful questions. Her nervous energy never failed to overwhelm her senses.

When Dallas' phone rang, he jerked, startled from a quiet daydream. He looked at the clock. Who could be calling at this hour? The time was too late for a social call. He didn't believe either Helen or Ian would call when it was after ten thirty. Both would have appreciated the fact Dallas needed time to adjust to all the newness of having two parents she didn't know. They would never intrude on their privacy unless there was some sort of emergency.

Easing out of bed as he hoped not to wake Dallas, he padded to her phone. He meant to look to see if the caller was important. First, he let it go to voice mail. He didn't recognize the number. The call wasn't local. Rafe waited several minutes before he used her password to listen. Under the circumstances, he didn't think she would mind. The last thing he wished to do was disturb her sleep.

He tapped on the voice mail. The words he heard were clear and concise. The first he heard gave him a start. Shivers of dread sneaked down his spine. He slanted a look at Dallas. She still slept.

This is the police in Inverness. I need to talk with Dallas Shaw immediately.

Rafe's heart skipped a beat. His breath caught in the back of his throat. No! This couldn't be what he was thinking. Something more for Dallas to deal with. If he could do this for her, he would without hesitation. He couldn't be certain. Because of his thoughts a few minutes ago about Gordon and Tinley this call seemed more real than her father appearing after more than twenty years missing. Was this what was meant by the power of suggestion? Rafe didn't want to give that idea further consideration. He needed to forget but couldn't. He felt certain the police would pursue this case whatever it was.

Damn. This must involve those two men. There would be no other reason the Inverness police would ask for Dallas. Didn't make sense. She had no connection with the men. Once…once months ago she knew the men. Could she have left something to identify her with one of them?

How?

How would the police think to contact her? He needed to take this call in her behalf. The police might not talk to him. Nothing ventured nothing gained. He would give this a try.

A million thoughts rifled through his head. None of which he liked. The breath he tried to hitch into his lungs stalled at his throat. He coughed. Cleared his mind of various scenarios. This wasn't something he wished to tell Dallas. The sooner he got the call over with the better. He made his decision.

Drawing in a deep breath of air, he tapped the button that would connect him with the Inverness police department. To his surprise, Rafe discovered he held his breath. He let the oxygen go with a slow whistle while he waited.

With all his nerves stretched tight, he listened to the phone ring. Ideas rambled through his head. When the call was answered, he froze for a few seconds, his heart seeming to cease.

Identifying himself, he began, "This is Rafe Frasier. Dallas Shaw's husband. Someone from this department called a few minutes ago. I'm returning the call for my wife. She is unable to come to the phone. What can I do for you?" He needed to ask what the call was about even though he felt the police would never hand out the requested information.

"This is one of Inverness' homicide detectives. We need to speak with Miss Shaw. This is important. When can we talk?"

"Mrs. Frasier," Rafe corrected. "We're married. Whatever you need to tell Dallas, you can tell me, her husband."

"That's the problem, sir. Over the phone and without her permission, I cannot. Put your wife on the phone. I'll make this brief. She needs to be apprised of an event that might concern her."

Rafe stepped from the bedroom, closing the door behind him. It latched with a soft snick. He hoped this didn't wake her. "Dallas has had a difficult day. She's just gone to sleep. I'm not waking her. Tell me what you need."

"I must talk with…Mrs. Frasier as soon as possible…in person."

"Not tonight." Rafe held his ground. He wasn't going to wake her to more turmoil. Now, there wasn't a single doubt in his mind this would be disturbing news.

"Have her at the station in Inverness tomorrow morning to meet me. I'm detective Michael McKay. I'll talk with her then."

"She is otherwise engaged tomorrow morning. If I'm going to bring my wife into Inverness, you are going to have to give me more information." His heart pounded. This must have something to do with Gordon and Tinley. What did Dallas ever do to deserve all this upheaval? She would have been better off if her father and Aaron didn't return…at least not yet. To deal with one emotional crisis at a time would be easier.

"I see. Could you get her here by…say…four o'clock?"

"Again, I would need more information. It's a long trip. One she is not up for. My wife has had several shocks today. Another surprise could be devastating to her emotional stability. I have to think of her first. Whatever might be going on at your end, can wait." Rafe new he was laying this line on pretty thick. He did want to make a point. Dallas hadn't done anything wrong. These people would need to be patient if they wished to speak with her.

The man on the other side of the line cleared his throat. "This concerns the death of a man and what she might know about him."

"What makes you think…"

"Her driver's license was found on a person, now referred to as John Doe.

~ * ~

"Here we are again," Ian McDonell said as he and Aaron McKenna walked from a ring of stones in a sparsely inhabited part of Scotland. Long grass waved in undulating rhythms. Over the western craigs the sun was beginning to dip behind ragged peaks. The two men had been in this position twenty or more times over the years. He hoped this was the last time. With each journey through the stones, it seemed they just missed the date they needed. There were no guarantees. The two learned the fact a long time ago. He, for one, hoped John Shaw was still alive. For what the man put him through, he wanted some form of justice meted out to the man. Whether it was McKenna justice or public justice, he didn't care. John Shaw must pay for what he did.

"How many times have we done this?" Aaron laughed as if he found the situation amusing. Neither man did. "Seems like one hundred, though I know it hasn't been that many." Aaron mused thoughtfully as they walked along a well-used path that led to a road.

Highland cows grazed on grass. A warm wind seemed to blow down from the craigs. The scene wasn't any different than the last time they stepped from the stones. "Lost count also," Ian mumbled. "What I do know is that we left those stones somewhere around twenty times, give or take. The only idea that's been a constant on this unwanted journey is that nothing is the same each time we walk away. Every time we reached the inn, it's been different, more modern. That fact has to be to our advantage."

"Don't know about you but I'm exhausted. Feel as if I'm at the end of my tether. I need to find my bed. Sleep the night away with my wife. Sometimes I wonder if she is still alive. My children too…" Aaron let out a long breath of air while he rubbed the back of his neck. "I'm done. Don't know if I've got the strength of will for another try if this one fails."

"We're getting old. Missing out on our lives. Figure we're both in our mid-forties now. Lost so much time to all this traveling into unknown periods. It will be interesting to learn the date of our arrival. For certain, we are not the same as when we left." Ian cleared his throat before he continued. "We both understand we'll never stop searching."

Yes, Ian did feel old. Knew the lost time could never been relived. Wondered what his daughter looked like. If her life had been happy, filled with love along with joy. "This must be our last stop. If not, well, I'm not certain I wish to walk back into those stones again despite all we've missed out on. Just as you are, I'm beginning to feel as if I'm an old man. Old as those hills over there."

Aaron pushed an errant strand of hair from his face. The steel gray of his eyes focused on the building just over the hill. "Do you think the inn will be there? Whorehouse? Tavern? Inn? What will the building be this time? If we need jobs to move on, will we find work?"

"I hope the place is an inn or a tavern that rents rooms. I'm in great need of a bath along with something to eat. I'm starved." Ian thought about all the times they walked the short distance from the Kinnel Stones to the same building. Short distance...ah it took about fifteen minutes to get there. He guessed the distance to be around a mile. In the past, the building had been a whorehouse or a tavern with rooms upstairs. One time, the place was an inn where food could be had as well as rooms to be rented. What the building was today, neither had an idea. Might not still be standing. Over the years they'd seen the changes, the improvements made. The last time they arrived, a new wing had been built to accommodate more rooms for rent. There were also several cabins nearby for visitors to use; visitors from other countries who came to this part of Scotland. The scenery was beautiful, rugged. Seemed the place kept up a lively tourist trade.

The first time they stepped from the stones had been in the early eighteen hundreds. The building was a tavern owned by a man named Cal Ferguson. Once they learned this was not the date they were looking for, they worked for the man. When next they tried the Kinnel Stones, the huge boulders rejected them. Tossed them out on their butts. That was an exaggeration. Nonetheless, the stones didn't send them anywhere. During the interim they served drinks, sang old Scottish ballads for the crowds who gave them coins for their work. Aaron learned to cook. He cleaned the rooms. They spent the better part of a year at the place before they tried one more time to gain entrance to the stones. Failing, they walked back to the inn to resume their employment, as well as to pray the next time they tried, success would be there's.

The two worked at the inn for three years before embarking on what turned out to be another futile try at the stones to bring them home. The last effort during that century. They were both fearful another attempt would result in death. As much as they both wanted to return to their families, they didn't wish to have their lives end when they were still young men.

The subsequent endeavor landed them at the end of the nineteenth century. The tavern was no longer a place for a man to wet his dry throat. Well, that wasn't entirely correct. A man could get more than a couple of glasses of ale at the Seven Sister's Whorehouse which was run by, yes, seven sisters. The seven women were all beauties. The oldest told him they were tired of men telling them what they could as well as what they could not do. All seven were in favor of women's rights. They applauded the women who stood up for the rights of other women. They figured in their own way they were doing the same. They made more money at their chosen profession than they would have working other jobs.

Aaron and Ian worked as bouncers for the seven sisters. The women didn't call them bouncers at first. They were their protectors; some men got rough with ladies of the evening. They stayed there for a few years. Seemed the stones weren't always receptive to men coming and going through time. They always needed to wait until the stones would accept them.

There were different encounters. Even though they met beautiful women, both men stayed true to their mates. Time passed with the speed of a lumbering tortoise. The scenery changed. This time, when the two stepped from the boulders that had been part of their lives for far too long a two-lane road led up to the tavern. In this year, the building was a tavern again. Bright lights shone from the interior. For Aaron and Ian, the sight was a welcome one, homey. That building over the last few years was their only constant. Thoughts of the seven sisters was also a constant in Ian's mind. He'd respected the women, despite, or maybe because, of their vocation.

"Well, do you think we're in the right era?" Aaron asked, looking ahead as they strode beside the road. "I pray we won't have to do this again. My gut tells me we are home."

"We've been closing in on the year we are looking for. Since we both appear our age, I'd be guessing that we won't see our children the way we left them. Dallas wasn't walking yet. She crawled. Pulled herself up to stand. Watched her shift to her beautiful kitten one time." Ian felt as if the earth had been ripped away from his feet. Thoughts of missing his child growing up turned his stomach sour. He wasn't the type of man to dwell on what was fair along with what wasn't. He'd expected to have several children. In the highlands, one always understood life was hard and was not always objective. He would never have more than the one child. That fact he regretted. He always loved children. Hoped to father two or three. As they walked, Ian hoped this was the end of their quest to come home. Prayed his little girl had become a fine young woman. He wondered how old she was now. With any luck he would soon discover the answer to all his questions.

"They'll be all grown up," Aaron said as he let out a long sigh. "My son along with my daughter. They could be married with kids. That would make us grandparents."

Ian acknowledged that thought as one he'd yet to envision. "I've got a good feeling about today." With that, Ian picked up the pace, eager to see what was ahead of him. His steps felt lighter. The spring breeze was warm. A brilliant sun was sinking in the west, turning day into night. He had the uncanny suspicion today would be the real beginning to the rest of his life. Soon, he might hold Helen in his arms again. He'd missed his mate. Longed for her with every breath he inhaled. Over the years he stayed true to her as Aaron stayed faithful to his wife.

Inside the tavern, the two seemed to take a deep breath in unison. The place was much the same, yet the interior was different. The color of the walls was a light gray. People sat on a porch where they ate and drank in the fading light of the day. Heaters were interspersed along the porch to supply warmth for the patrons. Just as the other times, the chatter was lively. People held things to their ears while they talked. Some seemed to play with the devices. A modern invention that neither he nor Aaron understood. In any case, this didn't matter to them. First things first, the date needed to be discovered. After that they could proceed further. Getting to the McKenna keep might be difficult. After discussing the matter, they both agreed that would be the place to go first.

Yes, this was the time. Ian could feel the truth deep in his bones. Felt so close to Helen it seemed he could reach out and touch her. His body shook with emotions as well as very real hope. This was the first-time hope had become a deep-seated part of him. Ian didn't quite understand how he knew this for a fact. He did. Leaving Aaron behind, he walked outside the tavern.

The newspaper in the stand read February seventeenth, two thousand twenty-five. Ian couldn't imagine seeing that date. With quick mental calculations he determined his age at the time. This was the first they entered a period they might have lived through. Nonetheless, the date on the paper seemed to correspond to the way he aged. He would be forty-five years old in this time. The age was how he felt. His daughter would be twenty-two.

Who would she be? What would she be like? Ian understood John Shaw orchestrated this scenario that sent him away from his family for more than twenty years. The man had a lot to account for. How would he prove foul play? Because Aaron had the misfortune of being in the wrong place when all this took place, he too was sent into the Kinnel stones. John wasn't about to leave a witness.

~ * ~

Ruby and Cole stood on the highest part of the keep, looking over McKenna land. The two spent many nights this way since Aaron disappeared. Ruby insisted on going this evening after returning from dinner at the Frasiers. Cole was not surprised when she told him how close she felt tonight to her husband. She told him she felt his presence with every breath she inhaled. He was out there…somewhere…close.

"What do you think to see?" Cole asked, a bit amused at his mother's wistful expression. He'd enjoyed the evening. Dinner with the new married couple had been interesting. He understood both families were hurting, Dallas was confused, and Rafe's first consideration was to his mate. "Do you think father will walk up the road?" Cole pointed in the direction his mother stared.

"No, he'll have caught a ride from someone. Oh," she turned to him, startled at what she said. "I understand you must think I'm a crazy old lady. It's just that…I feel him, Cole. She took his hands in hers. "He's in every breath, ever beat of my heart. Deep in my soul I feel him. He's out there somewhere. Aaron is close at hand. If I had any idea where, I'd have you drive me in that direction. I can't wait to see him."

Cole had a moment's misgiving. They talked endlessly about hopes as well as dreams. Spoke of the idea they might never see his father again. He needed to back his mother in whatever direction her mind took. Mates had uncanny ways of being together, of understanding each other's minds. He tried to think of all the possible scenarios. "We could head to the Kinnel Stones," Cole was hesitant to volunteer. Still, he felt supporting her was necessary. "Can you reach out to him in your head? Ask him where he is? That would be a definite help in finding Father." He wasn't certain why he was giving his mother advice in communicating with her husband.

"Yes…" When she turned to speak, her face was bleached of all color. She gripped the rail in front of her. "Yes…" The last word was murmured into the heat of the late spring day.

"What is it?" Cole was concerned, terrified he'd said something wrong, that perhaps he asked too much. When she looked at him with a watery smile, he began to understand how she felt. Their feelings were in agreement.

"I'm afraid," she spoke with a whispered softness that stole straight to his heart. "Afraid to hope too much. If I reach out to Aaron and he doesn't answer, I'll be devastated. He feels so close to me. I feel as if I can put my hand out and touch him."

Cole picked up his mother's hands again. They were strong hands. He admired them as he met her gaze with his. "I am too. This is hard to put into words. Just as you do, I feel my father's presence. He is close by.

Close enough for me to want to connect with him. I always spoke to him when I was in your womb. Somehow, I've lost some of that relationship I had with him as a small child. Mother," he paused, rubbing her hands to give hope, "I feel him too. He is nearby. His spirit beckons to us. So very close that, just like you, I think I can reach out and touch him. You're not imagining anything. Neither are you a crazy old lady."

She wiped moisture from her cheek. Cleared the dampness from her throat before she continued. "You do? You feel the same as me? I would... I thought I was half foolish and more than wishful. Believed my imagination was working too hard. After all this time, do you think...?"

Cole touched a drop of moisture that slipped from her eye. "Our prayers have been granted. Perhaps. What do you think? Should we take a chance? Drive to the Kinnel Stones? We might miss him if he's caught a ride. If he hasn't, we might find him walking alongside the road in our direction." Cole found he was holding his breath while he anticipated an answer. An hour ago, he walked Phoebe to her room at the keep. He didn't dare visit her again tonight. For him, keeping his hands to himself when she lived so close to him was growing increasingly difficult. Taking his mother on a search might be best for all concerned.

"Do you wish to bring Phoebe?"

"No," the answer came too fast, so fast his response startled his mother. "I cannot. She is dear to me as well you know." Neither did he wish to explain, nor did he understand why he kept his distance when she was willing to be intimate with him. This was the way their life together was supposed to be.

"The two of you have grown too close for your plans, I see. I expected that. She is an attractive, sensual woman, even though her age is not that great. She will make you a fine wife. You've always been a stickler for plans. Wanting your life well-ordered. Maybe it's time to make new plans where your mate is concerned. If we've learned anything over the years, life as we see it can change in a blink of the eye."

"I'm afraid that time will come sooner than I planned. Doubt if I can wait two years for her as I intended." He held up his hands, a gesture of surrender. Capitulation...held a new connotation for him. "I shouldn't be speaking so plainly to my mother. Could turn out to be embarrassing for both of us." As if he brought on the emotion by mentioning it by name, the heat of embarrassment climbed to his face. The rise of color was a new experience for him. He realized his mother would see then interpret the truth. The fact remained, Phoebe was still chaste. Her innocence was still intact. If they waited two years for the wedding, that fact would not be true when he claimed his mate. He doubted if it would be true in a couple of months. Cole found he needed her as much as he needed to breathe.

"You're right. What happens between you and Phoebe is for the two of you to decide, as well as to know. I play no part in your decisions. Nor do I have a need to know. I promise I won't ask for more information. Though you did volunteer, I wasn't prying into your life." Her grin was wide, amused at his discomfort. "I'm looking forward to grandchildren. Most McKenna children arrive a *wee* bit early. There is no shame in that. For me, considering all I've lost over the years, the sooner you take care of business the better."

"Shall we take a ride North. See what we can discover?"

"I believe that is a splendid idea."

Chapter Ten

Rafe asked Dallas if she was up to visiting her father this morning. At the mention of the appointment, her stomach somersaulted. The truth…she was petrified. The man she was about to talk to was unknown to her. What if he didn't like what he saw? He might be just as jaded and insincere as John Shaw and her mother. How could she accept that? She couldn't breathe. Every breath of air stuck in her throat. After Rafe stopped the car, she couldn't make her legs move to get out. Ruby assured her they would have the necessary privacy to talk with freedom, to ask questions that might arise in her head. No one would interrupt. That information failed to ease the ache in her heart or the pain in her stomach.

Walking toward the meeting, Cole in front of them, she thought this must be the way a person condemned must feel on the walk to the gallows. She had to reinforce the notion she wasn't sentenced to death. She wasn't walking toward her execution. This was a meeting she could abandon anytime it suited her. Right now, she could turn around. Walk away from the reunion. For her, there were no obligations. She was doing this at her father's request. The man deserved some consideration. None of what happened to him was his fault. She needed to learn how his disappearance came about.

In front of the door, Dallas held back, her blood pounding in her head, rushing through her ears. Feeling lightheaded, she clung to Rafe. Her fingers bit into his arm. He remained stoic. When she started to turn away, Rafe held her wrist, stopping the movement to give her time to reconsider. With gentle encouragement, he brought her back to him. She felt the hard warmth of his body, the hard planes and angles. His hands rested at the small of her back as he held her. She sucked a gasp of air and turned to look at him. The steel gray of his eyes shimmered with compassion.

His whispered words were spoken close to her ear. Strands of her hair tickled her cheek where his breath fluttered across her face. "I know you're terrified. If you don't wish to do this right now, I'll make your excuses. We can go home or drive to the village for a cup of coffee if you think you might have a change of mind. Your parents need to understand this from your point of view. They must be patient."

She found herself nodding, wishing she dared wait for another day. If she did put off the confrontation today, one day would turn into two then a week. She doubted if she would ever gain the nerve to sit down to talk to them. She swallowed, closing her eyes. Rafe was right about all he spoke of. Her throat was parched. Holding onto Rafe's arm, she leaned into him. His closeness steadied her enough so she could think with a more open mind.

"I don't know what to say to the man. I've never known him. Don't know him even though he is technically my father," she whispered, her heart thrumming. She tried to make herself become calm. Attempted deep, even breathing. In then out. Again.

Rafe had to bend close to hear her words. "You..." he paused, touched his forehead to hers, "don't need to say anything. Your father has a story to tell as does your mother. Helen needs to explain why she treated you the way she did. Right now, they are two strangers to you. All you need do is listen. Even if they ask you a direct question, you can defer to me. I'll answer for you if that's what you would wish."

"I know. You understand me better than anyone. You've always been with me. That's what has me shaking. How does one talk to strangers? To people they don't know? What is said between us cannot be called small talk." Dallas mulled over what Rafe told her. She didn't need to do the talking. He said she should listen. She nodded as she formed the conclusions that would allow her feet to walk into the room. "I can do that; listen. I don't have to decide anything."

"Good girl. As we talked about, all you need do is listen to what the two people sitting in that room have to say. Ian needs to tell you what happened to him. Why he was away for over twenty years. You should learn the truth. After you discover the facts, you can make decisions. Your mother has her own apologies to make. She needs to help you understand what motivated her to treat you the way she did. All those years when you needed her the most, she was no real mother to you."

"My life would have been so much different if he'd been here. At least I think it would have been." She felt as if she scrambled for words, needing to believe her true father would have changed her life for the better.

Rafe brushed an errant strand of hair behind her ears. Smiled when she questioned with her eyes. "It was sticking out," he explained, his voice a tender murmur. "I don't want you to be frightened. Remember, I'm here for you. Always have been. Always will be. Whatever you need, Dallas, you can count on me to deliver. I believe you know that."

She did know Rafe would always be there for her. Wasn't he her rock? Hadn't he always been? Leaning into his hard body, Dallas absorbed the warmth coupled with his strength. She straightened, ready for her life to make another dramatic change. Hoped that transformation would be for the better. "You will hold my hand?"

"I will. Whatever you ask for."

"Deep down somewhere beyond the terror, I do want to meet the man who is my father. I do hope to have a mother who will care for me. Though…" Dallas stopped, unable to walk another step before she spoke an absolute to Rafe. "I no longer need those feelings. You've always been there for me. I've made it past my desperate need for loving parents."

"I am here for you now."

"I know."

"Take a deep breath, love. We're either going to venture into that room together or we will leave. If you decide to leave, we can set a date for another time. Ruby or Cole will take care of those arrangements. You need not speak to anyone."

Dallas did take a deep breath, then let it out slow. She stepped back. Rafe still held her hand. "Do I look all right?" Somehow worrying about her appearance made her laugh. "Stupid thing to say under the circumstances," she muttered. "Though my appearance has always been a sore point between me and my mother."

"To me, you always look beautiful. It's not stupid to care about your appearance, though unnecessary in your case. I've always told you how I feel about the way you look, even though you never listen. Perhaps you've never believed me." He sounded petulant. "You will be beautiful to your father too. I promise."

"You think so?" She understood eagerness was displayed in the tenor of her question. She wanted her father to feel that way about her. Time had passed since her high school days when her insecurities showed on her face. College wasn't much better, though her doubts about herself lessened. She felt that way now; insecure as well as tenuous. She always wished she was thin. Rafe never cared. He liked her the way she was. She wondered how her father would feel. When she lived at home, her mother reminded her every day she needed to diet.

Rafe leaned forward, his hand on the handle of the door. He looked at her. She nodded, a grim determined expression on her face. He opened it then stepped aside so Dallas stood in the entrance. Her chin tilted. Her back stiffened. If she was going to meet her new life, she meant to do so with courage not trepidation.

Courage, she didn't feel. Bravery, what was that? Her hands held tight in front of her, she stepped inside. Her hesitancy didn't go unnoticed by Rafe. He set his hand at the small of her back. Her gasp at the sight of her father caught her mother's attention. Ian did look the exact duplicate of John Shaw. As far as she could tell there weren't even subtle differences. They were carbon copies of each other. Copies, except in the way they treated people. At least she hoped that was true.

Ian stood. His gaze focused on her, a slight smile on his handsome features. His eyes seemed to shine with appreciation as he watched her. Waited. Seeming insecure, he held out his hand to her, then let it drop back to his side when she didn't reach out to accept the gesture. Rafe ushered her to a chair which faced her parents. He stood behind her, his hands on her shoulders. A gentle squeeze gave her a tiny measure of encouragement. That small signal gave her a boost of comfort. Her insecurities lessened.

Rafe told her it wasn't up to her to make conversation. All she need do was hear what this man had to say. He told her that her father had a story to tell. One she should give him a chance to speak. It was his history of the years away from his family. Her heart fluttered at his short perusal of her. His smile was soft. Warm. She felt a melting of her hardened resolve. That smile was nothing like John Shaw's. The smile in some ways reminded her of the way Rafe looked at her when he wanted to erase all problems from her head. She felt as if her father, the real one, Ian McDonell, cared for her. Maybe they weren't duplicates of each other after all. That single thought boded well for their future together.

"You've grown into a beautiful woman. I regret missing out on your life." When he spoke his voice was hoarse, husky with emotion. "You should listen to what I have to say. At least I hope you will hear me out. I don't wish to miss out on the rest of your life. Neither does your mother."

Dallas nodded but she didn't offer any words of encouragement. She turned to Rafe then back to her father.

Rafe still stood behind her. He looked to her mother then back to her. "You're angry with me. I don't blame you. I'm angry with myself. Furious. I made a stupid mistake. One that should not have been made. I trusted. The fact cost us all."

"No...no," Dallas found herself shaking her head. "How could I be angry with you?" She thought of her tumble through time. Nothing...nothing...there had been nothing she could do to change what happened to her. That day there had been other factors at play. None of which she controlled. He said he made a stupid mistake. Was it stupid to trust someone? The only person she ever trusted was Rafe.

"You have a mutinous look on your face. Is it directed at me?" His smile reached his eyes. He saw some humor in her expression which wasn't so much mutinous as curious. Thoughtful. She needed to digest his words, come to understand what made his trust turn on him. Dallas figured he must have put some faith in John Shaw in order to call what happened stupid.

As to the small bit of humor, Dallas didn't believe her father laughed at her. He was here to set incidents gone horribly wrong to right. "Not you... Not anyone. How?" She was becoming more curious about the circumstances that took him away from her. "How did father...no...John Shaw get you into the Kinnel Stones? Is that the unwise blunder you are speaking of? Is he the one you trusted?"

Ian lifted his shoulders in a reluctant shrug. His mouth set in a grim furious line. "Yes, and yes. The man had a gun. I did not. I wasn't into arguing with the man who pointed his gun at me. Never thought for a moment I'd be gone from my family for half my life."

"You thought you would take your chances inside the Kinnel Stones?" Dallas asked as she took interest in his story. "Before these last few days, I'd never heard of the stones. Never thought they would take a person to a different time and place. That's not how I left this century to end up in the past." She understood Ruby would have told him about her journey.

"There were rumors," Ian said, "if one listened to clan stories. We Scottish can be a superstitious lot. Most of us anyway. Some not so much, I suppose."

"I fell into a different world, too. Not through the Kinnel stones. I searched for the stones on Google. They look like huge boulders sitting in the middle of farmland. Just as you didn't have a choice, I wasn't given one either. The moment just happened. I didn't expect to find myself in another period. I slid down a hill to find myself in the eighteenth century."

Ian's gentle smile undid her. "I didn't believe we were taking a chance. Neither did Aaron. Walk into the stones or take a bullet in the head?" His eyebrow arched toward the ceiling. "Didn't seem I had a choice either." He held up his hand as if to stop her next question. "We'd heard rumors about the place being bewitched. Stories cautioned people to stay away. We didn't believe the stories, thought we could hide behind one of those big boulders, as you call them, then when John left, we could march right out unscathed."

A small smile made its way to her mouth. She watched her father's look of chagrin as he told the story. "That didn't happen. Why? Why did you trust that man? He's a horrible person, was an even worse father." That was the truth. Behind her, Rafe gave her another tiny squeeze to encourage. She felt pleased with herself. They were talking. So far, her mother remained in the background, silent.

Ian slid his fingers through his hair as he continued with his story. "I'd known John for years. He always coveted your mother. I didn't think anything of that. Helen was mine. *Is* mine. Didn't expect…" He tossed up his hands in obvious frustration. "I was a fool. John Shaw had a plan. Get rid of me then he could have Helen all to himself. I never believed Helen would allow that to happen. From what your mother has told me, she fought him every way she could."

Dallas closed her eyes. Swept a gulp of air into her lungs. She found herself denying the rapid bombardment of sensations. The feeling as if her father didn't understand all that was done to her. "He took over my life. Commanded me. The man beat me after I tried to shift. He loathed you. Hated all shifters." She sounded bitter. Was vehement. "He made me feel…" A sob ended the words she was going to say. Her gaze shot to her mother. Saw the rise of color on her face. "Rafe saved me. He took me under his wing. Helped me with difficult times. Understood my fears when no one else cared."

"I'm relieved you had someone in your corner. A friend to hold your hand. That's important when there is no one else for you." Ian appeared to study Rafe for a short time. A brief nod in her husband's direction reassured her. Not that his approval meant anything to her as yet. Perhaps it never would. "Good to have a person you can lean on. Helen has told me her part in your early years. How, as well as why, she abused you. She despised every time she was forced to do you harm, whether that hurt was inflicted verbally or physically. She regrets everything. Had to proceed the way she did. How she acted was to keep you alive. John never saw you as his daughter. He saw you as my brat. John wanted a child of his own. Helen denied him the one thing he coveted. He didn't like the fact she kept from conceiving and took his anger out on you. He couldn't keep his eye on your mother all the time, neither could he keep her locked away. She was punished for that also."

"Oh." Her heart pounded against her ribs. When she looked at her mother there was a watery smile on her face.

There was so much more to the story. Ian continued for another fifteen minutes or so, telling them about his journey through time and the places where they'd ended up. His laughter when he spoke of the Seven Sister's Whorehouse surprised her, as did his admiration of the seven women. In the end, Aaron's wife and son, sensing he returned, drove to the Kinnel Stones. They found he and Aaron walking along the side of the road, eager to return home.

Later, much later, the two couples walked out of the keep together. While all emotions, along with hurts inflicted by Helen, were not all put aside, Dallas decided she would give her mother a chance. Out of hand, she didn't forgive her. Though she might in time find the necessary strength to do so. In the present, given all that happened to her, she could not yet find the power in her heart that would erase the memories from all those past years.

Before Helen and Ian got into Helen's car, Dallas stopped them. Her hand placed on her father's arm. Ian turned to her. The steel gray of his eyes flashed with remorse. "I need a few days to think about all that has happened. Everything you told me. I'm confused yet thrilled to have you back, even if you might not see that fact in my eyes. Know that I'm pleased to have my real father with me." She looked to Rafe as if asking permission, yet she wasn't. He wasn't the type of man she needed to ask for his approval.

Clearing her throat, she took Rafe's hand into hers. His strength guided her. "We'd like to have the two of you to dinner. A couple of evenings from now? Would that work out?" Dallas held her breath while she waited for an answer. "I love to cook."

Rafe's chuckle was soft, throaty. From the sound of his voice Dallas understood he had something in mind for their return home. "My Dallas is a fantastic cook. Though…for…last night, she made so much food, we could probably still munch on leftovers two days from now."

"Absolutely not!" Dallas said, seeing red at his horrific suggestion. There would be no leftovers served when her parents came to dinner. "What do you like to eat? Simple or fancy? I prefer fancy if the dish challenges my cooking skills."

"Anything you want. Something easy," Ian said, his reply appearing on the heels of her declaration. "Suit yourself. Try a new recipe if you like. Give us leftovers if you like. Time with my daughter is what is important."

"…or complicated." Rafe pointed out, sounding bemused at the interplay between father and daughter. "Dallas enjoys fiddling around in the kitchen, getting the dishes dirty. Using all the pots as well as the pans. That way she keeps me busy. Since she is the cook, I get to wash all the dishes."

"Rafe!" She pushed at his arm. He held still.

The grin he shot her was wicked. *I love all the things we do on the kitchen table too. Don't you?*

Rafe! Not now. Not here.

Love the color of your cheeks when I say something scintillating. All your cheeks, all four, when I say something that brings the heat to your face. You blush with rare beauty.

"I do believe we have some inside communication going on right now. How long have you been married?" Ian asked, studying his daughter. "The two of you have the look of newlyweds. Don't tell me I missed my daughter's wedding by a few days? Maybe we should redo the night. A father should be able to give his daughter away. I didn't get to watch the Clan Chattan ceremony either. I've missed out on too much." From humor, the tone of his voice turned to disappointment. "I mean to make up for this tragedy the rest of my life."

"We won't tell you," Rafe said with no tone. "Though you did miss a lot of firsts. We are newlyweds, I'm still fascinated with every aspect of my wife. We are just getting to learn more about each other."

If she was warm before, she flamed now. *I'm going to get even with you for this, Rafe Frasier. I won't cook your dinner for two weeks. If you ever tell Ian about the fact I pose nude for you... Don't tell him!*

I'm certain I'll be the beneficiary, no matter what you plan as my punishment. I made certain the kitchen table was empty of all items before we left. If you want to play, that is. The first round for this afternoon can be there. As for cooking, you've asked your parents to dinner in two days. What do you plan on doing about that?

You can cook.

If you want a disaster on your hands, I'll be happy to oblige in any way.

Pay attention to...

"Mother, Father," Dallas brought herself back to the present. Haggling with Rafe over anything never got desired results. Not that she minded using the kitchen table for what he was implying. This afternoon they didn't have the time. He told her while they were driving into Inverness but never gave her the reason why.

I heard that.

317

No, you didn't. It's not what you think.

Dallas lifted her chin. She wasn't going to hug either of her parents. They weren't that far along in their relationship. Ian, she didn't know. Her mother, she never hugged. Never remembered doing so. Given the circumstances of her life, she wasn't certain that was something she would ever be able to do.

"We'll see you in two days," Helen said, as she finally contributed to the conversation. During the visit she hadn't said a word. With a quiet demeanor, Helen watched and listened to the conversation going on around her. It seemed obvious that she didn't want to defend her actions. She had little defense.

While Ian backed up, then turned the car, Rafe wrapped his arm around her. The gentle touch lifted her mood. She heard the steady beat of his heart. Felt each breath he inhaled. Basked in the warmth of him. She let loose the breath she'd been holding while her parents drove away. "I wish I could forgive her everything. I just don't know how to do that."

"Forgiveness takes time. Learning the truth is not enough sometimes. Truth often doesn't replace bitterness. Be patient with yourself. I've a feeling Helen is beating herself up over her actions against you," Rafe walked with her to their car. She mulled over all he told her.

"What is enough? How much time is required? I would have an answer or two. I don't want much from this except understanding." No answers came to her mind. There were times in her past when she tried to get into her mother's head. Wanted to understand why. Could never reach into her thoughts. She didn't remember if she was ever able to see into her father's head; read his thoughts without having them spoken.

"I believe the word is show. Helen needs to show you her feelings and her behavior toward you have changed. One can't say, 'I've changed' then expect to find themselves believed. Sometimes actions will speak louder than mere words. As we've said before, this will take more than one or two meetings with your mother."

"All right then…you're telling me to be tolerant. You understand patience is not one of my stronger traits." Dallas thought he'd choke after she mentioned the fact she never possessed patience.

"True to both. Where your mother is concerned, can you wait a month, even a year? Can you give her the chance to prove herself? I believe that is all she asks of you. Doesn't expect your forgiveness today or tomorrow."

"That's a question I don't have an answer for. My father told me he was stupid. He trusted someone he shouldn't. Couldn't he be describing me if I trust Mother now?" There was something inside her telling her to be cautious. It seemed that now she was older and better able to understand, her mother could have given her some hint as to why she acted the way she did.

"Yes, but…I don't believe he is. Imagine your mother was as much a victim as you were. The difference being your mother understood what she was doing. You didn't understand why everyone who should love you, treated you as if you were dirt beneath their shoes. If what she has told you is correct, she treated you the way she did to keep you alive. Would you have done otherwise if put in your mother's position?"

That was something she'd never thought of before. One could never say for certain how they would act. "Suppose that sums it up. That is how I feel. You've been with me so long…what do you think? Should I give my trust to a woman who has betrayed me for twenty-two years along with a man who can see no fault in that woman? It is obvious Ian dotes on her."

"You noticed that too?" Rafe's voice held a wealth of amusement. Then with a tone that brooked no argument. "She is his mate. Do you suppose I adore you? If you haven't considered that thought, you are remis. You are my heart as well as my soul. I would give you the world if I could. As things stand now, all I can give you is myself. Hope that's enough."

Rafe said the words as if they told the true story. Maybe they did, it still didn't change her feelings. "All I can promise is that I'll try for patience as well as tolerance. Will give Mother time if she wants it."

"I feel the same about you. I would defend you no matter what you did. In this instance, your father has good reason to endorse her actions. They were both put in an unconscionable position. Something neither one dreamed would ever come about. Now, twenty some years later they have to renew a relationship that never got very far off the ground."

"I didn't think of that. Do you suppose Ian loves her? They'd only been together for a few years when he disappeared without a trace."

"Can you imagine how you would feel if that happened to us?" Rafe spoke as he walked with her to the car. "As to love? I can't speak for them."

"No…maybe…since it has in a way…happened to us." Didn't all mates love each other. Was that thought just hopeful thinking on her part?

"What if we had an infant? A child who could shift? A young woman who might find herself ostracized because she was different?" Rafe asked. "What if's…"

"I don't know. I would love her with all of my heart." They reached the car. Rafe steadied her as he helped her to sit. Once inside, she let her head settle on the back of the seat. She found exhaustion seemed to be overwhelming her.

"A man was taking her husband's place without her permission. Because you were there, in his way, he threatened your life if your mother didn't concede to his wishes. He despised you for being Ian's child."

Dallas couldn't stop the ensuing sigh of displeasure…of fatigue… she wasn't certain. "There had to be another way. Someone Mother could have turned to," Dallas was certain this argument was good. She believed there was always a choice. Didn't her mother have friends? Someone to fall back on?

"If Aaron McKenna had been there, she could have looked to him for help. The McKennas rule the Clan Chattan. Have for centuries. Aaron would have taken care of any problems she was having. He was gone, disappeared the same time Ian did, and all her options vanished without a trace."

"I see." Dallas wasn't positive she did see anything.

"I hope so. Cole wasn't very old at that time. He couldn't help your mother. He was a young boy with no power. His mother was not a shifter. She also held no power in the clan. Neither would have come with the supremacy of strength to help Helen. There was no one for her to turn to for assistance."

~ * ~

The emotional drain he felt from this encounter went soul deep. Having been inside Dallas' head for the duration, he absorbed her feelings into himself. He couldn't image how Dallas must feel. She would be exhausted. They were headed to Inverness now. He intended to spend the night there. Go out some place nice to eat. Relax at a nice hotel. Treat her to whatever she wanted.

Rafe experienced everything his mate suffered today. He was one with her during the ordeal. Now, there was another encounter that needed to be satisfied. He wasn't looking forward to telling her what they were doing. So far, he'd told her only about his romantic intentions. The real reason for driving to Inverness, the meeting he never apprised Dallas of. Never told her about the phone call from the detective last night. Understood she would learn soon enough. He would not be able to put off the inevitable much longer.

They stopped by the house long enough to pack a few things needed for the brief sojourn in the city. Rafe hesitated to call what they were doing a honeymoon. He didn't believe the first part would leave even one pleasant sensation. The thought that Dallas had to identify Gordon Mathew's dead body troubled him. During the morning confrontation there was no need for Rafe to keep his considerations blocked from Dallas. She was so engrossed with her parents, her mind never traveled in his direction. Now he needed to be certain she didn't see into his head. She would be able to read his unease with this trip to the city. No matter how he tried to spin what was about to go down, he couldn't make it pleasant.

"What are we doing in Inverness? I've been perplexed since you brought it up. Thought we would spend the evening at home. Just the two of us, a bottle of wine and..." Dallas said, as she turned to look at him. They had been silent for the last hour. Each seemed to be engrossed in personal thoughts. With her head on the back of the seat, coupled with her closed eyes, half the time Rafe thought she was sleeping. "Tell me...this isn't some pleasant excursion to Inverness, is it? Why are we going into town?"

The long-expelled breath of air would tell Dallas he didn't wish to talk. Still, since this concerned her, he needed to speak the truth. He'd put this off for as long as he could. Now, seemed to be the time. He didn't want to spring anything on her that she needed to absorb. "Last night you received a call, on your phone." Beginning at the first seemed appropriate.

"I got a call last night? I don't remember, must have been more tired than I thought." She was looking through her purse pulling out one item after another. "Here it is. Knew I had one in here somewhere." Dallas held up a pen as if she found a thousand dollars somewhere inside that big bag of hers. She carried all her necessaries in that bag.

With an inward chuckle, he kept his gaze on the road in front of him. She was always losing stuff inside that huge container. They passed the entrance to the falls where she slid into another time. He felt her tiny shiver of apprehension. Reaching over, he clasped her hand in his, brought the back of her hand to his lips for a quick kiss. He needed to explain the phone call along with his meddling. He had no right to answer her phone. Yet he did, and he didn't regret taking the call for her.

"You were asleep, I answered for you." His shrug was meant for himself. The slight lift saying he would do so again in a similar situation. "You don't mind, I hope?"

Stunned, she looked up. "Why didn't you tell me? Maybe I do mind."

Rafe didn't know if her tone was one of outrage or indignation. "Do you care that I answered your phone? You were sleeping soundly. I didn't wish to wake you," Rafe asked, holding on to what little oxygen was left in his lungs.

"Not if you thought answering was important, no, I don't mind. I've nothing to hide. You know all about me," she told him, studying his face as he looked straight ahead. This time when she rummaged through her big purse she came up with her phone. She looked at the front screen for a few minutes, tapped on the phone, then previous calls. "I'm curious."

"To be honest, I didn't recognize the number. No name flashed on the front of your phone. Under the circumstances I sensed the call might be important, so I answered."

"Was it? Was the call important? Why did you push the button?" Her brows drew together. There was nothing on the screen to give her the information she searched for.

Pinching the bridge of his nose, he began to tell her why, then realized there was only one reason he could summon that could be believable. "Gut. My gut told me I needed to see what or who was on the other end of the line."

"Suppose you found out," she told him deadpan. "Was it important?"

"Very and…I'm also glad you didn't take the call. Relieved that you were asleep. The call would have been something else for you to worry about today." Rafe stole a quick glance in her direction. The frown was still plastered to her forehead. Her lips were pursed. He wanted to kiss her. She was adorable. Dallas wanted answers, not kisses or sex.

"Is this something you plan to apprise me of or keep me guessing? Seems you could just shoot out the needed information. From your mouth to my ears." She seemed put out by his reticence. Her sarcasm didn't go unnoticed. He wouldn't give in to her ploy. "I would know who called as well as why. In case you haven't guessed, I'm entitled. It is my phone. The call was for me. Not you." She slipped the phone back in her bag. After that she graced him with a 'you can go to hell' look she perfected long before they were wed.

Rafe could tell her he didn't blame her. Dallas was right on all counts. She knew it too. "Don't wish to do either." Putting off the inevitable was first as well as foremost at the front of his decisions. He didn't plan on upsetting her. Explaining the nature of the conversation would do just that. This morning, along with last night, had been hard on her. This afternoon wasn't going to get any better. All along, he understood it was a body or bodies she would be summoned to identify.

"Well…" Dallas felt a loss of words. She had the appearance of a lost waif. Now both confused as well as irritated.

Realizing his time for silence was coming to an end, he put all thoughts of saying nothing to the back of his head. She would rebel if he didn't give her some clue as to the nature of the call. "A detective at the Inverness police department was on the other end. He didn't tell me much since I wasn't you. Said he wished to speak with you this morning."

"This morning?" Dallas questioned with a puzzled look. "What he had to say was that important?"

"He seemed to believe it was. I told him you weren't available in the morning. If it was convenient for him, we could try and come to the city this afternoon."

"That's what we are doing now? Not a honeymoon? Didn't think so. Would have been more pleasant tonight to stay at home. So…?" *The kitchen table had nothing on it. Was that your doing?*

Unable to stop himself, his laughter howled from him. He brought himself back to reality. Rafe understood there were more questions rambling around in her head. She wanted to blast them out. Restrained herself as she waited for him to be more forthcoming. "True, we are on our way to speak with the man. Michael McKay is his name. He seemed pleased with the fact we would talk to him. Said the meeting was important."

"You have an idea as to the nature of what he wants from me?"

"I've a guess," Rafe agreed, without saying more than she needed to learn. "He wouldn't tell me any details because I'm not you."

Dallas quirked both eyebrows upward. "You weren't that forthcoming. How did he know you weren't Dallas? Dallas…the name could be a man's name."

"He has your driver's license. The picture told him you are female." He sucked in a deep breath of air. "Has it been missing for long? Your license?" Rafe held that airtight after he asked. Sounding sarcastic was not how he wished to go about addressing Dallas. It wasn't as if her life since returning from the past had been even the least bit normal. For the moment, she seemed to be taking everything in stride.

"I didn't know it was missing." Shaking her head, she reached inside her purse to pull out her wallet. Stared at the slots where her license should be. The document was missing as was one of her credit cards. She dropped it back into the purse, accompanied with some noise that must mean disgust, Rafe was positive. "How? How did anyone get these things? Wouldn't someone steal the entire wallet? They would have had to have time to rummage through my things. Who?"

"Those are all good questions, none of which I've an answer to. You should think back in time. Could have gone missing several weeks ago, don't you think? Doesn't have to have been recent. Might have happened when you slept in the same apartment as Mathew Gordon. Would clarify what you described. I believe either Mathew or Tinley is the source of the missing documents."

With that said, Rafe saw wheels spinning wildly in her head. Heard the silent curse ruffle through her mind. He was tempted to laugh. Held his amusement to himself. "So, where did they find it?" She didn't' sound upset or uneasy. Seemed to take the missing documents in stride. "I'm also absent a credit card. Suppose I should take care of that missing piece right now. I've not had any unusual purchases." She tapped her nails on her jeans. The nervous gesture didn't go unnoticed.

"The detective didn't mention the card. Imagine they didn't find the other piece in the same place as your license." He didn't appreciate the direction this was taking. Didn't want to worry about someone using her card. She would call. The company would issue her a new one.

"I'll have to call and have this number discontinued. Don't use it much anyway," Dallas was muttering about things going from bad to worse. The waste of precious time on a phone call such as the one she was about to place never failed to exasperate. Time on hold when waiting for someone to take the call was always annoying.

"Put things in perspective, love. Finding your father is not a bad thing. A complication of sorts for you. Ian is a much better man than John Shaw. I'm certain in time you will agree with my deduction. As to your missing license and credit card. those are easily taken care of. I'm positive the license will be handed over to you today."

"I'm certain I will…put this all into perspective…given time," she shot back, her annoyance at his flippancy was easy to read. She was dialing. It must be the credit card company. She was also avoiding him. Apparent to Rafe, she'd had enough conversation with him giving unwanted opinions. It might be prudent now to keep his thoughts to himself.

While she spoke to the people on the other end of the line, Rafe found his teeth clenched tight along with the tight stretch of his nerves. He was doing all in his power to ease her hurt feelings along with protecting her from what was to come. She would be furious when they reached the station and she discovered what he guessed. There was little for him to tell. Forewarning her would serve no purpose except to make her more mistrustful. Waiting for the actual moment seemed necessary. The surprise would jolt her. He would be relieved if his guess was incorrect. Didn't suppose it would be wrong.

This invitation to the police station was about Gordon and Tinley. That was the notion that hit his gut hard last night while he spoke to the detective. He'd seen both men at the docks, talking to a man who appeared to be a drug dealer. He was afraid she was going to be asked to identify the bodies. She would balk at the notion. He felt positive one or both overdosed on whatever they bought that day or the next one. After the earlier part of this day, he wasn't certain how Dallas would handle round two.

They were in the city. His GPS was giving him advice on the best way to proceed to the station. She hung up. Glared at him. He saw the color blossom in her cheeks. Was pleased by her spunk. She would weather this storm as well as any that might come later.

"Is everything taken care of?" he asked, while pulling into the parking lot. "Your card? We'll have your license back before we leave. You could drive home if you'd like." Not that her driving was a real option. He'd never been a good passenger.

"All's fine. There weren't any purchases, which is strange. Who would take a credit card then not use it? As to driving, I'm positive we'd both be more comfortable if you continued the role of chauffer."

"Someone who didn't know what it was for?" That thought surprised him. Those two seemed to enter this century knowing how to do everything a modern-day man would comprehend. He knew Gordon drove. He brought her to his house one of the first nights she returned. It was the time he knew she was his mate. That kiss, the touches between them, he'd never forget the moment his mouth captured hers. The inferno that ignited between them. So, why didn't they use the extra money? From what he saw on the docks, they could have used clean clothing. Food. A place to stay. All which a credit card could be used for.

Needing to feel her in his mind, to sink into her thoughts, he held her hand as they walked from the parking lot. He massaged her wrist with his thumb. Felt her shiver of pleasure. Once inside, he gave her name to the person at the desk, along with the information about the phone call. They were shown to the correct office. The sign on the door read, Detective Michael McKay.

The man behind the desk stood, extended his hand. His smile didn't reach very far. His eyes were cold, fathomless. He was a tall man. His hair cropped short; he stuffed his fingers through the short hair, doing little damage, and held out his hand. "I'm Michael McKay. I assume you are Dallas Shaw. It's nice of you to come down to the station."

"Dallas Frasier now…of less than a week. I didn't know my driver's license was missing. Where did you find it?" She sat down on the edge of the seat, her back stiff, chin tilted in the air. It didn't seem she was going to waste time with frivolous words. Dallas must have thought the missing ID was the reason she'd been called here. It wasn't. She would learn the real reason soon enough. Though it was the ID that brought her name to the detective's attention.

Michael McKay cleared his throat before he shot a glance at him then to Dallas. "

An unknown man, a John Doe, was in possession of the document. Seems your ID was in the pocket of his jeans. We hope you can tell us something about how it got there, as well as information about the deceased. If possible we will hope for a name."

At the word deceased, Dallas' face turned as white as new fallen snow. She gulped in a smattering of oxygen while her mind dashed in several different directions, never connecting with coherent thoughts. Dallas must have guessed something of the reason she was here. Rafe saw her shaking her head. Her fingers were woven together so tight her knuckles seemed to be turning white. He realized with a jerk she might faint.

Calm yourself, love. Breathe deep. Easy in, easy out.

Rafe reached out to her in the only way he understood, with his mind. After his words, she corralled her thoughts along with her body. He watched her breathing out. *Remember these men wished to harm you. If one or both are gone from this world, you will have less to worry about.*

"The pocket of his jeans," Dallas murmured, her lashes lowering for a moment. "You searched him? He allowed it? Oh…" She realized what she overlooked. When her nerves took over and she wasn't at home to cook, she always tapped with her fingers. In the car, he caught her doing that, tapping. At this moment, Dallas was tapping on her leg. He hoped she would switch to the wooden arm of the chair. The noise would do more for her than the silence.

"Yes," Michael said, his voice soft, seeming to notice the distress in hers. "I need to have you identify the body. Because of your driver's license, we have reason to believe you might know him." The last was said with a cautionary note. Michael seemed to have taken notice of her lack of color as well as the possibility she might faint. "You do know that man well enough to make an identification?"

With the assimilation of his words, Dallas slumped. "His body? What happened? Was he murdered?"

Rafe could tell she was hanging on with every possible part of herself. He wondered why she jumped to that question. Rafe answered for her, to give her some much-needed minutes to mull over the words. "Perhaps you should give her a moment. As I told you on the phone, the last two days have been trying. Her father returned from the dead. Well, he'd been gone for more than twenty years. Not of his choice. Gone, nevertheless. She is still adjusting to that knowledge. There were other things too. Of course, none of this pertains to what you've requested of Dallas." Rafe wasn't going to get into any more elements of her past.

"I'd like a glass of water," she told the detective. *Need to be alone with you. Can't think here or breathe in this stuffy room. It's airless. Feel as if the walls are closing in on me and the floor is turning in circles.*

I know. The water might be doable. However, the man is not going to allow us privacy even if we ask. Let's get this over with so we can get out of here. Once we're alone we can talk about what has happened. The repercussions of his death. You must have guessed this man is either Tinley or Mathew. What we do know is that the man won't bother you again. The next question is what has happened to the other one..

Did you know about this?

Yes, in part. I guessed this had to do with those two men. Knew one was gone. Also guessed that one or both might not have made it after what I saw. I'll explain later. There is no time for that now. Concentrate on what needs to be done in the here and now. Get out of here as soon as possible.

Michael returned with water for her. "I'm sorry for your loss," he told her, sounding serious.

What the detective could never understand was that Gordon did not represent a loss to her. The man was a villain. Threatened her life on more than one occasion. Wanted her to the point he was willing to rape her to get what he coveted.

She looked at the detective. Tears slid down her cheeks. Her mouth opened then closed as she seemed to grapple for words. "The man was not a loss to me. He threatened me with both my life as well as rape. How he had my license is unknown to me, though he might have sometime had the opportunity to go through my purse. I don't know. Anything is possible." Dallas held out her hand. "Can I have my license back?"

McKay tapped the card on the desk a few times before handing it over to her. Now the detective sounded hopeful. "Can you identify him? There is no one else that we know of."

"Yes. How? How did the man die? What happened to his friend?" It seemed she was opening up, needing knowledge.

The detective lifted his shoulders. The shrug was careful not to let more intense feelings show. "Overdose. The man overdosed. As to this friend of his, I've no idea where he might be. Couldn't tell you. Was this friend also using?"

"Oh…he wouldn't have understood how drugs work," Dallas muttered. "As to Tinley, he would do whatever Gordon did. Suppose he was probably using the same drugs."

"How so? In a time like the present, who doesn't know about drugs. Seems you don't know your friends well."

Rafe understood she let something slip that would be better left to some other time and place. "He…" She began. He needed to finish off the sentence.

"Neither Gordon or Tinley were very smart about things. He wanted what everyone else had. Wasn't satisfied with…oh, I don't know. Can we get this over with? I need to take Dallas somewhere she can relax." Sleep was more what she needed. He would let her sleep twenty-four hours if she needed.

A half hour later, they sat in his car. Silent tears streaked down her beautiful face. Her shoulders were trembling, vibrating with the force of her sobs. She knuckled her watery eyes before she turned her gaze toward him. The soggy smile she gifted his way left him stunned. Silver streaks created by her tears painted her cheeks. He watched a teardrop fall from her chin. This was so much more than she should have endured. While Rafe understood her thoughts about Gordon, she would never wish for the man's death.

She reached out for his hand, and he enclosed his fingers in hers. Held tight. Her hand was so cold. The decided lack of warmth startled him. After she looked up, she spoke, "I've never seen a dead body before. That…that was horrible. I thought I would faint."

He found himself at a loss for words that would soothe her. Taking her into his embrace, holding her until she felt warm again, was what Dallas needed. He couldn't hold her now. He searched for the right words, necessary words. "Not something most of us experience. I haven't either. Let's try to forget this afternoon. Put it in our past as we've done so many other things. Do you want to stay in the city or drive back? I made reservations…"

"Please no… I want…need…to go back home. Sleep in our bed where it's warm. We can do this some other time; have fun in the city when there is nothing to remined us of death. Maybe after all this is far enough away from us, we won't care." She pushed back her long hair before securing the strands in a ponytail. "Rafe, if you're not up to driving, we can stay here. If you are, I want to be in our bed tonight. I can deal with whatever you choose."

With you. I need for you to hold me. Must hear the beat of your heart as it melds with mine. Know the even sound of each breath.

"I'm fine with driving home. It will be late when we get there. You'll be exhausted. Never mind. You're overtired now." His heart went out to her. The day was both heartfelt as well as tragic. Bittersweet. Hopeful. The atmosphere left a person on tenterhooks. A man she hoped would disappear died instead. That was never something she wished for. On the other hand, this morning's events promised untold happiness. If all her hopes with the beginning of her life with her parents were fulfilled, she would find joy with each new day.

"I have you with me. That will help. I can sleep in the car. Rest while you drive," her words were spoken in an attempt to reassure.

"We'll stop. Pick up something to eat before we leave the city. Do you have anywhere you'd like..." he stopped speaking when she interrupted.

Dallas was massaging her temples. "I'm not hungry. Food in my stomach would keep me awake. I'd not wish to toss what I ate in your car. Go anywhere that suits you. I'll be fine."

"Alright. I'm still going to buy you something. A cookie maybe... something to drink. Coke?" He asked, hoping to encourage her. "Soft drinks can soothe the stomach. A little sugar always helps."

She tossed a half-smile his way. "Fine. Something to drink would be nice, lots of ice. If I get thirsty, I can sip. I will be asleep for most of the trip. Can't seem to keep my eyes open." Dallas yawned once then again. At first, he thought it was feigned. It was not.

She leaned back against the seat, closing her eyes. He kept looking at her, hoping she would fall asleep with no trouble. His hopes came to pass. In minutes, she was sleeping. He understood her exhaustion. For him, staying at a nice hotel would have been preferable to driving home. For Dallas, the need to be centered, to find stability was what she needed. She could only do that in their home, beneath their roof. Dallas was his first priority.

By the time they pulled up in front of his house, her head was on his lap. She'd been sound asleep a few minutes ago. Now, she straightened, smoothing long strands of hair from her face. Her eyes were sleepy bedroom eyes. He knew the way they looked when she reached that sweet pinnacle of bliss as well as just before. There would be no play tonight. They would find their way straight to bed. This was where she wanted to be.

"How are you?" he asked while he watched her stretch then yawn. enjoying the way her lush curves responded. "Can you walk into the house on your own? I could carry you...if you'd like."

"Yes, I can walk. How are you? You had to drive... Maybe I should carry you." The *gamin* grin sent lust straight to his groin. Sleep must have been good for her.

Ignoring her comment, "We'll be in bed soon. I find the thought of lying down next to you makes the bed more welcoming. All those years I was by myself are now in the past. If you can get yourself inside without help, I'll bring the two overnight bags with me."

He stepped from the car as Dallas was walking toward the house. The crash on the back of his head sent him staggering to his knees. The second blow landed harder than the first. While he fell, he wondered what happened to his cat senses. Instinct should have warned him of the danger. He'd been thinking only of lying in bed with his wife, holding her, making love to her. In the distance, he heard Dallas scream his name. Stunned by thoughts of Dallas, he floated in the air for what seemed an eternity. Fell. Hit the ground hard with a bounce. All else went blank. Colors turned from the darkness of a night with moonlight to black velvet.

The odd thing was he could hear Dallas. She screamed his name then whirled. Heard the sound of air. Now she yelled at the person who hit him. Her voice loud, threatening. She was outraged. Out of control. She pummeled the person. Her fists bounced off the man's body.

"What the hell do want here? There is nothing for you! Go away! Go back from wherever you came from! That dark hole can have you!" Silence swept around him for a few seconds. *I'm not going with you! Never!*

Who? His mind splintered. Pain sparked bright lights in his head before they once again blackened.

"You know damn well I need to go back there. The devil take ye. Want to fall through that black hole so I can live somewhere I understand. You killed him…Gordy. You're going to help me. Must go back. There isn't any other choice!"

"Tinley," Dallas' voice sounded calm. Distant. Seemed as if she spoke in a void. "I didn't kill Gordon. It was the drugs the two of you bought that killed him. He overdosed. Why didn't you overdose?"

Rafe didn't quite believe she asked Scratch that question. Almost sounded as if she wished he'd taken too much of whatever killed Gordon. Dallas wouldn't think that way. *I'm trying to get to you, Rafe. If you're alright let me know. Need you now. He's waving this gun around. He means to kill you. To hurt me. Help us. Wake up!*

Don't understand why I'm hearing you. Can't move. Can't see anything except the black hollowness that seems to be in my head.

Please...Rafe...Get help!

The voices were gone. He no longer heard Dallas in his pounding head or otherwise. His groan sounded hollow, far away as well. The black emptiness where he'd been sent changed to dark grey. Flashes of white and blue light split through his head as if the glows were lightning slashing through the sky.

"Rafe! Wake up!"

Hands were shaking him. His mind struggled. Seemed sluggish. This time the groan sounded more real. Someone moved him. Shook his shoulders. Shoved him to his side then his back. He lay on his back staring into the steel gray of Ian McConnel's eyes. Someone came to help him.

"What? What happened?" Rafe touched the back of his head. His hand came away smeared with blood. "How long have you been here? Did Dallas call for you?" So many questions whipped through his head. He needed answers to all of them.

"Not long. You've a bump the size of a goose egg on the back of your head. No time to see to it now. The lump will wait. Someone has Dallas. We need to move before they get too far away. Do you know who he is or what the man wants?"

"He hit me. I..." All he understood now was that Dallas needed him. When she couldn't find him, she must have reached out to her father. "Why are you here?" Rafe asked, but he had a good idea why Ian showed up. "Dallas called me for help. Did she call you too?"

"She did." Ian pulled him to his feet. "You have any idea where they would go?"

Rafe wasn't certain. When he reached out to Dallas, she didn't respond. He hoped that didn't mean she was unconscious too. "It's someone..." There wasn't time to tell Ian details about Dallas' fall through the portal by the waterfall. "How much has Helen told you?" Hell, Helen didn't even know what happened to Dallas except that she was gone, then she was back again. She wouldn't be able to tell him about her travel to a distant century.

"Someone? Hope you got more than that to go on."

"I believe I might know where they are going, since I know who took her away. Tinley Scratch, if I don't miss my guess. He's going to the falls. It's an attempt to return to his time. If we don't stop him, he'll try to take Dallas with him. She won't let that happen. Not if she can help it."

"What's my daughter like? Will she fight this man who means her harm? Would she venture to change…" Ian left that part off seeming unsure of asking.

"Dallas will fight. Yes, she'll fight. Might change to her cat. I don't know. There is no place for her anywhere but here with me. She knows that better than anyone." There were no guarantees. Tinley would go back to that time where he wanted to live. The time he knew as well as understood. If possible, he would drag Dallas with him for revenge. He must blame her for his friend's death.

"You're in no condition to drive." Ian helped Rafe to his feet then into Helen's car. "You need to show me which way to drive. We will get there in time." The last was said with the conviction only a father or husband would have.

Rafe's head hammered both with the pain from the blow he took and his fear for Dallas. Dear God, they couldn't be too late. He wished he could hear from her. Wished she would reach out to him. He needed to get inside her head. Needed to know everything. More than everything.

He called out. His voice was met with nothing except silence. The cringe of fear rumbled up from the pit of his stomach. Terror surrounded him. He hesitated to think the worst, yet knew he had to remain calm. Must continue to search for her in his head. That was the only way he would know where she was.

All he registered was a jumbled mess of conflicting thoughts. Dallas would be terrified. Tinley would hold the gun to her head to force her to do his bidding. The man blamed her for the death of his friend. The man was a maniac. He blamed her for their travel through time to the present. She was the means for him to enact his vengeance over crimes he perceived were committed.

"How are you doing?" Ian asked as he pulled off the highway onto the exit for the falls. They drove down a forested road that twisted and rotated every which way. They turned into the parking lot and Ian clicked the key to stop the engine. He rested his head on the top of the steering wheel. "Can you get around without help? I can leave you in the car. Go after her by myself," Ian told him.

"The man has a gun. You cannot go alone. She is my wife."

"My daughter."

"Who you barely know. Who's to say she won't be as frightened of you as she is of Tinley or the travel into another century?"

"I know." Ian stopped to study him with a hard stare. "We might need to shift. I brought extra clothes. Are you up to that? Shifting. Will your head withstand the difference?"

Dallas told him what she recalled about the last time she was here at the falls. Someone had been shot. She saw that through a murky haze. "We're battling a gun. One that fires more than one bullet without reloading," Rafe said as he thought about what might happen. The odds were not good. Dallas wouldn't think to shift. She was far too new at the game. She might not understand her strengths in doing so, along with her weaknesses. She would hold back. Maybe not. They practiced. Instinct might take over. She possessed a cat's sense of survival.

Take care. Don't do anything foolish. He reached out one more time. No one answered.

"Let's just see what is going to transpire. Maybe he just wants to go home and sees Dallas as his ticket," Ian said as he studied the water fall in front of him. He might not care if she comes or goes. There were few vehicles in the park. Most everyone had gone home a long time ago.

"He came for her with a purpose in mind. He wants her. Intends to take her with him wherever that might be. The man wants revenge. He's terrified with Gordon's passing."

"We are wasting time then," Ian murmured. "Let's take care of business before it's too late."

"They'll be on the other side of the falls. We should hurry."

~ * ~

Tinley didn't know what to do. His mind was in a jumble. The girl,

Dallas, fainted. He didn't have the strength to move her from the car. He wanted to take her with him. Needed her to help him find that damn black hole again. She would know where to look for the hellish' place. What good would she do him in this state? She was a dead weight, holding him back. He couldn't carry her. She was too damn heavy.

She moaned. He shook her hard trying to wake her up. Her body was limp. Useless. In this condition, she wouldn't be able to walk a step. "Wake up, bitch! Wake up now!" he yelled, frustrated as well as angry. He slapped her face. The woman annoyed him. He hated her. Every time he thought of the damn pepper spray she shot in his eyes, they stung. She wouldn't do him any good like this, all floppy and pathetic. She couldn't help him unless he could get her to wake up. He shook her again. Hit her face so hard, her head jerked back. A red mark the shape of his hand formed on her face. "Open your damn eyes!"

She cried out with the blow. Whimpered. Her lashes blinked once then twice before they closed again. "Oh…" her moan was thin. Her head turned to the side. He shook her again. Tried to make her stand. Weak kneed she fell, the side of her head pressed against the dashboard of the car.

Gordon had wanted her more than anything, more than what was prudent or right. Had raved about how it would feel when he could be inside her. Wanted her to fight him. Always liked a woman to battle until his masculine supremacy won. Said that subduing a woman made him feel like a real man.

He'd wanted her too, but not like Gordon. To him she was just another whore. His friend was obsessed with having her. Spoke of little else…except the hellish pills. They had other women in the camps. Ones that didn't complain when they took them hard, spilled their seed inside their hot channels. They spread their legs for them as if they needed a good poke. Drugs. He warned Gordon about those pills that didn't make him feel right. Gordon liked that sensation. He went back for more pills. Didn't have the funds to use on something that didn't feed them. Gordon decided he would make money by selling the tiny pills.

Except for this incident, his friend was always the smart one. He relied on Gordon to keep them alive, to make certain there were women to ease them. Gordon made all the crucial decisions. Now that Gordon left him, all he had to count on was himself and this woman who despised him, loathed him to hell and back. The girl who was knocked out in a dead faint on the seat of Rafe's car. When he hit her, he thought he got through to her. All she did was moan. If he wasn't certain of his need to find that black hole, he would spread her legs and have her here outside the damn car. He didn't care if anyone watched. He needed to see why Gordon wanted her so much. Soon…soon, he would have this lush creature all to himself. He would keep her in their hut. Keep her all to himself. Poke her whenever he wished.

On the way here to this god forsaken place, she'd been swerving from one lane to the other. Fearing for his life, he told her to pull over. When she ground to a halt, the force of the stop sent him forward into the windshield. He cracked his head. Blood spilled. His temples pounded. Took him a few seconds to recover, for him to focus. Even though he drove the car only a couple of times, he could keep the damn thing on the right side of the road. Maybe she was on those little pills or foxed. He could understand foxed. She might have drunk herself into oblivion when the two lovebirds were driving home from their visit with the detective.

Before they exchanged places, he stuffed his gun into the back of his jeans. She groaned. Clung to him while he dragged her from behind the wheel to put her into the passenger side. On impact, she must have hit her head too, maybe on the steering wheel. Now that they stopped, he had to figure out how to get her around the falls to the far side. Behind the falls was where the place was. That terrifying spot was where he was going to return to his time.

Hefting her, his hand under her arms, he dragged her along the trail, stopping for a few seconds to suck in air before he started again. For a few more minutes staggered breaths of air were all that made their way into his lungs. He felt as if she dug her heels in to stop his process. No, the woman, Dallas, was limp. She remained in the dead faint. She couldn't help him. Hell, she couldn't move.

Unable to take one more step, he dropped her. She lay on the ground, her head lolling to one side. He vacillated from one thought to the next while he leaned against a rock, gulping air. He didn't need her. He did. If she also returned to his century, he would have his vengeance. He would keep her in the cabin he and Gordy built. No one would learn of her existence. She would see to his needs, every last one of them. Those times were the good life. He'd have his whore in his home with him. She would service him whenever he beckoned.

First, he had to find a way to the other side of the falls. Once he got her there, if she remained unconscious, he could roll her down the damn hill. That would be fine with him. If he got her a little bruised as well as disoriented, she would be easier to handle. Gordy would have liked to be here with him tonight. He learned just before he died, he wished they would have found a way to go back to the century where they'd been born. Should have insisted two days ago they find some way to get here. If they had, Gordy might still be alive. Couldn't get those damn little pills in their time. Gordy would no longer crave them. They would have been just fine if they could have found their way home.

Tinley figured out if he could get her arm around his shoulder, he would be able to walk with her. Her head would still droop, her feet drag on the ground. If they saw anyone, he could tell the person she drank too much. Pretend they were lovers going behind the falls to have sex. People would believe him. He would make certain of that.

The one couple they encountered decided in his favor. Either that or they just wanted to look the other way. Tinley sniggered, pleased with himself. People weren't much different now than they were back then. Most, except the damn McKennas along with the Frasiers, seemed to want to ignore whatever appeared to be wrong rather than do something to fix the wrong. Though, Tinley admitted, the way she leaned into him gave the impression they were lovers.

Together they made it beneath the water pouring over the edge, to that spot behind the falls that sloped down to the clearing where the fuckin hole opened up to suck them inside. He did as he decided before they started walking. Setting her down, so she was sitting, her side pointed downhill. He gave her a hard kick then stepped back to watch her somersault then roll down the incline. He heard the loud thumps each time her body hit the ground hard. A whimper of pain every once in a while, echoed to him as he dashed after her body. He didn't wish her dead, just down the damn hill.

He didn't know what he'd find at the bottom. For all he knew as he watched her bump and bounce along the high grass, she would be dead at the bottom. When she stood, he saw the quivering of her body. A moment of fear branded him. He realized what all the shuddering meant. He'd watched shifters change. Fuck! The tossing and turning must have brought her out of her stupor. He watched as all her clothing ripped from her. Startled, beyond speech, he remained frozen.

Dallas was a cat. One of those hell cats. The devil's own hell cats. He thought Rafe Frasier, her husband, might be one, but never suspected that Dallas could turn. With a mighty roar he recognized as not being as fierce as Roc Frasier's, she leapt up the hill. She was coming after him. He needed to run. Instead, for too many seconds, he froze. Understood the danger racing to him.

Tinley forgot everything, except getting away from her claws as well as her fangs, turning to tear up the hill. He tripped on a tree trunk, tried to right himself. Found all he could do was move on all fours as he fought for air. Terror engulfed him. He was going to die. She would rip out his jugular. Knew that for a fact. Soon, he'd be joining Gordon in whatever hell waited for him. He didn't want to die.

After Dallas landed on top of him, his face hit the ground hard. He felt the press of his nose on inflexible earth. He ate grass along with dirt. A stone nicked the corner of his eye. Blood flowed from the wound by his eye to his mouth. To his surprise, his lips were covered with blood. His blood. He expected she would go for his throat.

Tinley lay in the dirt, panting, shivering, listening to the beat of his heart. Silence clung to him. Movement was not possible. Afraid if he did try to run again, she would pounce on him one more time. Her teeth caught hold of his collar, his shirt was ripped from his pants then torn away from his back. The gun at his waistband was pulled away. He felt her teeth rake the small of his back. The sound of the weapon landing in the brush somewhere brought the fact pulsing into his head that he should have used the weapon to blow the cat away. He lost his chance.

The sickening sense that something more was wrong came to him in a rush as he was hauled to his feet.

"No!" Tinley stared into the steel gray of Rafe Frasier eyes. He'd been on that end often enough to recognize the color, along with the heated intensity, the cold hard unrelenting look. Though the ones he stared at weren't Rafe's. They were someone else's. Another shifter by the look of his eyes. Who the devil was this man?

"Yes…" was the silent yet deadly reply.

Once again, all his plans were for naught.

The blow hit him hard. Knocked his head back while all his teeth jarred. He worked his mouth to see if any were loose. The next blow sent him whirling around to land on his hands and knees. While he tried to crawl away, he found himself hauled to his feet another time. Hit again then again. The blows rained down on him until he was senseless. All the muscles along with the joints in his body ached. He fainted into oblivion.

When Tinley woke, it was to bright lights flashing around the parking lot while hitting the waterfall, to turn the sprays to beautiful transparent colors. His hands were cuffed behind his back. He sat on the cold cement, leaning against the police car. Blood, his blood dripped into his eyes. Even though his future didn't appear to be bright, Tinley was thankful he was alive. As he thought earlier, life at this point didn't look promising.

Rafe Frasier was speaking with someone. Tinley imagined the person on the other end was one of the cops. Maybe they would feed him in jail better than he'd been eating in the homeless camp. He could always look on the brighter side of life.

His head pounded so hard everything was fuzzy. The man with the steel-gray eyes beat him harder than necessary. He wondered what was going to happen to him now. In this century, what was the penalty for kidnapping? Not one doubt in his mind existed that Dallas and Rafe, along with the man who pounded him to oblivion, would seek to have the harshest possible sentence inflicted. Perhaps more, though he didn't know what that would be.

This was the last chance he'd had to find his way home, to his true home. He didn't like to think he would wither away in this century. Gordon might have been right to seek solace along with oblivion in the pills. If he still possessed the gun he'd stolen, he'd put it to his head. End his misery.

Epilogue

Three years later

Dallas posed for Rafe in the upstairs studio. He told her he would position her just as she had been the first time he painted her naked. Today there was a major difference. She was eight months pregnant with their second child. Dallas swept her hands across her belly, pushing in elbows or knees so she would be more comfortable.

The sweetest thing was that Helen and Ian had a son who was a few months younger than their first child. They were both so pleased the pregnancy went well. Helen was younger than Ian by more than a few years. Neither expected they would have another child. This was their chance to do everything over. Second chances were always appreciated.

A month ago, Rafe found the painting Roc did of Lainie so many years in the past. It was hidden behind a panel. Until then, Rafe never new about the secret cubbyhole. He came across the hiding place quite by accident. The portrait was rolled up and tied with two faded blue ribbons. Rafe framed the picture then hung it beside the nude of her that Rafe painted before she traveled through time. The two portraits were so similar, looking at them together stole her breath. That painting was of her in another time. She could only be grateful. Through her help, Lainie found her way to Roc. According to legend, if that had not happened, she and Rafe would have never been together. Max, along with this second little boy, would never have been born.

They could both see subtle differences between the two portraits. Their one-year-old son knew which portrait was of her. She wasn't at all certain she liked the child seeing her nude body, especially when he grew older. Somehow that seemed wrong. At this time, he was a toddler. What about when he was a teenager. Dallas was beginning to think both portraits should be rolled up then put in their rightful place behind the secret panel. She didn't wish for anyone except Rafe to see either painting.

"Mama…" Max pulled himself up on the bed where she posed. Pointed at the portrait that was her. "Mama. My mama." The toddler touched her rounded stomach. "BroBro." He grinned. The smile resembled his father's ridiculous grin. Both were such dears. So sweet, so very gentle…she loved them both with all her heart, her unborn son also.

"I told you we should wait until after he goes to bed," Dallas told him, indignant with the prospect of discarding the robe so Rafe could paint with her son ever the observer. She wasn't about to take the robe off in front of their little boy, even though they shifted together a few times. Decided she was going to put an end to disrobing then changing shape in front of Max. That was Rafe's job…to teach. If she were to join them in their cat, she would shift in private. She could play with the two of them under those circumstances.

"Ah, but I couldn't wait for that." Rafe winked at her before waggling his eyebrows. He was such an incorrigible flirt. "I want to look at you."

She snorted a patch of air. "You're going to have to wait until your son goes to bed." Dallas meant to stay firm on that account. She wasn't going to pose naked for Rafe with the little man looking on. Even as a toddler, the boy was too old to see his mother naked. Rafe's paintings would have to be done at night. While she didn't object to the boys seeing nude pictures, ones of her were off limits.

"Why?" Rafe smirked, as if he understood the reason but wasn't about to give credence to the viability. "Seems the boys need to understand life. This is art not porn. A man cannot hide from the realities of the world."

She didn't think Max was old enough to decipher the distinction. That was another job that would go to Rafe. He needed to make certain the boys understood the difference. "I'm not taking this robe off until he's put down for the night. It's bad enough he sees me naked in that portrait. In the future, this little boy, and the one I'm carrying, are going to find this room off limits. Locked. Either that or you must put the portraits back into their hiding place. I'm not…" she was stopped short by his easy compliance to her dictates.

"As you wish."

She blinked a few times as if that small gesture would clear her head. In her mind he gave in far too easily. She expected an argument. Rafe would believe it was perfectly logical that the boys see their mother nude. She didn't agree with the man. For the argument that would occur with time, she needed to make certain all the salient points were in line...all her ducks in a row.

"If they were girls, would you feel the same?" Rafe challenged every instinct within her, and still with that silly half-grin that told her his thoughts were wicked. "You wouldn't have one objection. I know the way you think. Your opposition is a bit one sided. Nevertheless, I'll broker an apology."

"That question is not fair! An apology be damned!" She pointed a finger at him, her brows drawing together in silent protest before she reiterated her statement with more enunciation to each word, as well as less volume. "Not fair at all. Not by a long shot." She scooped the boy into her arms then sat on the big, overstuffed chair in the corner of his studio. Max's fingers dipped behind the fabric. He wanted to nurse. He'd just eaten. Didn't need her for nourishment. This was his way of going to sleep. All her little man wanted was the comfort of his mother. She was just as loathe to give these moments up as Max.

"I believe it is. Don't you stand for equality in all things? Women's rights? What about men's rights? The male of the species should also be treated with equality. Don't you think?" He lifted his shoulders in an all-masculine shrug. "At least, I thought you did."

"This is different, and you know that for a fact. I won't have my son ogling..." Dallas found herself cut off before she could finish her statement.

"I'm putting him to bed." Rafe interrupted with another wink. "I want time alone with my wife. As to the topic of men's rights, there is no need for more discussion. I understand as well as agree. All men should garner the same rights as women. This is a woman's world. You know that, right?" Rafe scooped the boy from her arms into his then disappeared.

Dallas leaned back. Her head settled against the soft cushions. She closed her eyes, listening to the fall of Rafe's feet as he walked down the steps to the second floor. The door to the nursery closed. Rafe sang to their son. She loved listening to him sing, his rich baritone floating up the narrow staircase to the third-floor studio. He would be back as soon the baby fell asleep. She appreciated his teasing remarks. He did have a way of making her think along different lines. On this issue, her mind wasn't going to change.

She ran her hands along the contours of her belly. Felt the baby kick. The *wee* lad was strong. At times he spoke to her just as Max did when she carried him. The conversations were always enjoyable. She was eight months pregnant now. Didn't understand why she agreed to pose for him in this condition. She could change her mind anytime. Should change her mind before he began to work. Once he started, Rafe would cajole and finagle to get his way.

Their second little boy would be a shifter just as they were all shifters. Max began changing into his cat as soon as he could crawl. He was just as adorable as a kitten as he was in his little boy form. His changing ability seemed a bit early to her. Rafe took it all in stride. Loved to shift with him when it was bath time. Together in their cats they would wrestle. Even at the tender age of one, Max understood this was the only time changing shape would ever be allowed unless they traveled into the privacy of the highlands.

The boy sported his father's thick black hair, coupled with his steel gray eyes. His sense of humor seemed to develop with his growth. Max laughed at everything, especially his father's antics. Rafe loved to perform as did Max's Grandfather Ian. The two could play with the boy for hours heaped upon more hours. Her mother turned out to be a loving, nurturing mother as well as grandmother who loved both her daughter as well as her grandson. She was also a doting mother to her son. The change in her mother both surprised as well as pleased her.

Dallas loved bringing Max to visit, as well as cooking dinners for her parents. Before the first year was out, she'd forgiven her mother. Found she loved her father so much more than she ever would have expected. The fact she now had a real family never escaped her. She vowed to always cherish her family, every last one of them. For the first time in her life, she felt loved by her parents.

Tinley spent his remaining years behind bars. He died in prison two years after his aborted attempt to flee this century. She could never feel sorry for either Gordy or Scratch. They were terrible humans, bringing their dire fate upon themselves.

"You're lost in thought?" Rafe scooped her from her chair into his arms before settling her on his lap. He ran his hand along the rounded curves of her body. Paused for a moment where their son kicked.

"I was thinking about how good our life is. I can hardly wait for this child to be born. Max will be a good brother to this little one. Already loves the new babe. Can we try at least one more time for a girl?" Dallas understood that thought would please Rafe. He would give consent to as many children as she would like. She thought three were enough. Maybe not. She did hope for a girl.

Rafe smoothed her hair from her neck, placing tender kisses along the back. "You do know how much I love you. You give me every wish I could ask for."

"Hmm... Rafe's every wish fulfilled. I like the sound of those words. I love you too. We are lucky all turned out the way it was supposed to be."

His hand slipped inside her robe. Cupped her breast. Ran his thumb across a nipple.

"What about you? Has Dallas' every wish been fulfilled?"

"Yes..." she breathed softly as Rafe gave up beginning the new portrait to make love to his wife.

Coming Soon

Georgia's Rebellious Heart
Sweet McKenna Book Eleven

London 1758

Rain sluiced from the dark-clouded sky. Chandler would be here soon. She did and she didn't want to see him. After his last ultimatum more than two months ago, Georgia acknowledged the fact she would never be able to trust the man…her person forever…her mate for now and into the future.

She loved Chandler.

She would never confide in or rely on the man. Would never be able to trust him with her heart or her soul.

He had insisted she stay the remainder of her contract after she gave birth to their little girl. Maintained she owed him. In her mind, Georgia didn't believe she owed him anything. He threatened her. Told her he would give her to Bertram, a man she despised, for his personal entertainment if she didn't continue to work the nightly shows. Also told her he would auction her to the patrons of his shows. If he did that, she would find herself on her back in the rooms on the third floor entertaining the highest bidder. Her favors sold to the men as if she was a common whore. At the thought her stomach cramped. She was no whore. The only man she'd ever been with was Chandler.

Never, would she ever go back. Her future along with her daughter's and her unborn child lay ahead of her.

Giving into his demand was a lesser evil than the other choices he presented her with.

She endured the month and a half left on her contract. Escaped him. Now, she owned a home. Was beginning her career as a professional caterer. She did enjoy cooking. Loved to visit with her clients while they planned menus for their gatherings. With this job, she could bring her daughter with her along with her bodyguard Hollis.

The situation was strange. Chandler insisted she hire Hollis. She smiled thinking about this man, who wanted to see to her protection even though he didn't love her. Chandler would never love anyone except himself.

Hollis was the largest man she'd ever known. His dark black skin glistened while the muscles of his forearms bulged. Each and every time he smiled, the white of his teeth gleamed against the background of his face. If Hollis wished, he could lift her with one hand. His thighs were the size of tree trunks. Dark, very dark brown eyes, gifted his handsome face. He always treated her with respect. When Chandler visited, he remained close. Surprising Georgia, Hollis was loyal to her, not the man who hired him.

Once she arrived in this small cottage just outside the busy city of London, Chandler would attempt to convince her to return to the fold. Her return to that decadent lifestyle would never happen. The five-month-old daughter she cradled in her arms was too important to spend her formative years living in a high-priced brothel. Maeve was the most important person in her world. Her hair was as black as midnight, her eyes the color of a vibrant summer sky. The little girl resembled her.

Chandler didn't like the name she gave her daughter. Wished she called her something less Irish. Too bad. That was all right by her as long as he never abused the baby or the girl as she grew into womanhood. While he never hurt her, Georgia acknowledged the fact he harbored a mean streak. Recalled when he hurt his sister-in-law. Resented his immediate family for disavowing him. Promised revenge.

Now that she was free of the brothel where he made his money, he continued to attempt to bring her into the world she left. Maeve would never see the inside of that whorehouse. Would never learn about her mother's participation in the debauchery within. With Chandler, she never cared who watched them while they were intimate. Didn't even mind the participation of Jimmy along with Johnny when they fondled her breasts. Sometimes the scenarios excited as well as pleased. When he brought his best friend, Bertram, into the mix, she drew the line. Bertram disgusted her.

Her future was ahead of her. Their daughter's potential would never be compromised by the filth of her father's world.

Georgia let out a slow breath of air. She loved Chandler with all her heart. After some time, she came to realize he would never love her back. He was too enamored of himself to give his love elsewhere. This egotistical nature of his actions blurred anything that was good in him. He was unable to give of himself even though he was her mate.

The loud boom of thunder startled her. A tiny noise escaped her. Within her arms, she rocked Maeve. The noise frightened the child. Tears filled her beautiful blue eyes. The babe let out a thin wail of distress, her head bobbing against her as if she searched for something that would give solace. Georgia brought her little love to her shoulder, smoothing her hand along her back to calm the infant. Maeve's entire hand found its way to her mouth as she tried to soothe herself.

"Hush, little one, this is just a storm. It will pass then the skies will be sunny as well as clear again. Nothing for you to worry over. You will have to get used to the tempest outside as well as the ones that will be brought to you because of your father. Your papa is not a good man." A long slow breath of air left her. She should never prejudice her daughter against the man who sired her. Time would explain to Maeve who her father was as well as what he was.

Setting her hand on her stomach, she thought about the tumultuous days as well as nights with Chandler. She was pregnant again. Georgia wasn't positive how she felt about another pregnancy so soon. It would be difficult to raise one child by herself let alone two. Now she would have two little ones to be responsible for. The man made certain of it before he allowed her to set out on her own. She still didn't believe he would, in truth, give her to Bertram. Mates didn't treat each other that way. They were possessive as well as demanding of their partners.

Humming to Maeve, she strode around the room. Stopped to peer out the window. Set her forehead on the cold pane of glass. Maybe the storm slowed the man down. Perhaps he had a change of heart. Maybe an accident. The thought caught in the back of her throat. While she didn't wish to have anything more to do with Chandler, she didn't want any harm to come to him.

She hoped the storm would slow his progress. Maybe the wheels of his carriage would get stuck in the mud. Perhaps he would turn around. She wasn't looking forward to the argument that would ensue upon his arrival. Chandler argued they should marry. Told her she should return with him so they could be together. She opposed a marriage between them. Never wanted him to own her.

Never!

Never say never too often. It might come to pass.

Gritting her teeth against the thought of being under his thumb, she forced herself to stay strong. When she pushed her chin in the air then stiffened her back, the act would help. Considering this scenario, being weak would do her no good. Shivers pounded down her spine when she thought of those last days of her contract. Fear of what he could do to her or Maeve if she protested held her at his whim. That last month and a half, she did all he asked. Some of those nights, he would leave Bertram to stay with Maeve as a reminder of the command he held over her.

Maeve's daddy is not a nice man.

Never did understand why he forced her on stage when she didn't wish to be there. The audience witnessed her reluctance. That fact brought in more groats than the previous performances. Forced her with threats. Except for the nights he sat with Maeve, Bertram was always close. Always nearby to carry out Chandler's wishes if he asked. To her disgust, sometimes he participated.

Until she arrived on the scene, the two men always shared their women, their conquests. To her knowledge, she was the first female Chandler and Bertram didn't share. Well…that fact was one point in his favor.

"You are Winter Snow, the ice maiden," he told her with a grin that didn't reach his eyes. "Your fans want to see you with me. Once, you enjoyed the lovemaking in front of an audience. You will again. Your unwillingness is an aphrodisiac to my audience. They wish to see you struggle against my attentions. Perhaps I should tie your hands above you. Leave you open to whatever my audience asks of me. We could allow them to write the script for us to play out. I am certain the play would be titillating."

She didn't enjoy the last days of her contract. The different scenarios she found herself forced to endure were horrible. Her mind would be with Maeve, sheltered upstairs. While she never believed he might hurt the child, she could never allow herself to trust him or Bertram. Must take care to give into all his dictates. The time would pass. If anything happened to her, Chandler would become the child's guardian. As soon as she escaped Chandler, worked the ensuing weeks of her contract, she would set about making her father, Cormack O'brien, Maeve's legal guardian.

The knock on the door startled her. Her stomach turned over while her heart pounded hard against her ribs. Before she walked to the door, she swallowed the huge lump of fear lodged in her throat.

Chandler…

A long deep breath helped for a swift moment. He was here. Would insist on staying the night. Could hold the horrific weather as the reason to remain. If he stayed, he would expect to share her bed. Chandler needed to realize she wasn't going to change her mind about their future. While she would never stop him from seeing his child, soon to be children, she didn't intend to share intimacies with the man. She couldn't bear to have him in her bed. Didn't wish to be reminded of the intense feelings she had for the man.

Taking her time, she brought Maeve to her crib then set her inside. Kissed the baby's forehead before drawing a light cover over her tiny body.

"Sleep tight, my darling. I won't let anyone hurt you." Beside the crib, Georgia lingered. "Your father is here now. I'll check on you as soon as possible."

The knocking on the door became more insistent. "Open the damn door!" The uttered words sounded frantic.

Father!

Georgia rushed to the door, unlocking then flinging it open. So thrilled to see him, she was in his arms before he could step inside the door. She heard the strong, steady beats of his heart. With each breath he inhaled, she felt the movement of his chest. His strong arms locked around her. As she pressed herself against his large frame, the moment was not much different than when she was a little girl. She wished she could keep him here with her forever. Wished he could protect her from Chandler. No one except herself could manage the feat. She needed to rely on her wits as well as her strength of will.

Cormack O'brien set her back to look at her. His smile was just as she remembered. "That was a nice welcome." The ensuing pause seemed significant. His brows furrowed together. "Are you alright? The bastard hasn't hurt you? Has he?"

She couldn't stop the cringe at the label her father gave her mate even though it was true. "I'm fine. Can I take your coat? Get you something to drink? You do know I wasn't expecting you. You didn't write." She sounded as if she lectured her father even though she was certain the surprise visit was meant to be just that…a surprise. "You're a long way from Belfast."

"A nice hot cup of tea with a wee splash of brandy to help warm my chilled body would suffice. For the time being, I intend to take up residence in London." Cormack shrugged from his coat. "Where's little Maeve?"

"Asleep in her crib. While I get your tea, you can look in on her." Georgia smiled at her father's back as he made his way to the nursery. "Don't wake her. If she is awake, bring her out to the front room."

Cormack was such a loving father. What happened to her broke his heart even though he understood finding her mate was a necessity along with the claiming. After she discovered her mate, there was no backing down. She realized proceeding with her plan was a necessity. Well, Chandler, with his father's help, learned the ceremonial words that would result in his ability to mark her as his.

While he claimed her, she did experience past lives together. Acknowledged the fact their line would continue. Some of what she saw was turbulent. Other times they were so in love the sight of them together made her shake.

Forgetting what happened between their meeting and the claiming would never happen. Nor would she ever regret those experiences with him. Some of those moments were wild. At times exciting. Chandler understood all her weaknesses. She would never regret those twelve months, the good along with the bad. Maeve was the result of her first few encounters with Chandler. In less than five months, God willing there would be another child.

The teakettle had been on the stove warming. It would not take much time for the water to boil. She pulled cookies from her cookie jar to set on a plate. Arranged the teacups along with the plate on a tray she would bring to the front room. Brandy, lemons and sugar were included to add to the plain drink.

Before everything was ready, Georgia heard Cormack. When she brought the tray into the room, he was staring out the window at the pelting rain. His hands were behind his back. When he heard her walk through the door, he turned. Gifted her with a smile she realized he didn't feel into his heart.

"Thought you might wish for something to eat as well." Walking into the room, she set the tray on a table.

She poured the tea then handed her father the bottle of whiskey while she doctored her tea with a bit of lemon and milk. To sweeten, she added a spoonful of sugar. Wasn't eager to tell her father she was expecting Chandler. Since he'd yet to arrive, thought the storm might have made him change his mind. Chandler was a man who loved his creature comforts. To be out in a night such as this one went against his natural behavior.

"Always thinking of others." He tested the temperature with a small sip. "Good, glad you remembered the whiskey. Warms my innards on this cold November day." With his look of concern, he seemed to see into her soul.

"I know you, Father. Understand your likes along with your dislikes. Try a cookie. Baked them yesterday. It's a new recipe I'm trying out for my business. You can tell me what you think." Her attempt to keep his mind off her relationship with Chandler wasn't going to work. She could tell by the way his eyebrows drew together.

"You plan to go forward with this foolishness? I can't believe you are going to cater to the rich and arrogant in the city." He quirked a graying eyebrow to the ceiling appearing to test her mettle with her plans. "This is too much work." He paused again, tapping his finger while he appeared to be thinking.

"My ideas are not foolishness. I need to support my daughter. While I've some money put away, the two of us will go through it if it's not supplemented. Before my eyes, she is growing, sprouting up so fast."

"I will continue with your allowance." His voice was so stern she brought her head up to look into his eyes. "There will be no need to supplement your income." Cormack bent over, his forearms resting on his thighs. "I will see to all your needs."

"I understand. I will accept if I need money. Don't mind if you continue to put my allowance into the account you set up in London in my name. The only coin I intend to use unless there is an emergency is what I've added to the account."

"Stubborn girl…" Cormack muttered under his breath. "What did I do to make you so willful that you won't listen to good common sense?"

Yes, she was stubborn. Meant to forge a life along with a future for her and her children. "Thank you for being here for me. Having you here makes me feel less uneasy. I also need to find a nanny for Maeve. Any suggestions?" Even though her father had many negative opinions, he could be helpful. Cormack had her best interest in his heart. Helping out his daughter was his role as he saw it.

He grumbled for a few ticks of the old clock on the mantel above the fireplace. "A grandmother, yes, she lives too far from her grandchildren. Met her just the other day while she was shopping for groceries. With you in mind, we had a nice long chat. She would treat Maeve as one of her own. Lives here in London. Doesn't have much. Certain there is plenty of room for her in your little cottage."

Georgia didn't repress the giggle on the tip of her tongue. "The cottage is not so little. Did you know it had a name? Of course, you did. Orange Blossom Cottage is not what I intended. I assume you put a hefty downpayment on the home. Otherwise, I doubt if I could have afforded the monthly dues." The extra money her father had a way of dropping on her was both appreciated and was not. If she were to make a go of this independent life she saw for herself, this was something she needed to accept. "I do intend to pay you back at some time in the distant future.

Cormack looked up, surprise registering in his eyes. With a slight tilt to his head, he began with a snort. "No…no I didn't place a downpayment on the Orange Blossom Cottage though doing so did cross my mind. Nor did I negotiate the price down. As you asked, I stayed out of the affair. You did tell me you intended to do this on your own. I accepted your wishes even though I disagreed with the concept."

So startled by the revelation, the teacup she held slipped from her hand. Hot tea splashed around her. She stood to shake the water from her skirts then picked up the broken cup. With some of the napkins on the tray she wiped up the mess she created. Dazed by the revelation, walking into the kitchen she mulled over all he told her. Nothing made sense. If he didn't, who did?

The man didn't lie. If he told her he stayed out of the picture because she wanted him to do so that was the truth. What was left was something she didn't like. Didn't want to owe Chandler anything. He was not supposed to have stepped into the negotiations or paid even a single penny for this home. She stuck her chin in the air while she poured more tea into her cup. Her back stiffened while she thought on the repercussions of her new discovery.

Bloody eyes, Chandler was trying to buy her. The man meant to orchestrate her return to the brothel by putting her in debt to him. Seemed he would stop at nothing. She sipped in a deep breath of stuffy air. Tried to stiffen her backbone against him. He wasn't going to succeed. With a fresh cup of tea in hand, she sat down across from her father. Her fingers shook, the cup rattling on the saucer. She set it back on the tray, unnerved by the revelation.

Rubbing his jaw, Cormack stared at her. "Chandler? Do you think he discovered who our agent was? I didn't tell him."

"Through the Wolcott name he has unbreakable connections. Through his business he has the ability to blackmail any number of important people. Besides you, he is the only other possibility. No one else would toss money my way." For a few moments, she fiddled with her skirt. Looking up, she tilted her chin. Her gaze focused on her father, "I'm not certain what I should do at this juncture. I cannot give him funds I don't have. I'm certain he…well…he would not take the money from me even if I had the needed amount. His intention is to use this situation to bend me to his will."

"I will see to this problem. Don't wish for you to worry. With the child along with the new baby on its way coupled with the business you wish to create, you've enough on your mind. I'll also see to the hiring of the nanny for you. The lady is wonderful. Positive you will appreciate her skills."

"The woman will be a godsend. I will look forward to having

female company. While Hollis is a dear, he doesn't talk much. Do you think the woman will enjoy coming with me when I cater? I'm still…" Georgia wasn't certain if she could speak of breast feeding with her father. Seemed to be something she didn't feel comfortable addressing the subject.

"You still need to feed Maeve. I get that. Of course, she will wish to follow along with you and the child. If you are agreeable, your new nanny might also wish to help with the cooking. She told me she is skilled in the kitchen. However, I believe she was hoping to invite me to dinner. We were interrupted before she could issue an invitation."

The loud wail brought both their attention to the nursery down the hall. "Speaking of feeding the babe. Maeve must be hungry or frightened. The storm is still loud. She doesn't like the thunder or loud noises." Wind howled around the eaves. "Excuse me for a moment. I'll feed her then bring her out. You can play with her."

Georgia took her time changing Maeve's diaper then sitting down with her while she nursed. Her father gave her a great deal to mull over in her head. She wasn't certain how to proceed with Chandler other than to continue on this same course. Everything she decided on was difficult. If she didn't love the man, none of this would matter.

Debating with herself, she couldn't make up her mind whether to confront the man about the downpayment or ignore what he did. In any case, Georgia didn't believe what she did would change the outcome. She didn't need to decide this instant. Part of her decision would occur made when she discovered his motive.

After she finished feeding Maeve, she brought her out to see her grandfather. Cormack held out his hands to her while Maeve gifted him with a huge smile then a little squeal which sounded much like pleasure. It was obvious to her that Maeve loved her grandfather. When he visited, he always made time to play.

A thick wool blanket was spread on the floor for Maeve. Cormack lay down beside the baby, handing her different toys for her to peruse. Everything he handed her found its way to her mouth. She seemed to like the cloth doll the best. She was propped in a sitting position. It would not be much longer before she would be able to sit by herself. She was growing up way too fast.

While the two played, Georgia tidied up the front room before heading for the nursery to rinse out the diaper. Once she thought this type of work would not suit. Now, she found everything, even diaper-duty, was something she could do without complaint. Humming to herself, she left the nursery. Wandering to the front room, with her arms crossed she leaned against the wall and watched. Maeve reached for the wooden toy. Started to topple. Her grandfather caught her then lifted her high above his head. Georgia thought she could watch these two forever.

All this time, she forgot that Chandler was supposed to arrive. He was late. Tardiness was not something unusual. Chandler did what he wanted when he wanted. Didn't care for time restrictions. She acknowledged the fact her father would not leave just because Chandler showed up. Cormack meant to stay. Tonight, because of the storm, she would have two men under her roof. Two men who despised each other.

Chandler would want to occupy her bed. His doing so was not going to happen. Not in this instance. Keeping him from her bed when he visited was difficult. He knew just how to seduce her. Never stopped with the word, no. Thought he had *carte blanche* with her body. In some ways he did.

Once, one time, he managed to seduce her. He made love to her, carrying her to her bedroom. He set her with gentle ease on the bed. The mating was hard…messy. In this instance, she felt shame at what they did. Felt dirty. After that, Chandler grinned at her. Believed he made his point clear. Whether or not she lived with him, she was his. After the one and only episode, she tried harder to remain strong. Attempted to stay away from him. Let him play with his daughter. Watched. Was always amazed at the tenderness he showed their baby. He never left the cottage without making love to her at least once.

With the new pounding on the door, Georgia realized this small period of tranquility had come to an end. Chandler was here. He would attempt to dominate everything. His wishes would be made clear. The rest of the evening would become a battle of wills between her father and Chandler. This evening, she was glad there would be a buffer between them. Chandler would stay more than one night. If her father knew, he might also choose to remain at the cottage longer. Feeling the stress, she pinched the bridge of her nose. Tried to breathe.

Before she could reach the door, Cormack with little Maeve in his arms, tugging on his ear, opened the door.

"Chandler." There was no emotion in his voice. A cold chill enveloped each word. "What are you doing here? Don't believe you are welcome."

"Cormack." Chandler was just as frigid. "I'm here to see my daughter along with her mother. You can't stop me. Both are mine." He pushed passed her father, shoving him aside. Stopped when he spotted her. "Winter…you are looking lovely this night."

Her father could be a cold man when the purpose suited him. Cormack was unforgiving for the time she spent with her mate in the brothel. Intolerant about some of the things Chandler orchestrated during those months. Though she told him less than nothing, he heard tales of what went on behind the closed doors. She signed a contract saying she was willing. The contract for a year was binding. What Georgia would never forgive him for was what happened after she gave birth. Would never pardon him for the threats he made to her person along with the threats to their daughter.

Chandler could be even colder. Could be mean as the devil. Georgia recalled what he did to Harris, his brother's wife. That was all before he made his first fortune with the whorehouse. Now, he was among the wealthiest men in London.

"Came to see Winter," Chandler nodded toward her. "My mate," he added with emphasis for her father.

"Her name is Georgia," Cormack ground out through clenched teeth. His hold on Maeve tightened.

"Not to me," Chandler pointed out as he stepped into the room. "Winter Snow is the woman I've known in so many different ways. I've seen as well as touched every delicate, white part of her all her pretty pink places too." Chandler's insulting gaze traveled the length of her then settled on her face. "She is the woman I claimed. If you've any doubts, all you need do is look at her shoulders. Those are my claw marks. Winter is mine. The babe is mine."

"Don't elaborate, Chandler. What you said to father should not have been expressed," Georgia pushed away from the wall. Walked toward Chandler but stopped before she reached him. "I'm not going anywhere.

There is no need for the two of you to argue. Maeve won't like the loud voices. You'll scare her. If the two of you continue in this manner, the both of you will make her cry." Just with the few minutes while the two males bristled for superiority, her nerves stretched. She set her hand on her somersaulting stomach. The stress was almost too much to bear.

"Why is your father here? Had plans to have a discussion with you…an important one. Can't speak to you with company." He looked her over. Once he perused her from her head to her toes, Chandler stopped at her breasts before lifting his gaze to her eyes.

Georgia understood he would have made some other comments if her father wasn't in the room. She wasn't positive why that would stop him. Though she did appreciate the small effort he made.

"Hollis has made up a room for you if you wish to stay the night. The storm is still howling. Father is staying here too. You are also welcome to spend the night in the guest room." The words of welcome caught in her throat even though he always stayed at least one night.

Dinner would be a tense affair. Already she felt the pressure building between her father and Chandler. What she didn't say was that he wasn't welcome in her bed. Couldn't say that in front of the man who sired her. Even beginning the night in a separate room, she would not be surprised to find him beneath the same covers by morning. She would think of a way to keep her distance. Chandler thought of her as his possession. Her deflection from his brothel, infuriated him. Tonight, she intended to sleep in the nursery. Hollis would have her bed. If he did seek her out in the middle of the night, he would find Hollis, not her. The thought brought a smile to her lips, one she needed to hide from Chandler.

She hoped that with time he would begin to understand this was the right thing to do for their child. Ignoring the babe, he stepped up to her. Placed his hand on her belly. Grinned. Caressed. Smiled again.

"Your bump is growing…a promise for my future. Do you think this one is a boy?" he asked as his fingers moved across her. "I hope so. A son I can mold to be like me."

"No!" Georgia moved away from him, surprised by his words. She prayed for another girl. "Never…you won't have the opportunity."

The fury in Cormack's eyes was undeniable. "Leave off. You've no right to touch my daughter. Didn't hear her give you permission to set your hand on her stomach," he growled, his voice low and deep.

"You can't stop me, old man," Chandler spoke with an air of superiority. "You can't stop me and neither can your daughter. If it's a boy she is carrying, he will live with me. Perhaps, Winter will return to me so she can be near her second child."

Maeve let out a tiny whimper at the harshness of her grandfather's voice. Georgia paled at Chandler's words about a son. Her breath wobbled in the back of her throat as she tried to grasp the new threat. Cormack's retreat from his building anger was undeniable. Her father would do nothing to cause her more discomfort. Chandler's look of victory was also undisputable. He was filled with himself. Caught up in the moment. He would use the baby anyway and anytime he could.

Hollis, bless his heart, seemed to understand what was happening. He stepped between the two men. She found she could breathe again. "Father, would you put Maeve to bed. She is tired. Sing a song to her. She loves your voice." The two men needed distance between them. She needed to make certain her father never showed up here unannounced again. Two bristling male peacocks were too much for her to deal with.

Her bodyguard sat on a large chair near the fire. His hands were folded in his lap. His legs were stretched out in front of him. He didn't say anything. His size alone would intimidate most men. She walked to the kitchen. Dinner was roasting in the oven. Vegetables were ready to steam. She hoped Chandler would sit down in the main room. Wasn't surprised when he shadowed her to the kitchen. Set his hand on her shoulder. She flinched away from him.

"Why is your father here?" Chandler's harsh voice reverberated behind her. His hands were set with possession on her shoulders. She tried to shrug them off even though she understood the attempt would be useless. He brushed his lips across the back of her neck. Bit with a light touch that was meant to tempt her to his wishes. The contact gave rise to a shiver she needed to ignore. He understood how to touch her.

Stiffening, she cut vegetable. Chopped hard as if she was cutting into him. To answer him would give him more questions. Not answering him would enrage the man. She didn't wish him to be angry. He was hard to deal with when he was calm. This was not how she planned the evening before her father showed up unannounced. Catching her lip with her teeth, she tried to keep her mind focused on preparing the dinner. Realized Chandler wasn't about to let up. He would continue until he got what he wanted from her.

"Why is your father here? You knew I was visiting. Tell him no next time or I won't be responsible for what happens. Not willing to share my time with you. Hollis living here is bad enough. Though I do acknowledge the need for a man to protect you when I'm not here to do so."

"Don't need protection except from you."

She swallowed her anger along with her fears. "To see Maeve, I believe that is the main reason my father arrived here during this storm. I had no idea he intended to visit. He never wrote." She also thought he would try to make her see everything from his point of view. Every time her father visited, he spouted new examples as to why she would return to their home in Ireland.

~ * ~

Chandler slipped his hand around her to cup her breast. Heard the tiny hiss of pleasure. Ran his thumb across the tip. Since she was nursing Maeve, she wore only a chemise beneath her gown. He held on to the taunt crowns, twisting. Bloody eyes, but he missed her. Missed all of her. Needed to feel her sultry heat surround him. It didn't make a difference that her father was here. He meant to sleep with her tonight. Would do so.

"What do you want?" she asked, her words clipped while she placed the chopped vegetables into the pan.

"Shocked you need to ask. Thought what I wished for in this cottage was you…or did you think I came to see the baby?" Chandler didn't care much about Maeve. Girls had one reason to be on earth…for a man's pleasure. Otherwise, females were worthless. When she was old enough, he would choose her husband. Find a rich titled man for her.

His thumb continued the lazy path across her nipple. Felt some moisture as he touched her there. Some of her milk leaked. He liked that.

"Sit down, Chandler. Burning the dinner would not be pleasant." She tried to twist away from him. His hands slid to her hips. Held her still.

"Ah, you can't concentrate on two things at once?" Chandler bit the back of her neck again before moving one hand back to her breast, squeezing the hard tip he'd been massaging. He did as she asked. "Don't like your father. You know that though. He wants to take you back to Ireland with him. You understand I would never allow that."

He sat down at the small kitchen table. They'd eaten breakfast in here each time he visited. Did so once a week. Georgia brought him a snifter of brandy. He studied her. She was always so bloody cool. Her emotions were like ice.

"Join me?" Chandler asked. He held up the glass. Knew she would decline. The few times she drank, she didn't hold her liquor all that well. Wouldn't mind if she became a bit fuzzy-headed before bedtime. He wouldn't feel one moment of guilt. "Sit down. Have some wine."

Guilt was lost on him. As far as he was concerned, the feeling was a waste of time. Thought of the show in London that was going on right now. Ah…it was Summer along with Autumn who would be on display this evening. When he wasn't participating, Jimmy was the one to play with his little school girl. Summer played other parts with him, all virgin parts. After a year she was not the virgin that came to him. Though he was working on a new script for the woman. Wasn't surprised when she signed on for a second year. Her family still sacrificed her for his entertainment. They needed the money. Summer didn't like the work. Didn't enjoy the auction where men bid on her for their personal use. Didn't enjoy being a whore. His clients loved her. Paid top dollar for her charms.

"No. Don't want wine tonight." She stirred the vegetables. Seemed she was trying to keep her distance from him. Her ploys would never work.

"I think you will." Chandler found the bottle of wine. Splashed a good amount into a glass. "Drink." He didn't know if she would comply to his wishes. If she didn't, he had ways to make her drink.

He was pleased with his efforts when he saw her chin tilt and her back stiffen. He liked it when she thought she could get her way. Winter understood he would insist then continue to insist until she drank. He eyed the almost full bottle then Winter. She would down the bottle before the evening was finished. He would see to it. Maybe begin on a second one.

"You realize I don't like to drink." Opening the oven door, she bent over to check the meat. Her delicious rump was presented to him. He didn't think she would bend over in front of him if she understood what the sight did to him. Chandler imagined thrusting into her from behind. He could set her face down on the little kitchen table. Toss her skirts…ah… So swollen with lust for her, he had to adjust himself.

"Drink the glass of wine." His voice held a hard edge as he confronted her disobedience. She would do as he wished. "Drink, then I'll pour you more. You do understand I'm not giving you a choice."

Winter nodded. Drank the half the glass before she wiped her mouth with the back of her hand. After she swallowed, he smiled while he watched her body shudder. It was obvious she didn't enjoy the taste.

"The rest of it…" He pointed to the glass while he held the bottle up to her. Winter would understand, she would finish the bottle before the night was finished.

He hooted his laughter when her brows drew together and her lips thinned with her burgeoning anger. While he didn't hold all the cards tonight because her father was in the house, he still had the winning hand. Their daughter was vulnerable. Winter understood he could do what he wished. Told her if she disobeyed, he would find the worst workhouse in the slums of London. Almost the moment Maeve was born, he made the fact clear to her that the baby was expendable. If she behaved, he would grant her some leeway. Nonetheless, Maeve's future rested in his hands.

Finishing the glass, Winter slammed it on the table. "Are you satisfied?" Her eyes blazed with fury. She was passionate. He'd felt her passion many times. Watching the rise of anger now pleased him.

His grin turned into a low chuckle. "Not yet. No, not satisfied at the moment. By tomorrow morning I'm certain to be feeling better…more than quenched by your fire." Again, he laughed at her. Saw the look of defeat in her sparkling blue eyes. With Winter he would always have his way. He allowed her to leave the brothel. Didn't think he could ever be so generous. The feeling that he would gain more sway over her if she wasn't with him every day of the week was a top priority in his mind. The more he granted her the more he held over her head. The more she would owe him. Chandler wished for Winter to owe him the world then more.

"You are not coming to my bed." She pointed the serving fork at him, her brows drawing together as if that scowl would stop him. The one she tested the roast with. "Not while my father is in the house. I swear…" Turning her back to him, she pulled dishes from the cupboard then silverware from the drawer clattering around her.

"We shall see." He grinned at her stiff back. Decided she needed more wine. The sooner she felt the influence of the alcohol the easier it would be to seduce. She would still tell him no. He would say yes. As always, she would melt around him. Chandler knew just the right places to fondle, to massage with serious concentration.

In one lithe cat-like move he rose. Chandler was beside her before she could step back. Pulling her to him, he pressed her length against him. His hands cupped her sweet butt. Her large breasts pushed against his chest. When he brought her closer, he knew she would feel his arousal. He wanted to be snug within her. Intended patience.

"No, Chandler. You cannot have me anytime you wish. I don't want you in my bed. Do not threaten me with our daughter. You would never do the things you say just to get yourself into me. You are not as ruthless as you wish me to believe." Winter didn't struggle against him. No, she held herself very still. Frozen, just like the ice queen she was. She would not give into her passion as long as she was fully clothed. He wanted to change that situation. With her father as a house guest, he didn't intend to mortify her to the tips of her toes if Carmack entered the kitchen.

"I know your ploy, Winter. Doesn't make a bit of difference if you act frigid. Nor does it matter to me if you say no. Your no doesn't mean a damn thing to me. I will have you tonight. Understand how to make you want me." Chandler kissed her hard. He needed to savor the taste of her. Thrust his tongue deep into her just as he wished to thrust his sex inside her small body. Wanted to become part of her while she moaned and heaved beneath him. She didn't move. Her hands remained limp at her sides. There was no response from her. He groaned at the quick rise of sexual power he experienced. Tugging on her bottom lip, he sucked the sweet flesh inside.

While he continued to kiss her, he slipped his hand inside the bodice of her gown. Held his hand against her where he could feel the rapid stamping of her heart. Floated his hand across her hard-tipped nipple. Delicious feminine sounds floated from the back of her throat. His smile was one of victory. She was not as immune to his seduction of her as she tried to make out. She couldn't freeze him out of her bed. He wanted to kiss her again. Decided against that when he heard footsteps. There would be more time to grant her the pleasures of the flesh he knew she craved. His Winter could never remain frozen against him for long.

"Finish dinner," he left her side to return to the chair along with his brandy. "Believe I'll watch you. Love to see your breasts move when you do small things. They are so large. Firm ripe melons meant for our pleasure. The small damp spots on your shirt are such a delight. Those two beautiful globes are so much larger now that you've given birth and Maeve is suckling on your tits. Think about me sucking on each one. Pulling your breast so far into my mouth that you scream with the pure delight of the ecstasy I give." After filling her wine glass again, he stretched his legs in front of him. Sipped on the brandy.

The next ten minutes, he studied her. Sought means to get her to admit she wanted him. Bloody hell, Chandler knew she loved him. Begged him to claim her. They made love the night of the claiming. He'd taken her several times before they fell asleep. He never believed she would leave the brothel. Never realized she was serious. That's when he made his threats to give her to Bertram. She detested his best friend.

Winter refused to marry him. Refused! Told him she didn't want him to own her. Said now that he claimed her as his mate, she didn't need marriage. All was done that needed to be done to secure their passage through time. Had the gall to tell him, she hoped he would be a better man in the future.

The table was set. Maeve was asleep for most of the night. Chandler wondered how often Winter fed the little girl. She was five-months-old now. Surely, Winter didn't get up more than once. Maeve was eating some solid food. Maybe she slept through the night. The last few times he visited, he didn't pay much attention. Every time Winter allowed him to seduce her she swore to him that was the last time.

"Dinner is ready," she stood in the main room wiping her hands on a towel. Hollis along with her father rose.

The meal was eaten in silence. Chandler continued to fill her glass with the red wine. She drank. He was content. Acknowledged the fact she would never argue with her father in the room. Would be compliant to his whims. With dinner finished, Cormack settled in a big chair facing the fire. For his further amusement, Chandler decided to help Winter with cleaning up. Well, he wasn't going to help. He meant to fondle all those beautiful body parts of hers he adored as well as missed during the long week. Meant to caress her breasts, her hips, the soft damp parts between her legs. Her breathy little sighs of pleasure would lend encouragement to his plans. By the time he finished, she wouldn't be able to refuse him. Winter would come to him warm and willing.

Opening another bottle of wine, he spilled more into her glass. By the expression on her lovely face, she wasn't pleased. Her hands were in the sudsy water. He held the glass to her lips. If she didn't open her mouth then drink, the liquid would spill down to her lovely breasts. The thought of sipping the wine off the tips gave him something to think about. Another time perhaps, when there weren't so many people in the house. He saw himself pulling her corsage down to her waist while her hands were immersed in the sudsy water. Seducing Winter would satisfy him. Perhaps he didn't wish to wed with Winter. The woman could be a demanding shrew. She always had a plan contrary to his. This arrangement almost suited him. As soon as he could convince her she wanted him in her bed, he would be more than pleased. Perhaps she would return with him to the brothel. No, he doubted that would happen.

She drank. He didn't put the glass down. When Winter gasped wine slipped from her mouth to run down her chin. He followed the path of the drops with his lips, touching her chin then sipping wine from her long slender neck. He paused at the racing pulse at the base of her neck. Sucked then nibbled. Felt the shuddering rush of pleasure from her slender body. As he charmed those evocative places, he knew would bring her to the point where she wouldn't snub his efforts. He would continue this until she begged for more pleasure.

Ah, but the evening would drag on before he could climb into her bed. Before he could have his way with her delicious body. He missed her. Was used to having her every night, showing her off to the lecherous people who paid to watch him give his ice queen her pleasure. Loved to see her reach that beautiful pinnacle more than once in the evening.

"Don't…" Winter's eyes were closed. Her shoulders stiff. "Please don't. I don't want anything more to drink. I'll get sick. The wine can't be good for Maeve. She is such a tiny little thing. Chandler, no…"

"Open them. Open those pretty eyes of yours. I want to see what you're feeling. Do you realize you are an open book for me to read?" He watched the slow move of her lashes. Gazing into her eyes he saw her anger flare along with fear of him. Chandler didn't like seeing fear in her eyes. Though he understood at one time he enjoyed seeing terror in the eyes of a woman. He shook his head. He wasn't like that anymore. Found he liked to see desire in a woman's eyes, in Winter's eyes. Winter wasn't afraid of him. She loved him. Had said the words the night of the claiming. If she loved him, why didn't she want him in her bed? That was a question that befuddled his mind.

Chandler scrunched the fabric of her gown in his hands while he brought the material higher up her leg. With his boots between her feet, he pushed them apart. Felt the fine shiver of desire rush through her. He teased her soft flesh. Rested his hand on her belly. Cursed the fact the house was filled with people.

"I don't want you to touch me there." Her muted voice told him of her arousal. The words she spoke weren't true. Soon she would beg for him to bring her to the point where she lost command of her body.

"Where?" He didn't care what she wanted. He told her that numerous times. "Where is it you don't want me to touch? Here? Or there? Maybe over here?" His hand roamed. Scorched her flesh with its presence. For about the hundredth time tonight, he wished they were alone and she was naked.

The wine glass at her lips stopped her from replying. She drank more. Swallowed the potent liquid. She was on the second bottle of wine. He smiled with thoughts of desperate pleasure rumbling around in his head. She might have a raging headache in the morning. What did he care if the wine gave him better access to her feminine endowments.

He wanted to come into her from behind. With her father sipping brandy in the front room, she wouldn't let out even a squeak. She would hold the yell of ecstasy inside her mouth. After setting the glass down, he ran his hand along the inside of her leg. Touched her. Fondled the softness welcoming his attention. Found her dampness delightful. Thrust two fingers through the soft welcoming folds that were even now pulsing, milking his fingers with her need. Her body was crying out for him.

"You want me."

"No." In defiance of her word, her head was thrown back. Rested on his shoulder. He watched the frantic tick of her pulse at the base of her neck.

Stroking her, fondling her with intimate precision, he understood she would climax in a matter of seconds if he continued. Not wishing for her to reach her pleasure, Chandler brought his hand away. Heard the tiny noise of disappointment. Touched her cheek with his wet fingers. Sipped on the back of her white neck. Thought to travel lower. He did. Tested the flesh along her shoulder. Unfastened several buttons as he slid the fabric aside.

"You want me," he repeated. "You can deny with words all you want. Your beautiful woman's body is telling a different story. If I allowed it to happen, in another second you would have screamed your pleasure."

"No."

"Come, finish the dishes. Believe I heard your father retiring for the night. We can go to your room as soon as you..." He paused while he looked her up then down. She must be blocking her thoughts from him. He wished to listen to what was in her mind. "I'll undress you. You can do the same for me. We will sleep naked after I've given you more pleasure than you deserve for denying yourself what you want."

"You're not going to sleep with me," Winter continued on that vein. "Not going to sleep with me or give me pleasure."

While he wasn't known as a patient man, he felt as if he exhibited a great deal of patience where his ice queen was concerned. A bit of standoffishness was alright. Winter caried the aloofness to an extreme.

"We will see," his soft murmur surprised him. His feelings for this woman shocked him. Chandler denied to himself the tenderness he felt for her. He didn't love Winter. Acknowledged the fact he was a man incapable of love. Lived on the seedier side of life which he enjoyed to his immense delight. Every day of his life there were women vying to gain his attention. Since Winter surged into his life, he'd not wanted any other woman. He forced himself to play with a few he employed. Couldn't stand the thought that he only wanted to have Winter in his bed. When he returned, he would take Celine to his bed while Summer Passion watched. Next, he would give Summer more pleasure than she merited. The girl was too standoffish though that act was part of her charm. The men loved to bring her down a peg or two.

Winter turned on him. Her hands pressed against his chest. Her eyes blazing with emotions, she told him again her thoughts on the most prevalent topic on his mind. He'd gone without long enough. She wasn't going to escape his attentions tonight. All he meant to do was give her the sweetest climaxes imaginable.

"You are not..."

Chandler held up the glass that was still half full. "Finish this. Once I'm finished with your lovely self, you will sleep soundly." All tolerance with her denials fled. "I will come to you as soon as the house is quiet. Though your father should understand that I belong with you. He knows I claimed you. With that done, Cormack would also comprehend you are mine."

Winter shook her head. She tried to push away from him. Her breasts shimmied across him. He groaned his delight. "No. Don't come to me. Can't you understand? I don't want you. You need to comprehend. Stop coming here."

Chandler didn't wish to admit to the emotion. He was hurt by her comments by her denial of him. Retaliated to her negative words. "Yes." He helped her finish the wine. Held the glass until she drank all the liquid. Set his hand at the small of her waist. "Come, you look tired. You need to rest." He steadied her when she missed a step. She was just where he wanted her to be. Winter would be pliant as well as willing when he came to her in another hour. He loved waking her from a deep sleep. Would kiss her closed eyes, the tip of her nose. After that he would fondle her mouth with his lips then his teeth. He would caress those sweet pink parts of her that were his favorite places. She would be warm and wet. Ready to accept his full arousal. When her eyes opened, he'd thrust inside. Would fill her to the brim then more. Would then take her cry of pleasure into his mouth. No one in the home would be the wiser.

"I don't," she swallowed her words. "Don't...no...in my bed. Can't." She leaned into him, pressing her weight against his chest.

On his shoulder, her head lolled. She stumbled again, steadied herself with her hand. "Yes, in your bed, Winter. That's where I belong. In time you will see things my way." They walked past the nursery.

"No."

"Do you need to see to Maeve?" He wanted her to be done with the nursing then waiting for him. She would unveil her breasts. While he watched, he would see his little girl suckling at her breast. It was a fine sight. Though he threatened her with Maeve, he would never do anything to harm the baby. In the present, the child made Winter vulnerable. He appreciated that aspect of the child. If he would mold Winter to his wishes, she needed to be defenseless.

"No."

At the door to her room, he gave her a gentle push before walking away. He was going to have a few words with Hollis then retire to his room. Thought he should have helped her out of her clothing. Did enjoy disrobing her. Before he sought Winter's bed, he would wait until the house quieted. Until there were no sounds disturbing the cottage. He stepped into the front room, lighted with a few lanterns. Outside the wind still howled. It was a miserable night for anyone to be outside. Inside the fire warmed the home. He stuck his hands out to receive some of the heat generated.

"Hollis," he said as he settled into a large chair with a glass of brandy in his hand. He held it with both hands warming the liquid as he rolled the glass between his hands. Watched the amber liquid catch the warmth of the fire.

"Chandler. You will behave yourself tonight." Hollis' sigh after the words held a wealth of meaning. Hollis would understand his words meant nothing to him. Hollis was a good man. He was glad he protected Winter. He was loyal to her as well as Maeve. Tonight, he wished him to be gone.

"You should remember who pays your salary. The big man would never stop him from seeing to Winter. Winter Snow was his. He created her. Gave her work when she came to him with a willing as well as an open mind. By God, she signed a contract then thought to renege. That act of defiance forced him to threaten her. "I always behave myself," he returned as he chuckled at the humor those few words produced.

"I remember," Hollis said what sounded like a snort of disgust.

Hollis understood what he would do. What he wanted. Winter in his arms. Damn, but he just couldn't keep away from the woman. After she left the brothel, he intended to do just that. Stay far away. Why did he want a woman who didn't wish to have anything to do with him? Supposed this mate thing was what drew him to her.

He wouldn't allow a woman to control his desires. There were plenty of women who wanted him. He could have his pick of all of the women at the brothel. Crook his little finger at whoever caught his eyes. The girl would run to him. Would want him to do anything he chose to her female parts. At one point, he thought to take Summer to his rooms upstairs. Summer could never replace Winter. Sitting back in the big chair he closed his eyes. All he could see was Winter's breasts. Her other wonderful female endowments. She was so beautiful. Made for his enjoyment. Thoughts of her naked and in his arms caused his stomach to cramp with need. Bloody everlasting hell, she was his. Only his. She forgot that small fact. Forgot they were a couple through all eternity. She bedeviled him.

The groan stopped in his throat. Didn't want the big man to see his obvious need. Hollis rose. Seemed he meant to retire for the night. The big man rubbed his hand behind his neck. Seemed to start to say something then didn't.

"Good night. If you can behave yourself, know the little mama doesn't wish for you to be in her bed," Hollis said before he left the room to walk down the hall to his room. All was going as planned.

Chandler couldn't see him. Heard his door open then close. He wondered how long he should wait until Winter slept. She drank so much wine. Must be asleep by now. He could go see her. Slip inside. Lean against the wall so he could watch her sleep. That all sounded just fine to his way of thinking.

He quenched all the lights before following Hollis down the hall. In his bedroom, he leaned against the door. Closed his eyes imagining Winter on his bed. His dream was for her to come to him. Her hair down and with no inhibitions. Naked. Realized he needed her the way they used to be. Didn't wish to pursue her this diligently. They had another child on the way. Before she left, he made certain she was increasing. Took her both night and day as well as any time he felt a need for her.

Sitting down, he removed his boots then the rest of his clothing. Just thinking about Winter made him ready for her. He slipped on a dressing gown before lying down on his bed. His hands were behind his head. Rain pelted the window. Trying for patience, he counted the beats of the clock. Time crept by with the speed of a slug.

Fifty-five minutes passed. He was about to rise. The sound of footsteps caught his attention. A gruff clearing of a man's throat told him either Hollis or Cormack was awake. He cursed. Swore out his frustrations while he was forced to wait for the house to grow silent again. He closed his eyes. Awoke with a start to a loud wail from the nursery. Would nothing go his way tonight? Was beginning to doubt he would have his wishes fulfilled. Cormack would leave tomorrow. At least he hoped the man would return to London. When that happened, he only needed to deal with Hollis. The bodyguard held no sway in what he did. He didn't hear the light fall of Winter's footsteps headed toward the nursery. The crying stopped. Winter must be in the room nursing Maeve. Another half hour passed. He didn't hear her return. Realized her steps must be so silent, he wasn't able to hear them.

Another few minutes ticked by. Chandler decided he was out of patience. He rose, strode to her door. Opened it. For a few seconds he leaned against the doorframe studying the form lying on the bed. The body was way too large.

Bloody eyes!

Hollis turned over then sat up. He grinned at what must be his startled expression. "Looking for someone?" he asked with nonchalance that surprised Chandler.

"You damn well know I am!" Chandler exploded into his surroundings. "Where is she?" He stalked into the room, his fingers tightening into fists. Looked in all the corners as if he could conjure her. It was obvious she wasn't in the room. Winter played him for a fool.

Hollis let out a long deep breath of air. "Won't do any good to keep the truth from you. If I don't say, you'll wake the household looking for her."

"She's in the nursery!" Chandler remembered the single bed in the room. Winter must have slept there when Maeve was sick. He knew she had the crib in her room for the first few months. "Damn her lily-white hide."

He didn't slam the door even though he wished to do so. Winter wasn't going to get away with avoiding him. If she didn't know this now, she would. The bed in the nursery was big enough for both of them. When he opened the door, she was sitting in the rocking chair, Maeve in her arms. Maeve had her fist stuck into her mouth, her eyes closed tight.

"Chandler," she said her voice all quiet and serene. He wished he could shake her. "Maeve is frightened of the storm. If you wish, you may sit on the floor. If not, go back to bed. I will be here all night. Believe this will be a long night for both of us." Winter brushed a soft kiss on the child's forehead.

"Why was Hollis in your bed?" he gritted out, asking the question even though he knew the answer.

"Believe you know the answer to the question. I did tell you I didn't want to sleep with you. The fact you didn't listen to my wishes doesn't surprise me." Winter yawned, placed her hand in front of her lips. The very ones he needed to kiss.

"You intend to sleep in the baby's room every time I visit?" he asked again knowing the answer. "You don't sound muzzled any longer." Chandler was furious with her. Should have made her drink all of the second bottle of wine.

"I'm sitting. If it's any consolation to you, I had a terrible time walking to the nursery after you left me at my door. My mind is hazy. Not hazy enough to let you fondle me. That's not ever going to happen again."

"You understand that sleeping in the nursery won't deter me. You are dead wrong if you think I won't ever again be deep inside you while I take you to that place you so love." His words didn't have the ring of truth. Sleeping with a baby next to him, held no appeal to chandler. He would be forever conscious of any sounds they made. Winter's little feminine, throaty purrs delighted.

"Go to bed, Chandler. As you must be able to tell, I'm staying in this room while you are visiting. You will just need to get used to this arrangement."

There were other times to make love with his mate. Didn't need the night. Nor did he need a bed. She wasn't a damn virgin. The hell of it was he wanted her now.

"Put Maeve in her crib. She's asleep."

"No."

~ * ~

"Bertram!" Chandler bellowed when he arrived at the brothel three nights later. "Get over here!" He slapped his riding gloves on his leg. "I'm out of patience. What the blessed hell are you doing? Bring me Summer."

The show featuring Summer and Autumn was about to begin. Bertram looked up at the bellow of rage he heard from his friend of fifteen years. He was seeing to last minute details. Chandler would understand that fact. The women keeping the body cooling fans going were positioned in strategic places wearing see through gowns. They were all beautiful women. All signed contracts giving the patrons permission to have sex with them. The fan maidens were next in line to be auctioned at the end of the night for any man's pleasure who had enough coin to buy them. The bodyguards were situated around the room. One night a fight broke out. It was then Chandler decided they needed a few men who would protect the women from someone who lost control. At times the audience became frenzied with their frenetic desires. Bertram loved watching men lose themselves in a woman's soft body. He never could believe his good fortune when Chandler derived this idea.

He chuckled when he looked at Chandler. His smile was broad. The reason behind Chandler's bad mood could only be credited to one small woman who always bedeviled him. "You're in a bad mood tonight. Did nothing go as planned?" Bertram asked as he watched his friend pace the floor. "The little harlot refused all your advances. You don't need her permission to take her any damn way you wish. You do know that? Of course, you comprehend you are bigger as well as stronger than Winter." He wished for his old friend to return. Liked him better before Winter changed him. Looked forward to the nights they shared their women.

"Horrible. She wouldn't…hell she worked everything out so it was impossible for me to get to her. The devil knows I tried. She outwitted me, damn her soul. She believes she can set rules. I won't allow that. Next time, I will win. I'll push her up against a wall right in front of Hollis if she doesn't give me an alternative to that." He circled the room before stopping at a window that looked down at the street below.

His chuckle at Chandler's distress bought him a scowl from the man. Bertram frowned. He wondered about Chandler's intentions for tonight. "Do you wish to perform tonight? Summer always gives herself as much as is possible to you. After that first time the woman understands her place. We do need to think of some other script for the pretty lady.

Believe our audience is tiring of the little girl act. All realize she is no longer a virgin. What do you think she should become? Perhaps a nun. That role might be fun."

"Believe I'd like to let off some steam that's all bottled up inside me. Yes, I want Summer. Need to punish her for her naughtiness. We will put our heads together to come up with a unique scenario for her. Maybe we could reenact how we discovered her. Pushed her up against a store just to talk to her. Do you recall that day? We brought her to her parent's home. Made her father a proposition he couldn't refuse. Her being a nun sounds intriguing." He turned, his fingers beneath his chin while he tapped them. "I'll think on the two scenarios. Perhaps both roles in one night. That would put a new twist to the script."

Bertram nodded. "Oh yes." He rubbed his hands together anticipating the pleasure. The two left the rest of the evening's details to Jimmy and Johnny, the twins they had with them from the beginning. The thought of watching Chandler take Summer multiple time appealed to all his sexual fantasies.

Once the new thoughts were mulling around in his head, Chandler poured them both a glass of whiskey. Bertram spoke from the heart. Worried about his friend. He wasn't acting normal. Hadn't been since Winter gave birth then left the brothel. Chandler had not been the same since.

"Tell me everything. You can't keep going to the cottage then returning in a royal snit. You become a bore for the next few days. Bring her back with you. You're stronger than she is…bigger."

Chandler rubbed the back of his neck. Winced as if the movement caused him pain. "You realize, I've thought about doing that more than once. I just have to find a means to deal with this obstinance or hers. She is only a woman and thus inferior. A female doesn't have the wit to outsmart a man."

While he listened to the beat of the clock on the shelf, Bertram wondered if Chandler believed what he spouted. Though he never enjoyed giving a woman the credit of possessing a brain, he was well aware of the fact many were smarter than some men. They did possess a different way of thinking about things. Some managed to have their way over a man's desires. Seems Winter had Chandler wrapped around her fingers.

"I believe we should drink to male prowess…to their competence in all things. To outwitting all the females of their knowledge." Bertram held up his glass in salute. Grinned at Chandler. He enjoyed women with no ability to think for themselves. A woman with a mind was dangerous to his wellbeing. Twits were convenient. They were easily molded into the woman Bertram wanted at that time.

He tossed the remainder of his drink down his throat then grimaced. "Winter blocks her thoughts from me. She doesn't have the right to do so. I'm her mate!" He splashed more brandy into his glass. "I'm supposed to know what's in her mind. Need to get inside so I can understand if she is in danger."

"You are too new to shifting. Have some patience. Together we can work on that point. Does she read your thoughts?" Bertram decided he was just the man to teach Chandler how to best his woman at her game.

"She must read my mind. Winter seems to know what I'm going to do before I've cemented a plan. Most of the time she is two steps ahead of me if not more. I don't like it. Not right for her to have so much power over me."

Bertram watched Chandler pace the room. What he needed was a woman to ease the ache between his legs. He must have spent two days in a state of arousal that he couldn't ease. Chandler didn't appear to be in any shape to perform tonight. Not even with Summer playing the school girl. He thought about Summer as a nun. Perhaps he could arrange a costume before they came on stage. A new script would be just the thing for Chandler. Would put bounce back into his step. Would give him the confidence he needed to confront Winter in another week or two.

He heard the chime of the clock. It was eight o'clock. No, there wasn't enough time to set up the new script. Next time…for tonight, he could send her to Chandler after the show. Summer would lose out on the auction. Would not gain the extra blunt. That didn't matter to him. His friend sexual health mattered.

"I must go. Why don't you watch through the viewing room you had built. Might get you aroused enough to make an appearance. Could send you Celine or one of the other girls."

Connal's Eternal Love
Sweet McKenna Book One

A few days shy of All Hallows' Eve Connal McKenna, Laird of Clan Chaton stands on the parapets of his castle. Bonfires line the hillsides while his clan prepares for the upcoming festivities. Drawn by the whispering of the wind, Connal McKenna feels a strange restlessness in his soul. Setting out to discover the wickedness that is calling to him, he discovers his mate. With gentle words and sensuous kisses, the auburn-eyed highlander conquers his mate, the beautiful, defiant Wynnie Adair who he comes upon during an evening ride. She must ultimately put her trust in the only man who can save her from the ruthless plans of her father and succumb to his gentle coaxing.

In Brady's Arms
Sweet McKenna Book Two

Forced to run from the only home she knows, beautiful, headstrong Lillian Townsends seeks shelter in the wild highlands where the McKenna clan live. Trying to avoid a betrothal contract signed by her stepfather to an aging lord, she is desperate to find a means to sidestep the inevitable, including a marriage to the oldest son of the laird. Lilly is enamored of the young lord who pursues her with unrelenting determination flashing his devilishly handsome charms. She is hard pressed to resist.

Besotted from the first moment Brady McKenna sees Lilly, he is determined to find a means to coax her into his arms and bed. With only the promise of carnal pleasure as his mistress, Brady relentlessly pursues the woman who has unwittingly forged a place in his heart. She is like no other woman, proud, defiant and enchanting. Despite his father's advice to stay away from her, he cannot. He boldly seeks her out and makes her his own.

Nobody but Walker
Sweet McKenna Book Three

The Highland Lass...

She was brought up, adored and loved by a doting mother and father ardently protected by her brothers. She was everything sweet and innocent until she was faced with betrayal and an unexpected and out of wedlock pregnancy. When she gave her love to a man who couldn't return her passion and commitment, she was left devastated and furious. Faced with the loss of her child if she didn't comply to his demands, Crissie McKenna followed him to Belfast then on to his country home to discover he was already married.

...The Irishman

Stunned to find out his one and only encounter with the woman he wanted to love forever created a child, Walker Endicott, Earl of Briarwood, claimed his child as his only heir. Walker threatened all her previously held values even while he thrilled her senses. From the moment he first saw her to the second she ran after him begging him to make love to her, his captivating masculinity held her fascinated. In his arms she would know tempestuous passion, bitter despair, and a soaring joy that would humble them both before the power of love.

Roby's Moonlit Night
Sweet McKenna Book Four

Once she'd been a pampered child with high expectations for her future blessed with love. Then she became an innocent pawn in a terrible game of greed and power. Now, with a noose around her neck, Pippa was to hang before she had the chance to unveil the men who drove her from her home, before she had the chance to live.

Roby McKenna was a man blessed with endless charm and wit. While he searched for his eternal love across the Atlantic in a new land, he would have to come home to find her. His silver blue eyes could sparkle with amusement or harden to steel gray with displeasure. He had all the women a man could want or need. As he grew older, mistresses were not enough. A quirk of fate brought him to the gallows, a spark of destiny made him claim the condemned Pippa as his bride.

Made for Houston
Sweet McKenna Book Five

Leah Kennedy is as wary of people as she is strikingly beautiful. However, the shocking death of her father that forever changed her girlhood has left her terrified of the very love she desperately longs for. Only in the untamed splendor of the Scottish crags does she feel safe from the feelings she stirs in men and the cruel mockery of Selkirk's villagers.

Debonair, well-educated doctor Houston Stuart has turned his back on social privilege along with professional honors to set up a medical practice in the lowlands of Scotland. There, serving those who need him the most, he hopes to forget the bitter memories and disillusionment that disturb his days.

Coincidence brings the cultured doctor and this fey mountain girl together. Something as bizarre as destiny disrupts the obstacle of birth and breeding, stubborn pride and fear which has kept them apart...as each seeks to heal the other's wounds with a raw passion neither can deny and all the odds against them cannot defeat.

Say You Love Kit
Sweet McKenna Book Six

Fascinated...

When the woman stepped through the door of the pub, the sun setting her fiery red hair glowing around her delicate features, Kit Stuart finds himself captivated by the sight. The moment he sees her he knows she will be his. Convincing the fire-haired lady of that fact isn't easy. After she calls out another man's name when he kisses her that night, he is instantly enraged as well as jealous. The road they travel is fraught with secrets that neither can tell. Trust is an elusive quality that neither can give.

Intrigued...

Forced to run for her life, desperate and afraid, Aila MacDuff willingly enters into the Kinnel Stones, a mysterious place where people disappear then appear magically in different times. At the first sight of Kit, she finds herself inexplicably drawn to him. She's been told to search for her mate and that she will know when she finds him. Aila doesn't know what this man's name is or what he looks like. Nonetheless, she is certain he will be similar to her mate from one hundred years earlier. Despite the fact she is falling in love with Kit, he can't be her mate. Her mate is a shifter. Kit is not.

It Had to be Riley
Sweet McKenna Book Seven

Her anger assured retaliation...

Shawna's only concern with the contemptable scoundrel she had been forced to wed was the return of her dowry. She had not seen her husband in three years, and now Riley Stuart furiously repudiated there had ever been a marriage. He even went as far as to tell his family he'd never seen her before this day.

...Her passion promised love

In the heather clad hills of the beautiful Scottish crags surrounding the small village so near to the Mckenna keep, the ferocity of her loathing yields to the intense hunger of unquenched longing. In the powerful arms of the dark and handsome husband she thought she reviled, Shawna shivers with the honeyed torment of awakened desire and powerlessly submits to the wild, enchanting ecstasy of burning passion. Together they abandon themselves to the exquisite pleasure of the love their hearts cannot escape.

The Magic of Hawk
Sweet McKenna Book Eight

With her extraordinary silver-mauve eyes, Maisie McRae struggles with the return of her lost love. She finds solace living with her half-sister and existing on dreams. After three long years the man she once dreamt of marrying asks her to make the same foolish mistake again. Holding herself aloof from the arrogant man, Maisie refuses to let his sweettalking words seduce her into his arms.

Smitten from the first instant Hawk Frasier sees Maisie, he is determined to find a means to entice her into becoming part of his life. A missing letter keeps the unlucky couple from realizing their dreams. Defeated by her rejection, Hawk searches for a way to ignore the woman. Unable to forget the way she feels in his arms, Hawk returns from the colonies, ready to try again. Despite the chance of a second rejection, he forges ahead. Boldly, he seeks her out and makes her his own.

Roc's Steadfast Heart
Sweet McKenna Book Nine

Dallas Elaine Shaw, on a photo shoot for the magazine she works for, tumbles down an incline to find herself catapulted into the eighteenth century. Facing three men, one of those men, the one with laughing silver blue eyes commands her attention. The other two stare at her with leering, malicious intent. She finds herself rescued by the man with the intense eyes. Terrified of horses, she discovers herself riding in front of the arrogant man who saved her. In a few short minutes, he sends a multitude of sparks simmering within her.

When Roc Frasier sees the woman sprawled on the ground, he thinks he's gone to heaven. This is the woman all his dreams are made from. Her body holds the enticement of lush bountiful breasts, curved hips he could hold onto. She is his dream come true. What he doesn't understand is this woman has traveled through time. She comes to him to complete the interrupted circle of life. This woman is his soulmate. His life's blood. She wants nothing more than to leave him, to return to her time. She can't. They are each other's destiny.

Harris' Reckless Heart
Sweet McKenna Book Ten

The Highland Lass…

Harris Frasier was raised and adored by a devoted mother and father, zealously sheltered by her two older brothers. Harris is everything sweet and spicey, trusting and loyal until she is faced with what she believes is betrayal to all she holds dear within her heart. She gives her love to a man who confuses her. A man who she doesn't think can return her loyalty. Given no viable choice, Harris is forced to follow him to London then on to his home near the Dover coast to discover she is correct in all her assumptions about his fidelity. He is a womanizer. Harris cannot abide a life with a man who will not remain faithful.

…The Sassenach Soldier

Stunned to discover the woman he will love forever then into eternity believes he is a cad and a philanderer. Ashton Wolcott realizes the uphill battle in front of him will worsen before Harris will learn to trust his word. He isn't anything like the man she assumes him to be. Ash endangers all her previously held values. Even while he delights her senses, she battles misconceptions. From the moment he first sees her sunning herself naked by the loch to the moment she runs after him begging him to compromise her, his captivating masculinity holds her in thrall. Within the shelter of his arms, she will learn all-encompassing passion, loyalty, and joy and the lasting power of love.